Edited by Radclyffe and **Stacia Seaman**

Erotic Interludes

Erotic Interludes 2: Stolen Moments

Erotic Interludes 3: Lessons in Love

Erotic Interludes 4: Extreme Passions

Erotic Interludes 5: Road Games

Romantic Interludes

Romantic Interludes 1: Discovery

Romantic Interludes 2: Secrets

Romantic

INTERLUDES 2: SECRETS

edited by

RADCLY*f*FE and
STACIA SEAMAN

2009

ROMANTIC INTERLUDES 2: SECRETS

© 2009 BOLD STROKES BOOKS. ALL RIGHTS RESERVED.

ISBN 10: 1-60282-116-X
ISBN 13: 978-1-60282-116-3

THIS TRADE PAPERBACK ORIGINAL IS PUBLISHED BY
BOLD STROKES BOOKS, INC.
P.O. BOX 249
VALLEY FALLS, NY 12185

FIRST BOLD STROKES PRINTING: SEPTEMBER 2009

"A TRUE STORY (WHETHER YOU BELIEVE IT OR NOT)" COPYRIGHT © BY LESLÉA NEWMAN FROM *SECRETS* (NEW VICTORIA, NORWICH, VT). REPRINTED WITH PERMISSION OF THE AUTHOR.

THIS IS A WORK OF FICTION. NAMES, CHARACTERS, PLACES, AND INCIDENTS ARE THE PRODUCT OF THE AUTHOR'S IMAGINATION OR ARE USED FICTITIOUSLY. ANY RESEMBLANCE TO ACTUAL PERSONS, LIVING OR DEAD, BUSINESS ESTABLISHMENTS, EVENTS, OR LOCALES IS ENTIRELY COINCIDENTAL.

THIS BOOK, OR PARTS THEREOF, MAY NOT BE REPRODUCED IN ANY FORM WITHOUT PERMISSION.

CREDITS

EDITORS: RADCLYFFE AND STACIA SEAMAN
PRODUCTION DESIGN: STACIA SEAMAN
COVER ART: BARB KIWAK (WWW.KIWAK.COM)
COVER DESIGN BY SHERI (GRAPHICARTIST2020@HOTMAIL.COM)

CONTENTS

INTRODUCTION

Love is one of those rare, elusive states of being that defies definition, and yet is universally recognized and often the object of lifelong quests. We don't understand it, but we write songs and poems and love stories about it. Love is not only "a many splendored thing," it is also infinite in expression and changes with us as we risk and lose and dare to love again. Twenty-three celebrated authors explore the hidden layers of love, reminding us that no matter how many times we fall in love or how many years we've been in love, each moment has the potential to bring new wonder and surprises. Romance is as varied as the individuals captured by it, and these stories reflect the diversity of our experiences with humor, poignancy, and sometimes, by imagining whole new worlds entirely. Surrender to the unexpected, succumb to secret desires, and embrace the hidden power of our most intimate associations...no matter how near we come to understanding the mysteries of love, there will always be another secret to savor.

Radclyffe 2009

With love comes secrets. There are the secrets individuals hide from the world, from forbidden love to hidden identities; the secrets couples hide from others, from role reversals to secret fantasies; and the secrets lovers hide from each other. In the stories contained in this anthology, join the authors as they explore—and celebrate—the secrets of love.

Stacia Seaman 2009

COLETTE MOODY is a resident of southeastern Virginia. Her turn-ons are classic movies, witty banter, politics, and women with big sexy brains. Turn-offs include rainy days, frowns, misogyny, and the blind renouncement of science or human rights. Her first novel *The Sublime and Spirited Voyage of Original Sin* was published by Bold Strokes Books in March of 2009. Her second novel for BSB is *The Seduction of Moxie*, a historical romance (September 2009).

Moonlight Serenade
Colette Moody

I had always been in love with Marjorie Stein—always. At least since eighth grade when her family had moved to town. Of course, I'd never shared that with her.

There were two main reasons for that. One was that in the America of the early 1940s, lesbianism was not only never discussed in polite company, but sex of *any* kind was completely taboo.

The young women of my generation seemed perfectly content to wait until they married to see what their "wifely duties" entailed. But it was the women who *didn't* wait—who were out late at night with their underpants around their ankles—who were my friends. I envied how easily their sexual experimentation came to them, perhaps because they were straight. Had I known another lesbian in my town, I would have experimented too—until my tingly bits just rubbed clean off.

The only "good girl" I associated with was Marjorie—which brings me to the second reason that I'd kept my love for her to myself. Marjorie was profoundly and heartbreakingly heterosexual.

As the years passed and we both grew up, I stood by and longingly watched as Marjorie's mother arranged dates for her with all the eligible Jewish boys in town. I listened to her as she pined over the boys we went to school with who weren't Jewish, lamenting that her parents would never condone her seeing someone outside her faith. It therefore seemed utterly impossible to dream, knowing that not only was my family Protestant, but that I had supple woman-parts where my circumcised penis should be.

With every crush that she shared with me through our high school years—every admission that she found some fella handsome—I died a little inside. In her senior year of college, when she told me that she and her steady beau Alan had gotten engaged, I wept on and off for two weeks. I exerted a Herculean effort to appear happy for her, and when Alan was called up into the Army to help fight the war and shipped off to Europe before their wedding day, I tried just as hard not to feel elated...well, maybe not *just* as hard, but I did try.

I, on the other hand, had not bothered with college, instead choosing to work at the hometown bar my father owned—which I was now running single-handedly while he too was off at war. When I wasn't consorting with the town sluts, or hanging on every breath that Marjorie's magnificent body exhaled, I was driving over two hours to Mo's, a small lesbian bar on the outskirts of the city. It was there that I was able to meet women like myself, learn how to flirt with them, and experience my sexual education. But my sprees never amounted to more than flings to sate my hunger and loneliness, because after all, none of those women were Marjorie.

One breezy spring night at Pop's bar, I was busy wishing that I had closed early and gone into the city to sow my wild oats. It was the middle of the week, and though everyone was still deep into war rationing and penny-pinching, I can say with certainty that somehow people still managed to do plenty of drinking—except for this night. By 9:30, all of my regulars had gone home except for Mr. Brewster.

He remained perched on his bar stool, nursing what was his fourth scotch and soda. Because Mr. Brewster lived within walking distance of the bar, he and I had an agreement that as long as he wasn't driving anywhere, his cut-off point was a little higher than most patrons'. I had already learned that he never wanted to talk, no matter how depressed or troubled he seemed. So I poured his drinks and, as was his preference, left him in silence to wallow in the pain that was his life.

I had reconciled myself to wait Mr. Brewster out, and so I sat on the glossy mahogany bar, listening to the Wurlitzer 950 jukebox I had purchased and reading a smutty novel. Pop had been against getting a "coin-operated phonograph," saying it would never pay for itself. But I knew it would generate revenue, so I bought it while he was away— convinced that I'd show him what a moneymaker it was once the war was over. It would still be several months before I'd learn that Pop wouldn't be coming home.

The book I was rereading was called *The Scandalous Spinster*. Years later, lesbian-themed books would become a bit more commonplace, though they would suffer from the same curse as this one—meaning that typically any characters who so much as acknowledged that another girl was pretty met some unspeakable fate. In *The Scandalous Spinster*, the protagonist engaged in some heavy petting with a few young ladies and she was consequently killed in a freak thresher accident. Ironic, I thought, since she clearly didn't live long enough to become a "spinster." As this was the fifth or sixth time I was perusing it, I chose to only read the dog-eared pages—which were, of course, the racy parts. I'll admit they got me plenty hot.

The silver bell jingled as the bar door suddenly opened and in strode Marjorie. My breath caught in my throat as she stood for a moment silhouetted by the blue neon of the sign in the window. She was amazingly beautiful.

"Hey," I said. "What are you doing here so late on a school night?"

"I need a drink," she said sullenly, sitting on the stool directly to my right.

"You don't drink," I told her, sliding off the bar.

"Well, now I do, okay?"

"Okay," I agreed, walking behind the bar and assuming my work stance. "What'll you have?"

She seemed caught off guard, as though she didn't realize that there was more than one drink—just booze. "Uh…" As though conjured by her bewilderment, the Andrews Sisters' "Rum and Coca-Cola" started playing on the jukebox. "That's what I want," she said, seeming to take it as divine inspiration. "Give me a rum and Coke."

Curious, but wanting to frame my questions carefully, I nodded and made her drink—sliding it in front of her with flair. I looked over and saw Mr. Brewster staring at us morosely, and found it somewhat unnerving. "Marjorie, this is Mr. Brewster. Mr. Brewster, this is Marjorie Stein."

Though she was clearly distraught over something, Marjorie forced a warm smile anyway. "Nice to meet you." God, it tugged at my heart when she did things like that.

Mr. Brewster nodded back at her dismissively and then audibly belched. I smiled at Marjorie, giving her a look that I hoped explained that Mr. Brewster never got any friendlier than that. "Want to talk about it?"

"No."

I knew she was lying. I mean, why else would she have driven twenty miles from campus this late at night? She took a tiny sip of her drink and was visibly repulsed by it. "You can't even trust the Andrews Sisters anymore," she sighed, propping her chin in her hand.

"Well, they are singing about hooch and whores," I muttered softly, lost in the amber flakes of her brown eyes. "Tell you what," I said, taking back the glass. "Let me make you something you'll like, okay?"

She nodded sadly and glanced over to my book. "What are you reading, Laney?"

I slid the hardback under the bar self-consciously. "Nothing. Just some smut that I got from Patty." That was essentially a true statement. I had learned long ago that there was no lying to Marjorie. One skeptical arch of her eyebrow had me confessing everything to her…and God knew I didn't want *that* to happen.

"Why are you friends with Patty, Laney? She's not a very…nice girl."

The truth was that because Patty was the town tramp, she was one of the only people I felt I could confide in about my sexuality. Patty didn't judge me because I didn't judge her. It was a symbiotic relationship. "She's not so bad," I said, mixing Marjorie's new and improved drink. "Maybe I'm not a very nice girl either."

She laughed, no doubt because in her mind I had never had a steady boyfriend, so how could I *not* be a nice girl? She had no way of knowing how I spent my evenings at Mo's. What's more, if she had been aware that I'd had several sexual partners already, she would never have suspected that as I made love to them, I always imagined they were her. I had dreamt so many times of the feel of Marjorie's body, tongue, and fingers that I had convinced myself that I knew it all by rote.

Mr. Brewster stood, wobbling only slightly as he took out his wallet and dropped a few bills on the bar.

"Have a good night," I called after him as he started out the door.

"See you tomorrow, Elaine," he slurred softly.

"He's here every night?" Marjorie asked after he was long gone.

I nodded. "He's a practicing alcoholic. It's like a religion for him." I set another drink in front of her.

"That's sad."

"Sad is that he lost his wife three years ago to cancer, and now both his sons in the war."

"So he's all alone now?"

"Unless you count Johnnie Walker, yes." I leaned toward her on my elbows. "So are you ready to tell me why you're here?"

Marjorie shook her head unconvincingly. "I don't want to bother you while you're working."

I sauntered to the door and locked it, turning off the bright neon sign in the window and pulling down the shades in the windows and door. "There, now I'm not working," I said, walking back, picking up Mr. Brewster's cash and ringing it into the register. "Did you try your drink?"

"No, not yet."

"Go ahead," I said. "If you don't like this one, you don't have to drink it."

She tasted it hesitantly at first, then took another, larger swig. "What is this?"

"It's my own concoction. I call it a Betty Grable. So you like it?"

"Maybe," she replied, taking another sip.

"Okay, spill it, sister."

She removed an envelope from her handbag, set it on the bar, and slid it over to me. I could tell by the return address that it was from Alan overseas. At least he was still alive, I thought reflexively, having known too many lost in the war already.

"Open it," she said, not looking at me. "Read it."

Pulling the letter out, I was surprised at its brevity.

Marjorie,

> *There is no kind or simple way to tell you this, so I'll just get right to it. I've met someone here in Italy, and fallen in love with her. I never meant to hurt you, and I hope you are able to move on with your life. If you like, you can keep the ring.*

> *I wish you the best,*
> *Alan*

"That son of a bitch!" I spat. I couldn't imagine *anyone* not wanting Marjorie. I was angry and stunned. Then I remembered that she probably was too…perhaps almost as much as I was. "Are you okay?"

"I'm not sure. I have…mixed feelings."

I squinted at her. "How so?"

"Well, part of me feels kind of…relieved, I guess. I mean, maybe Alan wasn't the one for me."

"I could have told you that when he gave you a waffle iron for your birthday. What the hell kind of a gift was that?"

Marjorie laughed—a lilting, spirited sound that tended to make my heart feel like it was about to explode.

"So how does the other part of you feel?" I asked.

"Destroyed."

I walked around to the front of the bar and took a seat on the stool beside her. "I'm really sorry. What did your mother say?"

Her expression became instantly contrite as she bit her lower lip. "I haven't told her yet. I'm actually considering letting her think that I'm still engaged for a little while."

"Wow. How long can you keep that up?"

Marjorie took another sip of her drink and started to fish for the maraschino cherry at the bottom of the glass beneath the ice. "You just don't know what it's like to have all your dates arranged for you."

"True," I admitted with a shrug.

"I mean, I've never dated a guy who hasn't met my mother first. Everything is orchestrated at temple. I think part of the reason that I accepted Alan's proposal in the first place was just so I wouldn't have to get fixed up with every available Jew within a hundred-mile radius."

I put my chin on my fist. "So you're saying there's a couple of Hebrews out there somewhere who haven't gone out with you yet?"

She laughed, which had been my intention. "There may be one or two who've not had the pleasure. What about you?"

"If I dated a Jew, I wasn't aware," I said, being purposely vague.

"Well, are you seeing anyone?"

I winced, my discomfort plainly evident. "I go out. But I'm not seeing anyone in particular."

"You never talk about your dates, Laney," she said, finishing off her Betty Grable. "Do yours make you as miserable as mine make me?"

"I just don't get serious like you do," I replied weakly.

"On purpose?"

"I suppose so." This line of questioning needed to end quickly. I hopped up and walked back behind the bar. "Do you want another drink?"

She seemed to stop and consider the question before nodding, so I started mixing the ingredients.

"You know," I suggested, as I rattled the cocktail shaker in front of her, "I'm thinking that you didn't really love him." I know that was certainly the thought that I was consoling myself with.

"Maybe not. I don't even know anymore. I can't seem to tell the difference between what I want and what I'm *supposed* to want." She blew her bangs out of her eyes in what was patently the most adorable fashion I had ever seen.

I set the glass before her and watched her take a large gulp. "You really should slow down," I advised. "You don't want to make yourself sick. I'm probably not the best person to clean you up and see you home afterward."

"Oh, I don't know about that," she said, squinting at me.

What the hell did *that* mean? Before I could even form the words to ask, the jukebox started playing part one of Benny Goodman's raucous "Sing Sing Sing."

"I *love* this song," she said. "Dance with me."

Now before you get the wrong idea, Marjorie and I had jitterbugged about a thousand times before. In fact, we both learned how to dance by dancing with each other. I won't lie and say that those weren't some of the happiest memories from my teen years, but we were young women in our early twenties now. It had been years since we had danced together.

"I dunno," I said sheepishly.

"Come on. It would make me feel better," she replied, entwining her fingers in mine and tugging playfully. And since I was not genetically coded to tell Marjorie no, I came out from behind the bar, confidently took her in my arms, and we began to dance.

I had forgotten how wonderful it felt to hold her—spin her—fling her around. I know I was grinning like a Cheshire cat, but part of that was because so was Marjorie. We were great together, I decided.

I really could have danced like that with her for hours—relying on pure adrenaline and pheromones to cancel out what would undoubtedly become exploded patellas and bloody stumps where my feet once were. But Wurlitzer would not have that. He had something else in mind for me, that wily bastard.

Marjorie and I were spinning as the song ended, and to make sure that I didn't send her flying headfirst into the wall, I had a very tight hold on her. Our rotation slowed as the record switched, the thumping swing replaced by the lilting melody of Glenn Miller's "Moonlight Serenade."

I contemplated letting go of her until I recognized that she was still holding on to me. "This is my favorite song," she whispered as she moved her hands into position so that I was now leading her in a slow dance.

Feeling like I might never have this opportunity again, I started moving her lithely around the floor. My right hand settled on her hip—as I had dreamt ten thousand times before—and it felt just as incredible as I had imagined.

"You're really good at this," she said, sounding surprised.

"Thanks."

"Do you go dancing a lot?"

Crap. Somehow we were back to me and my love life. "I've spent a little time on the dance floor," I replied evasively. "But you're by far the best partner I've ever had."

What the hell was I saying? Had I gone crazy? Was I actually flirting with my best friend? The straight one? The one who up until this morning was engaged to be married?

Before I chastised myself further, I fell into the dark chocolate of Marjorie's eyes. She was looking at me in a way I could easily get used to. Perhaps it was the romance of the song, I reasoned, or maybe it was her emotional state.

When her index finger slid slowly up the side of my neck to the base of my hairline, I got goose bumps. Approaching sensory overload, I closed my eyes, afraid that I would not be able to hide the lust she was evoking in me.

"Laney, why can't relationships with men be as easy as it is with you?"

Jesus, this was killing me. I opened my eyes, and the intensity I saw in her gaze stole my breath. "Because they don't love you like I do."

I had answered honestly without thinking. But her expression remained unchanged.

"And how do you love me?"

I was unable to even try and craft a cute, pithy response, which left me with nothing to fall back on but sincerity—something that had rarely worked for me in the past.

"Completely," I rasped, as our bodies continued to sway to the music. "Without limits or conditions."

The words left my mouth and I was only partially cognizant of what I was admitting. But that tiny sliver of me that was lucid was bracing for the inevitable response from her of horror and rejection. I studied her face and none of that registered.

Her finger again lightly traced the back of my neck, and the realization began to dawn on me that she *wanted* me to kiss her. Before I could rethink it and convince myself otherwise, I leaned in and brushed my lips softly against hers.

The music and our surroundings melted away as our mouths moved sensually against each other. It was all I had ever fantasized it would be, and so very much more. I would have been convinced that my heart had stopped beating were it not for the pounding pulse that was rushing through every extremity of my body.

Her lips tasted like grenadine, coaxing my tongue inside to savor whatever other sensations awaited me there. Her mouth was warm and sweet, and the kiss became deeper—hungrier. My hands framed her face as our dancing stopped. Marjorie grabbed a fistful of my hair, and the feel of it consumed me with an ardor that, were I thinking clearly, I would not have allowed myself.

I'm not sure how long we kissed, but when we finally broke apart, we were both breathless—our eyes glassy with a smoldering, consuming heat.

"You're really good at that too," she finally said. A response that I had to admit was far superior to any that I had previously fictionalized on the many lonely nights I spent imagining this moment.

"Marjorie, what are we doing?" I finally asked. I searched her eyes cautiously for any sign of remorse.

I waited for her answer, my hands sliding tentatively around her waist. Instead of replying, Marjorie—my unattainable Marjorie Stein—lifted her hand to my cheek and brushed her thumb tenderly across my lower lip. And that was all the answer I needed.

I kissed her again, adequately convinced that I was not the only one who wanted this. My thumbs lightly brushed across her nipples, and I felt them stiffen through her cardigan before my hands moved to caress the small of her back and her sumptuous backside.

"I've wanted you for so long," I whispered near her ear as my tongue snaked along the lobe.

"I know," she said.

"How long?" I asked, moving to her collarbone.

"I don't know." Her voice softly trembled. "I told myself that I should stay away from you. I should listen to my mother and get engaged to a nice boy with money."

"Look where that got you," I said, my teeth grazing the skin of Marjorie's shoulder.

"Of course, I had no idea that you would be so"—she moaned provocatively, and I made a mental note to keep doing everything that I was doing at that precise moment—"damned…skilled. Should I ask where you learned how to do all this?"

Was that what all her questions tonight had been about? "Nothing matters now but you. Come home with me."

I pulled back to gauge her response and was pleased to see her hunger unabated, her swollen, freshly kissed lips curving into a small, somewhat naughty grin.

"Aren't you worried that you're taking advantage of me?" Her palms traveled down my chest to my stomach, and then around my waist. "I am, after all, emotionally vulnerable."

"Just how I like 'em," I said glibly.

She chuckled, but her gaze looked as though she wanted to devour me. "And I am just the tiniest bit tipsy."

"Doubtful," I replied as I slipped my fingers inside her sweater and stroked the outside of her silky bra. "There wasn't any liquor in that drink."

Marjorie's face registered shock, perhaps partially from what I was doing to her under her clothing, and partially from my admission. "No?"

"No. The Betty Grable is just like the Shirley Temple…just sexier-sounding."

Our mouths met again, and I thought I would combust when she playfully nipped my bottom lip with her teeth.

"Then let's go," she murmured against me. "Because I'm all out of excuses, Laney."

I nodded. "I am too."

I closed my eyes and silently thanked that bastard Alan…and the planets that had somehow inexplicably aligned in my favor. And of course Glenn Miller, who created the most perfect love song there has ever been.

LESLEY DAVIS lives with her American partner Cindy in the West Midlands of England. She is a die-hard science-fiction/fantasy fan in all its forms and an extremely passionate gamer. *Truth Behind the Mask* from BSB is her newest romantic fantasy novel.

THE TWELFTH ROSE
LESLEY DAVIS

Danya registered her door opening but it was the strong aroma of coffee that drew her attention away from her computer screen.

"Cassie, you are a life saver," she told her colleague.

"And you need to come out of this damn office," Cassie huffed. "Stretch those legs, rest your eyes, maybe even fetch your own coffee once in a while!"

Danya cringed under her friend's well-meaning advice. "I just need to finish this proposal and then I can relax a little." Her attention drifted back to her screen where the facts and figures swam before her eyes in a mass of charts and equations.

"You never relax, Dan, that's your problem. You are too pretty to waste away behind your computer screen. Get out there! Meet Ms. Right!" Cassie slipped back through the door with one final parting shot. "Find out who your secret admirer is!"

"Yeah, yeah, like that's going to happen any time soon," Danya grumbled, staring at the luscious red roses that sat in a vase on her desk. Eleven blooms that had mysteriously arrived one a day to steadily fill the vase. She rubbed her temples, hoping to alleviate the headache brewing there.

Sipping the coffee, Danya leaned back in her chair and deliberately ignored the screen. Her office was bright and cheerful. She enjoyed her work. But it just wasn't enough anymore. She wanted more from life than spreadsheets and projection forecasts. She shook her head, surprised by her uncharacteristic musings. She wasn't the kind of person to waste time worrying about what she didn't have. After all, she was happy. Wasn't she?

Her computer chimed and a small pop-up box appeared in the middle of her screen.

I have this indescribable ache for you.

"What?" Realizing she'd spoken out loud, she quickly checked to see if anyone had heard her. No one in the large office beyond her partially open door was looking in her direction. Another chime sounded.

I need to tell you how you make me feel.

"Oh," she said softly, her skin tingling at the intimate words. Then she frowned, wondering if she was being set up by one of the office clowns. She heard the chime again as she was casting a more critical eye over the people directly in her line of vision. No one seemed to be looking her way.

This isn't a joke, I promise you.

Danya laughed. "Oh, first you're inside my computer and now you're reading my mind. Who are you?"

Will you accept these messages?

. "Sure, let's see who you are." Danya moved her curser to highlight the "continue" arrow at the bottom of the box.

I'm the one who desperately wanted to send you roses on Valentine's Day but couldn't work up the courage. I've been making up for it every day since.

Smiling, Danya reread the words and gently stroked the soft petals on an open red rose. Their appearance every day was a mystery to her and a major cause of speculation through the office.

I like knowing that I'm the one who brings that beautiful
smile to your face when you see the flowers on your desk.
I watch you smell them every morning.

Danya slowly lowered her hand from the bloom and again cast a
wary eye around the office. She searched the faces of the people who
could see inside her office and who could have witnessed her delight
at the flowers' daily arrival. Her gaze fell on the oldest member of her
team, but he was staidly married and going on sixty. He was also *so*
not her type. The girl next to him was too flighty to even work out
how to switch her own computer on, let alone send private instant
messages. Just behind them, though, at a smaller row of desks sat the
IT Specialists. Danya couldn't help but stare a little too long at Brynn,
the tall, slender woman who could resurrect dead PCs with her capable
touch and fix errant e-mail without uttering a word. Danya had been
undeniably drawn to her since she'd joined the IT team two months
ago. *Could it be?*

Work pressures, her usual excuse, had kept her too busy to start up
a friendship, let alone anything else. But that hadn't stopped her from
looking, and she found Brynn very charming to look at. Her sandy-
colored hair was cropped short and her lean body belied the strength
she displayed when moving office equipment around. Danya's body
tingled whenever Brynn was near her, yet they'd hardly spoken beyond
the typical formalities.

I've wanted to approach you for so long but I've been
afraid. Stupid insecurity, I know, and I can't hold it in any
longer. I need to do more than give you roses to show you
how I feel.

Danya's hand shook where it rested over the mouse. No one
had ever said such things to her, with so much passion that the words
reached out from the screen to caress her. A hot shiver ran through her
body. She liked how it felt.

Do you know you take my breath away when you come
into the office every day? The scent you wear stays in the

air only for a sweet while, teasing my senses. I want to get closer to you, to discover your own even sweeter scent.

Danya swallowed hard as a rush of heat settled in her belly. She could almost hear Brynn's deep voice whispering to her, suddenly feeling warm in places that had long been left cold.

Can I tell you that you dominate my dreams? You leave me breathless and aching for your caress. Then when I see you, the reality of you makes my desire so much stronger. I have to struggle not to touch you whenever you're near, to prove to myself that you are not just conjured from my desperate longings.

Trembling, Danya surreptitiously watched Brynn rise from her desk and waited, holding her breath, for those dark eyes to look over and find her staring. But Brynn just handed a folder to a neighboring colleague and sat back down. Danya's chest ached before she finally let out the breath.

"What on earth is wrong with me, lusting after a woman in my office I don't even know? Besides, she's probably not the one sending me roses." But she didn't return to her work. She stared at the computer screen, willing another message to appear.

I long to run my fingers through your hair and feel the curls wrap themselves around me. I want to lift it from your neck and press soft kisses there, feel your pulse beneath my lips...hoping you want me as much as I want you.

Danya shifted on her seat, praying her face wasn't as red as it felt. Her body was hot and every nerve sang in tune when the chimes rang from her computer.

I find myself fascinated by your hands. While the other women in the office marvel at how pretty your nails are manicured, all I think about is them raking across my back.

Danya found herself looking at her fingernails. Short and

manageable to cope with the endless typing. She never paid much attention to them other than to keep them brightly colored when she needed cheering up. Suddenly she saw them in a whole new light.

Would you be as taken with my hands? They're not soft like yours, but would hold you so tenderly that maybe you could forgive their broken skin and rough texture?

Closing her eyes, Danya imagined being held by strong arms, feeling her face caressed by fingers that were just rough enough to cause a delicious friction. She shivered as she envisaged those hands going lower. She shot up in her chair and looked around, flustered.

"This is totally inappropriate behavior in the workplace," she grumbled, although she was one of the few who hadn't been caught up in an office romance at one time or another. She kept watching the monitor, waiting.

I find myself watching you as you deal with the others here. Would you be as kind and considerate to me as you are with your colleagues when they need assistance, or would you be passionate and forceful, as I've heard that you are in the boardroom as you drive a point home?

"Which would *you* prefer?" Danya asked as if someone might answer.

I would want all of you. Every facet, every emotion. I want to be a part of everything you see and feel and experience. And I would give you the same—all of me. I want you to see me.

"I want to see you too," Danya whispered longingly, desperate for more messages, savoring the connection with this invisible someone more than any of the relationships she had blundered through recently. She'd tried so hard to find someone who saw *her*. And that someone had been here, in this office, all along.

I want us to get to know each other. I feel I know so much of you already. Everyone here admires you. They share their confidences with you, turn to you for a kind word and support. Do you need a shoulder *you* can lean on, someone who will take your confidences and keep them tucked away in their heart for safekeeping? I would hold you when you need to be held and let you go when you needed to be free, safe in the knowledge you'd come back to me.

"I'm tired of being free," Danya sighed, resting her chin in her hand. "It's not all it's cracked up to be."

I wonder if you know who I am? Are you as aware of me as I am of you? I think you are. I catch you sometimes looking at me and it's all I can do not to race to your side and do whatever you wish from me. Do you miss me when I don't come into work? I find myself pining for you in your absence and then, when you return, all seems right with my world again.

Danya found her admirer's honesty and sweetness irresistible.

I have noticed that whatever your mood, it's reflected in your clothing. When you are ready to do battle, you wear the black pinstripe suit with the white lacy shirt. The darkness gives you a projection of power while the lace shows that you are still decidedly feminine in this male-dominated office. When you are happy, you wear the vibrant blue dress that complements your bronze hair and sends my pulse soaring because it fits your curves so beautifully. It's strange how, when you are happy, it lifts my day too.

Why haven't you come to me sooner, Danya thought, astonished by the insights. She *did* indeed wear her pinstripe to try to look somber and severe when going up against the good old boys of the business. And a friend had pushed her into buying the summery blue dress, saying it complemented her unusual coloring and hugged her in all the right places.

What would you see in me, though? I am all dark clothes for business, and I'm not the least bit gregarious like your friends seem to be. I come in, do my work, and then go home alone. My work used to be everything—all I had in my life. I wanted nothing else.

Danya waited. The chime was oddly quiet and for a long, endless minute she feared the writer had gone. She stole a look out of her office and saw that Brynn was still in her seat, head bowed before the computer.

And then I saw you.

Danya sighed, torn between getting up to search the office for the writer or staying put because each word was a treasure.

You make me breathe the air anew. You cause my heart to soar when I hear your laughter. There has truly never been a more beautiful sound. I want to make you happy just to hear that sound directed at me. I want your hands on me, bringing me peace and love and hope. Delivering me to you.

Danya leaned closer and closer to her screen, trying to get closer to the person behind the words. When she realized what she was doing, she purposely pushed back.

I'm taking the coward's way out telling you how much I adore you this way when really I should just get up from my seat and come to you. I should walk right into your office now, shut the door behind me, close the blinds against prying eyes, and push you away from that desk you appear to be chained to. Then I would sink to my knees, resting my body between your legs, spread apart your thighs with my hands, push your panties aside, and...

The words struck Danya like a caress. Her insides clenched at the bold and blunt words, her body all but ready to explode from the visions that slammed through her head. She let out a strangled gasp, her arm jerked across the desk, and she spilled her coffee all over the keyboard. Crying out as the liquid soaked her desktop, she just managed to push herself away before being splashed.

Everyone in the work area turned to see what the commotion was. Cassie hurried toward Danya's office, but Brynn appeared out of nowhere, cut her off, and entered the office first.

Danya's face burned with embarrassment. "Sorry, everyone, I just spilled my coffee everywhere."

Brynn pulled tissues from a box to mop up the spillage, then said over her shoulder to the gathering throng, "Nothing to see here, people, just another christening of a keyboard because you lot will keep drinks on your desk."

Suitably chastised, everyone began to drift back to their own seats.

"Have you burnt yourself?" Bryn asked quietly once they were alone.

"No, the coffee wasn't all that hot. I'm fine, but my keyboard is swimming in mocha." Danya realized that from where Brynn was standing she could easily read the pop-up message still open on her screen and hastily hit the Control-Alt-Delete keys to lock her screen.

"Secret admirer?" Brynn asked softly as she went about the business of detaching the ruined piece of equipment from the computer.

"Hopefully not so secret for much longer," Danya said honestly, watching as Brynn took her keyboard aside and carefully tipped it over the large leafed plant that stood in a corner of the room.

"Not sure if your plant will appreciate the caffeine fix, but hopefully it won't be too wired." Brynn met Danya's gaze steadily. "I'll get you a new keyboard."

Danya nodded then decided, secret admirer or not, she was going to do something bold for once. "Would you care to join me in a cup of coffee away from my desk?"

"I'd like that very much."

Brynn's shy smile gave her courage. "Are you free now?" She gestured to her desk. "I have a good excuse to be away from that computer for once."

Brynn nodded. "Just let me go take this back to my desk, and I'll be right with you."

Danya's heart lifted as she watched Brynn walk away with her ruined keyboard in hand. She gazed at her screen, the instant messages hidden by the company screensaver.

I should walk right into your office now, shut the door behind me...

"I hope my heart is right," Danya said softly, "because the only one I want closing my door is the one who just walked through it."

❖

Brynn leaned the soaked keyboard against her chair and swiftly keyed in her password to exit the program that had been running and to lock down her own computer screen.

"Geez, Brynn, I've never seen you move so fast!" Jeff, a tech seated nearby, grinned at her.

"Coffee in the keyboard, it's a nasty business." She handed him the item in question. "Here, you can dry it out."

He whined pitifully. "Why do I have to do it?"

Brynn shrugged while reaching into her desk for the twelfth long-stemmed rose she'd hidden there. She slipped it into a folded newspaper and casually put them both under her arm.

"Because I have a date...for coffee."

LESLÉA NEWMAN is the author of fifty-seven books for adults and children, including the novel *The Reluctant Daughter*, the poetry collections *Nobody's Mother* and *Signs Of Love*, the short story collection *A Letter To Harvey Milk*, and the children's books *Heather Has Two Mommies*, *A Fire Engine For Ruthie*, and *Mommy, Mama, And Me*. Her literary awards include creative writing fellowships from the National Endowment for the Arts and the Massachusetts Artists Foundation. Nine of her books have been Lambda Literary Award finalists. She is happily (and legally!) married to Mary Newman Vazquez and lives in Massachusetts. www.lesleanewman.com.

A True Story (Whether You Believe It or Not)
Lesléa Newman

This is a true story and it happened to me, Zoey B. Jackson, on the twelfth of May, whether you believe it or not. And to tell you the truth, it's kind of hard for me to believe it myself. It's the sort of thing someone would make up to impress a girl they just met at a party or something. But believe me, I could never make this up. I could never even imagine such a thing happening and least of all, happening to me. But it did, sure as I'm standing here telling about it.

Well there I was, in the Famous Deli (which isn't famous for much except maybe its slow service) waiting for Larry, the kid behind the counter, to make me two BLTs on rye. I was just standing there minding my own business, studying the different cheeses in the deli case wondering how they make one cheese taste different from the next and why do they bother? I mean, cheese is cheese as far as I can tell. Cheddar, Muenster, Monterey Jack, do they use different kinds of cows for different kinds of cheeses or what?

I guess my mind was a little fuzzy, sort of like a TV that's out of focus. I had just spent two hours trying to get a cat down from a tree and I wasn't in the greatest mood of my entire life. When I joined the fire department two years ago, cats stuck up in trees wasn't exactly what I had in mind. I wanted to be a fireman ever since I was a little girl, only my mama said I couldn't—little girls don't grow up to be firemen or policemen or businessmen or garbage men or any other kind of men at all.

But I didn't care what my mama said. I used to dream about riding in a fire truck with all the lights flashing and the sirens screaming, wearing a big red hat and racing through town with a black and white dog wagging its tail on the back. I got a piggy bank shaped like a fire truck for my birthday once and I used to sleep with the thing. Still have it too.

So when I turned forty, two years ago, I decided to come work for the FD as a present to myself. I didn't want fame or glory or anything, but I did have visions of myself on the front page of the *Tri-Town Tribune*, all dirty and sweaty, having worked all night putting out a fire and saving a couple of lives. I was in the paper, actually, but not for any heroic deeds or anything, but because of my size. I don't know whether it's something to be proud about or something to be ashamed about, but I'm the smallest person in the history of the whole state to ever join the fire department and only the second woman. Probably the first lesbian too, but you know they didn't put that in the paper. I'm just about five feet tall when I'm not slouching, and I weigh about a hundred pounds soaking wet, but it's all solid muscle. I can whip that hose around like nobody's business when I have to.

But that night I didn't have to do anything fancy. I mean, whose idea was it to call the fire department to get a cat down out of a tree anyway? People watch way too many cartoons, that's what I think. When we got there (we meaning me and Al) old Mrs. Lawrence was standing under that tree crying and carrying on like it was her husband or one of her kids up there instead of her stupid old cat Matilda. She had Matilda's dish out there full of food and all her favorite toys—a wiffle ball, a sock full of catnip, and a tangle of yarn, and she was practically on her knees begging that animal to please, please come down. Mrs. Lawrence was promising her all sorts of things; she'd feed Matilda fresh fish every day, and she'd let her sleep in bed with her and she wouldn't yell anymore when Matilda sharpened her claws on the living room furniture if only Matilda would just get down.

I guess old Matilda had been up there for most of the day yowling and by this time it was ten at night and the neighbors were trying to get some sleep. Half of them were out there in their pj's in Mrs. Lawrence's yard trying to figure out what to do. It was probably the most exciting thing that's happened in that part of town for about ten years.

So me and Al made a big show of getting the ladder out and climbing up there and getting Matilda down. Ornery thing she was too—sank her claws deep into that branch, fluffed out her tail until it was fat as a coon's, and hissed at Al fiercer than a rattlesnake. He finally grabbed her, getting his face scratched in the process, tucked her under his arm, and climbed down the ladder with everybody cheering except poor Mrs. Lawrence, who couldn't even bring herself to look.

Once Matilda was safe in Mrs. Lawrence's arms, everyone went back home to bed, and me and Al got into the fire truck to come back to the station and make out a report. We stopped at the deli first though, for something to eat like we usually do. For some reason, most food tastes better at midnight than it does in the middle of the day. We usually get sandwiches, sometimes coffee and a piece of pie. Al likes strawberry, I go for apple or banana cream.

So Al was sitting in the truck outside waiting, and I was standing by the counter inside waiting, and I was beginning to think Larry was standing behind the counter waiting too, for the bacon to be delivered maybe, or for the pig to grow old enough to be slaughtered or something, it was taking so goddamned long. But then in walked this woman and all of a sudden I didn't care if those sandwiches didn't get made until half past next July.

She sure was pretty. More than pretty. Beautiful. Gorgeous. A real looker. Awesome, like the kids on Mrs. Lawrence's block would say. I knew she was a stranger around here because I know every woman in this town—those who do, those who don't, and those who might. This one would, I was sure of it.

She was wearing jeans that fit her just right—tight enough to give a good idea of what was under them, but loose enough to keep you guessing just a little bit. She had on this red shirt that was cut straight across the shoulders so that her collarbones were peeking out a little bit. And I could just see the edge of her bra strap, which was black and lacy. She had on these little red shoes that damn near broke my heart and a mess of silver bracelets on her right arm that made a heck of a noise sliding down her wrist and all crashing into each other when she reached into her purse for her wallet. There must have been fifty of them or more. Her pocketbook was red too, and so were her nails and lipstick. Not too red though—not cheap red or flashy red. There's red and there's red, you know what I mean, and this red looked real good. She had silver hoops in her ears, to match the bracelets maybe, and she was a big woman, which suited me just fine. I like my women big, you know, like those old painters like Renoir used to paint. None of this Twiggy stuff for me. I like a woman you can hold on to. A woman you're not afraid you're going to break if you squeeze too tight. A woman with a little meat on her bones.

Well, I took all of this in in about two seconds flat and then I looked away because I didn't want her to think I was being impolite. I know my manners. My mama taught me it's real rude to stare but I just couldn't help it and before I knew it, I found myself looking at her again. Mind your manners, I said to my eyeballs, but they just wouldn't. I watched her unzip her little blue change purse and take out four quarters for a soda, and then before I could say boo she was looking right at me with her deep brown eyes the color of a Hershey's Special Dark which happens to be my favorite candy bar. She smiled at me slow, a real sexy smile like she knew she was looking good and I knew she was looking good and she knew that I knew that she was looking good and that made her look even better.

"Hey, Zoey, here's your chow."

Wouldn't you know it? Just when things were starting to get interesting, Larry got my order done. I took my sandwiches, paid for them, and would have tipped my hat but I'd left it out in the truck with Al. I just kind of nodded my head at her or made some such gesture that was meant to be gallant but probably looked foolish. I walked past her, catching a whiff of perfume that almost made me dizzy, and left the deli with another vision to add to my fantasy life, which is about the only action there is around here for an old bulldyke like me. I don't know why I stay in this town giving all the PTA ladies something to gossip about. I could tell them a thing or two myself, but that's another story.

Well, we weren't back in the fire house for more than ten minutes when the phone rang. I let Al get it since my mouth was full of sandwich and he had downed his in about three seconds flat.

"It's for you," Al said and I don't know who was more surprised, him or me. I never get calls at work. We're not supposed to tie up the phone in case there's a fire or another cat stuck up a tree or something, and anyway, I keep my personal life, what little there's left of it, pretty much a secret though it's crystal clear I'm queer as a three-dollar bill even if I don't wear purple on Thursdays. I think it was the first phone call I got in the whole two years I'd worked there. I wiped the mayo off my chin with the back of my sleeve, took the phone, and spoke in my most official-sounding voice. "Hello?"

"Hello. Is this Zoey?"

I knew it was her. I couldn't believe it, yet I wasn't surprised. A little startled, a little shook up, even shocked maybe, but not surprised. She sounded like she looked. Good. Sassy. Sure of herself. And hot.

"Yeah, this is me." God, what a dumb thing to say.

"My name is Natalie and I was just in the deli a little while ago. I don't know if you noticed me or not"—yeah, right—"but I noticed you and I was wondering if you'd like to go out and have a cup of coffee with me sometime."

How about right this second, I wanted to say, but I didn't. Get a grip, Zoey old girl, I said to myself. Don't rush into anything now.

"Uh yeah, sure, that'd be great," I said, sounding about thirteen.

"How about tomorrow then, around four?"

"Sure," I said, "you know where Freddy's is?" Freddy's is the only place in town that sells a decent cup of coffee and doesn't have a million high school kids throwing spitballs at each other in the middle of the afternoon. It's a little out of town, not sleazy or anything—it's not far from my place, as a matter of fact, but not smack dab in the middle of town either. I told her how to get there and then there wasn't much left to say.

"See you tomorrow, sugar," she said, and I swear I could feel her tongue licking the inside of my ear right through that telephone.

I hardly slept at all that night, I tell you. I was more than a little curious and more than a lot flattered, and hell, I figured that any woman with that much sass deserved at least an hour of my time and hopefully more. I wondered where she had come from and what she was doing out there by herself, all spruced up like that in the middle of the night. But to tell you the truth, I didn't really care. I was just glad she was where she was when she was and I was there too.

I tossed and turned, too full of BLT and lust to sleep, but I must have dozed off sometime because the next thing I knew it was ten o'clock and the sun was coming in through the windows heating up my eyes like they were two eggs cooking on a grill. My bedroom is tiny—one wall is mostly all windows and the bed takes up almost the whole room. I don't mind though; in fact, I kind of like it like that. Feels sort of like a nest, though why I have a double bed at this point is beyond me. Nobody's been in it since Sally left over two years ago. Hard to believe it's been two years already. Time sure does fly, I guess.

But it must have been because she left right before I turned forty, right before I signed up at the fire department. That's one of the reasons I did it. With Sally gone there was this empty space in my life, this aching in my belly I didn't know how to fill, and I just couldn't face all those awful lonely nights by myself. So now I sit in the firehouse two, sometimes three nights a week playing poker with Al.

I sure didn't want to be thinking about Sally this morning, so I got up, plugged in the coffeepot, and went into the jane to splash some cold water on my face. "Looking good, old girl," I said to myself in the mirror over the sink, which I noticed was speckled with old toothpaste. "Who says Zoey B. is over the hill, huh? Women are still beating down your door, old gal." I winked at my reflection—I am a pretty good winker if I do say so myself. I can also raise one eyebrow at a time; it's not as hard as it looks if you practice. I looked at myself and wondered what Natalie—God, even her name was sexy—had seen last night standing in the deli that made her give me a call. Your basic brown eyes, an ordinary nose, average lips, nothing special.

Maybe it was the uniform. Some girls really go for that sort of thing. Or maybe it was the gray hair at the temples, makes me look kind of distinguished. Some girls like older women. I wondered how old Natalie was and if she did this sort of thing often. Maybe her buddies, whoever they were, had put her up to it. Maybe a whole gang would be waiting at Freddy's to laugh their heads off at the old bulldyke who'd been taken in by the first pretty face that's shown up in this pint-sized town since 1959. Or worse, maybe there'd be some guys waiting with chains and billy clubs ready to kick ass. Like I said, it's no secret who I am and it's no secret that some folks in this town don't exactly like it either.

That was really hard on Sally, one of the reasons she left, I think. Nothing ugly's ever happened, but we were always thinking it might. Sally took herself to San Francisco, where she says the streets are paved with queers and she can even hold hands with her new girlfriend all over town and nobody bats an eye. Not even the cops because even most of the goddamn cops are queer themselves. Now that's something I'd sure like to see.

I drank my coffee and messed around most of the day, cleaning up the house and doing chores. My place is small, just the bedroom, the kitchen, the living room, and a small spare room where I keep all my stuff—my tools and papers and stuff. Used to be Sally's painting room—that's what she does, paint—watercolors mostly. She even had a show of them in San Francisco, sent me a postcard about it.

About three o'clock I started getting nervous. First of all, what the heck was I going to wear? Not that I had much choice. It was either jeans or jeans. Jeans with a ripped knee, jeans speckled with white paint, or jeans with two belt loops missing. I could wear my black chinos but that would look awfully funny, me so dressed up in the middle of the day. I put on the jeans with the belt loops missing and a white shirt I thought about ironing and my sneakers. By the time I'd finished fussing with my hair, which is only about two inches long and not all that much to fuss about, it was time to get my ass out the door. I sure didn't want to be late—something told me Natalie wasn't the kind of woman who liked to be kept waiting.

It only took me ten minutes to walk to Freddy's. I got there at four o'clock on the nose and she wasn't there. Well, fine, I told myself. I don't care. Wouldn't be the first time old Zoey B.'s been stood up, not the first time she's looked like a fool. I sat myself down in a booth toward the back, ordered a cup of coffee, and looked at my watch. Four minutes after four. Oh well, I thought, ripping open a packet of sugar and dumping it into my cup. I knew it was too good to be true. These things don't really happen. Not in real life anyway.

At exactly ten past four, the door to Freddy's swung, and I mean swung open and in walked Natalie like she owned the whole goddamn place. She was looking so good I almost dove right straight into my coffee. I held on to that cup for dear life as she stuck her hands on her hips and looked around like she had all the time in the world. When she spotted me, a slow smile crept across her face that said, I knew you'd be waiting for me. I smiled too, thinking to myself, fool, of course she'd be late. She didn't just want to meet me here. She wanted to make an entrance.

I watched Natalie walk across Freddy's slowly, giving me plenty of time to admire her as she weaved her butt in and out of tables and chairs on her way over to where I was sitting. She was wearing this white, blousy kind of thing with a belt at her waist with these pink pants that had little black designs on them all over the place that reminded me of slanty tic-tac-toe boards. She had on little pink shoes too, that knocked me out; round pink earrings that looked like buttons; and hooked over her arm, a shiny black purse. It's those little things that separate the femmes from the butches, you know. Sally taught me that. Accoutrements are everything, she used to say, and of course I had to ask her what the heck accoutrements were. They're just a fancy word for accessories, which is just a fancy word for earrings and pocketbooks and stuff. Sally was always throwing those fifty-dollar words around when she was angry at me, or frustrated at being stuck in this peanut-size town.

Anyway, I don't know a thing about accoutrements. I have an old leather wallet I stick in my back pocket, two pairs of sneakers, and earlobes as unpunctured as the day I was born. But Natalie, boy, I bet she has a jewelry box the size of Montana and a closet full of pretty little shoes that could just about break your heart. She was wearing those same silver bracelets again that clattered down her arm in a fine racket practically every time she moved. It was like each one bracelet wanted to be the first to get down to her wrist and maybe win a prize. Her lipstick was one shade lighter than yesterday, her smile one shade darker.

"Hi, honey, sorry I'm late," she said in a voice that let me know she wasn't sorry at all. "Have you been waiting long?"

All my life, I wanted to tell her, just to hear a woman like you call me honey. "Nah, I just got here myself," I lied. Both of us knew I had been waiting and would have kept waiting forever, and then some if I'd had to.

She slid into the booth, put her purse beside her and leaned back against the seat looking at me.

"Want some coffee?" I asked.

"I'll have tea," she said and leaned toward me with her elbows on the table as if deciding to have tea was an intimate secret just the two of us were in on. Her blouse moved when she leaned forward, revealing the top of her cleavage, and I almost forgot how to breathe.

"Hey Freddy, bring this lady a cup of tea," I hollered over my shoulder. Natalie smiled and settled back in the booth and her blouse settled back over her skin and her cleavage disappeared to wherever it is cleavages go to when they're not out there in the open calling to you practically by your own name.

We kind of looked at each other again, with me grinning like a fool because I just couldn't believe I was sitting there in Freddy's with this absolute doll who had come out of nowhere, and she smiling that I-know-what-you're-thinking smile and playing with one of her bracelets.

"So, uh, here we are," I said, always brilliant at making conversation.

"Yes," she said. Not yeah or yep or uh-huh, but yes. "Thanks for coming out with me."

"My pleasure," I said and I hoped she could tell I meant it. "I was very flattered that you asked me."

Now she smiled a real smile and I could see her beautiful white teeth. She even blushed a little bit, which only made her prettier because I saw that maybe she wasn't as sure of herself as she thought she was.

"I didn't know if you'd be glad or not. But when that boy behind the counter at the deli called your name, I knew it would be easy to find you. How many Zoeys could there be at the fire department of a town this size?" She waved her hand around like the whole town was sitting in Freddy's, and that sent her bracelets rushing back down toward her elbow this time, sounding like a million tiny little bells.

"I'll have to remember to thank Larry next time I see him," I said.

"Yes," she said again. It sounded almost like a hiss, like she had just run into the room and was a little out of breath when she said it. "I wanted to meet you."

"Why?"

"Because," she said, staring straight into my eyes, "I've always been interested in fires. Ever since I was a little girl."

"Really?" I couldn't believe it.

"Yes. And when I saw you in your uniform," she lowered her eyes and lifted them again, "I knew I could ask you some questions about fires and maybe you'd have the answers." She leaned forward. "Now why, for example, do you sometimes fight fire with fire, and why is it sometimes better to soak the flames until everything for miles around is wet through and through? Then I've heard that some fires," she paused like she was really thinking this out, "some fires burn even hotter when you try to put them out. And some fires can burn for days, weeks, months even, and there's just no stopping them." She started stroking my arm, which felt like it was on fire itself, and her fingertips were soft as feathers. "I thought maybe you could explain," she went on, "why some fires are just warm enough, some burn so hot they destroy you, some go out in a minute, some need to be stoked to keep them going, and some will just burn and burn on their own forever."

"Let's go," I said.

We stood up and I threw two bills down on the table. Freddy was just coming over with Natalie's tea, but we just walked right by him without saying a word. We didn't say anything to each other either as we walked down the street. I just listened to Natalie's little heels clicking and my heart beating and thought about the fire burning deep inside my belly and wondering how in the world it could ever be put out. I never wanted anybody the way I wanted Natalie right that second and I didn't care if the whole town knew who she was and who I was and what I hoped we were just about to do. It was all I could do not to take her in my arms right there on the street. But hell, this isn't San Francisco. The six blocks between my house and Freddy's seemed like five hundred miles.

Finally we got to my place, and my hands were shaking so bad I could barely get the key in the lock. There goes my suave bulldyke image, I thought, if I ever had one to begin with. I kept fiddling with that door for what seemed like forever until it finally gave way and we stumbled inside. Or rather I stumbled. I don't think Natalie's ever stumbled a day in her life. Natalie entered my place. She sauntered, sashayed, swished and swung those big luxurious hips from side to side, checking out the place like it was something special, like Buckingham Palace. We were standing in the living room, and she had her back to me, looking at this painting of a sunset that Sally had done.

I didn't want to tell her about Sally. I didn't want her to know I had ever been with another woman before or ever would be again. Nothing mattered but this moment. Nothing mattered but her. She filled my house with all the longing I had ever known in my whole life, and I knew if I didn't have her that second, I would burst and maybe even die. With my heart beating in my throat like a big bullfrog, I walked up behind her and cupped my hands under her gorgeous behind. She leaned back slightly, letting her weight settle into my palms, like she was sitting in them, and I thought of that song for a minute, called "He's got the whole world in his hands." But just for a minute because Natalie turned her head and whispered into my neck, "How about showing me where you live, baby?"

I turned Natalie around and put my mouth down on hers for an answer. She was about the most kissable woman I ever met in my whole life. And even though I'm hardly a Casanova or Don Juan, I've known a few women in my time. None of them kissed like Natalie kissed. Natalie sucked, nibbled, bit, chewed, licked, rubbed, stroked, caressed, and damn near danced with those lips. And the things she did with her tongue I don't even have words for. I was dying. My knees got all rubbery and I thought they'd give out on me for sure. Finally she, not me, led us to the bedroom, like the tough femme she was.

But once we got there, she knew her place. She kicked off her shoes, slid all those damn bracelets off her arm, lay back on my bed, and let me undo her buttons one by one, setting loose her glorious body an inch at a time. Her breasts were round and full as the moon, the perfect size for me to get my mouth around. She pressed my head into her harder and harder and I made love to her breasts for hours, weeks, years, it seemed and that woman just couldn't get enough. Finally she took my hand and put it where it belonged.

I took off her pants and her pink lace panties gently, and slid four fingers inside like a diver hitting the water in one clean, easy motion. She took me in all the way, and inside there it was soft as…soft as… hell, she gave a whole new meaning to the word soft. Soft and sweet and wet and wonderful. Oh I tell you she was all woman from those deep dark chocolate eyes down to the soles of her pretty little feet and I should know because I explored every single inch of her. I felt like a kid in a candy store—my eyes just got bigger and bigger and bigger and I wanted everything. And each kiss I gave her, each touch, each lick, would make her catch her breath in the sweetest little gasp, like that was the first time anyone had ever touched her in that spot before. I tell you, some women are just made for loving and Natalie was one of them, that's for sure.

Before I knew it, it was dark outside, with the windows all filled up with black and a little sliver of a moon peeking in. I could barely see Natalie's face though I could feel it an inch away from mine. Maybe that's why I let what happened happen. It's almost like I didn't even know what was going on until we were in the middle of it, but before I knew anything, there I was flat on my back with Natalie up above me, unbuttoning my shirt and sliding my jeans down.

Now I'm usually clear about who's the butch and who's the

femme, and I like my women to just lay back and enjoy themselves while I give them what they want. That's how I always get my pleasure, from giving pleasure. That's the way it's always been and that's the way it's always going to be and that's the way I like it. But Natalie had me under some kind of spell. My whole body just wanted to leap into her mouth—breasts, belly, legs, elbows, you name it. So when she finally reached for me down there, I didn't give her my usual, "No thanks, babe." I let her.

Listen, I sure don't want this getting around the PTA or even to my friends who are queer like me, because it's a known fact, in certain circles anyway, that Zoey B. Jackson is a proper, old-fashioned stone diesel dyke that doesn't flip for nobody. I've never been a rollover butch but that night stands apart like it was a whole lifetime by itself, or a dream maybe, or a visit to another planet. No one I knew had ever met Natalie or ever would. My instincts told me that. And I was safe with her. And that for some reason beyond what I could understand, I needed her to do to me what no one else had done, though more than a few had tried.

"Silky," she whispered as her fingers stroked me. "You're as soft as silk, see?" And she took her pink lace bra, which happened to be real silk, and rubbed it all over my body. I went wild, I tell you. Then she kissed her way down from my breasts to my belly and beyond, and when her mouth landed down there, I thought they'd have to pick me up off the floor in a million little pieces. I wondered why it had taken me forty-two years to lay myself down for a woman. I sure hoped all the women I ever made love to had felt that good. Just thinking about it got me even more excited and before I knew what was happening, my whole body exploded like the fireworks they set off down by the high school on the fourth of July and I was gasping and moaning and carrying on like a banshee.

I felt a little shy after that but Natalie just laughed and came up to kiss me. I tasted myself on her lips and I tell you, that got me going all over again. I'm usually a once-a-night girl—I don't need all that much to keep me satisfied—but that night I lost track of how many times I did it to Natalie and she did it to me and we did it to each other.

What a night. I tell you we didn't even think about getting any sleep until about six in the morning when the windows were a pale pink and the birds were singing their wake-up song in the trees. I held

Natalie tight and she laid her head against my chest and filled up my arms with all the sweetness in the world. I fell asleep with one of her legs braided between mine and her soft breath tickling the base of my neck.

When I woke up hours later, the sun washing my face with heat, she was gone. Gone. I couldn't believe it. Lock, stock, and pocketbook, gone. I got up and paced around the house, fooling myself every two minutes. Oh, she must be in the bathroom, I'd tell myself, and go looking. Or maybe she's in the kitchen making coffee. Nope. Maybe she's in the spare room looking at my stuff, spying on me. I wouldn't mind. But it was useless. She was gone. I climbed back into bed, forlorn as a big-pawed puppy whose owner just hollered at him to go on home.

I stretched out flat on my back with my hands behind my head, thinking. I could still smell her, hell, I could practically still taste her in my mouth. I wanted her again so badly I almost touched myself. I don't want this going any further than you, me, and the lamppost, but I even cried a little bit—just a tear or two leaking quietly out the corner of my eye. I buried my face in her pillow then, the pillow she slept on, that still smelled like her fancy perfume. And when I turned over and reached my hands up under my head again, I felt something cold, round and hard. One of Natalie's bracelets. She'd either forgotten it or left it under the pillow on purpose, for me.

I put it on and a second later took it right off. It looked silly, like an ankle bracelet on a dinosaur. I've never worn a bracelet or a ring or a necklace in my whole life. But when I got dressed later, I surprised myself and put it on again, just to keep her near me. I pretended like we were going steady and I liked the feel of that bracelet sliding up and down my arm like a kid on a water slide. I wished I had given Natalie something and I probably would have if she'd stuck around a little longer. Or maybe what I had given her was enough.

So that's what happened to me, Zoey B. Jackson, on the twelfth of May. It's a true story and here's the bracelet to prove it. Funny, I feel almost naked without it, wear it all the time now, in case she comes back. Well, that's not really why. I guess, I know Natalie isn't going to pass through this town again except in my dreams maybe. Hell, who knows how long I'm going to stay in this town anyway? Been thinking I might get myself to San Francisco one of these days, see what Sally's up to. Bet I could get myself a job there, and wouldn't that be something, riding up and down those San Francisco hills in a big red fire truck? I'm not really a city person, but I don't know, these past few weeks, this town has felt too small all of a sudden, like a sweater that shrunk in the wash one day and doesn't fit right anymore. Al says there's something different about me too, but he doesn't know what. Oh, he noticed the bracelet right off—said it looked real fine, and was I going to start putting out fires in high heels and skirts now? I must have blushed real red when he said that. If only he knew what I knew. And don't you dare tell him.

MEGHAN O'BRIEN lives in Northern California with her partner, young son, and gang of four-legged friends. She is a dog lover and a gamer who lives to tell stories. She has two novels published by Bold Strokes Books, *Thirteen Hours* and the e-book *The Three*. She also has had selections in *Erotic Interludes* 2–5, as well as *Romantic Interludes 1: Discovery*. Her romance *Battle Scars* is forthcoming in 2009.

Devil and the Deep Blue Sea
Meghan O'Brien

The frigid rain plastered Coast Guard Executive Officer Erin Brooks's hair against her face, where it quickly froze to her skin. Her uniform was soaked through, and even with her free hand jammed in the pocket of her thick coat, her fingers had gone numb. The medium endurance cutter *Storis* pitched and rolled on the waves, tossing her this way and that on the well deck. She had to clutch the ice-cold railing just to stay on her feet.

But Erin was oblivious to her own body, and to the fierce rocking of the ship that knocked a seaman onto his ass just to her left. She'd stopped registering the cold an hour ago. Eyes narrowed, she struggled to keep sight of the seaman, just a yellow slash bobbing up and down in the choppy gray sea, and the woman who was towing him to the safety of the rigid hull inflatable boat. The storm raged around her, wind howling, but the only thing she could hear was her own heartbeat, thundering in her ears.

"XO Brooks!" Petty Officer Jackson shouted from her right side. The tone of his voice made her suspect that he'd been calling her name for a while. "Ma'am, you're shaking."

Erin said nothing. Katy finally made it to the RHIB and two other rescue swimmers reached out to pull the drowning man inside. Seaman Young lay at one end of the boat, head lolling against the side in time with the massive waves. If Katy hadn't gone out there when she did, he would probably be dead.

Until the chief warrant officer made it back on board the *Storis* with her charge, that thought was cold comfort.

"That's the last one," Jackson said. "Ma'am, why don't you head to the bridge? You've been out here for two hours straight."

"When they're on board," Erin answered. One of the sailors manning the RHIB caught the back of Katy's suit and tugged her into the rescue boat just as a particularly massive wave soaked all its occupants. Erin's heart leapt into her throat and only started beating again when the water receded and she could make out Katy clinging to the man she had just rescued, keeping him anchored in the RHIB. "I'll go in once they're on board. Thank you, Jackson."

He nodded crisply and made his way across the deck, moving hand over hand along the railing. He took his place at the crane that would raise the RHIB from the water. Erin leaned over the rail and watched Katy intently as the rescue craft approached the starboard side of the *Storis*.

Jackson was right, she was shaking. Hell, she was scared to death.

Katy and another sailor worked to attach the RHIB to the crane that would hoist it back aboard the *Storis*. The coxswain was clearly struggling to keep them in position as the nearly ten-foot swells battered the small boat and its occupants. Erin held her breath as the stern line was ripped repeatedly from Katy's hands.

"Come on, come on," she whispered.

Despite the coxswain's efforts, the RHIB jerked sharply as rough water lifted it, then sent them riding down the face of the giant wave. Erin's stomach dropped. The rescue swimmers and the last of the survivors from the *Merry Lady* were in serious danger of capsizing. If they pitch-poled, it could be all over.

A seaman brushed against her as he slip-slid purposefully across the deck. All around her, people went about performing their jobs, just as their shipmates were doing in the sea below. Erin tore her eyes away from the RHIB for the briefest of moments to glance up at the bridge. The CO, Atkins, was up there looking down on their efforts. What must he think of the vigil she was keeping?

A shout arose from the starboard side, and Erin refocused on the RHIB. Katy had managed to attach the stern line, and now the small boat was ready to be hoisted aboard. But first all its occupants would have to board the *Storis* using a rope ladder thrown over the side of the deck. Erin hated this part. With the way the waves tossed about the

RHIB in counter-rhythm to the *Storis*, the able-bodied would likely have to jump to grab on to the lowest rung. They would lower a Stokes rescue basket for the injured.

Erin could barely stand to watch when it was Katy's turn to scale the ladder. The waves pounded the ship relentlessly, and a large swell crested just as Katy jumped for the bottom rung. To Erin's horror, one of Katy's hands was torn from the ladder and she dangled precariously for what felt like an eternity before regaining her hold. Erin knew Katy was operating on pure adrenaline at this point. She should be too exhausted to hold on to that ladder, or to power her way to the top. But somehow she did. Two seamen pulled her onto the deck and supported her until her footing was secure.

The boatswain's mate assembled his crew to start the arduous process of hauling the RHIB aboard, but Erin's only concern was Katy. Katy shouted to the other members of her team, her words lost on the wind. Then her gaze shifted to Erin.

Erin knew she was showing more than she should when their eyes met. She felt open and exposed, raw and battered by the emotional toll of the last hours. It took her more than a couple of breaths to regain her composure, and Katy's face told her that she had just revealed everything in those few moments of pure, utter relief. Erin broke their gaze first, and turned quickly to shout to the sailor who was helping carry Seaman Young, the injured crewman, across the unsteady deck.

"Take him to see the corpsman!" It was a ridiculous order. He already knew what to do, but he gave her a polite nod anyway.

"Yes, ma'am," he said, never faltering in his quick transport.

Erin nodded curtly, then turned to make her way back to the bridge. Even though all she wanted to do was reassure herself that Katy had made it back in one piece, she didn't trust herself to hide her emotions from the curious eyes on deck.

"Ma'am!"

Swallowing, Erin stopped mid-step and swiveled. Katy stood no more than five feet in front of her. Erin's knees nearly gave out at the sight. Katy's short, dark hair was a mess, stuck to her face, and rivulets of water coursed down her smooth, tanned skin. Her brown eyes burned with some unspoken emotion, her lips tinged blue from the cold. Erin gripped the railing for support, and Katy did the same.

Erin pulled herself together the best she could. "Yes, Chief Warrant Officer?"

"Ma'am—"

A wave crashed into the starboard side and soaked them both, knocking Erin off her feet and into Katy's chest. A strong arm caught her there and kept her from taking a header onto the deck. How could Katy be so warm when she had just been pulled from the Bering Sea? For a moment Erin allowed herself the pleasure of being held, then she pushed away from Katy with both hands on her chest.

"Report to the corpsman, Ms. Ortiz," Erin said, forcing steel into her voice. She grabbed the railing again and concentrated on stopping her legs from shaking. "Good job out there."

"I'm fine, ma'am. I promise." Katy took a step away from Erin, as if sensing she needed the space. "Seaman Young took the worst of it."

"You were in the water for a long time. Two hours, seven rescued. Go see Doc right now. That's an order."

"Yes, ma'am." Katy bit her lip, then searched Erin's face. "I appreciate your concern."

More than anything, Erin wanted to touch her, to reassure herself that Katy was very much alive. But that was impossible. With a tight smile, Erin locked all her personal feelings away. There was no place for them here.

"That's my job," she said, and turned to go to the bridge.

An hour later, Erin stretched out on her bed, wrapped in a warm robe. A hot shower had her blood moving again, but her fingertips still tingled from the previous cold. She stared at her stateroom door, afraid of hearing the knock, hoping for it all the same.

As much as she needed to see Katy, she didn't know how she would maintain a professional distance tonight. Though Erin had stood vigil during perilous rescue situations before, never had it been so personal. Never had she stood watch as Katy's lover. She was shaken by how frightened she had been, and by how unimportant their secret had seemed in those moments when she wasn't sure Katy would make it back to the *Storis* alive. It had taken everything Erin had not to kiss her when that wave sent her crashing into Katy's arms. She doubted she would be so controlled in the privacy of her own stateroom.

Their one unspoken rule was no physical contact when they were at sea. It was just too risky, and it would be too easy to get carried away. If they were discovered, they could both be discharged. No matter how much she hated denying what they shared, Erin wasn't ready to give up the Coast Guard yet. She didn't think Katy wanted that, either.

Yet Erin couldn't imagine not holding her tonight. Just one hug, maybe. Or was that too dangerous? Erin held vigil on the door, willing the knock to come. Could she really stop at one hug? If she had Katy in her arms, it would be so easy to kiss her. And then what?

No, it was probably better if she didn't see Katy at all tonight. She needed to touch her so badly and if they were alone together, she was afraid she'd give in. Erin sighed uneasily. Shouldn't Katy be done seeing the doc by now? What if something was wrong?

Erin closed her eyes. Watching the door wouldn't make Katy appear. And even though she didn't know how she would sleep until she saw Katy again, she needed to try. They would see each other tomorrow morning on duty. For now, that would have to be enough.

A knock at her stateroom door brought Erin upright, her heart pounding. If she were smart she would ignore the knock and hope that Katy would go away. But what if it wasn't Katy? Erin's throat tightened. What if something had happened to Katy and this was someone coming to her with a report?

"Just a moment," Erin said, and glanced around for her uniform. Her head felt strangely light. "I'll be right there."

"It's me, ma'am," Katy said. "Katy."

As though Erin wouldn't know her voice anywhere. For a moment she sat paralyzed, unsure what to do next. If she let Katy in, she wasn't sure what would happen. But she didn't want to tell her to go away.

"Please, ma'am." Katy's voice wavered, so full of emotion. "May I talk to you for a moment?"

Erin got to her feet and crossed the small room in three steps. Though she knew she should get dressed before answering, she didn't want to take the time. She could hear the raw need in Katy's voice, and her body responded. Throwing caution to the wind, Erin opened the door and tried to keep her own voice steady. "Yes, Ms. Ortiz?"

Katy stood in the hallway wearing dry uniform pants and a navy blue *Storis* T-shirt. She squared her shoulders and gave Erin a sharp salute. "XO, I just wanted to make sure that you were all right."

Even having spent the past two hours battling the Bering Sea, Katy looked gorgeous. It had been three weeks since they last kissed, let alone made love. Normally a patrol lasted only a month, but this one had been extended because of repairs. Erin didn't know how she would make it another three weeks. Surely she would die of wanting before then.

"Ma'am," Katy said quietly. "May I come inside?"

Erin's face burned in a way that didn't seem connected to either the cold rain or the hot shower. She poked her head out into the hallway, checking to make sure it was empty, then gestured Katy inside. "Come in, Chief Warrant Officer."

Katy stepped into the stateroom and closed the door behind her. Her posture was ramrod straight, but her expression was open and full of need. "Ma'am, I apologize if I'm being presumptuous."

Too worn out to keep up the formalities in private, Erin murmured, "You can drop the ma'am stuff, Katy."

Katy's whole body relaxed. She leaned against the stateroom door and smiled, so unthinkingly beautiful that it sent an ache to Erin's stomach. In an instant, the chief warrant officer became the lover she cherished in port. And immediately Erin regretted letting her guard down. How was she going to stay in control with Katy looking at her like that?

"I really am okay, Erin." Katy reached out, and after a moment's hesitation, put her hand on Erin's arm. "I promise."

"You were out there a long time," Erin said under her breath. The walls were thin enough that she didn't feel comfortable speaking at full volume. "You were in the water too long."

"I'm tough." Katy pulled her hand away, leaving Erin empty with its absence. Grinning, she whispered, "You know that."

"Tougher than me, I guess." Erin blinked back the tears that threatened to escape and leaned close so she could whisper in Katy's ear. "You have no idea how hard it is not to kiss you right now."

"I have every idea how hard it is." Katy's cold lips brushed against Erin's earlobe, making Erin shiver. "But to be honest, at the moment I don't care much about keeping secrets." Despite her words, she made no move to touch Erin.

Exhaling, Erin said, "We can't."

"Okay." Katy drew back and gave Erin a sad smile. "I understand."

"I'm sorry," Erin mouthed. The tears spilled over then and she turned away, embarrassed by her naked emotion. Resisting temptation was the right thing to do here, wasn't it? So why did it make her feel so bad?

"I'll see you tomorrow, ma'am." Though Katy did a hell of a job keeping her voice steady, Erin could hear the sorrow in her words. "I'm glad you're okay."

Erin closed her eyes, torn apart by the return of formality between them. She didn't want Katy to leave, but it wouldn't be fair to either of them to let her stay. One of them needed to be strong, for both their sakes. No matter how much she needed to feel their connection right now, no matter how strong her emotions, she had to let Katy walk out that door. There was no other option.

Erin jerked in surprise when Katy's fingers touched her face, gently wiping away her tears. "None of that," Katy whispered. "It's all right."

The tenuous hold Erin had on her control snapped. She opened her eyes and stepped forward without thinking, taking a fistful of Katy's T-shirt and pulling her close. Their first kiss was clumsy, all passion and no technique. The second was perfect, familiar and life-affirming.

Erin struggled not to moan when Katy's tongue dipped into her mouth. She sucked on it lightly, and felt Katy shudder. Erin broke their kiss and released Katy's shirt, shaken by her own weakness. She had promised herself she would never cross this line on duty, and yet all she could think about now was kissing Katy again.

"You should go," Erin whispered, not daring to meet Katy's gaze. "Before we do something we'll regret."

"Okay," Katy whispered back, but she didn't move. "You want me to go?"

Gathering her courage, Erin looked at Katy. What she saw made her legs shake. She could feel how much Katy loved her every time they touched, and she had heard the words so many times she'd lost count. But right now Katy's eyes said more than her mouth or hands ever had. Erin placed her palms on either side of Katy's face, wishing she could capture this moment and keep it forever.

"No," Erin whispered. "Don't go."

Katy dropped her hand to the belt of Erin's robe and tugged the knot loose. Slipping her hands inside, she grabbed Erin's hips and walked her backward until the corner of Erin's desk dug into her back. Without missing a beat, Katy lifted Erin onto the desk and spread open her robe.

"Quickly," Erin said, so softly she wasn't sure Katy could even hear the words. "Quiet."

Nodding, Katy ran both hands over Erin's breasts. Her fingers were still cold from the sea, and she left Erin's nipples almost painfully hard. Erin gritted her teeth so she wouldn't cry out, it felt so good to be touched. Erin gripped Katy's biceps, shivering when Katy pressed her bare thighs apart.

Erin leaned her forehead on Katy's shoulder and anticipated the first cool touch on her overheated pussy. Even expecting it, she jerked at the chill of Katy's hand. Still she craved it. Needed it, more than she had ever needed anything in her life.

Katy's fingers found her wetness, and Erin tightened her grip on Katy's arms. She spread her legs as wide as she could, desperate for Katy to go inside. Her heat warmed Katy's fingers. She needed Katy to fill her, she needed the undeniable proof that Katy was alive. That she was right here.

With one hand on Erin's hip, Katy slipped a finger into her pussy, then two. Erin let her head fall back, soundlessly parting her lips and wishing like hell that she could moan out loud. The emptiness she always felt when they were forced to be apart on patrol was gone. Erin squeezed Katy's arms and mouthed, "I love you."

Katy nodded, curling her fingers to brush the spot that would make Erin come quickly. Erin already mourned the inevitable end of their lovemaking even though she knew they couldn't take their time—not here, not now. But as soon as Erin gave in to her orgasm, Katy would leave, just as Erin had asked. Erin closed her eyes and concentrated on holding off as long as possible, not wanting to let Katy go.

But Katy followed orders, pumping her fingers hard, just the way Erin loved. The pleasure built rapidly in the pit of Erin's stomach. Her limbs growing heavier by the second, Erin grasped Katy's arm as it worked between her thighs, marveling at her strength even when she knew she must be exhausted. She could feel so much love in every stroke, and when Katy's thumb landed on her clit and circled quickly, Erin was utterly and completely lost.

Head thrown back, she came in a silent roar. Katy wrapped her free arm around Erin's back in a fierce hug and held her close. Erin could feel Katy's rapid heartbeat against her bare breasts and she closed her eyes and savored the strong rhythm. Too quickly Katy kissed her cheek, whispered, "I love you," and withdrew. She walked to the sink on the other side of the room and washed her hands in silence.

Erin slipped off the desk, wobbling on unsteady legs. She pulled her robe closed and tied the belt tightly. Too late for propriety, but she had to pull herself together somehow. She watched Katy dry her hands then turn back to her, professional mask firmly in place.

"Thank you for your time, ma'am." Katy saluted crisply, then smiled briefly. "I should be getting back to my rack."

"I was proud of you out there tonight, Ms. Ortiz," Erin said. In all her worrying, this was the one thing she hadn't said. It just so happened to be the most important thing. "Well done."

"I was just doing my job," Katy said, but her smile grew.

"Doesn't make me any less proud." Erin took a deep breath and opened the door, glancing outside to make sure the hallway was empty. Coast clear, she gave Katy a halfhearted smile. "Dismissed."

"Thank you, ma'am." With a curt nod, Katy stepped past her into the hall.

Before Katy could walk away, Erin murmured, "Ms. Ortiz?"

Katy turned back. "Ma'am?"

"Thank you for stopping by. I appreciate it."

After glancing around to confirm they were still alone, Katy grinned. "That was my pleasure, ma'am."

CLIFFORD HENDERSON lives and plays in Santa Cruz, California. She runs The Fun Institute, a school of improv and solo performance, with her partner of seventeen years. In their classes and workshops, people of all genders and sexual orientations learn to access and express the myriad of characters itching to get out. When she's not teaching or performing, she's writing, gardening, and twisting herself into weird yoga poses. Her first novel, *The Middle of Somewhere*, was released by Bold Strokes Books in 2009. Her forthcoming novels include *Spanking New* (2010) and *Maye's Request* (2011), from Bold Strokes Books. www.cliffordhenderson.net.

BOILED PEAS
CLIFFORD HENDERSON

Penny's heart had been trampled so many times she often thought of it as raw hamburger. Or an overripe persimmon pecked to death by birds and then dropped—*splat!*—from a tree.

True, she was overly sensitive. Or that's what her mom always said when she came to visit. Which she just had. And although her mom lived 4,915 miles away, her words had a way of sticking around after she left. They'd wrap around Penny like an itchy blanket. "You ask too much. Want too much. Quit looking for the pea, princess." The pea line was her mom's favorite.

Penny ripped open the bag of frozen Safeway peas and let them tumble into the boiling water. It was her twenty-fourth birthday and she was celebrating with a bottle of Veuve Clicquot and boiled peas. She wanted to accept her fate. Swallow it down. The too-picky princess who could never be satisfied.

Her cat Screech looked up from his nest of pillows on the couch. He was always interested when she was in the kitchen.

"Believe me, you wouldn't like this," Penny said to him, then went back to studying the dancing peas as if they were tea leaves.

It was silly really, to be obsessing over her mother's words this way. She was twenty-four now. And had a good job as an intern at the Natural History Museum. So why couldn't she be more confident? Like her friend Kai.

Kai was a sculptor who taught yoga at a local spa to pay the bills and didn't even want to fall in love. "Why would I want someone to muck up my perfect life?" she'd said to Penny just the other day. But it was different for Kai. Kai enjoyed one-night lovers.

Penny broke up a clump of frozen peas with a spoon while

picturing Kai and someone equally flexible contorting themselves into Kama Sutra–like poses, and thought to herself, *I could never do that with someone I'd just met.*

It took Penny time to trust a person. She needed to feel loved.

She popped the cork on her bottle of Veuve Clicquot and held it over the sink to keep the froth from getting on the floor. *What a waste,* she thought as she licked the expensive champagne from her fingers. She'd given up a haircut to afford it. Pouring the champagne into one of a pair of etched champagne glasses she'd given as a Valentine's gift to Phoenix, her last, and longest, love, she thought how sure she'd been that Phoenix and she would be forever. They'd even moved in together.

Then Phoenix's mentally unbalanced brother showed up and Phoenix told him he could stay until he worked something else out. It was pleasant at first. The three of them would have dinner together, and once they'd all gone to bed, she and Phoenix would talk about how well he seemed to be doing. Then he began to leave raw egg in the pockets of Penny's jackets. She'd reach in and her fingers would be covered in slime. She asked Phoenix if maybe this wasn't a bad sign but all Phoenix said was she'd talk to him. When he locked himself out and smashed the plate glass window to gain entry, Penny was almost relieved. Surely now Phoenix would have to ask him to leave. But Phoenix hadn't seen it that way. "He was locked out, Penny. What was he supposed to do? I'll talk to his doctor about adjusting his medication."

"But if he doesn't take his medication, which he doesn't, what difference will it make?"

"Give him a chance!" Phoenix yelled back. And so Penny had. Until he came brandishing the sewing scissors at the two of them, at which point Phoenix finally admitted his being around was a problem. But by then it was too late. Penny's trust was gone.

Before that there was her second-longest relationship, Mandy, who insisted her Great Dane sleep with them even though the flea-infested giant kept pushing Penny out of bed.

Maybe she did ask too much.

She dipped a spoon into the pot of peas, scooped one up, blew on it, almost placed it on her tongue, then let it plop back into the boiling water. She planned to eat a whole bowlful, every last one. Even if she did despise peas. She needed to accept the truth about herself. She'd never be truly happy. Never.

She took a sip of Veuve Clicquot to wash the pea flavor from her mouth. *Happy birthday to me.*

There was a knock at the door. She glanced at the clock. No one ever dropped by unannounced. The only apartment she'd been able to afford was too far away from the rest of her friends.

She tucked her pink fluffy robe around her and cinched it in so it wouldn't accidentally slip open, and went to peer out the peephole. Screech, who'd also been startled by the knock, glared at the door as if by sheer will he could make it go transparent and see through to the other side.

The back of someone's head was all Penny could see. Someone who had a lovely long black braid. No, two braids. One right on top of the other. Penny set the chain and cracked open the door. "Can I help you?"

The someone with the long black braids turned around, revealing a sassy-looking dyke wearing a low-slung tool belt weighted down by a hammer, tape measure, a few screwdrivers, and a bunch of other tools. In her hand was a toolbox decorated with vintage decals. She was tanned with lean muscles and her mouth tipped up to one side. Her T-shirt said: GIRL SCOUT GONE BAD.

"Sorry it's so late. But you contacted management about a flickering light?"

Which Penny had. Almost two weeks ago. She scrutinized the woman. How old was she? Penny decided they were about the same age. "Um. Yes I did. I most certainly did. Are you the new handyman— er, woman—they told us about?"

"I guess you could call me that, although I'd prefer if you'd call me Lil. I hope it's okay I just came over without you returning my call, but—"

"You called?"

"Yeah."

Penny glanced at her machine. Sure enough, it was blinking. "I must have been in the shower."

"If it's more convenient for me to come back..."

"No. No. This is fine."

"Again, sorry about being so late, but Mrs. Dunbar's drain in 6B was way clogged. Apparently she washes her Pomeranian in the sink."

There was a pause in the conversation and Penny realized they were still standing on opposite sides of the door with a chain lock between them. "I guess I should let you in, then."

"Only if it's convenient. Like I said in my message. I've got a slot on Thursday I could plug you into."

"Oh please. You're here. Why don't you just plug me now—I mean, *in!* Plug me in!" Blood flooded Penny's cheeks. "I can't believe I just said that! I meant, you're here, we might as well get *on* with it. You know, fix the light."

Lil smiled, her leprechaun green eyes flashing mischief, but Penny refused to be moved. She was not about to get sucked into another disappointment. No way.

"My name's Penny."

"So what say you let me in, then, Penny?"

Penny thought for a moment, then unlatched the lock. She *did* need her light fixed. As she opened the door, she became ultra-aware of how she must appear. It was a Friday night and here she was hanging around her apartment in her robe and holding a glass of champagne. Her hair was a mess. "It's…it's my birthday and I was kind of…celebrating."

Lil looked past her. "By yourself?"

Penny nodded toward Screech, who was cleaning his butt. "He may not look it now, but he's quite the party animal."

Lil set her toolbox on the floor and crouched down to massage Screech's chin. "Hey, bud, you gonna help Miss Penny celebrate?" Screech rubbed up against her hand. "He's a real lover."

Surprised to see her usually suspicious cat taking to Lil so easily, Penny said, "Yeah, he is."

After one final stroke down Screech's back, Lil stood. "So why don't you show me that light?"

"Oh, right. It's in the bedroom."

As Penny led Lil down the hall to the bedroom, she couldn't stop jabbering. "It's not that big of a thing, really. I mean, it still turns on. But about a month ago it just sort of started to strobe." She stepped into the bedroom and switched on the flickering light.

Lil placed her toolbox on the floor and looked up at the light. "I can't believe it took you two weeks to call. This would annoy the hell out of me."

"Well, I'd just had a problem with my dishwasher leaking, so it felt funny to call again in the same month."

Lil flicked the switch on, then off, then on again. "No one should have to put up with a light like this."

Penny, suddenly overly warm and horribly self-conscious, blurted, "Especially an epileptic," and then to her horror, began laughing so hard she snorted.

Lil looked away from the light fixture. "Hey, are you all right? You seem kind of keyed up."

"I'm fine," Penny said, pinching the top of her nose to regain her composure. "I think it's this birthday thing. It's got me kind of…I don't know…emotional."

Lil sat on the edge of the bed and began unlacing her boots. "So, if you don't mind me asking, how old are you?"

Why was this complete stranger taking off her boots—on *her* bed? Then Penny realized Lil didn't want to get the bed dirty when she stood on it. "Twenty-four," she said, admiring the cleanliness of Lil's socks.

Lil unscrewed the bulb. "Do you have a new one we could try?"

"In the hall closet," Penny said and went to retrieve it. She couldn't stop thinking how considerate it was that Lil had taken off her boots to stand on the bed. Considerate and oddly intimate.

"Here's a new bulb."

Lil screwed it in. The flicker was still there. "I'm going to need to turn off your breaker."

"It's in the—"

"Closet. I know. It's the same for all the apartments."

It was right then Penny smelled the peas. "Crap!"

"What?"

"My peas are probably dead by now."

"Your peas?"

"Long story," Penny said as she bolted for the kitchen.

The water was all gone and it stank. She turned off the stove and poked at the bloated peas on top; those underneath were black. She sighed. Of course she'd still eat them, or at least skim a few off the top. She had to. Because while princesses in fairy tales always got their wish and lived happily ever after, those in real life were invariably disappointed. And tonight was about accepting that—fully.

"It's about to go dark," Lil called from the hall. "Same breaker for the bedroom and the living room."

"Do you need me to hold a flashlight for you?"

"Naw. I got a headlamp. You just sit back and enjoy your birthday."

Penny took the pot of peas and bottle of champagne into the living room. She lit a candle. Screech stepped lightly onto her lap. She scratched behind his ear. "Thanks for coming to my party."

The sounds of Lil futzing around in the bedroom made her feel secure. She'd always liked people who could fix things.

She drained her glass and poured another, then another. There was no use rushing this concession to her mother. She had all night. And the peas sure weren't going anywhere. She peered into the pot, scooped out a spoonful of green mush and sniffed it.

A girl like her would never be satisfied. Her mother was right. She asked too much. Was too sensitive. She held the spoonful to her mouth—*Might as well*—shut her eyes, and prepared to shove the spoonful of disgusting peas into her mouth.

"Just wanted you to know I'm about to turn the breakers back on."

Penny opened her eyes and was dazzled by the spotlight of Lil's headlamp. She blinked a couple of times, the spoon suspended in front of her mouth.

"If you don't mind my asking, what are you doing?" Lil asked.

"Me?"

Lil looked over her shoulder. "Is there anyone else here I should know about?"

Penny let the spoon drop into the pot and blinked back tears. She was buzzed, no two ways about it. "Nothing. I was just about to eat my fate."

"Is *that* what's so stinky?"

"You've no idea," Penny said. Then something about being in the spotlight while seriously smashed on champagne uncorked Penny's bottled-up fears, and before she knew it she was spilling out all over the place, telling Lil about never being able to be happy, and the raw eggs and snoring dog, and her mother insisting that she was just like the princess who could feel a pea under twenty mattresses and twenty feather beds. Lil, who flicked off her headlamp and settled in on the floor across from Penny, just listened, the candlelight casting lovely shadows on her face.

When Penny finally ran out of steam, Lil said, "I think you're giving peas a bad rap."

Penny was indignant. Was that all Lil had gotten from what she'd said? "I don't see what that's got to do with…"

Lil raised a hand to shush Penny. "Could I take you somewhere tomorrow? If you're free, that is. I want to show you something. And then, if you still want to eat your gross peas, well, fine, eat your gross peas. But I really think you should see it before you go on with this."

Penny peered into the pot. The peas looked even more revolting now that she'd scooped into them. And tomorrow *was* her day off. "Um. Okay. I guess."

"I have to work in the morning, but I could swing by at about one."

Penny tucked a blond curl behind her ear. Should she be making this kind of commitment when she was on champagne? "Sure," she said, not at all sure that she was.

Lil stood. "Good. I'm going to turn the breakers back on."

A yawn slipped from Penny's mouth. She tried to disguise it with a smile. There was no way she wanted Lil to think the yawn had to do with their date. Or was it a date? Her brain was so muddled from the champagne she really had no idea. But she knew she had to say something. "You fixed it?"

"Won't know until the breaker's back on, but I found some loose wires. If this doesn't work, I'll come back tomorrow to check the switch. You want me to turn off this switch so you're not blasted by light when they come back on?"

Another yawn threatened to slip out, but Penny held this one back. "That would be nice."

Once Lil was out of the room, Penny stretched out on the couch next to a purring Screech. His soft rumble made her eyelids heavy. She let them close. Once again, she felt comforted by the sounds of Lil in the bedroom. She moved with such confidence, such self-assurance.

Penny pulled the throw blanket from the back of the couch and tucked it in around herself and Screech. What was she doing making a date with someone she'd just met? Again she wondered if it actually was a date. Maybe Lil just felt sorry for her. That seemed more likely. Who'd want to make a date with a sloshed crybaby obsessed with peas?

She woke briefly when Lil blew out her candle and slipped out of the apartment, clicking the door softly behind her. At some point in the night, Penny made her way to her bedroom where she slept uninterrupted until noon.

She awoke feeling refreshed, and excited, and a bit nervous about her date.

Once out of bed, she checked the light. Sure enough, the flicker was gone. She made her way to the kitchen where Screech rubbed up against her leg as if she might forget to feed him. "Okay. Okay. Hold your horses." As she reached for the cat food, she noticed a note on her counter weighted down by the pot of peas.

> *Miss Penny,*
> *If you've changed your mind about today, call me. 335-3700. Otherwise I'll see you at 1:00.*
> *Lil*

She smiled. No one had ever called her Miss Penny before.

As a reminder not to get her hopes up, she dumped the loose peas into the garbage disposal, then filled the pot with water to soak the rest of them out. *You barely know her.*

At one sharp there was a knock at the door. Penny glanced in the mirror. She'd been unsure how to dress so had chosen casual: jeans, her favorite tank top that showed just a strip of midriff, and sandals. She was glad for her choice when she opened the door. Lil was wearing shorts, a T-shirt, and work boots.

"You still up for this?" Lil asked.

Penny picked up her purse. "If you promise it'll keep me from eating those gross peas."

Lil laughed. "I can't promise, but I have a hunch."

As they walked down the stairwell, Penny couldn't help but feel sheepish about the night before. "Thanks for fixing my light."

"No need to thank me," Lil said. "It's my job. Besides, it was my pleasure." She unlocked the passenger side of an old pickup. "And this is my chariot."

Penny slipped in. The interior was spotless and smelled as if it had recently been wiped down with something slightly citrus. "Nice," she said when Lil came around the other side.

"Thanks. She might not be fancy, but she's paid for." With that, Lil turned the key in the ignition and pulled into the light Saturday stream of traffic.

A wave of panic passed through Penny. She barely knew this woman, and now here she was in a truck with her going to God-knew-where. She tried to think of something to say. "So, what was wrong with the light?" was all she could come up with.

"The usual. A few of the wires were loose. It can happen over time."

"Especially when you have a guy upstairs who jumps rope."

"In his apartment?"

"Monday through Friday. Six a.m. Right above my bed."

"You shouldn't have to put up with that."

"What choice do I have? He pays his rent just like I do."

As Lil seemed to be mulling this over, Penny sat back, trying to appear casual, and observed her driving.

She moved through traffic with confidence, like she belonged on the road. And she stopped for pedestrians. This was something Penny appreciated as she herself did not have a car so was often walking. And yet there was something about Lil's confidence that also frightened Penny. Where was she taking her? Just as she was about to ask, Lil said:

"I'm going to talk to Mr. Baratelli."

"The landlord?"

"Yup. He and I have a pretty good rapport. I'll let him know that the reason your lighting fixture needed work was because of unnecessary physical activity upstairs."

"You don't have to do that."

"I want to. I hate the thought—" Lil slammed on the brakes to keep from hitting a blue Mazda that ran a stop sign. Her arm instinctively reached across to protect Penny. "You okay?"

Shaken, Penny said, "Fine."

When Lil removed her arm, an unexpected longing passed through Penny. "My dad used to do that," she said.

"He didn't want anything to happen to his precious cargo."

"I don't know about precious."

Lil glanced at her briefly before returning her attention to the sudden cluster of traffic. "I do."

Penny looked out the window and said, "Thank you," very softly. Who *was* this Lil? And why was Penny still apprehensive?

A few minutes later they pulled up to a row of Victorians that had been split into apartments. "Mine's the blue and gray one," Lil said. "I'd invite you in, but one of my roommates is down with the flu. No need exposing you to that."

Penny cocked an eyebrow. "So why did we come here?"

Lil smiled. "You'll see. Now follow me." And before Penny knew it Lil was out of the truck and making her way down a small dark walkway between two Victorians.

Penny hopped out of the truck and trotted behind. What was this girl up to?

The walkway opened up onto a large community garden.

Lil stepped to the side of the entrance made of marvelously twisted wood, bent slightly at the waist, and swept her arm wide. "After you."

Penny, acting all serious, pretended to lift a heavy ankle-length skirt, tilted her chin toward the sky, and stepped through the arbor, then stopped dead in her tracks. The garden was stunning. Rows of raised beds, each meticulously kept up, filled the quarter-acre plot. And there were little sculpted sitting areas here and there—and wind chimes.

Penny walked over to a bed lined with luscious green. "Is this butter lettuce?"

"The best in the world." Lil grinned. "And completely organic." She broke off an outside leaf. "Want a taste?"

Penny opened her mouth and Lil tucked the crisp leaf between her lips. The back of her hand gently brushed the side of Penny's cheek.

Was that on purpose? Penny wondered. A slight shiver passed down her spine as, with great care, she closed her mouth around the lettuce leaf. It would be the freshest thing she had ever eaten and she wanted to savor it.

"Oh my God. It's so…"

"Buttery?"

"It is! Store-bought never tastes like that."

"Taste this," Lil said, ripping off a dark green leaf from another plant.

An impossibly sweet burst exploded in Penny's mouth. "What is that?"

"Italian parsley."

"Parsley? I thought parsley was just something you got on the side of your plate at a restaurant."

Lil popped a sprig into her own mouth, "I use it for a breath freshener," then walked over to a raised bed full of beets and carrots. "Soon we'll be putting in the summer stuff. You know, tomatoes, squash, eggplant."

"Who's 'we'?" Penny asked, suddenly praying it wasn't a girlfriend.

"Our collective. But I'm one of the main ones. I work out here almost every day."

Penny watched as Lil tenderly inspected the underside of a broccoli leaf. "I had no idea broccoli grew like that," she admitted.

"Isn't it beautiful? The heads are actually flowers."

The thought of eating flowers delighted Penny. She brought her nose to the broccoli head and inhaled. It didn't smell like a flower, but had a rich musky scent. "Yum."

"I'll make you up a bag of produce before you go," Lil said, taking Penny's hand. "But now let me show you why I brought you here."

Penny let herself be led to the back of the garden, loving the feel of her hand in Lil's. They fit so perfectly, Lil's larger, stronger hand wrapping around her smaller softer one. "Thank you for blowing out my candle last night."

Lil gave her hand a squeeze. "Seemed like you were having a pretty rough night."

They rounded a tall trellis covered in climbing green vines.

"Voilà!" Lil said. "My pride and joy."

Penny laughed. The vines were covered in pea pods. *Of course!* She stepped in for a closer look and noticed threadlike tendrils reaching out from the vines to curl around to the slender bamboo rods of the trellis. Along with the pea pods, each vine was sprinkled with the most delicate white flowers. Apparently peas started out their lives as flowers.

"Now *these* are birthday peas," Lil said. "Go ahead. Pick as many as you want."

Penny glanced at Lil, her grip on Lil's hand involuntarily tightening. "You expect me to eat these?"

"Why not? You were going to eat those crappy burned ones last night."

"But they're not cooked."

"Don't tell me you've never had fresh peas off the vine."

Embarrassed, Penny shook her head. Until last night, she generally avoided peas altogether.

Lil let go of her hand and plucked a pod off the vine. "Promise to keep an open mind?"

Penny nodded. What choice did she have? This woman, who she was finding herself more and more attracted to, was offering up what she called her "pride and joy."

Lil slid her finger down the seam of the slender pod and cracked it open, revealing six perfectly round peas. "Take one," she said as she stepped in close enough for Penny to smell her clean, parsley-scented breath.

Much as Penny was excited by the sudden intimacy and Lil's obvious delight in the peas, she couldn't help noticing a mild nausea heating up her belly. *What am I doing? I hate peas.* But she couldn't refuse, not after all the trouble Lil had gone to. So she braced herself for yet another disappointment, and said, "Okay. I'll try."

She chose the plumpest one, right in the center, and tugged lightly. The round orb popped out easily. Now she'd have to eat it. Or at least put it in her mouth. Lil's hopeful gaze was giving her no choice. She slipped the pea between her lips. The small hard ball rested on her tongue, so innocent, so devoid of expectation. She rolled it around in her mouth a couple of times, testing, then without another thought bit down.

"You like?" Lil asked.

Penny thought for a moment, and, to her surprise, found she wasn't the least bit repulsed. It was sweet. Fresh. Nothing like the bland peas of her childhood. She took the whole pod from Lil and, using her tongue, flicked the rest of the peas into her mouth.

Lil laughed. "I guess the answer is yes."

Penny wanted to say the answer was more than yes and that this was the best birthday present she'd ever received—in her whole life—even if it was a day late. But before she could put this thought to words, Lil pulled another pod from the vine, popped it open, and let the peas tumble into her palm; only this time instead of offering them up for eating, she just let them rest there. "It just blows my mind that inside each of these peas is the beginning of a whole plant."

"Kind of like people," Penny said softly. "Each one of us is full of so many things that nobody knows about. Like you with this garden."

Lil picked up a pea and pressed it to Penny's lips. "I'd like to know more about you. If you'd let me."

Penny let her lips curl around Lil's fingertip and linger for a moment, then took the pea into her mouth and circled it with her tongue before biting down and swallowing. "I should tell you, I'm not always easy. I can be kind of like…"

"A princess. You told me. But from what I've seen, you're the real thing."

An icy wall inside Penny began to melt, releasing a single tear. She brushed it back.

Lil let the peas in her hand drop into the rich soil, then rested both hands on Penny's shoulders. "What's more, I think real princesses deserve to live happily ever after."

The warmth of Lil's hands made Penny's knees go weak. "I'd kind of given up on that whole notion."

Lil cocked her head. "You'd given up on peas, too. So what do you say we give this princess thing one more try?"

MERRY SHANNON grew up a military brat. An avid reader with a deep love of language, Merry began writing at the age of seven and completed her first novel-length story when she was thirteen. She graduated in 2001 with a BA in English and currently resides in Colorado with one very noisy cat. Her Bold Strokes novels include the romantic fantasy *Sword of the Guardian* and the romantic adventure *Branded Ann*, a 2008 ForeWord magazine Book of the Year finalist.

The Whisper
Merry Shannon

Yawning, Jordan Gray shuffled into the kitchen, reached for the coffeepot, and winced as the movement sent a bolt of pain through her shoulder. *Another tough night*, she thought ruefully, and considered the glass pot in her hand. How easy it would be to send it floating over to the sink, to fill it up and empty it into the coffeemaker without having to move another aching muscle. The idea was incredibly tempting, but Jordan pushed it away with a sigh. She'd sworn long ago to never use her telekinetic powers frivolously. Frivolity was recklessness, and recklessness was how a person got caught.

So instead, Jordan carried the pot to the sink herself and prepared the coffeemaker by hand. When it was ready, she even pushed the little start button with her finger.

The scent of brewing coffee brought her roommate stumbling sleepily into the kitchen, curly hair wisping across her forehead.

"Oh, thank God." Dana plopped onto a stool at the breakfast bar, eyeing the coffeepot with anticipation as she automatically flipped open her laptop. "Jordan, you're an angel."

Jordan felt her cheeks warm. She didn't drink coffee herself, but her favorite part of every morning was the way Dana's pretty blue eyes lit up at that first sip. Not that she would ever tell Dana that, of course.

"Ah, she was at it again!" Dana shrieked delightedly.

"Who?" Jordan asked, though she already knew perfectly well. Just once, she wished she could take care of business without every reporter in the city clamoring about it the next day.

"The Whisper, of course! She's all over the news again this morning. Looks like she saved a bunch of people from an apartment fire last night." Leaning closer to the computer screen, Dana read aloud. "'At approximately two thirty a.m., a fire broke out in the Sage Hill Apartment Complex. Several people, including three small children, were trapped on the upper floors. Witnesses say the mysterious silver-clad heroine, known throughout Twilight City as The Whisper, entered the blazing building through a window. She levitated all eight victims safely to the ground just before the roof collapsed. No bodies were found in the debris, and authorities believe that The Whisper survived the collapse.'" Dana snorted. "Well, of course she did!"

Hiding a grimace as her sore shoulder protested, Jordan set a steaming coffee mug on the breakfast bar and retrieved her toast, Dana took the mug absently and raised it to her lips, then closed her eyes with a look of bliss. "Mmm."

Jordan was careful to quell her smile before Dana's eyes reopened.

"Look, the *Twilight City Gazette* posted a picture!" Dana swiveled the laptop around to show the blurry digital image of a shiny silver silhouette zooming toward the smoking apartment building. Jordan took a cursory glance and shrugged, and Dana let out a puff of exasperation. She turned the computer to face her again and gazed at the photo dreamily. "Have you ever seen anyone so completely, utterly *sexy*?"

Jordan choked on a mouthful of toast. "What?"

"Oh come on, even under all that quiet butch stoicism, I know you have the same fantasies as every other lesbian in this city. Telekinetic superpowers, heroic rescues, and will you just look at that body? I mean, those thighs…that ass! Just makes a girl wanna strip that mask off and…" Dana made a sexy noise in the back of her throat that raised goose bumps on Jordan's arms.

"I never really thought about it," Jordan said, embarrassed.

"If you'd ever been in her arms, you'd get it. She's so…damn, she even smells good. And when she whispers in your ear it's like warm honey poured right down your spine." Dana shivered, looking starstruck. "Best night of my life."

Jordan stared at her. "You were almost assaulted that night!"

"And saved by the most delicious woman on earth!"

Jordan turned to put her empty plate in the dishwasher, hoping Dana wouldn't notice the flush creeping steadily up her neck. "I gotta get to work."

"See you later," Dana mumbled, already absorbed in the computer again.

❖

"Mornin', Gray." Manny Lopez greeted Jordan with a friendly punch to the shoulder that made her gasp.

"Ow, Manny, watch it."

"Oh. Sorry, I forgot." He did sound apologetic, but there was a mischievous twinkle in his eye. "So tell me, how'd that little hottie you live with enjoy the morning news?"

"Not in the mood today, Manny." Jordan grabbed her hard hat from her locker and banged the door shut. She knew Dana would be attached to her laptop most of the day, posting articles to the various Internet blogs she wrote for, and the majority would be glowing commentary regarding The Whisper's latest exploits.

"That bad, huh? Gotta be just killing you that you can't tell her the truth. She start going on again about how the incredible Whisper saved her from those punks?" He fluttered his lashes as they walked to the construction site. "Ooh, The Whisper is sooo strong and brave. Ooh, how I'd like to get that yummy, shiny superhero between my—"

Jordan narrowed her eyes and sent a mental shove at Manny's chest. It was scarcely more than a thump, but she knew her irises would flash silver as she used her power, and that would be all the warning he needed. She was right; he shut up quickly.

"Geez, okay, I was just kidding."

"Well, it's not funny." Jordan kept her voice low as they passed some of the other workers. "What if someone hears you?"

"Hey, it's no big secret that you've got the hots for her, Gray. Every guy out here knows that gorgeous roommate of yours has got you wrapped around her little finger."

"That's not what I mean, and you know it." Jordan gestured toward the large sign posted nearby, which proclaimed the construction site as a forthcoming project of Wingate Industries, Inc. "You know what he'll do if he finds out."

"All right, all right." Manny ducked under part of the framing and reached into a heavy tool box. He tossed her a hammer, his aim off by quite a bit, but Jordan caught it anyway.

When he grinned, she rolled her eyes. "Let's just get to work."

By midmorning Jordan had shed her jacket and long-sleeved shirt and was down to just her tank top and coveralls. She could have used her telekinetic ability to make the work easier: the loads lighter to lift, the hammer strikes more forceful. But exertion was good for her. Her powers were far more effective when she used them to amplify her own strength rather than just reaching out with her mind.

Besides, there was something sweetly ironic about using Wendell Wingate's construction projects to empower herself—or rather, to empower The Whisper. She'd sought a position on this construction crew in the hopes of getting close to the corrupt corporate development tycoon. With incredible wealth and power at his disposal, Wendell Wingate controlled nearly all of Twilight City through a regime of intimidation and terror. The fire at the apartment complex the night before was likely retaliation for the owner's refusal to pay Wingate's "security fee."

Wingate had the police and the mayor on his private payroll, and The Whisper was the only force left in the city who could actually protect its citizens. Jordan fought back, donning the sleek silver bodysuit and mask and using her telekinetic abilities to thwart Wingate's schemes. She'd become a hero to the citizens of Twilight—and a much-hated adversary to Wingate Industries. Wingate would like nothing better than to get his hands on her, which was why Manny, her best friend since childhood, was the only person who knew The Whisper's true identity.

Her anonymity kept her alive, but there were times when the secrecy was nearly unbearable. Especially when it came to Dana Davis. Beautiful, brilliant, sassy Dana. Jordan hadn't anticipated what a problem it would be, sharing living space with someone she had fallen so hard for and could never, ever be with. The danger of her extracurricular activities negated any possibility of meaningful relationships. Before Dana had entered her life, Jordan had always accepted that just fine. Now, though, it seemed torturously unfair.

A loud screech of metal broke into her thoughts, and she looked up to see one of the chains that dangled from a crane to support a twenty-ton steel beam snap. Panicked shouts rang out as one end of the beam tilted downward, its immense weight easily breaking the remaining supports. Manny was standing directly beneath the crane, seemingly frozen in place as the enormous metal girder hurtled toward him.

"Manny, look out!" Jordan was more than a hundred feet away and she'd never physically reach him in time. Reflexively, she flung one hand upward, stopping the heavy beam in midair for a split second. With the other arm she made a sweeping motion that knocked Manny nearly five feet sideways. She released the beam quickly, and it crashed to the ground so hard she could feel the earth vibrate under her feet. Panting, Jordan ran to her friend's side.

"You okay?"

"Yeah. Think so," Manny wheezed.

Concerned team members surrounded them, all wanting to know what had happened. Jordan looked around nervously, hoping everything had transpired so fast that no one noticed what she had done.

❖

In his penthouse office downtown, Wendell Wingate took an urgent call from his construction foreman. "This had better be important."

"Oh, it is, sir. You have security footage of the Hampton project? Something just happened that you're definitely gonna want to see."

Wingate played the security video in slow motion on the big screen mounted against the far wall, taking in every detail as the support chains broke and a steel beam dropped from the crane. Workers scattered, but one of them, a woman, ran toward the plummeting girder. She threw out hers arms and almost imperceptibly, the falling beam stopped moving as the man standing beneath it was shoved violently out of the way, as if propelled by some invisible hand.

Wingate replayed the scene and zoomed in on the image. Closer... closer...and a little to the left...there. He sat forward in his chair and advanced the tape frame by frame, holding focus tight on the woman's face. She mouthed words, one at a time, and then suddenly, her eyes changed. In one frame they were dark, and in the next...

"It's her," he snarled. "Under my nose the whole time."

He snatched up the phone and punched a button. "Get me everything, and I mean everything, we have on this Jordan Gray. I want to know where she lives, who her friends are, what she had for breakfast. Now!" He slammed the phone back down and stared at the screen again. "I've got you at last, Whisper."

❖

Jordan's keys clanked as she wearily unlocked the apartment door. Why did she ever let Manny and the guys convince her to go out after work? It always resulted in loud, drunken carousing that ended far too late for her taste, even when they all knew they'd be getting up before dawn the next morning. But after today's near-disastrous accident, it hadn't seemed right to deny her friend the chance to buy her a drink.

She pushed the door open and fumbled for the light switch. Her mouth fell open. "What the—?"

The living room was a mess: papers scattered everywhere, one armchair upended, the sofa upholstery slashed, sharp bits of china and glass littering the carpet. Dana's laptop lay in one corner, the screen cracked and flickering.

"Oh God." She raced into the apartment. "Dana!"

She spied a piece of paper on the breakfast bar and grabbed it, her hands trembling.

Whisper—Be at Wingate Tower at midnight, or the woman dies.

Jordan slowly crumpled the paper. He knew. Wingate knew who she was, and he had Dana.

Closing her eyes, she extended her arms and rose from the floor. Fabric rustled and her work clothes disappeared. Her silver bodysuit materialized from its hiding place and quickly slid around her body like a shimmering second skin. Boots leapt from the closet to encase her feet, lacing and tying themselves securely. The hood came up around her face, covering her neck and hair, and a shining silver mask floated into her palm.

Jordan turned to the window, which threw itself open, curtains blowing in the sudden night breeze. She lifted the mask to her face and The Whisper soared out the open window and into the sky.

The doors to the main lobby were unlocked and Jordan glided into the building silently, scanning for any sign of movement. Wingate Tower was a work of architectural brilliance. From where Jordan stood in the center of the ornately patterned lobby, she could see all the way up to the glass paneled roof. Every one of the thirty floors wrapped around this central core, with the office spaces fronted by huge glass windows to allow light to filter in from above. The building was entirely dark save for one glowing ring of light at the very top—the penthouse office. It shone like the tip of a lighthouse, beckoning to her, and Jordan gritted her teeth. Wingate was calling her—taunting her with the fact that he had something she wanted.

Anger, and a sharp prick of fear, heated her insides. Never before had her battle with Wingate Industries been this personal, or this dangerous to someone she cared about. If she lived through this, she promised herself, Wingate would never, ever get such an opportunity again.

She soared upward, through the faintly glittering glass tunnel, and the shining ring of the penthouse above grew closer and closer. At last she reached the top, and there he was, sitting smugly at his mahogany desk behind a huge wall of glass. Two masked men stood to his left with Dana between them. One pressed a knife to her throat.

Jordan struck at the huge window that separated them, putting all her physical and telekinetic strength into the blow, and the window splintered in a shower of crystalline fragments. The impact sent cracks rippling all the way around the circular corridor, until every window seemed etched with spiderwebs. She flew into Wingate's office and surged toward him, but he calmly held up a hand. Dana's whimper stopped Jordan in midair.

She touched down on the thick office carpet as a tiny rivulet of blood trickled down Dana's neck, courtesy of the blade beneath her chin. Jordan froze, glaring at Wingate, her blood boiling at the terror contracting Dana's pretty features.

"Let her go," she commanded in the harsh whisper that had inspired her name. Wingate smiled and beckoned to another man who emerged from the shadows behind him. "I see even a glimmer of silver in those eyes, Whisper, and she dies."

The masked man closed in on her and abruptly punched her in the stomach, quickly following up with a second blow to her face. The strikes were sharp and powerful, but Jordan didn't dare use her powers to block them. Not when Dana was at risk.

She couldn't use her powers, but Wingate hadn't said she couldn't fight back at all. She retaliated with a fist to the masked man's jaw, careful to use only her natural strength. He reeled backward, and she lunged at him. Something heavy hit her in the back, and she fell to her knees. A second masked man joined the fight and kicked her solidly in the gut. She fell forward onto her hands, gasping for air. She tasted blood on her lower lip as she painfully straightened. Without her powers, she was not strong or fast enough to protect herself against two opponents at once.

Wingate laughed. "You have a choice, Whisper. Your life, or hers."

His men leveled handguns at her. Dana was still held at knifepoint. She looked terrified, her breath coming in frightened gulps.

"What's to stop you from killing her after I'm dead?" Jordan snarled.

"I guess you'll just have to take my word for it," Wingate said smugly.

"You leave me no choice," Jordan said. Wingate would never let Dana live, not after all Dana had witnessed tonight.

"No!" Dana thrashed in her captors' arms.

"Dana, don't move!" Jordan commanded, then raised her hands in surrender.

"Kill her!" Wingate ordered.

As the men fired, Jordan closed her eyes. She had only milliseconds to push a burst of energy from her palms, deflecting the bullets at precise angles, hoping against hope that her hurried mental calculations were correct. Dana screamed, men grunted, and Wingate howled in fury. Jordan opened her eyes.

The men holding Dana had collapsed, each one struck by a bullet meant for The Whisper. Dana appeared shaken but very much alive, the knife lying harmlessly at her feet.

Wingate gestured furiously at the two remaining men. "Don't just stand there, you morons, kill them both! Now!"

But now that the threat to Dana was gone, Jordan didn't bother to hide her telltale silver irises as she stretched out her hands toward the gunmen and closed her fists. The guns in their hands crumpled, like paper wadded into balls, and they dropped them with anxious yelps. Both men turned and ran, leaving their boss to face The Whisper's wrath alone. She turned her attention to him then, power crackling fiercely around her entire body, fueled by her rage.

Wingate backed away as Jordan stalked closer. "You've won this time, Whisper, but—"

In his haste, he failed to notice that he was standing just in front of the shattered office window. He took just one step too many; his heel dropped over the window edge and he lost his balance. For a split second his arms flailed uselessly in an attempt to right himself, and with a look of shock, he dropped out of sight.

Without thinking, Jordan dashed to the window and reached down for him, but it was too late. Wingate struck the lobby floor with a faint thump.

Dana appeared at her side and looked down at the motionless body lying far below. "Did you—?"

Jordan shook her head. "No. He fell. I couldn't stop it."

"Fine by me." Dana raised a hand to the cut at her throat. "Bastard."

"Are you all right?"

Dana nodded. "Thanks to you."

Jordan caught the adoration in Dana's voice and shifted uncomfortably. "You should get home."

Dana ran a hand lightly up Jordan's arm. "Will you take me?"

Jordan struggled to suppress the shiver that went through her at Dana's touch. Frivolity is recklessness, she reminded herself feebly. Her powers were almost tapped; it had taken every last bit of her concentration to redirect those bullets so quickly and with such precision. Still, Dana was watching her with such hope, such admiration…such *desire*. Jordan's stomach clenched. "All right."

With an expectant look, Dana slid her hands up Jordan's shoulders and around her neck. Dana's chest rose and fell rapidly and Jordan felt each hot, electrified breath on her own lips. With a gentle pulse of energy, she lifted Dana from the floor and into her arms. Now Dana's face was so close to her own, her deep blue eyes gazing hungrily into her masked ones and her body nestled snugly against the silver bodysuit. Every inch of Jordan's skin tingled.

"Hold on," she managed to say, then stepped through the broken window. They hovered for a moment as she sent another kinetic blast toward the glass ceiling above. Dana cuddled close to Jordan's neck as they soared upward through the shimmering, falling shards. Outside, the night air was cool and the blare of approaching police sirens sounded far below them.

"When they find your blood in Wingate's office they'll want to question you," Jordan warned.

"Let them," Dana replied vehemently. "I'm going to call them myself as soon as I get home. You should see what they did to my apartment! My roommate's gonna be so pissed."

Jordan would have smiled, but she couldn't waste the strength. She was already straining to keep the two of them flying. But the exertion was well worth it. She relished the feel of Dana clasped tightly against her, her mere proximity making Jordan's heart thud erratically. As exhausted as she was, and as much as she knew it was going to cost her tomorrow, she didn't care. She would make these priceless minutes with Dana in her arms last as long as she could.

Finally Jordan touched down on the apartment balcony. Reluctantly, she set Dana down.

"How did you know where I live?" Dana asked

Jordan couldn't think of a suitable explanation, as mentally she chastised herself for her slip. She couldn't reply, but Dana didn't seem concerned by her silence. She gently touched Jordan's swollen lip. "You're bleeding."

Dana's fingers sent a little electric jolt through Jordan's body, tightening her stomach and thrumming abruptly between her legs. Jordan caught her breath and dropped to the balcony floor.

"My God, are you all right?" Dana cried, her eyes widening.

"Fine. Just tired." Jordan struggled to stand again, but instead just managed to flop awkwardly onto her side.

"Stay right there." Dana disappeared into the apartment, and when she returned, she held a cup of water. Kneeling, she offered it to Jordan with a worried expression.

Jordan drained the cup and handed it back. This time she was able to make it to her feet, albeit unsteadily. "I should go."

"Not yet. Please?" Dana backed Jordan against the balcony railing, getting so close that their hips pressed firmly together. When Dana's leg slid, ever so casually, between Jordan's thighs, she closed her eyes.

"Whisper…you're shaking." Dana's tone was a mixture of wonder and arousal, and Jordan fought to suppress a groan. But when Dana's hands came up and tugged at her mask, Jordan caught her wrists.

"Stop. You can't."

Dana kissed her. Jordan was utterly unprepared for the heat of Dana's mouth, for the sweet, soft lips devouring hers. She gasped when Dana licked lightly at her lower lip, drawing it slightly into her mouth and releasing it in a slow, tantalizing caress when she pulled back. Jordan stared at her, unable to breathe, her pulse pounding in her ears. Again Dana reached for her mask, and though Jordan stiffened, she was now powerless to stop her. The kiss had left her head ringing, and nothing else mattered…nothing but tasting those lips again.

"Shh, it's all right," Dana murmured, removing Whisper's mask. "Oh my God. Jordan?"

The shock on Dana's face brought Jordan immediately back to her senses. What had she done? Jordan pulled away from Dana and tried to levitate from the balcony, but only managed to get a few inches above the ground before her powers gave out and she dropped again. Embarrassed, off balance, Jordan slipped past Dana into the apartment.

"I'm…I'm sorry," Jordan mumbled, keeping her head down as she headed for the front door. "I'm just gonna—"

"Wait! Jordan, wait!" Dana caught Jordan's wrist. She pulled back the silver hood and brushed her fingers through Jordan's short dark hair, tugging little pieces back into place around her ears. She ran her fingers down Jordan's neck and across her collarbone. "I should have known."

Feeling hot and queasy, Jordan repeated again, "I'm sorry." She should get out, run, but she had nowhere to go.

"You saved my life." Dana met her eyes intently. "Twice."

"Yeah." Jordan didn't know what else to say. She couldn't tell Dana what she felt, could she?

"And you sat here and listened to me go on and on about the incredible hotness of The Whisper every day, and you never told me."

"I'm sor—" Jordan was cut off by Dana's lips, pressed against hers once again. But this time, her kiss was softer. Deeper. Delicately she explored Jordan's mouth with her tongue and a light nip of teeth, slipping inside to tangle Jordan's tongue with hers. Every movement was tender, sweet, exquisite—and Jordan was stunned by the passion suddenly radiating from every line of Dana's body.

Unable to contain a moan, Jordan drew Dana into her arms, returning the kiss with everything she had, with all the feelings that had been hidden so carefully in her heart for so long. And though her powers were drained, some small reserve must have remained. Bits of paper and broken china rose into the air all around them. Then their feet left the floor and they floated blissfully in each other's arms.

Born and raised in upstate New York, ERIN DUTTON now lives and works in middle Tennessee. In her free time she enjoys reading, photography, and playing golf.

Her previous novels include four romances: *Sequestered Hearts*, *Fully Involved*, *A Place to Rest*, and *Designed For Love*. She is also a contributor to *Erotic Interludes 5: Road Games* and *Romantic Interludes 1: Discovery* from Bold Strokes Books. Her latest novel, *Point of Ignition*, came out in July 2009.

Better Than Fiction
Erin Dutton

W e'd like to thank you all once again for coming. This afternoon's readings will feature sneak peeks at some forthcoming novels from some of your favorite authors."

As the facilitator went on to introduce the first author, the twinge in my stomach grew increasingly noticeable. I fought the urge to shove my hands in the pockets of my jeans to hide the slight trembling in my fingers. Squinting against the bright sunlight, I regretted my decision to leave my sunglasses on the table next to the chair I had abandoned minutes ago. But I hoped the heat would provide an excuse for the flush staining my cheeks.

I stood off to the side of the makeshift stage, which was really only a clearing on the aggregate patio around the pool. Around me, women perched on folding chairs that had been placed between the already occupied umbrella-shaded tables. At the moment their attention was riveted on the dark-haired woman at the microphone reading from her upcoming espionage novel. When I'd read her last book I had been unable to put it down. But today, I couldn't concentrate on her words. I barely registered the accented voice I would normally have found sexy.

Public speaking always made me nervous. And as I awaited my turn at the microphone, I surreptitiously glanced at the papers I'd been holding so tightly that a crease bisected the passage. Since I was minutes away from delivering my own reading, there was little point in studying the words, but scanning them helped calm my racing heart.

I swept my eyes over the audience, then stopped as I met a pair of calm blue eyes. Despite her casual posture there was a seriousness in her expression that I knew was meant to reassure me. Her gaze was a silent reminder that I would do just fine, as I had during each of my other readings in the previous two days.

At that moment she glanced down my body and even from a few feet away I imagined I could see her eyes darken when they paused near my crotch. I felt the heat in my face ratchet up as I realized she was likely thinking about what lay beneath my jeans. The thin strips of leather hugging my hips and ass provided sufficient distraction from the waiting spectators, but now my nervousness took on a new edge. My fingers tingled with the temptation to discreetly smooth my hand over the fly of my jeans where I knew I would feel the ridge of the metal ring that for the time being remained empty. The rest of my equipment nestled safely in her purse on the table next to her elbow.

Earlier, she had watched as I dressed for the afternoon's events. When I had emerged from the bathroom unable to hide a shy smile, she crossed the room and deftly unfastened the fly of my jeans.

"Sexy," she'd murmured as she spread the soft denim. I glanced down and had to admit there was something hot about how the denim framed the silver ring lying against smooth black leather. She'd caressed the metal circle, lightly then more firmly, and an imprint of pleasure lingered on my skin long after she stopped.

She searched my eyes, as if trying to gauge my reaction to wearing the harness. I had put it on briefly before, right after we first bought it, just to see how it felt. I certainly wasn't a prude, but I had never felt comfortable confessing my curiosity about such things to any of my previous lovers. So I was surprised when I found myself having the conversation with her far earlier in our relationship than I would have expected. She echoed my interest as well as my apprehension and we had tabled the discussion until we knew each other better, which turned out to be only a few weeks later as we shyly wandered the aisles of a local adult shop. The rush of arousal and power when I first slipped on the harness had caught me off guard, though I still worried about my capability. I knew I could please her with my fingers, but would I be as adept at reading her needs without the feel of her pulsing around me?

I can't remember which of us first suggested I wear the harness during a reading, but we agreed the shared secret would be arousing. And as I stood next to my fellow authors gazing at her in the audience, I was quite aware that we'd been right. When I shifted my stance slightly,

I could feel how wet I was beneath the shield of leather covering my center, and the slight lift of one side of her mouth indicated she knew it too.

The sound of my own name startled me and I jerked my eyes from her face to that of our facilitator. Her expectant expression told me I'd missed my cue to go to the microphone, so I hurried over.

I smoothed the papers in my hand and mumbled a greeting into the mic, praying I could get through the next eight minutes without completely losing my composure. I made the mistake of seeking her eyes again and she was nearly my undoing. She pulled her lower lip between her teeth in a failed attempt to hide her smile and I was suddenly very aware that I was standing in front of a crowd of people wearing a strap-on harness. And that I was both turned on and terribly out of my comfort zone.

I cleared my throat and began reading a scene involving a first kiss between two women. When the characters, who had been arguing only moments ago, embraced just as passionately, I glanced up and my gaze crashed into hers. A quick look down confirmed the next sentence and I resumed speaking as if directly to her—describing the way they clutched at each other and their hips ground together. As I told of one woman's fist tugging impatiently at the other's hair, I swore I felt the sharp pull against my own scalp. I drew out the smoldering kiss, telling of one's tongue sweeping in the other's mouth. And somehow, I kept enough composure to go on instead of melting into a puddle when the tip of her tongue swept along her upper lip, even though for a moment all I could think about was the feel of that same tongue against my heated flesh.

I jerked my eyes away from hers and managed not to rush through the remaining two pages of my selection. Afterward, as I mingled among readers and fellow authors, I got the sense she was purposely staying away. When I circled in her direction, she sometimes let me close enough to brush her hand or catch the subtle scent of her perfume, light and airy, before drifting slowly away. I made my obligatory appearances only as long as necessary, all the while anticipating the moment when I could disappear with her.

When that moment finally came, I grabbed her hand and led her toward our hotel room, which luckily was less than a minute away. I pulled her inside the room and swung the door closed. She shoved me against it and my breath escaped, half gasp and half moan as my back met the door. I barely had time to fill my lungs again before her mouth covered mine. Her teeth scraped my lips and her tongue drove inside.

"I take it you liked the reading," I said when she let me breathe.

She grabbed my waistband and yanked me against her, then whipped open my fly. Shoving her hands inside, she growled, "All I could think about while you were reading was this." She pressed the leather against my center and my clit twitched. "And what you might do with it later."

I grasped her hips. "Is it later yet?"

"Yes," she whispered, then louder, "Yes."

She pulled her shirt over her head and unhooked her bra as she moved toward the bed. She had dropped her purse in the chair by the door as we entered and I reached inside it before I followed the trail of her discarded clothing across the room.

She now wore only pale pink cotton panties and she watched me watch her as she eased them off. I traced my fingers over her gentle curves and along the sides of her breasts. She pushed her hands in the open fly of my jeans again, then impatiently shoved them down and I kicked them away. Needing to feel her soft skin against mine, I quickly stripped off the rest of my clothes. When I eased her back and lay on top of her, she sighed and wrapped her arms around me.

"Kiss me." Her voice shook slightly and suddenly I was nervous and very aware of the harness tight around my hips.

I kissed her, pouring my need for her into each stroke of my tongue against hers. Slipping my hand between us, I caressed her breast and elicited a soft moan that turned deeper, more desperate as I tugged firmly on her beaded nipple.

When I cupped the back of her neck and trailed my fingers through her hair, she leaned into my hand as if drawing comfort from my touch. I pulled back slightly and searched her face for hesitation. I wanted her—wanted to share this with her, but her pleasure was most important.

With a fistful of my hair she guided my face close to hers. "Please," she rasped. "Touch me."

Now was not the time for teasing and withholding, and I immediately stroked over her stomach. I would give her everything she asked for and it would still not equal what she had given me. She filled an emptiness, eased an ache I had grown accustomed to holding deep inside me. Heat flooded me when I dragged two fingers between her legs and felt her moisture. She was ready and I knew I was wet too.

She thrust against my hand and I rubbed her more firmly.

"I need you inside." Her warm breath feathered against my ear.

"Not yet," I whispered despite the fact that my fingertips were already poised to enter her. I held back, fearing I wouldn't be able to stop.

"Now." She grabbed the straps at my hips and pulled me closer, grinding harder against my hand.

"Wait." I eased back, still kneeling between her legs.

I slipped the silicone dildo into the ring as quickly as I could and reached for a small bottle of lube on the nightstand. My heart raced as I pushed my hips forward slowly, slid inside her, and paused. She closed her eyes and tilted her head back with a moan. I gently kissed the soft skin of her neck. I was surprised at how comfortable I was, having expected to be more self-conscious, and I loved that she was willing to try this with me.

"Please."

Her softly spoken plea sent spears of arousal through me. I pulled back carefully before surging forward again.

"Oh, yes."

Her fingernails on my back urged me on as I stroked into her over and over, ending each thrust pressed as tightly as possible against her body in an effort to relieve the ache between my own thighs. Her legs came around me and she pulled me deeper each time.

I watched her face as I carefully matched my pace to the lifting of her hips. But the pleasure building in me propelled me on faster and harder. I hadn't thought I could come like this, with only the stimulation of leather against me, but the feel of her beneath me, meeting my sharp thrusts, hurled me toward the edge.

When her hips began to jerk almost erratically and she moaned with every panting breath, I hovered on the brink behind her.

"I'm so close. I'm going to go with you," I said as I grabbed her hair and wrenched her head back even further. I closed my teeth on her neck and plunged into her one more time. She cried out and wrapped her arms tightly around me. Unable to contain the pulsing tension that uncoiled like a spring, I tumbled after her.

"Stay," she said a minute later when I would have moved to her side. Her legs bracketed my hips and I remained inside her, holding her while we trembled through the aftermath.

"Always." I kissed her forehead, and smiled at our secret, a story much better than fiction.

ALI VALI lives right outside New Orleans with her partner of many years. As a writer, she couldn't ask for a better more beautiful place, so full of real-life characters to fuel the imagination. Her works include the Cain Casey Saga (*The Devil Inside*, *The Devil Unleashed*, *Deal with the Devil*), numerous romances including her most recent, *Blue Skies*, and the Lambda Literary finalist *Calling the Dead*, a novel of romantic intrigue.

HOOKED ON QUACK
ALI VALI

"We got it!" Beth held the phone in one hand and pumped the other fist into the air. "We damn well got it."

"They sent Chili into a room full of women and you had doubts about us getting the contract?" Paul shook his head. "Get real, Beth, she had them eating out of her hand."

Both laughed because, humor aside, the truth was, their boss's personality was hard to resist. It was the reason there was hardly any turnover on her team and a waiting list to come and work for her.

Christian "Chili" Alexander had come out of college with a head full of ideas on how to conquer the world, just not an idea of which particular world would be the subject of her conquest. On the way back to her home in New Orleans, a flat tire stopped her in a little town just east of the city. Stumbling into the small one-room campaign headquarters of Alvin Millet to use the phone, she found her calling instead. Chili considered Alvin the one candidate vying for a city council seat with the heart and drive to fairly represent the local constituents. What Alvin didn't have was money or a message, but after a thirty-minute conversation, what he did have was a new campaign manager. Chili still had a lot to learn after Alvin took his oath of office, but she'd found the one slice of the world she wanted to conquer—politics.

The Alexander team was the busiest and most effective unit in the Pellegrin-Morris Consulting Firm, handling campaigns from the local to the national level. Chili's offices took up two floors of Huey Pellegrin's refurbished building next to the Mississippi River in New Orleans, and from the moment you stepped off the elevators, you could feel the adrenaline flowing. Everyone there believed as Chili did—their efforts could change the world, and change it for the better.

Their latest challenge was Kathleen Bergeron, hopefully the first woman who would sit in the governor's chair in the state of Louisiana. Bergeron's campaign was the contract everyone in the business was hot for, and after two meetings with Kathleen's top advisors, it was Chili's to see to the end.

As the buzz went through the office, the elevator doors opened and Huey Pellegrin stepped out to what he liked to call his cash cow floor. His daughter Samantha stood next to him, smiling at all the backslapping going on. Chili had done it again and her team was ready to fight the good fight, each and every one confident of success with her at the helm. The hero of the day was still at Mrs. Bergeron's local office, but had called ahead so they could uncork the champagne.

"I see the jungle is going to be hopping today," Samantha said as she swept an errant lock of blond hair behind her ear. "After she gets back, they aren't going to get any work done."

"Honey, I think you're the only one in the building who's immune to the Alexander charm. You don't care for Chili much, do you? I thought after working with her on Senator Emory's campaign you would've warmed up to her some."

Samantha shrugged. "If other people think she's the end all, that's great. Hey, it's that much better for our bottom line. Just don't ask me to explain or try to understand it—that I really can't do."

At that moment the stairwell door opened and Chili stepped out. She took the eight floors of stairs every day, a couple of times a day, to burn off energy and stay trim. "Huey, what brings you down to the trenches?" She shook his hand not expecting too many accolades from her boss. It wasn't Huey's style and Chili wasn't the type of person who needed much praise. Huey shared her deep love of the political game. For both of them it was a passion whose fire would never go out. "And you come with such a lovely sidekick."

Samantha rolled her eyes at the comment but reminded silent.

"I came to remind you not to be late this Saturday. I expect you on the dock by five, Chili, no excuses." Huey turned and started for the elevator, looking back at her when the doors opened. "One last thing. Congratulations on Bergeron. Good job, kid."

"What's Saturday?" Paul asked as Chili made her way to her office.

"The Pellegrin-Morris annual duck hunting trip. There's no better photo op for any politician, Pauly, than to be seen brandishing a firearm. Makes them look tough on crime and strong to the ever-powerful gun lobby." With a flip of a switch the unique boards in the room rolled to fresh, clean white paper. Chili always thought better with a pen in her hand, and it was time to start strategizing Kathleen's campaign. Before long two of the walls in her office would contain the roadmap that would lead the woman who'd just hired them to victory.

"You're willing to kill some helpless ducks for a photo op?"

"Pauly, I'm willing to kill you for a photo op," Chili joked as she tossed a pile of messages in the trash. Most were from the other gubernatorial campaigns looking for some election-day magic. "I don't particularly enjoy spending my day in a duck blind freezing my ass off, but this event is nonnegotiable as long as I'm here working for Huey. It's his favorite event and I don't want to disappoint him. Besides, you know how much he loves dealing with the media."

"Does that mean there's a chance you'll be giving up duck hunting after this election, so to speak?"

The view out the two walls of solid glass overlooked the churning brown water of the river and parts of the port, and as it often did, it captured Chili's attention. She was silent for so long, Paul was about to leave her to her thoughts.

"In this business no one would blame me for giving it up," she continued his analogy. "The duck hunting, that is. But where I come from, you dance with the one who brung you, buddy, and Huey was my dance teacher. As long as he's leading the band, I'll be happy to duck hunt."

"Yeah, but one day Samantha's going to be sitting in the conductor's chair. What then?"

"Then we'll be singing a different tune, won't we?"

❖

An eerie mist rose from the bayou as the guides put the small boats in the water. A large group of people in camouflage stood around holding shotguns and trying to stay warm while eager media personnel moved around getting pictures and sound bites for the Saturday night six o'clock news.

Chili walked up with a beautifully tooled weapon that looked almost too fancy to fire. She held it casually and unloaded as she made her rounds, introducing Kathleen and her husband to the group of mayors, senators, representatives, councilmen, and other elected officials. Kathleen's campaign assistant hovered, her hand on Chili's arm. When the cameras were trained elsewhere, more than one bet was made along the way as to who would bring back the most ducks. Chili's record hung in the balance.

"Chili, you ready to go?" Jean Pierre, Huey's groundskeeper, asked.

Jean Pierre was always her ride out to her blind, the blind he'd built to her specs when she joined the firm. The night before, he stocked away the supplies she requested, probably laughing the whole time at the thought of what Huey would do if he ever found out how Chili spent her time out there. Chili was the only person every year who hunted alone, never minding the silence and isolation of the area.

"Let's get going before one of these guys fills my ass with buckshot."

They both zipped up their camouflage jackets when he pulled the starter on the small quiet outboard and pushed away from the dock. It was still dark, but Jean Pierre had grown up in the marshes they were headed into and could have gotten there blindfolded if necessary. Spending time with him, Chili had come to appreciate the beauty of the wetlands and had joined the growing consortium of concerned citizens to fight to save them.

"Pick you up at ten, so stay put." The pirogue glided into the bank and Jean Pierre killed the engine.

"Stay put, he says. Where in the hell do you think I'm going to wander off to? You afraid I'll go for a swim in the pond? The only way that's going to happen is if a Starbucks magically surfaces out of the water." The heel of Chili's Timberland boot disappeared into the mud when she stepped out onto the small island where the simplistic structure stood. She pushed off the boat, trying to keep her boots clean, and warned, "I'll give you a heads up, though. Ride clear of Councilman Smith's blind if you don't want an eye shot out. It's not six yet, but he's already sauced."

❖

Chili pushed aside the makeshift flap that formed the door to the blind and ducked inside to get out of the cold. She was sure this was the only one on the property with a butane heater, crude wooden floor, cot, CD player, and a refrigerator stocked with champagne and orange juice. On top of that sat a tray of fruit.

The place was warm since Jean Pierre had come by earlier and turned up the heat, so she left the muddy boots at the entrance, rested the gun in the corner, and hung up her jacket. With socked feet, she headed for the cot and put on the headphones. Vivaldi's *Four Seasons* lulled her into closing her eyes and crossing her feet at the ankles. She was as relaxed as she ever got and was still in the same position when her visitor arrived.

Chili opened her eyes when she heard the footsteps getting closer. The intruder hadn't bothered to remove her shoes. "If I get mud on my socks I'm going to be pissed." She removed the headphones and laced her fingers behind her head, wanting to admire the shapely derrière when the woman bent over to unlace her footwear.

"It'll make us even, then." A boot landed close to Chili's with a thud.

"Even on what?"

"If Kathleen's campaign manager had gotten any closer to you this morning, on the pretense of getting a look at your *gun*, I was going to have to do something about it. You not doing anything about her flirting pissed me off, so we're even." The other boot was thrown with the same precision.

Chili chuckled at the straight posture and balled fists. Charm alone wasn't going to defrost the mood. "I wasn't flirting—"

"The hell you weren't," was shot back before Chili could finish.

Chili stood up, the headphones dropping forgotten to the floor, and moved behind her. "Flirting is buying a woman flowers and serenading her from the street even though you can't sing worth a damn." That reminder caused the fists to relax and the rigid body to lean into her. "Flirting is wanting to find ways to get the girl of my dreams to kiss me every time I have her within reach. Flirting is also allowing said woman into my inter sanctum to enjoy the morning."

"Do many women fall for this bullshit?"

"One bouquet of flowers got me a date for dinner." Chili grasped the zipper on her visitor's coat and pulled. "The serenade outside her window got me an invitation up to her place for a drink." Chili unfastened a few buttons on the flannel shirt so she could slip her hand onto a smooth, warm stomach. A little scratch elicited laughter and an arm snaked back around her neck.

"She sounds easy."

"Easy?" Chili snorted. "She's my boss's daughter and it took me months to get her to notice me, so don't blame me for resorting to some rather corny dating maneuvers."

"Ah, but you did look cute with the mariachi band playing behind you. Until you started singing, anyway." Samantha pulled Chili's hand out of her shirt and turned to face her. She looked around the small space as if wondering how many other women Chili had brought here. "This isn't just about stolen moments with the boss's daughter, is it?"

"Let me show you what this is about so there won't be any doubts." With ease, Chili picked Samantha up and carried her to the cot. Outside the sound of gunfire started as the first fingers of dawn painted the cloudy sky. "I usually spend this time listening to classical music to drown out the barrage of gunfire and squealing water fowl, so stop your wondering." She smoothed the frown line that had appeared the minute Samantha started taking in the room. "Today, though, I thought I'd spend it showing you how much I care about you, and that has nothing to do with your last name."

Kneeling, Chili finished with the buttons and opened the shirt to reveal a camouflage bra. "I see you dressed appropriately in case you have to sneak up on a duck in your underwear."

"I saw it in that stupid catalog you gave me and I thought you'd like it."

Chili kissed the swell of one breast where it peeked enticingly over a demi cup. "I love it, sweetheart." The button of the pants came next and Samantha helped by lifting her rear so Chili could take them off. The matching bottoms with little flying ducks embroidered on the waistband made Chili smile. "This is as close to any ducks as I want to get today."

Chili kissed her, and Samantha felt the rush of passion that had been building since they'd first seen each other that morning. The mouth that took possession of hers, like its owner, had a way of stripping away her inhibitions and awakening a need she hadn't known she possessed. It had been this way since she'd first let Chili through her front door, and the reason she had tried to resist her for so long. Given a chance, she was sure this woman could make anyone a glutton for this feast of carnal desires.

"I want you to do something for me," Samantha requested when they broke apart.

"What do you want?" Chili put a knee up on the cot and Samantha hooked her heels under her butt, pulling her in. Fingers ran through her hair, pulling just to the point of pain, stopping her from claiming another kiss. She felt Samantha's lips move against her own as she whispered one simple word.

"Control."

Simple, but control was something Chili never gave to anyone no matter how she felt about them. It was one of the reasons she was so successful in business and had survived in her personal life so long with her heart intact. "What do I get in return?"

Samantha just placed one finger on Chili's forehead and pushed her away until she was sitting on Samantha's fleece-covered foot, then pushed her back a little more by moving the same foot to Chili's chest. The game had begun, and Samantha was so far ahead there was no catching up.

"Take it off," Samantha ordered, her voice husky.

Not wanting to give in too easily, Chili took her time with Samantha's sock, smiling at how erratic Samantha's breathing was becoming. If she bided her time, she'd have Samantha begging before she knew it. Except she made the mistake of looking down as the last of the sock made it past Samantha's toes. The first time she'd seen the sight was in a late-night work session in her office when Samantha had slipped off her pumps. The next morning Chili had found herself at the florist buying roses like a schoolgirl with a crush. Red toenail polish was her kryptonite, at least red polish on Samantha Pellegrin. To Chili it was the epitome of femininity, and if giving up control was what she had to do to get her hands on it, Samantha would get her wish.

"Whatever you want, it's yours," Chili said as she removed the other sock with more enthusiasm.

"Stand up." Samantha leaned back with no intention of removing anything else just yet. "Take your shirt off." She watched as long fingers flew to the buttons and opened the first two in rapid succession. "Slowly," she added, not wanting to cut her show short.

Chili's nostrils flared and her hands stilled. From the look in her eyes, Samantha could tell there was an internal war waging. There was only one way to tip the outcome in her favor. She sat up again and reached behind herself to the clasp of the bra. The cups slid down a bit when the back came undone, but Samantha held it in place. Chili's nostrils flared again, but now it was from frustration of a different kind. Samantha had never thought of herself as beautiful and desirable until the first time she saw this same raw hunger in Chili's face. The sight had awoken the woman Samantha wanted always to be, the only woman in Chili's bed.

As slowly as she wanted Chili to go, Samantha reached for one of the straps and dragged it off her shoulder. Every movement was carefully studied by Chili's blue eyes, and she smiled at the way Chili's fingers twitched almost as if she was fighting the need to touch her. The next strap came down just as slowly and, naked from the waist up, Samantha leaned back and ran a hand from her stomach to the underside of her right breast. Samantha pinched the already hard rosy nipple, then released a hiss of pleasure as she repeated the move on the left nipple.

Chili's head fell slightly in defeat.

"I believe I asked you to slowly take off your shirt," Samantha said, skating her tongue along her top lip.

Chili went back to unbuttoning her shirt, and it was agonizing to watch and keep her hands to herself. Chili finally finished, leaving the heavy cotton garment hanging open. Underneath she wore a tight sleeveless T-shirt and with a flick of her wrist Samantha indicated she wanted it all off. When the clothes hit the floor, Samantha licked her lips again. Chili's need for her was obvious, since her nipples looked hard enough to chip ice.

"Tell me, baby, are you wet?" Samantha asked.

Chili closed her eyes and took a deep breath in an obvious effort to center herself. "Are you?"

"Do you want to stop?"

Chili's eyes flew open at the question. Stopping now was most definitely the last thing she wanted, and she relinquished the last of the fight in her. Whatever Samantha wanted, she was going to give it to her. "No, I don't."

"Then answer my question."

"I'm very wet," the admission came out as a whisper, "and it's because of you."

"Take your pants off and let me see." Samantha wasn't finished playing yet. "And don't forget to go slow."

Following orders, Chili unbuttoned the hunting pants and let them drop to her ankles. It left her in a pair of tight white briefs, and for once she saw Samantha's breathing catch. She wasn't the only one fighting for control. The underwear wasn't coming down without help, so Chili bent over to pull them off along with the pants and socks. When she straightened out, she faced Samantha naked, waiting for her next set of directions.

"Do you know what I've been thinking about since the last time we were together?" Samantha sat up again and set her feet on the floor. Her lover shook her head, visibly bristling with energy, reminding her of a thoroughbred in the starting gate. Given permission, Chili would explode with a burst of power.

"I've thought about how your mouth feels on me." Samantha parted her legs and, with a crook of her fingers, called Chili over. She ran her fingers lightly along Chili's sex, feeling her confidence grow at what she found. Chili was indeed wet and more than ready. "I've been dreaming about your tongue right here…" Samantha leaned back on one hand and slipped the other into her underwear, mingling the evidence of their desires together. When her fingers reappeared, they were glistening. "About how I can taste myself on your lips when you kiss me after, and how it makes me want to do it all over again when I do."

Rocking on her heels, Chili swallowed hard. "Sam, please."

"Hold me," Samantha said softly. She sighed when Chili leaned over to engulf her in her arms, the act so sweet, despite how turned on Chili was, that she almost told Chili how she felt. But fear of Chili bolting kept her quiet when Chili reached to pull off the last barrier between them. "On your knees, Alexander."

This time there was no argument and Chili groaned when Samantha painted her lips with her wet fingers. When she was done, their lips came together again and Samantha smiled fleetingly when again Chili ceded control, letting her lead this dance. When the need for air became paramount, Samantha pulled on Chili's hair again, guiding her head lower.

Like she was presenting Chili with a gift, she lay back to give Chili what they both wanted. "Make my dreams a reality."

Weaving their fingers together, Chili lowered her head and ran her tongue through the wet heat. Before either of them was ready, Samantha held Chili's head in place and gave her last order. "Now, baby, now."

Chili's fingers sliding easily into her sex took away the last of her resolve and she exploded against Chili's mouth and fingers, yelling loud enough to scare the few ducks that had landed outside. The feeling of possession was so complete that Samantha was sure she'd never give this part of herself to anyone else, even if Chili was too afraid to give in to her feelings.

"Wait," she panted when Chili went to start again.

Chili rested her head on Samantha's abdomen, and the position seemed to give her the courage to say what she had never even alluded to in words up to this moment.

"Do you know what I think about?"

The quiver of uncertainty was so evident in Chili's voice that Samantha ran comforting fingers through her hair. "Tell me, it's okay."

"I think about our stolen moments like this, and it isn't enough for me."

"What are you saying?" A tentacle of fear reached into Samantha's chest and she thought the pain of it would constrict her lungs until she couldn't breathe. She looked down into Chili's blue eyes.

"I want all of you, Sam. I love you and I want all of you for as long as you'll have me."

"You love me?"

"So much that I'm going to talk to Huey today about my intentions for his little girl."

The tease had its desired effect and Samantha laughed. "You're going to talk to him while he's holding a loaded shotgun? It must be true love." She pulled on Chili's hand, needing her to hold her. Chili moved up and pulled her close and she tucked her head into Chili's shoulder. "You know, the first day I stepped into the jungle, I began my own campaign strategy."

"Do tell?"

"My father thinks I'm immune to your charm."

Chili laughed and slapped Samantha gently on the butt. "You are. I've never had to work so hard at getting someone's attention. For the longest time, I thought it would take begging for you to have a cup of coffee with me."

"I just wanted to make sure when I fell in love with you, you would be good and snagged, baby. This was one campaign with a lifetime term limit, so I wanted to win in a landslide." Samantha cradled Chili's cheek and kissed her. "I love you and I'll have you as long as my heart beats."

"Can we do something about that wanting me now?" Chili's low voice cracked when Samantha's fingers closed around one of her nipples.

"Only if you promise to leave this part out of your talk with my father."

Six months later…

"The new sign on the building made the *Post*," Paul dropped a copy of the *Washington Post*'s business section on the recently added partner's desk in Chili's office, "and you received an invitation from the new governor to the mansion for dinner as a way of thanking you for all the help."

"A sign is news now?" Chili glanced down at the article as she rolled the last of Kathleen's campaign plans away and replaced the boards with fresh paper.

"Tell the governor we accept," Samantha answered from the doorway. She threaded her arms around Chili's waist, admiring the bouquet of roses on her side of the desk—the desk that came with the position she'd inherited with her father's retirement. "And *of course* the new sign made the capital's paper. Alexander, Pellegrin, and Morris is the hottest thing going in politics these days if you want to get elected."

"I guess this means you won't be giving up duck hunting anytime soon, huh, Chili?" Paul asked.

Chili pulled Samantha into her arms and kissed her hello. "After winning the heart of the most beautiful woman in the world, and Huey's wedding gift of a partnership, it's safe to say I'm permanently hooked on quack."

CARSEN TAITE works by day (and sometimes night) as a criminal defense attorney in Dallas, Texas. Her goal as an author is to spin tales with plot lines as interesting as the true, but often unbelievable, stories she encounters in her law practice. Her first novel, *truelesbianlove.com*, was a pure romance. Her second novel, *It Should Be a Crime* (August 2009), is a romance with a heavy dose of legal drama, drawing heavily on Carsen's experience in the courtroom.

Privileged and Confidential
Carsen Taite

I want a divorce."

She watched me closely as if trying to gauge my reaction, but years of practice kept me from showing my shock. I leaned back in my chair and gazed at the woman seated on the other side of my desk. I never expected to hear these words. Frankly, I'd never expected Linda to marry in the first place, but she had wasted no time after she announced she had fallen head over heels into blissful romance. Within two months of meeting, she and Joan had dashed off to Toronto and acquired a marriage license. Many of our mutual friends predicted sure disaster for their rushed relationship, but I'd known Linda for well over twenty years and my perspective was quite different. In all that time, she'd expressed a reluctance to dive into love, especially the commitment part. I figured that whatever was driving her to hurry her relationship with Joan along was a strong and powerful force, destined for longevity. Despite my personal history with Linda, I was stunned by today's announcement, so stunned I forgot the fact she had actually called my secretary to arrange this meeting. I reached across the desk and grasped her hand.

"What happened?"

"What hasn't happened?" Linda said, looking oddly dispassionate. "She isn't who I thought she was. She made herself out to be a caring, responsible person. She is cold and careless. We're not emotionally or financially secure and she doesn't seem to care. She doesn't care about anything. She's not the person I fell in love with."

Twenty years of love and friendship between us and I still wasn't sure what to say in response to this cut-and-dried summation of her marriage. Part of me wanted to dig for detail and engage in familiar gossip, as friends often do, but this situation was different from all the other times we had dished over our failed love affairs. Linda and Joan had become a singular entity to me and my partner, Sydney. Since marrying Joan, Linda had transformed from the friend whom I went out with on girls' night into merely a component of the happy foursome we had all become. To talk about the failings of one of our group signified a destruction of the cohesive unit. I defaulted to what I knew best and delivered a professional assessment on the status of her two-year relationship.

"You can't get a divorce."

"Why not?"

"Because you aren't really married."

"The hell we aren't."

"Sure, you're married in Canada, but that doesn't mean a damn thing here in Texas. Texas doesn't consider you married, so you can't get a divorce. One of you would have to establish residency in Canada or somewhere else that recognized same-sex marriage in order for you to get a divorce, and you'd have to go through legal channels there."

"Fuck," Linda spat out, her opinion about my legal advice clear. "That's no help. What am I supposed to do?"

"Does it really matter so much to you if you're married somewhere else? You can accomplish a separation without going through the hoops of a divorce." I delivered these rational statements without a second thought. I took a dim view of what I called pseudo-marriage, much to the dismay of my long-suffering partner. Sydney had finally stopped hinting we should elope to Canada, Massachusetts, or California when she realized I could not wrap my mind around legal trappings that were anything but. I told her every day how much I loved her, and it was true. Sydney was my world. I loved her more than I could ever show and more than words could ever express. But marriage, in its current hazy, "some places it's real and some places it's not" state was out of the question to my logical attorney mind. There were so many ways I could show Sydney my love that I refused to buy into the notion that marriage had to serve as the pinnacle of our romance.

Linda's next words snapped me out of my reflections. "What if I want to get married again?"

I couldn't help it. I laughed out loud. Certainly she was trying to add some levity to the situation. A blunt retort about not making the same mistake twice welled up from my core and pushed its way toward the surface. The earnest expression on her face caused me to bite back a lecture. I could almost hear Sydney's soothing counselor voice in my ear: *"Honey, everyone doesn't have to share your opinion. It's okay to accept our differences."* She had a way with me.

I stifled my words and coughed away the laughter. "If you want to get married again, *legally*," I forced myself to say the word, "then one of you will have to live in Canada for a while. If you're serious about divorce, I can refer you to a barrister in Toronto so you can get the full details. In the meantime, you can take the necessary steps to separate your property, which is the gist of what you can legally do to accomplish a split here."

"Why haven't you ever gotten married?"

The non sequitur caught me by surprise for many reasons, primarily because I thought she should already know the answer. But now that I thought about it, I had tempered my rants about marriage in her presence, out of friendship mostly. She had been so giddy about the prospect of a wedding it had seemed a shame to rain on her parade. And it had only been in the last few years that everyone began rushing off to obtain trusty certificates and declare their vows in distant locales. We would have never had a conversation about marriage in our early days. It wasn't even on our radar.

Linda was still waiting for my answer and I conjured up a vague response. "Just hasn't seemed right."

"Maybe you just need the right person to make it right," she said quickly.

I've been told by many, Sydney included, that when I'm working on a case I have a singular focus. Meals, proper wardrobe selection, and a host of other personal matters take a backseat to puzzling out the problem I've been hired to solve. Now might have been one of those times, but Linda's tone had become sultry and she held my hand in hers. I recognized the look on her face. Combined with the other signals, I knew she had her sights on new prey. However, this time "new" was a relative term.

I drew my hand away, but she pressed closer to the desk.

"Seriously, Reed, remember how great we were together? Why didn't we give forever a chance?"

Because we were practically children when we dated? Because you cheated on me? I had a long list of reasons Linda and I wound up being no good together. Back then I thought our breakup was devastating. Ostensibly, we were the perfect couple. Young, good-looking professionals, we were happy lesbians with bright futures. But we were too blinded by the shiny shell of our relationship to recognize the lack of substance between us. If I'd known then what I knew now, we wouldn't have made it past our second date. Despite my present knowledge that we'd wasted a year together, each seeking something the other could never give, I couldn't bring myself to burst the bubble of her memories with my callous conclusions.

"That was a long time ago." Lame, but the best I could do.

"It's not too late." She purred these words into my ear. In my trip down memory lane, I had missed her movement around my desk. Now her hand was no longer in mine, it was sliding around my waist as she stood behind my chair leaning in. Vague wasn't going to work. I wrenched away and jumped up.

"Whatever the hell you're doing, you need to stop it. Now!" I glanced at the door, half wishing my assistant would hear my raised voice and charge in. Immediately ashamed for wanting rescue, I realized I needed to confront Linda's overtures head-on. "You need to go."

She looked as astounded as I had felt at her initial demand for a divorce. She had apparently expected me to melt in her arms and skip away with her to an idyllic ever after.

"You don't have to be such a bitch," Linda said. "I came here looking for advice and you're going to throw me out?"

"Apparently, you came here looking for more than advice." She was already setting up a plausible denial about her advances, but I was in no mood to play along. "I don't think I'm the one to help with any of your needs right now."

"Well, that's rich. I've always been there for you, but now that I need a lawyer, you're trying to turn me away."

It was true, we had always supported each other over the years, both during and in between relationships, but Linda had never been so inappropriate as to make an advance when she knew I was involved. There had been plenty of times, back when I was young and insecure enough to take back a partner who had once betrayed my trust, when I would have welcomed her advances. That version of me no longer existed. I was impossibly confident now, in part because of my rock-solid faith in Sydney's unwavering love. I would sacrifice even a twenty-year friendship to keep that bond secure.

"Yes. I'm turning you away." I let my tone tell her that legal advice was not the only thing I was declining to provide. "If you want a referral, I'll have my office call you with a few names."

She gathered her coat and purse and stomped toward the door. Just before she pulled it open, she looked over her shoulder to me. "Reed, I made an appointment to see you today."

"So?"

"So, I'm here consulting you as a client. I trust that everything I've told you will be protected by attorney-client privilege." She smiled, the corners of her mouth twitching. She had disguised her personal overture as a professional visit, knowing ethics would prevent me from telling either Joan or Sydney about what had just happened. *Perfect.*

❖

"Hard day at the office?" Sydney kissed me softly on the lips before reaching for my briefcase. I contemplated her question. Except for Linda's visit, it hadn't been. Before and after she disturbed my world, I had been drafting pleadings for an upcoming hearing, the kind of dull work I tended to embrace since most of my time was spent dealing with emotional crises and relationship ruin. Sydney, a licensed social worker, could read me like a book. If I launched into a diatribe about the evils of paperwork, she would know something deeper lurked beneath the surface. If I said nothing, she would think I was headed to the cave, my imaginary retreat from the day-to-day grind, where I became uncommunicative and unapproachable until I was ready to emerge. All I wanted right now was the comfort of her presence without having to share the reason I needed it so desperately. I handed her my coat and opted for a tiny lie.

"New client. Pain in the ass."

"Ah, I understand." And I knew she did. The nature of our respective jobs meant we each had an appreciation for the resulting drain of dealing with other people's problems. We also had a healthy sense of respect for privacy. Both of us had a duty to keep the confidences of our clients, which lent an interesting twist to the usual daily banter of dinner conversation about our workdays. We had developed a method of sharing details in a way that didn't compromise confidence, leaving out names, identifying characteristics, and even some pertinent facts just so we could share a portion of our day. Keeping completely silent about the woes of the individuals whose troubles consumed our working hours was simply too much.

The situation with Linda was different. I couldn't tell Sydney about Linda's pass and leave it at that. She would want to know more detail, deserved to know more detail, about the circumstances that led to Linda's crass intrusion on our happy home life. I was about to suggest a physical diversion to absolve me of the need to talk when Sydney's next words sank in.

"Joan called me this afternoon." Sydney's words were light, but I braced myself for the other side of the story. Did Joan know Linda had made a pass at me? Of course, if Joan had told Sydney about their desire for a divorce, that would free me to discuss the details.

"And what did she have to say?" Even as the words left my lips, I felt foolish. If Sydney told me now that Joan was pissed about what had happened, I would look stupid for not coming clean. I shrugged away the thought. My lover knew me better than that. She would understand why I hadn't told her, why I couldn't, and she would know beyond certainty that I would never do anything to jeopardize the bond of love and trust that held us together. Wouldn't she?

"She wanted to let us know she settled on Mario's."

"Mario's?" I didn't have a clue what she was talking about.

"For Friday night." Sydney must have read my confusion. "Linda's birthday dinner?"

I'm certain my jaw was hanging open. Sydney stared at my face as if trying to determine if I had lost my mind. It wasn't like me to forget details like friends' birthdays, and Friday was only a couple of days away. I wanted to respond that I hadn't forgotten about the dinner, I just didn't think there was any way it would still take place. Of course, I couldn't say anything, and now there was someone else I had to pretend around. Joan had no idea that Linda wanted a divorce. I didn't know Joan well, but in the two years we had shared dinner dates, I had witnessed enough of her insecurities to know she wouldn't purposely expose herself to a celebratory dinner when the demise of her relationship lurked in the background.

"Sorry—I didn't forget. But I'm not sure I can make it."

"Honey, it's just us four, we shouldn't cancel." Sydney's eyes said she knew something was up despite my attempt to sound nonchalant.

"I have a lot going on at the office." My excuse sounded feeble, even to my own ears. Sydney knew I didn't work late on Fridays unless the world was caving in. In this case, it would be me doing the caving. If nothing else, I wanted to avoid as much contact as possible with our friends' diseased relationship. "Oh, okay. I'll make it, but can we just meet them there?"

"Not a problem. Swing by my office and pick me up and we'll meet them at the restaurant." I could tell by her tone that she knew there was more to my request than convenience, but she didn't push and I didn't offer. During the rest of the evening, we shared dinner, TV, and bed without the kind of intimacy that invites sharing.

❖

Margaritas can make a good time better or a bad time worse. Linda should have ordered iced tea. From the moment we joined them in the booth, I felt a sense of dread. She leaned too close, taking every possible opportunity to touch my arm, grab my hand. Her animated bursts of conversation were all aimed in my direction, and she was downright snarly at any interruptions from either Joan or the waiter, whom she deemed incapable of quenching her thirst fast enough. I could feel the dull roar of Linda's need to erupt, to use Sydney and me as witnesses to the destruction of her relationship. Would she be so stupid as to declare her misplaced feelings for me in front of her wife and my partner? Part of me wanted her to drink faster in hopes she would pass out. I spent my days dealing with confrontation, but none of it was my own. I excelled at pushing other people's points of view, challenging opposition, but not when my own feelings were at risk. In this case, if Linda decided to blurt out her rejection of Joan and her attraction toward me, the person closest to me in the whole wide world would be hurt. The thought made me want to throw down a couple of twenties and dash from the restaurant.

"You two may have outsmarted us all by never getting married."

I shot a glance at Sydney and nodded at Linda's frosty glass. Her fifth. Hoping to keep the conversation from unraveling if I could just hold up my end, I shook Linda's grasp from my arm and tried for an answer that wouldn't invite discussion. "Oh, I don't know about that." Linda didn't take the hint.

"Look at all those people out in California. They ran off and got married and then months later, no one can tell them for sure if they're still legally married." Linda smirked in my direction. "Of course, Reed doesn't think these marriages are legal in the first place."

I wanted to ignore her, but I couldn't let her breezy summary of my stance hang in the air. I gave it weight. "I never said any such thing. All I've ever said is that until we all have the same rights, everywhere, we don't really have any rights at all."

"Blah, blah. I don't have a clue what the hell you mean by that." She probably didn't, but because of the alcohol, not due to any failing of her intelligence. She turned to Joan. "But our marriage is ironclad, isn't it, sweetie?"

"You bet it is." Joan smiled indulgently at her smashed spouse.

"Because we can't really get divorced even if we want to." Linda turned dramatically to face me. "Reed says so."

I felt Sydney's strong but gentle hand on my thigh. She always knew when I was seething, and hers was the only touch that could calm my swirling mind. I didn't let my gaze leave Linda's, but while I paused to temper my response, I placed my hand over Sydney's and squeezed back my thanks. The subject on the table was a sensitive one between us. Sydney and I had long ago agreed to disagree on the issue of marriage, and we avoided further discussion as futile since there really wasn't any room for compromise.

"I never said that." I turned to Joan and suppressed a wince at the raw questions scrawled into her expression. "I merely said that Texas doesn't recognize same-sex marriage and, as a result, they don't recognize the right to same-sex divorce."

"Reed says we would have to move away to get a divorce," Linda pressed on. "Maybe even to Canada."

Linda hadn't looked at Joan the entire time she had been talking, instead directing all her comments to me. What could have been mistaken at first for chummy conversation had dissolved into full-on hostility. Her sarcastic tone and look of disdain were unmistakable. Sydney would notice this detail and assign a meaning, but Joan merely seemed confused about the undercurrent of the conversation.

Joan leaned over to give Linda a kiss. "Well, we aren't moving anywhere, are we, babe?"

"No, dear." Linda tilted her cheek toward Joan, accepting a smack on the side of her face with a frown. "I suppose we're not."

❖

Sydney hung my coat in the closet and then pulled me into an embrace.

"Reed? Are you okay?"

"I'm sorry Linda was such a pain tonight." She couldn't see my face, but professional habit caused me to keep my expression blank.

"You're not responsible for her actions." Sydney cupped my chin gently, love pouring from her eyes. "*Any* of her actions. You know I know that, right?"

She knew. She always knew. I felt the knot of tension I'd carried inside all week unravel and I relaxed into the solid security of her arms. I would always be safe here. Actually, more than safe, cherished. Often I wondered if her sixth sense was the primary reason behind her success as a counselor. I knew it had to be a major factor. I nodded, telling myself that it took actual words to betray a confidence.

"I'm going to talk and you don't have to say a word, okay?" Sydney held me even more tightly and again, I just nodded. I could feel warmth on my neck as she breathed a sense of peace against me.

"Those two were never right for each other and they rushed into their relationship before they ever gave themselves a chance to find that out. I imagine Joan had no idea before tonight that Linda was contemplating divorce and had even gone so far as to talk to you about it." She paused and I struggled not to respond. "If they knew each other even a fraction as well as we know one another, surprises like that wouldn't happen."

Was that true? Were we so much a part of each other that surprise wasn't possible? Did I know how Sydney would react in any given situation, what she would say, what she would do? I knew the answer to each question was unequivocally yes. I might not know the specific words or the choreography of her actions, but I knew as surely as I knew anything on this earth that my lover's actions would always be kind and loving. When it came to me, or us, she would put my heart, my soul, first—before her own. Her love transcended any sense of selfishness. I had no doubt she loved me.

Here in her arms, I wondered if she felt the same sense of security. Could I be counted on to deliver comforting constants? Did she view my love as an unstoppable force, always present, always strong? I held her tightly, as if to squeeze out any doubt. She glanced up at me and when she did, I saw the answers to my questions in her eyes. She had no doubts about my love for her, either its strengths or its limits. Gazing at the unconditional love reflected back at me, I was overcome with the desire to shake her certainty, to make her question her well-grounded knowledge of all I have ever been. I wanted her to know that my love still came with surprises.

"Marry me."

VK Powell is the author of two novels of romantic intrigue, *To Protect and Serve* and *Suspect Passions*, and several erotic short stories, all published by Bold Strokes Books. Her third novel, *Fever*, set in Africa, is scheduled for release in early 2010. www.powellvk.com.

RETURN TO ME
VK POWELL

Ty dropped her bags at the terminal doors, blew me three air kisses, and disappeared behind the tempered glass. Each step she took was a blunt instrument gouging at my heart. She'd made me promise that I wouldn't cry. What a stupid agreement. The minute she vanished from view the tears started and wouldn't stop. Why didn't I try once more to tell her how I felt about her? Would it have mattered? "It's just another trip," she'd said. But it didn't feel like that. It felt like forever.

Three months turned into six and then twelve. Every place I went, every person I saw, and every sappy song on the radio reminded me of her. Each memory dredged up a fresh deluge of tears, regardless of time, place, or circumstance. The truth that everyone else seemed to know gradually registered and I finally admitted it. I was in love with my best friend. A cliché, but true. The real issue was whether I could convince her.

She was coming back for a visit and I paced the same airport terminal like an expectant parent. As I trod back and forth on the hard tile floor, I rehearsed a million suave and lighthearted greetings, but I'd have been happy with anything short of a blurted confession of love in a roomful of strangers. I'd glanced at the status board so many times, I felt like my head was on a swivel. Airport security was starting to regard me with more than a modicum of curiosity. But her flight had landed ten minutes ago, and still no Ty.

Eventually passengers started to descend the escalators. My pulse ramped up as I stood rooted in place and watched each person who wasn't her pass by. It had to be some twisted universal game that caused time to pass in direct opposition to your desires. My insides twitched like leaves in a stiff breeze as I waited—it seemed like eternity.

The first indication of Ty's approach was her well-worn UGG boots at the top of the platform, followed by faded jeans that hugged her muscular legs, and her signature leather bomber jacket hanging open over a turquoise T-shirt. My eyes burned as tears clouded my vision. I blinked, unwilling to lose sight of her for one second after waiting a year for this. Her baby blond hair, tanned face, and ever-present smile finally came into view as she ran down the steps toward me, shouting my name.

"Coop-a, Coop-a!" Her thick Australian accent made my name sound like it ended with *a* instead of *er*. "You're here."

She grabbed me in a full-body hug and swung us in circles. I grew light-headed but wasn't sure if it was from the merry-go-round greeting or her teacup-sized breasts pressed so closely under mine that they felt fused. I inhaled the light scent of her jasmine perfume hungrily. I'd tried so desperately to hold on to that fragrance after she left, whiffing everything that hinted at jasmine, but nothing approximated the combination of the aroma with her skin. My body tingled with the physical, visual, and olfactory presence of her.

Ty stopped her happy dance, held me at arm's length, and gave me a thoughtful appraisal. "You've lost a few pounds." Then she threaded a hand through my hair. "And gained more gray—gorgeous."

My heart pounded erratically. I tried to speak but my voice wouldn't cooperate. The words I wanted to say backed up in my throat. All those months of living without her had been hell, but now that she stood in front of me, I realized just how much more I'd missed her. If I opened my mouth, I knew my feelings would fly out. This was not the time or place.

"Aren't you going to say anything? Didn't you miss me?"

I managed to nod as the tears at last broke free. She cupped my face in her hands, brushed the tears from my cheeks with her thumbs, and whispered, "It's okay, Coop. Wait right here while I get my luggage and we'll get out of here."

As I drove away from the airport, my voice returned. "Where to?"

"She speaks."

"It's good to see you," I finally managed.

"So, what have you been doing? Or should I ask who?"

"Nothing and nobody." Since she'd been gone, my interest in other women had dwindled to a priestly level. I went out with friends to pass the time and to avoid becoming a complete shut-in. But my things-I-want-in-a-partner list had grown to voluminous proportions through the years, making it almost impossible for anyone to measure up. Maybe that had been my unconscious goal.

"I can't imagine the line of women at your door has gotten any shorter without me to cull out the unqualified."

"I just haven't found anyone I'm interested in." The role of noncommitted serial dater didn't really suit me anymore since I hadn't actually had a real date in over a year. But that was how Ty remembered me. I imagined it was the main reason she never took me seriously when I hinted at my feelings for her. She joked that I'd miss the other flavors if I settled for just one.

She reached over to where my hand rested on the console between us, covered it with hers, and squeezed lightly. The dim green glow from the dashboard must've concealed my blush because Ty didn't comment. It felt as if no time had passed as we caught each other up on mutual friends and family.

"How about some ice cream?" she asked. "You know where."

It was the last thing we'd done on the day she left. I hadn't been back since. We pulled into Maxie B's parking lot five minutes before closing and exited the shop with two double-scoop cups of Moose Tracks and Cappuccino Crunch.

"A year without Moose Tracks is cruel and unusual punishment," Ty lamented.

"I would've thought that alone was enough to bring you back sooner."

"Now that's the smart-ass Coop I remember."

We sat in the car eating ice cream and giggling like two kids playing hooky. Ty dug the vanilla from around the chocolate-coated peanut butter chunks and ate that first. She always saved the best for last. When she reached her favorite part, she stuck her spoon in my direction. "Want some?"

"You know I don't like to mix my chocolate with my peanut butter. It's not natural."

"It's as natural as a stoic old Aussie like me and a drama queen like you being friends for twenty-three years and never sleeping together. Why wasn't I ever good enough, Coop?"

I nearly choked on a glob of Cappuccino Crunch, which fortunately keep my mouth closed. I couldn't believe she'd asked *the* question. We'd been friends since childhood, went to school together, came out together, and even dated each other's exes. But neither of us had ever broached that particular question. Any time I tried to bring up the possibility, she blew me off with jokes. I was so stunned, I had no idea where to start or if I really should.

If she only knew that she was the standard by which everyone else was measured. I felt for her the one thing missing with everyone else—a heart connection. But how could I explain that to my best friend? What if she didn't feel the same way? If I had to choose between sleeping with her and keeping her as a friend, it was a no-brainer. The idea that I might have both never seemed a real possibility. So I erred on the side of caution. It was late. She was tired and this wasn't a conversation I wanted to have interrupted by yawns or pleas for a continuance.

"You were better than that, Ty. You were my best friend. Now, let's get you home so you can get some rest." If I could distract her momentarily she would probably let it go. Ty wasn't usually fond of discussing relationships or feelings.

"Home sounds good."

A feeling of warmth settled in my chest to hear Ty refer to my home as hers. Then a twinge of apprehension crept in as I realized that Ty didn't have a home here anymore and she'd be staying with me until she left again. Suddenly my three-bedroom home seemed too small.

A few minutes later, we deposited her luggage in the guest bedroom and I tried to sound like a calm, cordial hostess. "I've set you up here with the bathroom across the hall. If you need anything else, let me know. But you probably remember where everything is."

"Thanks. I think I'll just have a quick shower and turn in. Jet lag, you know."

Listening to Ty's non-melodic hum as she entertained herself with old Aussie tunes in the shower, I replayed the evening. She looked like the same person, smelled deliciously the same, and sounded like my longtime friend, but her foray into sexual innuendo was very un-Ty.

Before she left I hadn't thought of her in those terms since we were teenagers. A memory of two kids practicing kissing and ineffectively groping each other washed over me like an information overload. I gripped the kitchen sink like it was a life raft and I was drowning. I bowed my head and forced the trapped air from my lungs. Arousal swam through my system like an intoxicating drug.

"Are you okay?" Ty slid her arms around me from behind and hugged me to her freshly showered body. My shiver was involuntary.

"I'm fine. Are you hungry? Can I fix you anything?" I wiggled from her arms and opened the refrigerator, looking for quick distractions. Not now. Not the right time, I kept repeating.

"You're not okay. I know that frustrated sigh." Those sapphire blue eyes dug into my soul like a sensitive excavation tool. "What's up?"

"Nothing, really, Ty. Let it go."

"All right, but you're not fooling me. And I'm not letting you get by with it anymore. There are a few things we've let go between us. Starting tomorrow we're going to talk. I mean really talk to each other. But now I'm going to bed. Good night, Coop." She gave me a quick hug, went into her bedroom, and closed the door.

I paced the kitchen for a while replaying her words and wondering what she meant. I thought we'd always been the best of friends, sharing everything about everybody. The only thing we'd never talked about was us—how we really felt about each other. But some things didn't need to be said. You just knew.

On the way to my bedroom, I placed my hand on Ty's closed door and caressed it as if I were stroking her skin. I whispered *I love you* and went to bed. I tossed for what seemed like hours, chasing sleep and fearing it. When I finally drifted into a restless slumber, my deepest desire and my greatest fear came true.

A warm body spooned against my backside. I felt the thin layer of soft fabric between her breasts and my naked back as she pressed against me. Her hand slid across my abdomen, soft and tentative. I grabbed it and pulled it up between my breasts. When her hand started massaging my breasts and tweaking my nipples, I realized it wasn't a dream.

I sat upright in bed, clutching the sheet to my naked body. "Ty, what are you doing?"

"Nothing. I couldn't sleep." Moonlight through the partially opened shades cast a series of lighter and darker lines across her boxer and T-shirt clad body. She looked like a blond-haired minx. "I thought we could talk."

"Can I get dressed?"

"Lie back down. I've seen you without clothes hundreds of times. Besides, you've got your trusty toga draped around you like a shield."

I reluctantly lay back in the bed and turned to face her. "I thought you were tired. What do you want to talk about that can't wait until morning?"

"I was wondering about that question you avoided earlier. Why was I never good enough to be your lover? Weren't you ever attracted to me? Didn't you feel anything special for me? What was it exactly?"

"Ty, don't do this." She had no idea that every woman I had sex with was her in some way. And if the physical resemblance wasn't there, I'd close my eyes and conjure her up in my mind. But in the morning, there was just no substitute for the real thing.

"Do what? I really want to know." Her face took on a pained look as the light in her eyes faded and her smile disappeared.

I'd never been able to handle that hurt look. Anything that made her unhappy ripped at my heart like the talons of a wild beast. I could deny her nothing. "You're my best friend. I didn't want to mess that up."

"And sleeping with me would do that?"

"You see how well it's turned out with everyone else." I knew immediately that was the wrong thing to say. Her full lips pressed into a thin line of consternation, and she looked at me like I was the dumbest woman on the planet.

"But I'm not like everyone else. Haven't you figured that out yet? You've had a year to think about it."

My insides felt like they were going to explode if I didn't tell her the truth. It was now or never. She really wanted to know and I didn't think I could contain it any longer. "I love you."

"I know. And I love you, too."

We'd said those words a million times and they'd always meant *like a friend* or *like a sister*, never like a lover. This time I had to be clear. "I mean I'm *in love* with you. I think I've loved you since we were kids. And yes, I'm attracted to you, so much that it hurts to be around you without touching you. What I feel for you goes beyond special. It's everything I've ever wanted, needed, or imagined rolled into one blond-haired, blue-eyed, compact gymnast's body, mind, and spirit. I love you with all that I am." I waited for the inevitable string of reasons why that was impossible or unreasonable or my imagination. I waited for the joke that would let her laugh the whole thing off. But they didn't come. She just grinned. "Why are you smiling?"

"What part of being in love and having sex doesn't work for you?"

"The part that comes after the sex, the leaving part. I couldn't bear to lose you, Ty. All the sex in the world isn't worth it to me."

Ty's smile got bigger. "You think this is about sex?"

"What else?"

She reached for me and pulled me into her arms. "This is about love, Coop. I'm *in love* with you too. Why do you think I came back?"

"You returned to *me*?"

"Only you."

"Oh." The words I'd waited my entire life to hear hung in the air between us and I wanted to let them linger and swirl around me like her warm embrace. They sank into my brain and body one by one, releasing the hold I'd placed on my heart for years. The thread that had bound our hearts together strengthened and tugged me closer to her. I started crying and couldn't stop. "I'm sorry—" I tried to explain but the sobs robbed me of words.

"It's okay as long as those are tears of happiness."

I nodded as another wave soaked her thin T-shirt. She stroked my hair and rocked me back and forth in her arms. "I have missed you so much, Coop. I've had a year to think too and I know I never want to be without you again. We're meant to be."

"Really?" My heart swelled with hope in spite of the constant flood of tears.

"Australia is a beautiful country, but I can live anywhere. As long as I get to wake up to you every day I'm happy. But there is one condition."

"Condition?" I raised my head from her shoulder and held my breath. Was this the part where she told me she was only kidding? "Anything you want."

"Sex. There has to be sex, and it has to start now. I think I've been very patient. Twenty-three years has to be a record."

We kissed lightly, tentatively at first, as if unsure how to cross the threshold between friends and lovers. But that first intimate touch ignited the years of suppressed desire. Her lips were softer than I imagined, her mouth hotter, her tongue more probing and demanding. I moved against her and as our bodies entwined so did our lives—finally, completely, eternally.

JULIE CANNON, a native sun goddess born and raised in Phoenix, Arizona, is the author of six Bold Strokes Books: *Come and Get Me*, *Heart 2 Heart*, *Heartland*, *Uncharted Passage*, *Just Business*, and *Power Play* (November 2009). She has selections in *Romantic Interludes 1: Discovery*, *Erotic Interludes 4: Extreme Passions*, and *Erotic Interludes 5: Road Games*. Julie and her partner Laura spend their weekends camping, riding ATVs, or lounging around the pool with their two kids. www.JulieCannon.com.

MASQUERADE
JULIE CANNON

What do you do when you are so entrenched in something you can't even see the way out? So deep you have no idea even how to begin? Any time you think about it you feel foolish and embarrassed. And that's before anyone even knows you're doing something different.

I'm in that predicament. My name is Elizabeth Beckett, but everyone calls me J. No one knows my real name except me. I have no family, at least none that claim me or would even recognize me if I introduced myself. I ended up in foster care when I was twelve, my mom in jail and my dad long gone. But that's another story altogether and I don't dwell on things I can't change. What I can change is me, and that's my entire point here. I know what I want to do, but I am more afraid of doing this than I ever was of any dark street or mean foster parent.

If you were to look at me what you'd see is someone in their early twenties, dressed in baggy Dickies, a tight T-shirt, and utilitarian black boots. My hair is buzz short, #2 on the clippers if you know what that means, and I have a tattoo of a naked woman on my left bicep. You would have to look closely to determine if the bumps under my shirt were breasts or simply well-defined pecs. Most people think it's the latter due to the number of times people call me *sir* or *dude*. But I'm not. My hard exterior is an effective armor shielding my heart from pain.

Remember that foster care I mentioned earlier? Well, I was one of the unlucky ones who disappeared into the system. No one was there to protect me, so I learned early on to protect myself, my body, and my emotions. You know the old saying "sticks and stones may break your bones but names can never hurt you"? Well, let me tell you, it's bullshit.

Why am I telling you all this? Because I'm tired. Tired of the charade, tired of being what I'm not. Not really. You see, I don't want to be a bad-ass-baby-dyke anymore. I do all the work, make all the advances. I want to be a lady. Courted, cherished, and eagerly taken home to meet somebody's mom.

But how do I do it? This is where I live, where I've made my home. My friends are here, I can have just about any woman I want anytime, I own my own business that I can't just pick up and leave. Believe it or not, my roots here are deep, and much as I want to live my life differently, I don't want to pull up stakes and sever all ties with these people.

I know, I've read all the coming-out books and articles that say your friends will still be your friends no matter who you are. I'm a smart girl; my brain understands, but my gut and my heart can't stand another rejection. You heard me right. I said coming out because that is how I look at it. I would be coming out as someone very different than how everyone knows me. It's the same thing, isn't it? My friends might laugh at me, point their fingers and say I look like a dyke in drag. That would hurt.

What do I want? It's pretty simple. I want a woman to approach *me*, invite *me* for a cup of coffee, make meaningless small talk as she gets to know *me*. I want her to ask *me* out to dinner.

She picks me up at my front door with a little trinket—nothing serious, maybe a handful of daisies or something corny like that. She stammers, stutters, and her eyes pop out when she sees me in my short skirt, cute top, and snappy sandals. I invite her in and we have a quick drink.

She helps me with my jacket. She opens my front door. Holding my arm lightly, she escorts me down the stairs and holds open the passenger-side door of her car for me. Openly admiring my bare legs as I slide into her sleek machine, she can hardly breathe.

I want her to not be able to keep her eyes from sneaking another peek at my legs, exposed as my skirt rides up. When we arrive at the restaurant, she jumps out of the car and hurries to open my door again. She offers me her hand to help me out, taking another look at my legs, this time not bothering to hide it. She tells me they're beautiful.

She escorts me in, her hand lightly on my back, just above my waist. She walks beside me to the table, holds my chair as I sit down. She gazes at me across the table, refills my wineglass, makes warm, witty conversation intent on making *me* feel at ease.

She is dressed in a blue suit, impeccably cut to fit over her tall frame. Her hair is shoulder length, her eyes blazing blue, and her laugh deep and sensuous. She is an attorney, a successful professional and drop-dead gorgeous. We have dessert, coffee, and an after-dinner cognac. She pays the check with a platinum American Express card, her Montblanc pen boldly gliding across the bottom of the bill, without even glancing at the amount.

I feel her eyes on me as we walk out, and I add just a little bit more sway to my hips. She stands behind me, so close that her warm breath makes me shiver, and I feel her breasts press against my arm when she hands the valet the claim ticket. Not to be outdone, I brush by her as she holds the car door, giving her a whiff of my intoxicating perfume. Intentionally I hike my skirt even higher than before, giving her and the valet a bird's-eye view of what they've only imagined.

We go dancing, to an upscale club where women share their desire for each other, not play pool or grope body parts in a dingy, dark hallway. She asks me to dance, holding my hand, leading me through the throngs of people. We dance close, and *I'm* the one that dances backward. I follow instead of lead. The beat of the music picks up and her eyes burn as she watches my body move. My body burns when it slows again.

Getting late, she holds me closer, more intimate. During one particular song, she lowers her head and kisses me. She's gentle as if worried I might refuse. Her tongue asks permission to enter, giving me the option to refuse. I don't. The mating of our mouths and tongues symbolizes one of the most intimate of acts. I've never told anyone that I think kissing is just about as intimate as two people can get. Sometimes I think it's even more intimate than the other fabulous place mouths and tongues go. There's just something about it that makes me crazy. Quite a few times I come just by kissing, but no one ever knows.

She asks me if I'm ready to leave, and I slide my arm through hers as we walk to her car. Back at my front door she doesn't move to kiss me, but lets me take the initiative. By then I'm hers for the asking. She doesn't have to ask, I give willingly.

She sits on the couch in the living room while I make coffee. My hands shake so bad I spill the grounds all over the counter. I swear. I am way out of my element here. I am not the aggressor, the butch, the top, or whatever else you want to call it. I don't know how to act. I desperately want this to go right. I need this. This is who I really am.

Taking a deep breath, I ask myself why I am even bothering with making coffee. She wants me. She has made that very clear, yet I don't feel pressured into having sex with her. It's not payment for dinner at a swank restaurant, or dancing at an exclusive club. It isn't even expected because we've been dating for several months. I think that's what's so refreshing and frightening at the same time. Sex didn't come first with us and then we got to know each other. I know more about her than all of my previous girlfriends combined.

It's then I realize something. By being secure in herself she is, in fact, letting me lead. Everything we have done has been on my terms, my timeline. I'm not following her. She isn't in charge. But in some respects neither am I. I know I sound confused, like I can't make up my mind on who is doing what, and then the second revelation hits me like the frying pan that sits unused in my kitchen cabinet. It doesn't matter. There aren't any games here. No one has an assigned role they must play without improvisation.

I thought that being feminine meant giving up control. On the contrary, you actually have more control than if you were a big butch. You can be soft, tender, and submissive one day—or even one moment—and rough, aggressive, and dominating the next. It is the utmost sense of freedom.

My date rises from the couch when I return to the room. She does that—stands when I come to the table, or when I get out of my seat. And who said chivalry is dead? No one told this woman, and if they did she'd probably ignore them. With each step I take toward her, I feel more like a woman than I have ever felt before. My confidence rises and I lead her to the bedroom.

Slowly and seductively she unbuttons my shirt. My lace bra peeks out from the opening, my breasts swelling in anticipation. Lingerie makes me feel sexy and sensuous, even if no one can see it. There is a big difference between lingerie and underwear. I used to shop at Victoria's Secret for what it would do for me, seeing the woman I was within the scanty scraps of fabric. I bought this bra and matching panties for just this occasion—our first time together. Don't ask me how I knew tonight would be the night, and not the dozens of other times we've been together, but somehow I just knew.

She pushes my shirt off my shoulders and her hands shake when she slides my bra straps in the same direction. She licks her lips but doesn't move toward my breasts. Her eyes blaze a trail over my skin, the hardening of my nipples having nothing to do with the chill outside. It is warm under her gaze and by the look of ravishing desire in her eyes, it is going to get much, much hotter.

As she reaches around me to the back of my skirt, her shirt grazes my nipples and I gasp in pleasure. My nipples are ultra sensitive and it sends a jolt directly to my clit, not stopping anywhere in between. Her breath caresses my cheek an instant before she lightly kisses it. She is sweet and tender.

Deftly she slides my zipper south, her hands lingering on my ass when it can go no farther. She whispers that I have a great ass and I smile against her cheek. She steps back and I hold on to her shoulders as I step out of my skirt. Her hands leisurely trail their way back up from my ankles, pausing at the vee between my legs before settling on my thin waist.

She tells me I'm beautiful and I believe her. I've often said that myself to get a woman into bed. Most of the time it was true, but there is something in her eyes, the tone of her voice, that tells me loud and clear that it is not a line. She calls me Elizabeth.

We move to the bed and she lies beside me. Her hands gently explore every inch of my body, paying particular attention to the places that make me moan and laughing at the places that make me giggle. Her lips replace her hands and she smothers me with terms of endearment and praise. She moves on top of me. Then I am on top of her. There are no rules or mandatory positions.

Her touch is gentle. She worships my breasts, my thighs, the curves of my hips. Her long fingers enter me slowly and gently, but not before she looks into my eyes for any sign that I might not want this. Finding none, she fills me and I moan with desire. With infinite patience she moves in and out, each time sliding a bit deeper until I take all of her. Her thumb is on my clit, her fingers inside, and I have never felt so full. Her kisses become more passionate as my hips lift off the bed to match her strokes. Or is it the other way around? Her lips caress my neck, biting and nipping on the tender skin, then soothing with her hot tongue. Her mouth is a wonder on my flesh and she takes me over the top not once, or twice, but more times than I can remember. We make love. We don't have sex, and we definitely aren't fucking.

Satisfied, she holds me in her arms. My pleasure was her first priority, hers secondary. We cuddle, talking quietly about nothing and everything, her fingers running through my long hair. Her skin is hot under my hands and it's my turn to explore, discover, and please. She turns to me, and we make love again and again. The sound of my name on her lips is everything I have ever wanted.

In the morning she is reluctant to leave. She doesn't want to wear out her welcome or assume that we will spend the day together just because we spent the night together. I laugh at her shyness. Or is it politeness? Either way, she is endearing and I do want to see her again and again and again. I tell her so. She leaves me with a soft kiss filled with promises of the future.

So that's where I'm at. Well, actually I'm sitting in the back of my truck drinking beer with my fellow butches. It's what we do, what we've always done. Fine food, expensive wine, and classy women are not on the menu tonight. My homegirl tosses her can into the empty box.

"Hey, J, let's go get us some T and A."

Suddenly I'm not very hungry, and for the first time in my life I answer, "Not tonight."

YOLANDA WALLACE has written dozens of short stories which have appeared in multiple anthologies including *UniformSex*, *Body Check*, *Bedroom Eyes*, *Best Lesbian Love Stories: New York City*, and *Best Lesbian Love Stories: Summer Flings*. *In Medias Res* from Bold Strokes in 2010 is Yolanda's first published novel. She and her partner of eight years live in beautiful coastal Georgia. They are parents to four children of the four-legged variety—a four-year-old boxer and three cats ranging in age from five to eight.

SATURDAY NIGHT AT THE DEW DROP INN
YOLANDA WALLACE

The Bayou, 1932

The club wasn't much to look at, nestled in a thicket of trees deep in the woods. The weathered exterior was in dire need of a fresh coat of paint and the rusted metal sign on its roof was nearly illegible after years of exposure, but everyone knew about the Dew Drop Inn. A deeply rutted clay road led to the front door, but few people were brave enough to take it on in a car or even with a wagon. When the rains came and turned the road into more of a mess than it normally was, you could break an axle on one of those ruts or maim a good horse trying to pry the animal from the grip of all that mud. Besides, it was easier and safer to stagger home on foot. Those who didn't walk arrived by boat, maneuvering their handmade skiffs through the marsh with only the flickering light of kerosene lanterns lashed to the bows to illuminate the way.

The club might be small, crowded, and hard to get to, but the Dew Drop served up the best food this side of Sunday dinner and the most low-down, soul-shakin' blues in the entire Mississippi Delta. Shirley Robinson, the owner and operator, loved to say that her customers came for the food but stayed for the floor show. When the hooch started flowing, the sweat started pouring, and the rhythm worked its magic, it was no holds barred. Fights occasionally broke out as jealous rivals came to blows over a woman, but Miss Shirley's broad-shouldered sons Lonnie and Donnie were quick to make sure the altercations didn't last too long or go too far. And for the rare occasions that Lonnie and Donnie weren't up to the task, Miss Shirley kept a double-barreled shotgun behind the counter. Big Bertha was loaded and at the ready, but Miss

Shirley had needed to make her talk only a time or two. The sight of the massive woman with the butt of the long-handled gun resting on her hip was enough to cool most hot heads.

Neither Lonnie nor Donnie nor Big Bertha would be needed on this night, though. Not with Annie Simpson in town. Because when Annie took the stage, everything came to a stop.

When Annie, a big-voiced singer nicknamed the St. Louis Siren, was first starting out, the Dew Drop had been one of the first venues outside of St. Louis to put her on the bill. Miss Shirley had taken a chance by spotlighting an unknown, but the risk had paid off for both women. Annie eventually moved to New York in 1926 during the height of the Harlem Renaissance when Langston Hughes, Zora Neale Hurston, and Carl Van Vechten began to make real names for themselves. She became a star not long after, and her records were known from New York to Los Angeles and points in between. Despite her success—or perhaps because of it—the Dew Drop was one of her regular stops. Out of lingering gratitude and respect, Annie returned to the Dew Drop each year for a week's worth of gigs. During that week, she held the whole town in the palm of her hand.

People came to see her in droves, packing the club so tight that latecomers had to fight for seats in the rafters or crowd around peepholes carved into the side of the building. Because it wasn't enough just to hear Annie sing. You had to see her, too. Her dresses, short and sequined, were custom made and fit her like a second skin. Beaded headpieces covered her short, marcelled hair. In her right hand, she held an accordion-style porcelain fan that she never bothered to unfold. She didn't have to. No matter how hot it got on the tiny stage, she never seemed to break a sweat.

The same couldn't be said for the men in the audience, however.

"Mmm mmm mmm," one said as he passed a damp handkerchief over his glistening forehead. "Look at the way she *move*. Like she got a rubber band for a spine."

"Yeah, man," his friend agreed, reaching for the flask in his back pocket. He took a swig of the white lightning and wiped his mouth with the back of his hand. "She can snap that thing on me any time."

Watching from the kitchen as Annie performed her trademark belly roll, Miss Shirley shook her head with such force that the pearl choker around her neck rattled like dice in a craps game. "Thirty years and about as many pounds ago, I could do that, too," she said to no one in particular. She grabbed a freshly steamed crawfish off the prep table, snapped off the head, and sucked out the juice. "Annie is good for business, but she's bad for business, too."

"What do you mean, Miss Shirley?" Cora Davis asked. Though she was the youngest of the three cooks on staff, she was the unquestioned best. She had plenty of practice. "Blessed" with eleven children, most of them boys, Cora's mother had long depended on her to lend a helping hand in the kitchen. She had been tending to boiling pots and simmering pans since she was tall enough to see over the top of the stove.

"When she's out there tearin' it up like she is now, all the food and drink orders dry up. The people out there paid to get in, but all they're doin' now is takin' up space. That's not makin' me any money."

Cora smiled to herself. Though Miss Shirley constantly complained about how much things cost, everyone knew she had more money than she knew what to do with. She was the one people went to see when they were in need. If she really wanted to increase revenue, she would stop serving free meals or offering half-price admission to every Tom, Dick, and Harry who was down on his luck. But Cora knew that would never happen. Despite all her bluster, Miss Shirley was just too giving not to offer a helping hand whenever and wherever she could.

"That's okay," Cora said. "She can't sing all night." When the music stopped, the orders would come fast and furious again. It was just a matter of time. This was the quiet before the storm.

"You sure about that? She's on her fourth encore." Miss Shirley paused as the crowd treated Annie to another deafening ovation. "And from the sound of that," she continued, "they ain't gonna let her out of here any time soon. She might still be singin' when her train pulls out in the mornin'."

Cora took a peek at the stage. She had to stand on her tiptoes to see over people's heads and even then she didn't get to see much, but the little bit she saw was enough. It wasn't every day she got to see a genuine celebrity in person. In truth, she and the rest of the kitchen staff were enjoying the break. Before Annie began her set, they had been up to their elbows frying fish, baking pork chops, boiling shrimp, steaming crawfish, cooking grits, and digging pickled pig's feet out of a five-gallon jar filled with briny pink liquid.

Cora watched a handsome man in a gray suit and matching

homburg back a woman in a low-cut red dress into a corner and whisper something in her ear. Laughing at what the man said, the woman threw her head back, exposing her long neck.

"Nothing's that funny," Cora mumbled under her breath.

"Isn't that your man sidlin' up to Marie-Claire Boudreaux?" Miss Shirley asked, following Cora's gaze.

Cora frowned. "Lafayette Andrews ain't my man."

Miss Shirley bit the head off of another crawfish. "You could have fooled me."

Cora continued to watch them. Lafayette with his flashy clothes and flashier smile. Marie-Claire with her lilting accent and sensual beauty. Part Creole, Marie-Claire had green eyes, honey brown hair, and skin the color of lightly browned butter. Cora had to admit they made quite a pair.

"He's Annie's manager," Cora said. "He only talks to me long enough to tell me what Annie wants to eat after the show. Other than that, he don't want nothin' to do with me."

She didn't add that she didn't want anything to do with Lafayette, either. At the moment, what she wanted was to be in his place. To feel what Lafayette was feeling right now. She wanted the fingers sliding over Marie-Claire's smooth skin to be her own. She wanted the lips brushing against Marie-Claire's delicate earlobes to be hers. She wanted to be the one rounding those dangerous curves. But that wasn't the kind of thing she could say out loud. Not if she expected anyone to sympathize with her plight.

She and Marie-Claire had grown up together. They had been as thick as thieves from the time they were born until they turned fifteen. They had walked to school together. They had worked in the sugar cane fields together. They had done everything together. When they came of age, though, they had drifted apart. Marie-Claire had discovered boys and Cora had discovered that she liked Marie-Claire. Cora had never said anything to Marie-Claire. From the beginning, she had known that there was no point, but that hadn't stopped her from feeling the way she did. Nothing could do that.

As the years passed, they saw each other less and less as Marie-Claire went on date after date and Cora tried to insulate herself from the pain of watching the woman she loved fall for someone else. For men who treated her badly and who didn't appreciate her the way Cora did. Men who were looking for nothing but a night on the town, a good time, and a ticket on the first thing smoking.

Marie-Claire thought Lafayette could be her ticket to the big time. Her ticket out of town. She had said so time and time again. She threw herself at him each year when he arrived, but each year he boarded the train without her. Perhaps this year would be different.

As Marie-Claire and Lafayette ground against each other on the dance floor, Marie-Claire looked over her shoulder to make sure Cora was watching. Cora was, but not for long. Dropping her eyes, she returned to the task at hand. Each year, it was her job to find out what Annie wanted to eat after she finished performing, then prepare the requests, wrap up the plate, and deliver it piping-hot to Annie's hotel room.

"What does she want tonight?" Bessie Johnson, the oldest member of the kitchen staff and by far the most easygoing, asked while dishing up two plates of shrimp and grits for table number seven.

"The same thing she always wants—fried chicken, black-eyed peas, collard greens, cornbread, and peach cobbler," Cora replied. She dropped chicken parts into a brown paper bag filled with flour and shook the bag to make sure all of the pieces were evenly coated. Then she seasoned the chicken with black pepper, salt, and liberal dashes of hot sauce.

"For a skinny little thing, she sure can put it away." Bessie half filled two Mason jars with moonshine, put the jars and the plates on a tray, and prepared to fight her way through the crowd to deliver the order.

"This is probably the only week out of the year that she gets good meals," Miss Shirley said, puffing up with pride. "She says nobody puts their foot in it the way we do down here at the Dew Drop."

"Then I guess we down here at the Dew Drop are due for a raise," Bessie said, tossing a wink in Cora's direction. She knew talking about money was a sure way to get Miss Shirley's goat.

"Yeah, well, there's a Depression on, you know," Miss Shirley said, wiping her hands on a dish towel. Her fingers were stained red from the crawfish she had helped herself to. "Things are tough all over."

"Not for me," Bessie said, bumping the door open with her well-padded rear end. "I ain't had nothin' to lose in the first place."

Cora lowered the chicken into the frying pan, being careful not to crowd the pieces. She didn't want to lower the temperature in the pan too much. That would take the chicken longer to cook, making it soak up more of the grease. She wanted all her meals to be perfect, but this one especially so. It was Annie's last night in town and Cora wanted it to be a memorable one for all the right reasons. She didn't want Annie's last memory of her to be greasy chicken and watery collard greens.

By the time Annie finished singing the last scandalous strains of Ma Rainey's "Prove It On Me Blues," a song that the married but openly bisexual Rainey had written affirming her love of women, it was past one but the night was still young. On Saturday nights, the party at the Dew Drop didn't end until three or four. By the time Cora usually got home, it was almost time to get up for church. One Sunday a year, though, she was excused from having to attend services—the Sunday after she spent the night with Annie Simpson, helping Annie close out her affairs in town and pack her belongings so she could head to her next gig. On that day, Cora was allowed to sleep in as late as she wanted. Her family went to church without her and let her get some rest. When they got home, though, they would pester her for details about her night with Annie.

What had Annie said? What had she done? Were her costumes really as glamorous up close as they looked from afar?

Cora would dutifully answer all their questions but she wouldn't tell them everything. Some things—the most important things—she kept to herself.

She had just turned twenty and Annie had been a worldly twenty-five when it began. Annie had been coming to the Dew Drop for six years at that point and had been having her late-night meals delivered to the Rest Easy Motel for two. Three years on, Cora couldn't remember how it had started that first night, but she knew she didn't want it to end. It was one of the few things she had to look forward to.

Annie hunkered over her plate as if she hadn't eaten in days.

"There's no way I can eat all of this," she said, her voice slightly hoarse from all the exertions she had put it through. "Are you sure you don't want some?"

Draping a feather boa across her shoulders and doing a little twirl as she regarded her reflection in the mirror, Cora shook her head. Annie said the same thing every year.

"I know," Annie said with a wink. "You're waiting for dessert, aren't you?"

This time, Cora nodded. Annie said that every year, too. And every year it was true. Cora lived for this. For this one week a year when she could express her desire for another woman freely and without fear of rejection.

One hunger satisfied, Annie pushed her empty plate away from her and wiped her mouth on the linen napkin Cora had brought. Rubbing her full stomach, she looked at Cora with a different kind of appetite. She could have anyone she wanted, man or woman, but there was something about Cora that touched her soul. When Cora watched her perform, Annie didn't just sing the lyrics. She felt them. She lived them. Afterward, when they sat in the big claw-footed tub licking peach cobbler off each other's fingers, she lived that, too. She took those moments with her everywhere she went. If she had her way, she would take more than that.

Annie slowly extended her hand. Cora took it and they moved toward the bed. Their hands tugged at buttons, zippers, and hidden clasps until nothing stood between them except gently yielding flesh.

"How I've missed you," Annie sighed, finally able to relax now that the pressure to perform was over. Now that she had fulfilled her commitment. Now that she could be herself again, not the Siren. She licked her way from Cora's throat to her waist and back again, pausing to linger at Cora's full breasts. She loved to taste the salt on Cora's skin. It tasted like hard, honest work. It tasted like truth. It tasted like love. "I love you," she said as Cora's fingers slid inside her.

Cora stopped, even though she desperately wanted to move forward. Annie had never said that before. Before it had been about fulfilling a need. About satisfying an urge. About soothing an ache. Now it felt different. It felt like something real. Cora wanted to say, "I love you, too," but she couldn't form her lips around the words. She had never thought she would ever have an opportunity to say them. She had said them in her head a hundred times and in her heart a hundred times more, but not out loud. Not for someone else to hear.

"Come with me tomorrow," Annie said. She'd been offered the lead in a musical. A two-reeler, not a full-length motion picture, but it was still the lead. The film, the producers promised, would do the same thing for her that *St. Louis Blues* had for Bessie Smith—introduce her to a wider audience. When she and Lafayette boarded the train the next day, they would head for the West Coast instead of returning to New York.

Annie moved her hips against Cora's hand, waking it from its stupor. "Will you do that? Will you come with me?"

"Come with you to Hollywood?" Cora matched Annie's rhythm. She felt the heat build between them. Annie might not sweat onstage, but she was certainly sweating now. "What would I do?"

Annie clutched at her, looking for purchase. "Anything you want," she gasped.

Cora had never considered leaving town. Her family was there. Her life was there. But what kind of a life was it, really? It was existing. It was coping. It was getting by. It wasn't living. Living was what she did when she was with Annie. She lived for only one week out of fifty-two. What if the other fifty-one could be like that one?

"Don't make me dream of something I can't have," Cora said as Annie's walls closed around her fingers.

"I'm not Marie-Claire." Annie held Cora's face in her hands and kissed her fervently. "You can have all this and more if you want," she insisted. "Just come with me."

❖

"So it is true." Marie-Claire stared at the cardboard suitcase in Cora's hand before the porter whisked it away. She was wearing the same dress as the night before, though she and it both looked the worse for wear. The dress looked like it had been slept in and Marie-Claire looked like she hadn't slept at all. "You are leaving."

"Good news travels fast."

Cora looked up at the train as it idled in the station. Lafayette, his hat pulled low to cover his eyes, had already boarded and was asleep in his seat by the window. Marie-Claire's eyes pleaded with him to wake up and take her with him, but he didn't move. On the end of the platform, Annie was saying her last good-byes to Miss Shirley. Cora had said good-bye more times than she could count. She didn't know if she could take another. Especially not this one. Marie-Claire had meant so much to her for so long. Part of her still held out hope that Marie-Claire might one day feel the same way. She knew it was a pipe dream, but she'd already had one of those come true, hadn't she?

"It should be me, you know," Marie-Claire said.

The bitterness in her voice effectively put an end to Cora's fantasy once and for all. Marie-Claire sounded like she hated Cora. And for what? What had Cora ever done but love her and be there for her? How many times had she sat there miserable and quiet while Marie-Claire cried on her shoulder about some man who had done her wrong when all Cora wanted to do was treat her right? Had that been for nothing?

Marie-Claire's full lips curled into a sneer. "It should be me and not you."

Cora had stayed up all night trying to decide whether to go or to stay. Now she was certain she had made the right decision. "But it isn't you. It's me. I always used to compare myself to you and come up short. Now I realize I was using the wrong measuring stick. You're no better than I am. I just let myself think you were. I won't make that mistake again."

Annie stood nearby but didn't interrupt. When it became clear that Cora had said her piece and that Marie-Claire couldn't formulate a response, she offered Cora her arm and a reassuring smile. "Ready to go?"

They took their seats as the conductor shouted, "All aboard!" Looking out the window, they watched the scenery roll by.

"Thank you for saying yes," Annie whispered.

"Thank you for asking the question." Cora felt suddenly shy. She felt like she had on the very first night she and Annie were together. Like she was embarking on a journey she could never come back from. Like she could never go home again. Looking into Annie's brown eyes, she realized she was already there. And there was nowhere else she wanted to be.

Andrews & Austin are the authors of the Richfield and Rivers Mystery Series from Bold Strokes Books: *Combust the Sun*, *Stellium in Scorpio*, and *Venus Besieged*; and the romances *Mistress of the Runes*, *Uncross My Heart*, and *Summer Winds*. Andrews began her career as a broadcaster in NYC, moved into the advertising world as a writer/producer, and later became a movie studio executive. Prior to owning her own production company, Austin was co-producer and on-air host of a shopping channel. She partnered with Andrews in developing movies for studios, networks, and independents. Together, the couple owns a horse ranch in the Midwest and spends most of their time riding or writing. Strong, smart women and insightful dialogue are hallmarks of their work.

MADAME BROUSSARD
ANDREWS & AUSTIN

Women of a certain age were intimate with the shop on Rue de LaSalle—the whispered solution to inattentive husbands, less amorous paramours, and the sheer gravity of life that could weigh down one's sizeable assets—because the shop's owner, Madame Broussard, once the French Quarter's most notorious madam, knew precisely and to the hair's breadth what interested men, and it began with elegant silk lingerie.

Rumor persisted that the money to support Madame's luxurious lifestyle and lucrative business came from one royal client who had loved her so desperately that he left his wife and son to be with her, despite Madame promising him only one night with her. After that night, true to her word, she would have nothing more to do with him, and the thought of her with another man drove him mad and was rumored to be the reason he put a bullet in his head…demonstrating just how entirely mad he had been driven.

Madame Broussard was a striking woman, her high cheekbones, exquisitely pale skin, and voluptuous cleavage the envy of her clients. In addition to her slender creative hands and light brown satin eyes, she possessed a mass of red hair balanced atop her head in a huge swirl, tendrils dangling like succulent vines down her neck as if the wanton hair could not be counted on to remain in place, as could not Madame Broussard. She had traveled the world and met all manner of royalty, and the fact that she had chosen New Orleans's Rue de LaSalle as final port was hailed as a great coup for the wealthy women of this fine city.

In convincing me to shore up my marriage with a trip to Madame Broussard's, friends had conveyed the shop's lore. How each day, the small brass bell bearing the engraved initial *B* jangled on its sturdy metal post as the shop door swung open and Madame looked up, cocked her head seductively as if each new entrant were a lover, and said richly, "*Bonjour, madame*, I thought you would never come." Her lifted eyebrow and rakish smile suggested that the emphasized words might be a husband's lament unless, and until, the visitor took Madame's suggestions on how to please a man. Her greeting kept her wealthy clients atwitter, and they no doubt stayed longer and bought more based on her talents and reputation.

And so today when the door swung open ever so slowly, instead of a woman's voice, I was annoyed to hear the incessant and rhythmic pounding of repair work taking place inside the boutique, a constant hammering. I nearly turned to leave.

However, moments later, the work stopped and I, the woman referred to in society columns as "the golden-haired wife of New Orleans's wealthiest banker," shyly entered the shop. Having braved this new world only on the insistence of others, and having been told what to expect, I was surprised by Madame Broussard's slightly breathless greeting.

"*Bonjour, Madame Le Doux. Je ne penser que vous n'arriverais jamais.*" How did this woman I had never met, in a shop I had never entered, know my name? I would have left had it not been for the look in Madame Broussard's eyes—a hypnotic expression.

Madame excused herself from a customer for whom she was pinning a gorgeous train at the waist and, leaving the final touches to her assistant, swept across the room, her dress trailing the floor, and extended her hand.

"Please stay." She seemed to know that if she did not get a grip on me and block my path to the door, I would take wing like a frightened bird.

"So you look for something to—*je ne sais quoi*—enhance your already beautiful form." The way her eyes covered my body made me blush with pride. As if I'd been assessed and found to be desirable and, for some reason, that was pleasing—perhaps because Madame was a professional appraiser, having once chosen women's assets as a mainstay of her business success. And so to be deemed beautiful by Madame was a far greater compliment than could be paid by a mere friend, for the value of the former was virtually bankable.

"Yes. Uh, I'm going on a… I apologize. As you seem to know, I'm Emma LeDoux, Maxmillian LeDoux's wife, and we're going on a cruise and I want him to feel…" *I want him to feel…interested? Feel sexual? Feel damned near anything.* For my husband was a bit like an automated teller. If you fingered the right buttons, he mechanically delivered exactly the amount you expected.

"To feel"—the lilt encouraged me to complete my sentence and then she finished it for me—"young again. He focuses on erection, she on affection. Most often the issue." Madame angled her right arm at a doorway, brushing aside thickly beaded curtains that jangled as I entered through them and found myself in a completely mirrored room about the size of two normal dressing rooms.

"Ghastly." My eyes moved furtively from one mirrored angle of my body to the next, not approving of myself as I sucked in my stomach, pulled my shoulders back, and lifted my eyebrows to pull the lines from my facial expression.

Madame reached over and took my chin gently in her hand and turned my face to her.

"I will look at the mirror, you will look at me." Her voice was kind and I let out my breath. "A woman must love herself, without regard to convention." She winked at me and I blushed.

Madame appraised my figure as if deciding whether or not to purchase me, and prism-like images reflected in my peripheral vision: her eyes moved down my still-narrow waist to larger hips and back to my firm thighs. She stepped back and stared at my breasts. All the while I kept my eyes on the thick head of hair hypnotically bobbing around me, moving in, pulling back, until finally, Madame looked up and caught me by surprise with her completely captivating smile.

"Like a sinful dessert, you are." She disappeared through the beaded curtain, leaving me grinning at myself in the mirror, sucking in my breath and making cheerful bargains with my psyche about how much, if anything, I would ever eat again. *I would now rather be a sinful dessert than eat one.*

The curtain rattled again and Madame entered with several thin silk pieces of material over her arm. Without asking, she unbuttoned the small pearl-like clasps on the front of my sweater as I reached up to help but wasn't quick enough to accomplish what Madame had already done, the sweater falling open to reveal my bra. And for some unknown reason I began to question the quality of my bra—was it snow white or had it been inadvertently washed with darker clothing, giving it a gray cast? Did it look new?

"Tournez-vouz, s'il vous plaît." Madame pivoted me in the right direction and as I twirled, Madame unsnapped my bra and it fell into my hands. *What timing that took! How many women she must have undressed!* My back to Madame, I felt the silk fall over my head and drape around my shoulders. I turned to face her as Madame's hand slid over the pink silk front and cupped my left breast, startling me. "That is the fit we want, I think. Seductive, and yet it will still be comfortable in case you want to sleep in it." She beamed as if she'd just invented sleep.

I angled my body to look at myself, just as Madame took a white braided satin rope and looped it over my head, catching under my breasts and hoisting them slightly. Then she swiftly drew the rope up and back, holding me up against her chest, her chin on my shoulder, both of us looking into the mirror that looked back at us.

"We are a charming duo, are we not?" She laughed.

A little thrill rippled across my body, and I couldn't be sure if the satin rope or the sensual look in Madame's experienced eyes was caressing me.

She seemed frozen, as if caught in some thought she wished had not interrupted her consciousness. Suddenly letting loose of the rope, she swept her hands across my breasts in collecting and coiling it, and I shivered, then smiled and tried to make light of the moment.

"This is a bit like bondage for the banker's bride."

"Bondage?" She made eye contact for the first time. "Bound by love is for me more satisfying than bound by shackles." She glanced at my chest. "It's cold? I'm sorry. *Fini, alors.* I will have the braid sewn to the garment and, if it suits you, perhaps you will come back next week and we will try it on to be *certainement.*"

"We leave on our cruise in ten days." My voice grew softer.

"And this beautiful garment will leave with you, I promise."

I smiled at her charming accent and Madame flashed her beautiful smile in return. *"Merci, mon ami."* I tried out my French and she laughed.

"So you are French at heart. That beautiful body and gorgeous mouth, but of course. Your husband should count himself lucky. A banker with such a prize." Her emphasis on the word "banker" seemed to dismiss the entire financial community as unable to recognize value.

Madame exited the small dressing room and I felt weak. The power of this woman was palpable. No doubt she could command kings and courtesans. Why, with that power, was she here in this little shop on the Rue de LaSalle?

When I left the dressing room, Madame was nowhere to be seen. Her assistant stood nearby and I approached the young woman.

"Madame is such an interesting woman. Have you worked for her long?" I asked.

"I was a client at one time." When I looked surprised, she said, "I believed in her talent and wanted to be around her. She's like the pied piper. You will see."

❖

All week I thought of her. That vibrant red hair, the elegant way she drifted into a room, her refined hand gestures, and her gaze that made me feel there was no one else on earth, her focus so complete. Like a Raphaelian angel, she had blessed me and made me feel good about my body again.

Of late, Max had put me in doubt, suggesting I might want to hire a personal trainer or go to Europe to one of the spas. Never criticizing me really, just drawing attention to places where women's bodies could be overhauled like a Corvette, perhaps like re-stuffed upholstery and a new paint job.

By day Max kept himself buried in electronic ledgers and financial pro formas. He no longer smiled, thus robbing me of his nicest physical attribute. Romance was a nocturnal event scheduled much like a haircut and lasting far less time. I saw myself as diminished in his affection, no longer a partner or mate but more like a paid performer who had to prove to him that he'd purchased the best seat in the house.

But Madame Broussard was on my horizon and I couldn't wait for the days to pass. With each twenty-four-hour period, I became happier and giddier. Ironically, Max noticed and inquired as to my source of good humor. I said merely that I'd made up my mind to be happy and that alone had made me so. My response obviously not interesting enough to warrant further conversation, he shrugged and left the room.

I had a secret that made me happy: Madame Broussard, who knew what beauty was, had pronounced me beautiful. And once named, my beauty seemed unquestionable even to myself.

My hairdresser frosted my hair to even more golden highlights and I had a manicure. I took my husband's advice and went to the spa for a facial and massage. And on the morning I arrived at Madame Broussard's, I stood taller, my shoulders back and my head high. Madame, upon hearing the tinkle of the bell at the door, glanced up, and I thought her head snapped toward me just a few degrees before she caught herself.

"Madame LeDoux, vous êtes exquisite," she purred, in a tone that implied she did not greet everyone like this. She never looked up from the fitting taking place on a woman whom I immediately envied for Madame's fingers playing along her bodice. Looking into the mirror over the woman's shoulder, nearly as she had done with me, Madame spoke to her reflection, saying it now looked perfect, and then she directed her next remark to another young assistant, obviously having needed help from more experienced hands. "Be sure it drapes exactly so." Her hand made a swooping gesture as she stepped away and the assistant took over.

I stood like a trembling fawn awaiting instruction from Madame Broussard. Draped in purple velvet that dove down to her breastbone revealing just the interior edges of large and firmly supported breasts, she came forward and extended her hand in greeting. "You are back. My great fortune."

Without thinking, I kissed her on each cheek, noting that she smelled wonderful and wanting to know what tantalizing perfume she wore. Perhaps it would help me as well with my love interests, and I suddenly wondered if Madame had slept with many men or merely managed their affairs.

Her arm swept to the side, indicating another dressing room, and on the way, Madame signaled yet another assistant, ordering, "Madame LeDoux's apparel." The woman nodded and disappeared.

Inside the dressing room were two brocaded Napoleon chairs, across a table supporting a carafe and elegant crystal glasses, and at one end of the room a three-way mirror. The clothing hooks on the wall appeared to be vestal virgins, their urns extended to hold the padded hangers.

"Ah, the mirror," I teased, drawing back.

"The way you look, you should welcome the mirror. But for those who don't, we drink first." She smiled and I laughed lightly. "You are too beautiful to need it but for loosening your inhibitions...and your tongue. Claret?"

I tensed at her tone and nodded that I would take the drink. Madame poured it expertly, never spilling a drop, and then toasted.

"To all the men who've paid the price for all the priceless women." Madame downed her drink and I laughed again, following suit. As Madame refilled our glasses I was feeling warm from the wine, and emboldened.

"How is it that a woman of your charms and business acumen is here on the Rue de LaSalle dealing in lingerie?"

"I deal in dreams. Lingerie is merely the transporter. Some women use silk and lace to attract a mate, others to keep him, and some simply to make themselves feel better about who they are and what they do. What are *your* dreams?"

From anyone else, I might have thought that question impertinent, but then I had started it, hadn't I, asking why she was dealing in panties and corsets?

"Like everyone else, I guess, I want to be loved and desired."

"And Messer LeDoux does that for you." She stated it like a question deserted in the air.

"To the best of his ability," I said, as if no one could try harder than my husband.

Her eyes trailed across my drink glass to the overly large diamond that lolled its gleaming head on my ring finger, too drunkenly expensive to hold itself upright. "And he is a man who provides a comfort of sorts."

"Of sorts," I echoed.

"And so today, we improve your arsenal of weapons to further invade his heart." She stood up as if she knew that there would be a knock at the door, and at just that moment, there was. Her assistant arrived and hung the negligee on the vestal virgin, dimming the overhead chandelier upon her exit.

The door had no sooner shut than I stood in the dim light and dropped the dress I was wearing in one swift zippered movement, standing only in panties and hose, comfortable in the half-light. She froze as she had that first time. Perhaps she thought I sensed something in her look, because she said softly, "Close your eyes." At my puzzled expression, she continued, "Let me make it happen for you and then you will tell me if I have succeeded."

I stood still, hearing the rustling of her gown, which I recollected as being far too dressy for daytime and yet seeming to suit her royal personage. I had little time to contemplate the sound of her clothing as she stood in front of me slipping the garment over my head, and I struggled to remember to keep my eyes shut. The energy field between us was electrical, as if wired from her shock of red hair.

"No peeking."

Her hands smoothed the silk across my body, starting at the shoulder and running directly over my chest, and my face flushed as my breasts responded to her touch. But her hands moved on to my waist where they clutched me slightly, then to my hips. Now she was behind me and the rope pulled back and tightened and hooked, and one more time her hands traveled all over me, smoothing things out, and I was so aroused I felt I might lose my balance. She seemed to know and steadied me.

"You may open your eyes now."

In the mirror, the image was glorious. She had enhanced every curve and covered every blemish. I felt like a princess.

"It's exquisite. You're masterful," I said, twirling in the negligee and giggling over how elegant it made me feel. *"Merci, mon amour!"* I whirled and hugged her, realizing as I did so, that I'd used the wrong noun and thanked her as my lover. She pulled back and raised an eyebrow, giving me a seductive smirk. *European*, I thought. *Expressive and emotional.*

"So we are *fini*. Our time together is unfortunately over until you need something more from me."

"I do," I said suddenly.

She cocked her head in inquiry and I struggled to say what I needed. "Pants, perhaps, with a jacket, something I could wear on deck but then at the captain's table."

"I specialize in lingerie, and besides, you leave in only a few days."

"I could come every day if need be. I would really appreciate it if you would attempt it."

"You are a persuasive woman." Her eyes traveled over my body, taking in everything she had created. "I have memorized your size and it will take only one more fitting once we select the fabric. You will come with me to the fabric room?"

I said that I would and hurried to put my dress back on and followed her out the door like a schoolgirl.

"Giselle, please handle my next client." The assistant seemed anxious to obey and pleased to have been asked. Madame swept past her and we entered through a set of double doors at the far end of the shop. Before me stretched a glorious array of fabrics: every texture, color, pattern, and I realized that this small shop was just the front of a very large enterprise that Madame controlled. As we approached, several workers gave way and in doing so asked if they might assist. She thanked them but dismissed them with a hand gesture and they disappeared from sight. She slowed then, to allow me to fall in alongside her.

"Linen wrinkles, but its texture is comforting. Much more inviting than brocade. Of course, we could do something in Egyptian cotton." Her fingers ran along the bolts of cloth as she spoke, and I found myself following her fingers rather than looking at the material, and wondered why she was so hypnotic. I was aware in the distance several women sat at drafting tables apparently sketching clothing.

"You show?"

"Providing ideas for famous designers. My label invisible, if you will. They get the press and I get the money. Not unlike other businesses in which I've been involved." She grinned mischievously. "So what do you think?"

My head was swirling. I simply wanted to talk to her. Know her. "You pick the fabric and do the design. You're the expert. And instead of spending an hour in here, we could go somewhere and...sit and talk, perhaps. I would pay you. I apologize. I didn't mean that like it sounded. I meant we're not friends, so why would you waste an hour with me otherwise—"

She placed her hand on my arm. "Please. Let's go to my office and have tea." She moved ahead of me farther into the warehouse. Through another set of doors we entered an impeccably designed and decorated office. She quickly offered me a seat on the couch and poured tea. *And where did tea come from? Is it always sitting there waiting for her?* I felt I was on a movie set and a prop master was seeing to her every need.

Answering my unvoiced thoughts, she said, "I am a woman accustomed to satisfying needs instantly and expertly. Therefore, I have high expectations that my own needs be satisfied. My staff knows that the correct wine, tea, food must be in the exact place at all times." She smiled at me.

"Would you tell me about your other business? The one everyone speaks of?"

"That was a long time ago. Satisfied customers, isn't that what everyone wants? Mine were simply satisfied more quickly and at a higher price."

"It's rumored that a prince was so enamored of you that he killed himself because you would only sleep with him once."

"Yes, I've heard that repeated." Her noncommittal response made me smile. "After I made money, I slept with no one. It was the very thing that drove me to make money quickly. An empty bed was my reward. But you, your bed is not empty." The way in which she carefully spoke the words seemed to caution me that I was a married woman.

"I know you're busy," I said, stirring from the couch. "You're sure the pants will fit me? We haven't measured."

"I have a good eye, but if it will make you feel better, I'm happy to do it." She looked at me in a way that could only be described as seductive, but merely for a moment, then she got up slowly, moved to her desk, and pulled a pearled tape measure from a drawer.

"Should I take my dress off?" I asked, breathless.

"No, simply hold it up for me." I bunched the skirt up. She dropped the tape from my waist to the floor and then moved to her desk to jot down a number on a pad. Setting the pen down, she picked up a paper tape and, returning, wrapped it around my middle quickly and tightly, as if capturing me rather than measuring me. She flicked my tummy with her middle finger, teasing me into letting the air out. "Don't hold your breath or you'll be cursing me from the cruise liner. The pants should hang naturally."

She took the metal tape and dropped it down my inseam. "Do you like it here?" The back of her hand touched my upper thigh just below the crotch. "Or do you prefer it just a little tighter?" The palm of her hand cupped my crotch just for a split second and I nearly lost the ability to answer her question.

"Tighter," I managed to whisper, not really wanting my pants that tight but wanting that feeling again.

She cupped her hand there again without any emotion. "You might change your mind. Why don't we split the difference?" She moved away and jotted another number on the pad. "We'd best get you on your way."

She held the door and I sailed through it as if running away. I bade her good-bye and hurried to my car, still tingling between my legs. I drove home not knowing where I was until I pulled into the driveway and sat in the car still gasping for air.

I had forgotten to find out what time we were to meet over the next few days. And when I called the shop, I could hear repair work taking place again and inquired of the slight hammering. Giselle said they were in constant renovation and explained quickly that Madame had everything she needed from me and would call me when the garment was ready.

For two days I paced and fretted and checked with her assistants, but they said she was out.

The day before I was to leave on our cruise, a vacation I no longer wanted to take because it took me from her, a package arrived by messenger. Inside were a gorgeous pair of gold silk pants and a jacket, along with a note: "*Ma chéri*, my apologies for being unavailable. This is my gift to you. *Bon voyage*."

We took the cruise, Max and I, our stateroom luxurious. I never told him about the elegant garments that reminded me of Madame Broussard. I had them with me but kept them folded in my luggage where I looked at them and ran my fingers across them daily. I wanted nothing more of Max and, in fact, found her memory more arousing than his presence. And he, only slightly less interested in me, remarked after my refusing to sleep with him that he thought we should part. I was relieved because I had tried to form those very words but could not decide how.

When our ship came into port, I kissed him lightly on the cheek and told him my attorney would phone his. Then I hailed a cab and went immediately to the Rue de LaSalle. It was past five and I worried that the shop had already closed. When I got out of the cab, the storefront windows were shuttered, and I told the driver to wait.

Giselle popped her head out as if she'd been expecting me and waved happily. "Madame is waiting. May I take your cab?" I nodded yes and she hopped in. I thought how fortunate to have run into her and went inside, doing as Giselle asked, locking the door behind me.

"How was your cruise, Madame LeDoux?" Madame Broussard stepped into the room once so bustling with people and now entirely empty. She was wearing a strawberry-colored gown that matched her hair and looked breathtaking. "Was Messer LeDoux pleased?"

"No. Nor was I. We were not pleased with each other…and so I chose not to grace him with such gorgeous attire."

"Ahh," she purred. "Sometimes lingerie is not enough."

"I'm filing for divorce." I stepped closer to her and could smell her perfume.

"A step not to be taken lightly." She seemed to be referring to the step I'd taken in her direction. "Please come to my fitting room." She turned and led me into a room that was tufted and comfortable like a parlor, although clearly designed for fitting clothing.

She handed me a glass of wine. "Why have you come directly here?" This time her eyes rested on mine and the light danced in them.

"Why were you expecting me?" I asked boldly.

"Because years ago a Cajun woman read the tarot cards and told me that I would meet a woman who would come in on a ship from across the sea and we would be together. I took the shop on LaSalle so I could be near the ocean."

My throat tightened.

"You will need a place to stay. Will you come here?" she asked.

"Like one of your girls?" My question didn't seem to offend her.

"Not at all like that. By the way…" She leaned in and slid her hand between my thighs and held me there. "Were you happy with the fit?"

I grew weak as she pulled me onto the long tufted ottoman and began to expertly untangle my clothing, her nimble fingers seeming to caress as they undressed. Her lips, shimmering hot, covered mine and I moaned as her talented kisses liquefied me. Her hand expertly crested the top of my panty hose and slid down between my legs and into me, causing my body to undulate in waves as the tight garment pressed her even farther inside.

"We hardly know each other," I managed to whisper.

"How wonderful that is. Nothing to dislike and everything to love."

And as she rocked on top of me, driving herself into me, and I moved in ecstasy beneath her, one end of the ottoman hit the wood-paneled wall, banging rhythmically against it, and I remembered hearing that sound. Like a carpenter working, pounding something into the wall. And for one alarmed moment, I realized it was me being pounded and that perhaps this very scene had taken place before on this very couch.

But Madame Broussard's voluptuous breast was in my mouth and her hands were creating melodies inside my soul, and she whispered that I was the one the gypsy woman had promised her. And so I chose to believe the rhythmic sounds of the ottoman banging into the wall were unique to our lovemaking and unrelated to any more mundane hammering. After all, repair work went on constantly in New Orleans.

D. Jackson Leigh is a Georgia peach transplanted to North Carolina. She has worked the past thirty years as a print journalist and played an endless parade of sports. A hopelessly romantic Sagittarian, she has a deep-seated love for anything equine, her Jack Russell Terror, her blue-eyed partner, and women's basketball...not necessarily in that order. Her Bold Strokes novels include the romances *Bareback* and the forthcoming *Longshot* (2010).

Box Full of Surprises
D. Jackson Leigh

"Sky, what are you so nervous about?" Jessica clamped a firm hand on Skyler's bouncing knee and smiled at her partner. The long leg stilled, but Skyler's brown eyes continued to dart around the room as though she were a long-tailed cat and the women waiting patiently along with them were all sitting in rocking chairs.

"They're all pregnant!"

Jessica chuckled. "Well, that's why they're in Dr. Nichols's office, you goof. What did you expect?"

"Well, what if one of them squirts out a baby right here, right now?" Skyler's whisper carried, and a dark-haired woman sitting near them smiled into her magazine.

Jessica was having a hard time believing this nervous, apparently naïve, woman sitting next to her was the same six-foot, androgynous blond charmer who ran a large equestrian breeding and training facility. She wasn't even pregnant yet, and Skyler was a wreck. She was beginning to think having Skyler as her demanding trainer when she had prepared for the Olympics might have been easier than living through nine months of pregnancy with her.

"How can the sight of a pregnant woman throw you into such a panic? Is this what I've got to look forward to for nine months?"

"No." Skyler scowled and clutched Jessica's hand. "It's just… well…"

"Skyler, women, like horses, get pregnant every day. They carry babies full term, then have a normal birth—every day."

"But…"

"You've been watching *Emergency Doctors* on the Surgery Channel again, haven't you?"

Skyler shrugged sheepishly.

"Honey, they only show the bad cases on that medical show. Every pregnancy doesn't end in an emergency. This is not rocket science. We're just planning to have a baby."

"Okay. I know, I know. I'll chill." Skyler sighed and playfully bumped shoulders with Jessica. "We'll be fine."

"We don't have to do this, Skyler, if you're going to have a stroke over it."

"No. You know I want us to have kids. I love kids."

"I know, honey. By the third or fourth, you'll be an old hand at this," Jessica teased.

Skyler gulped. "Th-third or fo-fourth?"

"Kidding. I'm kidding."

Skyler blew out a breath of relief, her confidence returning. "On the other hand, four would be enough to have our own polo team."

Jessica gave Skyler a look. "Then you better be looking for maternity clothes in your size, too, or filling out some adoption papers."

"Ms. Black?"

Saved by the nurse, Skyler thought. She stood when Jessica did, shifting uncertainly from foot to foot.

"Do you want me…uh, you know, to go with you?" Skyler asked. They had discussed talking to the doctor together, but Skyler wasn't sure about being in the room while the doctor examined her lover.

"We're in this together, all the way." Jessica pulled her toward the waiting nurse, chuckling at Skyler's wide eyes. "Buck up, stud. At least you won't be the one with your feet up in the stirrups."

❖

"So why aren't we visiting our regular GYN for this?" Skylar frowned, uncomfortable knowing her lover was naked under a thin paper sheet and some guy was going to be coming in at any moment to take a peek under it. Dr. Taylor Nichols. Sounded like some preppy frat boy who went into gynecology so he could spend all day looking under women's paper things. She tugged at the covering, trying to tuck it tightly around Jessica's slim hips.

"Because, honey, Dr. Nichols specializes in in vitro fertilizations and fertility cases. Anita referred us here to give us the best chance of getting pregnant quickly."

At that moment, a knock sounded and a petite fortysomething woman hurried into the room. Jessica sat up on the table and Skyler stood protectively by her side.

"Hi, I'm Taylor Nichols." The woman smiled and extended her hand to Jessica. "And I'm guessing you're Jessica, since you're the one modeling our latest paper wear."

Then the doctor turned to Skyler and her smile became a grin. "And you must be Skyler, the bodyguard...I mean, partner."

Jessica snorted.

"Taylor is a *woman's* name." Skyler pointedly stared at the wedding rings on Dr. Nichols's left hand and muttered, "A straight woman."

"Isn't that a stereotype, taking for granted that my wedding rings were put there by a man?" Dr. Nichols asked good-naturedly. "Although in this case, you're right."

Skyler's eyes narrowed. This woman better be straight. She was just too cute to be putting her hands in Jessica's private places...places only Skyler touched now. Jessica laughed and wrapped a reassuring arm around Skyler's waist.

"Don't mind her. She's just a little—no, a *lot*—nervous."

"Fair enough." Dr. Nichols chuckled. "Now, lay back, Jessica, and let's check things out real quick."

The exam was fast. Fifteen minutes later, Jessica was dressed and they were all sitting in Dr. Nichols's office.

"Your lab work looks good and the exam was normal. I'm glad you've already begun charting your cycle. It looks pretty regular, which is very helpful. I don't see any reason why you shouldn't be able to get pregnant."

Skyler and Jessica smiled at each other.

"Now, are you planning to use a donor or a sperm bank?"

"I have a male twin," Skyler explained, "and he has agreed to donate to the cause." She was hoping, though, that the baby would have Jessica's dark hair and pale blue eyes.

"A twin? Excellent. You two are very lucky. So, do you want to do this in the office or at home?"

"Well," Skyler looked at Jessica for support, "my brother teaches at Princeton, but he's agreed to ship us some sticks. We'd like to try it at home. I think I know the fundamentals because I have artificially bred horses many times. It's basically the same equipment, isn't it?"

"Sticks?"

"Uh, that's what we call tubes of, uh, you know, when we breed horses. Popsicle sticks, because they come frozen." She was having trouble saying the word *semen* while talking about her brother.

"Well, yes, it is basically the same procedure. Your mission is to deposit the donated sperm so that it coats the cervix at the right time during Jessica's cycle. Orgasm at the time of insemination greatly increases the chances of fertilization by helping the cervix dip into the vaginal pool and suck up the sperm. The sperm is deposited most commonly with a needleless syringe. That's rather clinical, however, so one medical equipment manufacturer has just released a device that allows couples to simulate a more natural insemination if they wish. It is rather more expensive, of course."

Skyler didn't comprehend what the doctor was trying to explain, but Jessica seemed to.

"Do you have equipment you can show us?" Jessica asked politely.

"We keep a few in stock, so you can take one home with you today if you want." The doctor punched a few buttons on her phone and when the nurse answered, said, "Could you bring us one of the home kits?"

"Do you know what she's talking about?" Skyler murmured.

"I think so, honey." Jessica squeezed Skyler's hand. "Just wait, and we'll see."

After the nurse delivered a plain brown shoebox-sized box, Dr. Nichols handed it to Jessica. She peeked inside, then closed it again, brushing Skyler's hand away when she reached for the box.

"The instructions are there if you need any. It's pretty simple." Dr. Nichols's tone was totally clinical. "If you've handled livestock sperm, you're familiar with the basic precautions. This method is a little different because you have to remember to push the plunger slowly at the right moment. The ideal time to start pushing would be as the orgasm begins to build. This requires good communication and a sure hand. You want the entire sperm sample already deposited in the vagina when the orgasm hits its peak."

"You can handle that, can't you, stud?" Jessica teased softly.

Skyler was mute. Images of a naked Jessica, knees up, opening herself flashed through her brain.

"Of course, if you're unsure, we can do this in the office," Dr. Nichols offered.

Jessica tucked the box under her arm.

"No, no. I think we'll give this a try."

Jessica had learned during their past year together that Skyler's body language often screamed thoughts and feelings she couldn't voice. The flush on her cheeks and the faraway look made Jessica stop at the four-star hotel just down the road from the doctor's office. She didn't even mind the wink from the butch desk clerk over the "no luggage." She just smiled, grabbed Skyler's hand, and headed for the elevators.

When they reached the room, Jessica pulled Skyler inside, kicked the door shut, and pinned her against the wall. Their kisses were hot and deep. She made quick work of the buttons of Skyler's shirt, immediately found the clasp of her bra, and pulled a tight nipple between her lips.

Skyler moaned and her knees sagged. Jessica tugged at Skyler's belt buckle, then the zipper, before sliding the soft jeans and gray boy-shorts down Skyler's long, muscled legs. Her mouth watered at the scent of Skyler's arousal. She dropped to her knees and dove in without ceremony. Nothing turned her on more than this most intimate of acts.

Skyler's strangled "oh" and trembling thighs gave Jessica a sense of power that fired the heat between her own legs. She felt the pulse of Skyler's sex when she pressed her lips to it, then ran her tongue the length of her lover's clitoris to gather the growing moisture before grasping it in her teeth and sucking hard. It never failed to bring Skyler to a quick, shattering climax.

Skyler slid down the wall, her orgasm robbing her of her remaining strength. "Holy Christ, babe. Where'd that come from?" Jessica's stare was still hungry. "Not that I'm complaining, but you still have all your clothes on and I'm naked as a jaybird."

"Then we'll just have to fix that," Jessica said, pulling Skyler to her feet and dragging her to the bed. Skyler reached for Jessica's shirt, but Jessica grabbed her hands, stopping her. "No. You just stand there, lover. I'm in charge of this show."

This was the only woman who could tell Skyler what to do, but command her she did. Jessica would always own her, heart and soul. Skyler watched Jessica retrieve the box that she had dropped to the floor earlier and place it on the bed. Then Jessica slowly, very slowly pulled her polo shirt over her head. She ran her fingers over her lace-covered breasts and unclasped her bra, hook by hook. She pinched and pulled her nipples until they grew hard.

Skyler groaned when Jessica dropped her slacks to the floor, then turned her back to bend over and slowly lower her string bikini panties over creamy white hips. Jessica knew her backside was Skyler's prime trigger, and she used it often to torture her.

"I've been wanting to test-drive one of these with you," Jessica said, her voice low and silky, as she handed the box to Skyler.

Skyler felt her face and chest flush with arousal when she looked inside and found a firm dildo of simulated flesh with a thonglike latex harness. Unlike the ones available in an adult toy store, this one had a built-in syringe to load and ejaculate semen.

"Wow."

"I thought since we didn't have time to pick up any lube, I'd let you provide that for me," Jessica whispered in her ear, drawing her close. Their breasts brushed lightly, teasingly. Jessica pulled Skyler's head down for a heated kiss and then nudged her foot to encourage her to widen her stance.

Skyler felt the dildo, warm and firm, rubbing between her legs and across her still-hard clit. Her breath hitched. Her clitoris twitched at the contact. But before she was too far gone, Jessica knelt and secured the dildo against Skyler's throbbing sex. When Skyler reached for her, Jessica stepped back.

"Uh-uh, babe. You have to come to me."

When Jessica lay back on the bed and pulled her knees up, Skyler didn't know if she was going to faint or orgasm at the sight. Lord, what had she done to deserve this woman? Whatever it was, she wanted to keep doing it. Forever. And ever.

Jessica ran her fingers between her legs and then held them up for inspection. "This is what you do to me."

"My turn to show you what I can *really* do to you," Skyler growled. She licked Jessica's fingers clean before slipping her tongue deep into Jessica's mouth. She massaged Jessica's breast and maneuvered the slick cock between Jessica's legs. When she slowly slid it in, they both moaned.

They coupled face-to-face, breast to breast. Jessica's cry from her first orgasm still echoed in the room when she flipped over onto her knees and demanded, "Again."

Skyler's staccato grunts grew louder and her pace quickened. It was an erotic fantasy come to life as Jessica arched her back to meet her thrusts. The dildo's base rubbed the length of Skyler's clit with each stroke, making it feel as though it was, indeed, a part of her own body stretching her lover's warm vagina.

"Yes," Jessica hissed when Skyler rose up to her knees, pulling Jessica's hips upward to both increase and change the angle of penetration.

The tingling began building in Skyler's groin and she drove faster, deeper, flesh slapping against flesh. Her legs began to shake at the sight of the pliant prosthesis sliding in and out, filling and stretching, and she reached around to stroke Jessica's engorged clitoris with the same rhythm.

"Oh God, baby. Come with me, Sky," Jessica urged.

Crying out as one, they thrust together, riding out the last waves of their orgasms. Jessica finally collapsed onto the bed, exhausted. They lay together, their hearts pounding in synch. Jessica moaned when Skyler finally shifted her weight to pull the cock free.

"Damn, babe. You are really good at this," Jessica panted.

Skyler's chest puffed out at Jessica's compliment. She quickly divested herself of the equipment and flopped onto her back to pull her lover close. She loved the way Jessica's smaller body felt resting on top of hers. She ran her fingertips down the lightly muscled back and rested her hands on the firm buttocks. God, she loved Jessica's ass. She loved all of this woman, this wonderful woman who had given her lost and drifting soul an anchor. What had she given in return?

Skyler had only been at the bar to collect their drinks for a few minutes, but by the time she walked back to their table there was already a very attractive dark-haired stranger leaning close to Jessica, crowding Jessica's personal space.

"You seem to be conveniently alone." The woman leaned closer than was necessary for Jessica to hear her speaking.

"My partner is at the bar, getting us a drink."

The woman reached out, grabbed Jessica's left hand, and held it up to look at it. "Must be a business partner, because I don't see a ring on this finger. Or else this woman doesn't think much of what she has."

She saw Jessica pull her hand back and frown. Time to step in.

"Here you go, love. Are you about ready to hit the dance floor?"

Jessica took the offered drink and rewarded Skyler with a quick kiss. Skyler wrapped a possessive arm around her and looked inquiringly at the other woman.

"This is my partner, Skyler Reese," Jessica said. "Sky, this is…" Jessica raised a questioning eyebrow at the woman, waiting her answer.

The woman bowed slightly. "I can see it doesn't matter. Pardon my intrusion."

Skyler scowled as the woman retreated. The ring remark bothered her. She needed to do something about that.

"A penny for those heavy thoughts," Jessica said.

"Well, these thoughts are worth more than a few pennies." Skyler wiggled out from under Jessica's comfortable weight and padded across the room to retrieve her jeans. She really had planned to do this over a romantic dinner, not in the nude in a hotel room. But the moment seemed right just the same. It was the way she wanted to give herself to Jessica, exposed and vulnerable, emotionally as well as physically.

So Skyler knelt beside the bed. Her eyes brimmed with tears. After a long minute, she choked out what was on her heart.

"Jessica, will you marry me, be my partner for life?" She opened the jeweler's box to reveal a brilliant sapphire flanked by a pair of diamonds in a warm gold setting.

When Jessica pulled back in surprise, Skyler felt a surge of panic. That reaction wasn't what she'd expected.

"I'm not asking you to change your name or anything," she blurted. "It's just, if we're going to raise children together…no, that didn't sound right…" *Damn it.* She stared down at the bed. She could never seem to say what she meant.

Jessica smiled at her partner's consternation.

"Oh, Sky, it's so beautiful. Yes."

"Yes?" Skyler asked hopefully.

"Yes, I'll marry you…in front of the world, or in front of just a few friends. I could never love another like I love you, honey."

Skyler slid the ring onto Jessica's finger, tears finally spilling over.

"I love you, Jess. I would be so lost without you. I want to wake up next to you every morning for the rest of my life," she said, her voice cracking with emotion. "I want to raise children with you…children who will grow up knowing they, too, belong."

"That's exactly what I want, too," Jessica replied, gently wiping away Skyler's tears.

Skyler climbed back into bed and they held each other close, talking of the future between kisses, bonding gently, soul deep.

"You never told me you wanted to use…you know," Skyler said after a while. "I'm never going to be able to drive past this hotel again without getting horny."

"Me neither." Jessica blushed. "I wasn't sure how to bring it up. I meant to ask, did you remember to push the plunger at the right time?"

Uh-oh. "Was I supposed to do that?"

"What's the point if, when the time really comes, you forget to push the plunger?" Jessica laughed. "I think you're going to need a lot more practice, stud."

Skyler grinned. "I think I'm going to like this baby-making business even more than I thought."

NELL STARK and TRINITY TAM would like to blame Radclyffe for infecting them with vampirism. "Tenebrosidad" takes place one hundred years prior to the events of the novel *everafter* (October 2009). www.everafterseries.com.

TENEBROSIDAD
NELL STARK AND TRINITY TAM

I had been sneaking out of Villa Carrizo since my adolescence, but whereas before I had been running away from the drudgery of chores, the monotonous pettiness of my sisters, and the oppressive henpecking of my mother, today I was running toward my future. Throwing open the windows that led out onto my small balcony, I allowed the rope in my hands to uncoil and secured one end to the railing. I nudged the other end with my toe, sending it sliding off the edge and down through the leaves that crowned the quebracho tree growing in the gap between the side of the house and the wall. Knotting my skirt, I expertly slid a few feet down the rope until my feet connected with a firm branch. I steadied myself against the thick trunk before looping the rope around the branch and edging cautiously toward the wall.

Moments later, I had dropped down over the barrier that separated the villa from the outside world and was walking briskly toward town. Toward the small white house that stood on its outskirts, overlooking a bend in the river. Toward her, and the peace that only her embrace could offer. She had sent word yesterday of her return to Argentina, and finally—months after her sudden and secret journey across the ocean—we would be reunited.

Even in my memory, the beauty of her stirred me, jagged arrows of heat igniting beneath my skin. She had captivated me from the start…

I stepped into the circle of light around the bonfire, silencing the rumbling murmur of masculine voices as effectively as if I had slit their throats. The heads of five families stood in a knot close to the fire, as though it would afford them protection against the Others—their masters—who formed their own group, silent and apart.

Not their masters. Our. I took my rightful place among the mortals, tucking my arms beneath my breasts to hide the shaking of my hands. Some of the men regarded me with sneers of undisguised contempt. The others looked away.

"Solana Carrizo, we welcome you among us." The voice was smooth, confident in its softness. I hesitated before dipping into a formal curtsey. My father had neglected to instruct me on how to properly greet a vampire.

The meeting commenced with no further introductions. While the men discussed cattle, I discreetly examined the vampires before me. There was one more of them than there was of us—seven to our six. They ranged in height and age, sharing only their distinctive porcelain skin, untouched by the rays of the sun for God only knew how long. They were beautiful, as if by stilling the hands of time they had also learned to transcend the mortal aesthetic. A flicker of motion caught my attention. The seventh vampire had moved a few feet away from the others, clearly distinguishing herself as an observer. I started. Herself. Her long, dark hair was the same hue as the fabric of her trousers and blouse, and her pale, angular face rose above her high collar like a three-quarters moon.

She was stunning. As though I had spoken the words aloud, she turned to look directly at me. Clear blue eyes caught my own and held me. Legend had it that these creatures could bewitch with a glance, but I sensed no trace of devilish sorcery ·working within me—only the subtle force of her beauty. When her eyebrows arched and her lips twitched, I realized I was staring. Heat crept into my cheeks, and I quickly returned my attention to the meeting.

My father had told me—no, warned me—of their dangerous allure. Barely a week ago, in a startling deathbed proclamation that overturned decades of precedent, he had named me his heir. With his last breath, he had whispered the existence of a letter, tucked away in the hidden compartment of his desk. My last moment of innocence.

No. Not innocence—ignorance. My family name was steeped in blood, had been for generations. How, how had I lived for twenty years without perceiving the black bargain made between the landowning *estancieros* and the vampires of Buenos Aires? They gave us wealth and patronage, security in these tumultuous days at the dawn of a new century. In return, they asked for the blood of our people. Blood that was now my obligation to deliver.

"The Incas knew the wisdom of this kind of sacrifice," my father had written. "For generations, this family has provided for the needs of the one who calls himself Romero, and he has rewarded us for our faithfulness." I burned the letter after I read it, just as my father had asked. Only one in each generation was allowed to know the secret. My father's burden, and now mine.

I stole another glance at the female vampire. Her dark lips glistened in the flickering light of the bonfire. Who fed her, I wondered. A prickle of jealousy crawled up my spine, surprising me. I thought of what it would be like to wrap strands of her hair around my fingers, tugging her closer as she slid her teeth into my skin. The flood of heat returned, and I shivered at its strength. It wouldn't be a burden to feed her.

The meeting ended just past midnight. There were a few quiet, terse conversations amongst the men as we mounted our horses. No one spoke to me. I would not have allowed their reticence to bother me regardless of the circumstances, but now, I barely even registered the silence. Her face remained imprinted on my mind's eye, and as I wheeled my white mare in the direction of my estate, I could think of nothing else.

So distracted was I that I didn't perceive the oncoming surge of motion until the other rider was on top of me, seizing my horse's bridle with one large fist and wrenching at my arm with the other. Surprise and terror conspired to turn my scream into a low, choking gasp.

Diego Vargas, the leader of the *estancieros*.

In that moment, the irony that my attacker was not one of the monsters, but rather a man I had called "uncle" as a child, was not lost on me. I had underestimated all of them. I should have known that the other families would never stand for a woman who knew the secret. And now I would pay the ultimate price for my lack of foresight.

But just as I felt him gather the strength to throw me to the ground, I heard a sickly thud, and he slumped forward in his saddle with a loud cry. The movement almost pulled me under his horse's hooves, and I clung desperately to the neck of my mare, weaving my fingers into the strands of her mane. Neighing shrilly, she shied away, easily breaking his now-loosened grip…and I found myself staring in relieved horror at the ornately gilded hilt of a knife sticking out just below his left shoulder.

With no small effort, I reined my horse to a stop several yards in front of Vargas and sat trembling at the gruesome sight of him, now half dangling from his lathered mount, contorting himself in an effort to remove the weapon from his own body. When another horse and rider emerged from the dense foliage behind him, I gathered myself—whether to scream or to run, I did not know. But my mouth opened silently, and my hand on the reins was nerveless.

Her.

Again, our eyes met—hers brilliant blue and mesmerizing. Slowly, she raised a single, elegant finger to her lips, inclining her head in Vargas's direction. I wanted to convey my assent—to assure her that this secret, too, would be safe in my keeping. But my limbs were heavy, weighed down by fear. She finally looked away, breaking the spell, and withdrew a pistol from her waistband. I started in horror, but rather than cocking it, she urged her horse alongside Vargas's and dashed the gun against his head before he had even registered her presence. Grasping the collar of his shirt, she heaved his body backward. When the dead weight tumbled to the ground, the horse bolted. She let it go.

A long shudder ran through me then, returning the strength to my fingertips. I could only guess what she planned to do, and jealousy seized me again.

Jerking hard on the reins, I fled without looking back.

❖

She preceded me into the bedroom and bent over the nightstand. Seconds later, a match flared, and I watched as she lit two candles. She raised her eyes to mine then, extinguishing the match by pinching it between her thumb and forefinger. The unquenchable flame at the heart of me surged in anticipation at the thought of her touch on my skin.

If she heard the increase in my breathing, she gave no sign. She did not move. She did not speak. I felt her reticence for what it was—a gift. The temporary relinquishing of control. But my lingering doubts had been turned to ash in the crucible of our separation. I wanted her. I needed her, in my very soul.

My hands trembled at the buttons of my blouse, but not out of fear. She sighed as I pushed the fabric down my shoulders, revealing the light silk camisole beneath. Without hesitation, I drew it over my head, and this time her breath caught in her throat.

I smiled, feeling powerful as I first slipped off my sandals, then slowly slid my skirt down the length of my legs. I wore nothing beneath.

"Solana." My name on her lips was a prayer, charged with need.

"Your turn," I whispered.

She undressed quickly, efficiently, laying bare her strong, thin arms and the nearly flat plane of her stomach before reaching back to unclasp her brassiere. Her breasts were smaller than mine, their tips the color of coral. I wanted to kiss them.

In another moment, she too was naked. I watched the contraction of her leg muscles as she stepped out of her linen trousers…and then I allowed my eyes to feast, following the lines and curves of her, feeling my mouth go dry as I took in the dark patch of hair between her legs.

Desire propelled me forward—one step, then another. With only a few feet separating us, I paused, uncertain not about my choice but about what should come next. Sensing my confusion, she stretched out her hand, palm upturned, candlelight flickering off her pale skin.

I reached out to take it…

❖

I sat atop the wall that enclosed the villa, my location partially obscured by the gnarled tree that I had been using to reach this very spot since I was a child. It had been my first secret. I kept more now. Romero was a patient teacher and, I learned, a good master. He told me that he preferred to hunt and would rarely require my services to procure blood. However, the previous night he had come to me, face gaunt and eyes dark. I had known, without a word being uttered, that it was time for me to fulfill my end of the bargain. I led Romero down to the small stockade below the stables. We had caught a cattle thief three days before; he had tried to resist arrest and managed to break my foreman's arm in two places before we subdued him. I conjured up that image now, of the white bone protruding jaggedly from my man's bloodied arm while the thief pummeled him, foaming at the mouth like a rabid animal. Like an animal, I reminded myself as tears cascaded down my cheeks and I fumbled with the key to let Romero in.

In an effort to banish the memory, I took a slow, deep breath. The fragrant aromas of jasmine and ceibo mingled to perfume the dusky air. Strains of cheerful music wafted back from the courtyard, where my cousin would be celebrating her wedding until the dawn. I wasn't in the mood to celebrate. I turned toward the setting sun, allowing its last rays to soak into my cheeks. When it finally dropped beneath the horizon, I felt bereft.

"Your face is even lovelier in grief than it is in joy."

I started at the melodious voice that had interrupted my solitude, and looked around wildly for its source. She emerged a moment later from behind the tree, wearing a blouse and trousers so blue they were almost black. Resting one hand on the stone wall, she looked up at me. There was just enough light left in the sky to illuminate the slight curve to her lips.

"Take comfort," she said, her smile growing more pronounced. "They say it will rise again tomorrow."

My heart was thundering in my ears and my palms were

moist with sweat, but I refused to betray my fear. Or my excitement. "How long, since you have felt it on your face?" I asked, fighting to keep my voice even.

The quirk of one eyebrow was the only indication that I had surprised her. "One hundred and fifty-five years."

My breath left me in a sharp sigh, but I refused to cede more ground than that. "What is your name?"

She cocked her head, gazing up at me in frank curiosity. "Solana Carrizo, you are a bizarre and exotic creature." She held out her hand, then, and enthralled by her compliment, I reached down to take it. Her skin was smooth and cool. "I am Helen Lambros."

I smiled at her teasing tone. "Surely, there are many like me where you come from?" My eyes drifted downward over the swell of her breasts to the smooth length of her trousered thigh. "A land where women are allowed to dress like men?"

She tugged lightly, and caught off guard, I had no choice but to descend from my perch. "I come from many places, but in the span of two mortal lives, I have never met a woman such as you."

"There is nothing special about me."

Her arms slid around me as my feet met the grass, and I found myself pressed against her body. She leaned in closer and I felt the gentle caress of her breath against my cheek. "You are the only female *estanciero* in all of Argentina. You walk in dignity, not fear, amongst the men." She paused and her voice dropped low. "For the first time in one hundred and fifty-five years, when you look at me, the way you look at me, I feel the sunlight on my skin and I do not despise myself."

An electric thrill swept beneath my skin at the brief sensation of her breasts grazing mine, and I bit down on my lower lip to keep a cry from escaping. These feelings were not new—I had experienced them often during my adolescence, always in the presence of women. I had been wise enough never to speak of it, and had despaired long ago of finding anyone who shared my burden. My father would have called me a monster, had he known. How poetically just, to find a kindred spirit among the real monsters.

Helen inclined her head, and when her lips grazed my ear, gooseflesh rose on my forearms. "Dance with me."

Unable to speak, I nodded my assent. Wrapping one arm more securely around my waist, she gently took my left hand in her right and twined our fingers together. My head felt light, and I struggled to tame my short, sharp breaths as she began to twirl us adeptly beneath the boughs of the tree.

We didn't speak—we didn't need to. Overhead, the stars gradually emerged, called into existence by the death of the sun. What if she is no monster after all, I thought up at them, but one of you instead?

Returning my attention to the earth, I dared to lay my cheek against the cool silk of her blouse and finally find a measure of peace.

I heard the curtains flutter gently against the walls, compelled into movement by the sultry night breeze, but nothing could distract me from the storm that was rising in my blood. I knew that I would never forget this moment—my limbs pressed into the silky sheets by the body that hovered above mine, lithe and smooth, a study in elegant curves. I cupped her cool face in my palms, thumbs carefully tracing the sharp rise of her cheekbones, the delicate curve of her moistened lips.

I allowed my hands to coast up and down her arms, palms lingering on the subtle swell of muscle beneath smooth skin. When she bent her head, my heartbeat stuttered—but her mouth was ghostly, tantalizing me with unfulfilled promise. Her breath was cool against my face, and I arched up shamelessly, not caring that she saw my need.

She shifted her weight slightly, freeing one hand to touch me. Those elegant fingers began at my throat, lingering to feel the artery pulsing beneath, before trailing down, down so slowly, stroking with sure knowledge and gentle assurance. My back arched again, this time involuntarily...

❖

Cobalt clouds scudded across the night sky, alternately masking and revealing a crescent moon. The hot breeze lifted the hair from the nape of my neck and I sighed, leaning into Nature's caress.

"You are exquisite." The words came from behind me, borne on Helen's husky voice. I flushed, simultaneously flattered by the compliment and frightened to hear such a sentiment spoken aloud by another woman. Helen, I had realized, only paid lip service to local custom in order to blend in. Beneath her façade, she was radically different from anyone I had ever met, made alien by her perspective as one unchanged by the passing of time.

After an initial glance over my shoulder, I forced myself to turn back to the view of the waves, sparkling fitfully as they reflected the weak light above. Helen came up behind me, close but not touching. "This is a beautiful place," she murmured. I wished that she would slide her arms around me, or even simply rest her hands on my waist. I desired her touch with a ferocity that should have been disconcerting. We had seen each other often in the weeks since the wedding, but Helen had yet to betray any hint of the thirsty demon that lurked beneath her veneer of civility. She was disarming me. Lulling me. I knew it, and welcomed her seduction.

"It is," I agreed. "But its beauty is perilous. We call this place Maidenfall Cliff for a reason. Some say the land here is haunted."

Helen moved closer so that her breasts were subtly pressing against my back. My heart jumped within my chest. "The women who cast themselves off this precipice and into the water—what are they running from?"

I imagined taking the five steps that remained between myself and open air; I saw myself falling, white skirts billowing like the clipped wings of a swan as I plummeted toward the choppy waves. Would I see the faces of those I had sent to Romero as I descended? Criminals, all of them, sacrificed for the stability of our new nation. Would their eyes be accusing or forgiving?

"Who can say? The pressure of an overbearing

father. The shame of carrying a child out of wedlock. The overwhelming burden of working all day in the fields only to return at sunset to a cramped, dirty hut. Despair comes in many flavors."

Finally, finally she touched me, molding her hands to the slight flare of my hips. For a moment, I couldn't breathe. I felt her move until her cool mouth touched the shell of my ear. "And what flavor is yours?"

I turned to face her then, slowly and deliberately. She clasped her hands behind my back and I rested mine against her chest, looking up into the depths of her eternal eyes. "That I can never be more than the slightest ripple on the vast ocean that is your existence."

She stared down at me unblinking, the intensity of her gaze freezing me exactly where I stood. I wondered what she was looking for, and whether or not she thought she had found it.

"I am leaving on a boat tomorrow, for several fortnights. Perhaps even longer. But I will return."

I shook my head slightly as my body reacted—fear, loss, sorrow, even a tinge of aimless jealousy. Shifting my grip to the lean strength of her arms, I steadied myself. "What calls you away?"

She turned to look out over the ocean, and I feasted my eyes on the lines of her profile—strong yet feminine. "Business."

I let my fingertips trace the curve of her collarbone, feeling simultaneously excited by and embarrassed at my forwardness. I did not press her for more information. Her business affairs were none of my concern, unless Romero made them so. "Be safe," I whispered, thinking of the perils of the sea—of sudden storms and pirate attacks and treacherous shoals.

She unlaced her fingers, releasing me from her embrace—but before I could sigh in disappointment, her hands were cupping my face and her lips were pressing against mine, softer than rose petals. My sharp, muffled cry of shock and desire startled birds from the nearby trees, and as I felt the wind of their passage overhead, I wrapped my arms around Helen's neck.

The world spun as she gently parted my lips with her tongue, touching hers to mine and then withdrawing again. I moaned and was not ashamed. Gradually, her tender strokes grew bold, and I trembled in her arms as the stars wheeled above us.

Finally, she eased us down from that unspeakable high, pressing kisses to my nose, my forehead, the corners of my mouth. I clung to her, wanting more, ever more, certain only that I could never get enough.

"I will return to you," she said, breathing the words into my mouth.

And I believed.

As her palm skimmed across the curve of my hip, she finally kissed me. Her mouth was cool, and at the first soft touch of her tongue, I trembled.

"You taste like sunshine," she murmured, and I shivered at the raw longing in her voice.

Again, her lips met mine. And again. I silently rejoiced when she began to lose hold of her restraint—when gentleness gave way to need and tenderness to hunger. Her fingers were restless, and I moved like the ocean beneath her.

Her intimate touch woke fire in my blood. I thrashed in its grip, simultaneously begging for release and pleading that it would never die. Helen kissed the entreaties off my lips, stealing the words from my mouth before they met air. Her breasts slid against mine, beads of sweat rising between us to evaporate in the flames. She stroked me masterfully, but with an urgency that made me certain of her desire, her need.

Her need.

Even through the haze of the conflagration, I could sense her struggle. Her mouth refused to remain on mine, migrating repeatedly to the soft, pulsing skin of my neck, where her tongue traced exquisite patterns that only stoked the inferno raging inside of me. I wanted her to ask, but she hadn't. And she had promised, earlier tonight, that she wouldn't. "I don't want to hurt you," she had said, brushing her fingertips across my shoulders even as her tongue betrayed her words by skimming hungrily over her lips. "I certainly would never compel you. And regardless, it would…disgust you."

I hadn't argued, believing that after one hundred and fifty years of experience, she knew best. How, then, could I tell her now that I wanted to give myself to her freely? That in this moment, the thought of being the one to slake her thirst made me shiver only in anticipation? That whatever pain I felt would be well worth the knowledge that I was fulfilling the very essence of her?

I gathered my breath to implore her, but she chose that instant to slip inside me for the first time, her touch a cool counterpoint to the blaze consuming me from within. Reason fled. My lungs contracted in a moan—her name, a guttural prayer.

When she stilled her touch, my eyes snapped open and I struggled to focus. Her elegant face was a study in contrast—tenderness and ferocity, love and thirst. "You are heartbreakingly beautiful," she said hoarsely. "And you are mine. Finally mine."

The possessiveness of her words roused a memory in me, but then she moved even deeper inside, and rational thought fled before the gathering tempest. I shuddered in her arms, trying to force out the words.

"Take. Me. Helen…please…"

Her pupils expanded, black forcing the blue into the barest of rings. "You don't know what you're ask—"

"I do!" Cupping her face in my palms, I pulled her closer—not to my mouth, but to my neck. "Please, let me. Let me be this for you."

Her breaths ragged against my skin, she paused before suddenly shifting her fingers, wringing a sharp cry from my throat. Every single muscle in my body tightened at once, a knot on the verge of becoming unraveled.

"Are you sure?" Helen gasped.

"Yes!" I urged, driving my fingers into her hair. "Take it."

Her teeth sank into me, the sting immediately eclipsed by an ecstatic surge that spiraled up my spine. Her moan vibrated against my neck and I clutched desperately at her wrist as her fingers moved inside me. Heat poured from my veins, warming her everywhere our skin touched. I felt an unfamiliar twisting tension building low in my belly as her movements became more frantic, more erratic. My need was insistent but unfocused. More. I needed more.

"Helen," I breathed, tangling my fingers into the dark strands of her hair, "oh Helen, please."

Simultaneously, her teeth and her hand slipped deeper, molding my body into a taut bow. I could feel my heart pounding against my ribs as every ounce of my being raced toward…something. Something glorious. She held me at the precipice for an eternal moment, her suction at my neck pulling my pleasure right to the surface. She bore down with her thumb as her fingers twisted inside me…and the world exploded with impossible brightness, fire scorching along my limbs. Desperate to fuse myself with her, I slipped my thigh between her legs, glorying in the sensation of her heat against my skin. She thrust herself against me wildly and I dug my fingertips into her shoulders as my pleasure crested impossibly higher. Through the maelstrom, I clutched at my consciousness just long enough to feel Helen stiffen and then convulse against me as the ecstasy in my bloodstream slammed into her system and pushed her too over the edge.

❖

When next I could perceive sensation, Helen was leaning over me, holding a damp cloth to my neck. It stung slightly, but the overwhelming sensation throughout my body was a profound sense of peace. And joy. I smiled up at her, and she mirrored my expression. Tenderly, she peeled the cloth away, nodding slightly as though reassuring herself that she hadn't seriously injured me. I reached up to caress her face, and she turned her mouth into my palm, kissing it.

And then she pulled away, eyes suddenly sparkling. "Wait. Just a moment."

I watched her slide off the bed and cross the room to her desk, then extract something from its top drawer. The effortless grace of her movements was captivating. Unbidden but not unwelcome, the fire welled up again from deep inside, and I caught my breath at the force of my desire for her.

When she returned, I sat up to claim a kiss, but she pressed one finger to my lips instead. Carefully, she placed a rolled parchment in my hand. My mind was still muddled and the letters were foreign to me. "What is this?"

Her fingers smoothed my brow and danced through my hair. "A deed. The deed to my estate in London. Tomorrow I shall exchange it for Villa Carrizo and the rest of Romero's land. It seems that your old master has a thirst for adventure."

"My *old* master?"

She pressed a kiss to my forehead. "I will care for you, I promise—I will spare you from the guilt sown into your heritage by Romero and his appetites. You will be free of the devil's bargain. Free, as you deserve to be."

Her tone was so gentle, her words so beautiful. Could they all be true? "What about your needs? I will not have you suffer."

Her smile was patient and tender. "I can take care of myself. You and your family are released from this charge forever."

"But I want to feed you. I choose to sustain you. So long as my body draws breath, I will be yours until the end of my days." I caressed her face, trailing my fingers lovingly over her smooth skin and full lips.

"No one has to die, Solana." She leaned in past my questing fingers and captured my mouth in a soul-binding kiss. "My love. No one ever has to die."

And I believed.

KI Thompson is the author of three novels, *House of Clouds* (2008 Sapphic Readers' Award; 2008 Indie Book Award and 2008 Goldie Award finalist), *Heart of the Matter*, and *Cooper's Deale*. She also has short stories in *Erotic Interludes 2–5*, *Fantasy: Untrue Stories of Lesbian Passion*, *Best Lesbian Romance 2007*, and *Best Lesbian Romance 2009*. She is currently working on her fourth novel, *The Will to Wynne*, a historical romance set during the American Revolutionary War. KI lives in the Washington, DC, area with her partner and two much-loved cats.

CONSTANT COMPANION
KI THOMPSON

What time is it?"

"Late. Sorry to wake you."

I gripped the phone with my chin and squinted at the bedside clock. 2:07. "No, I wanted you to. How'd the meeting go?"

A tired sigh drifted across the country and caressed my ear. "Not as well as I'd hoped. About what I'd expected, though." Another sigh.

I strained to hear something else in the silence. I'd been doing that a lot recently, unsure of myself, and her. That familiar knot, my constant companion of late, settled uncomfortably in my stomach.

"It's been a long day and I'm tired," she explained.

"Yeah."

"I miss you." It sounded automatic.

"Me too," I said automatically.

"I really do," she whispered.

A remote corner of my heart began to beat again and I tried not to let the feeling spread. I stared up at the ceiling, noticing the old stain from when she had tried to repair the upstairs toilet by herself. We had laughed about it at the time, then called a plumber when the job proved too much for her limited skills. I'd never gotten around to painting the ceiling—too busy, I guess. In the dark, it took on a menacing, jagged appearance, splitting the plaster like an earthquake's chasm.

"You still coming home tomorrow night?" I asked.

"Yes. There's not much else I can do here. The client has made up his mind and I can't stop him from making a stupid mistake. Jesus, why do I keep doing this?" she asked for the millionth time.

"Because you care," I said for the million and first time. It was the same old conversation and the same circular reasoning.

"But lately it seems like I'm the only one who does."

"I care," I offered tentatively. It was a break from our usual routine, but she had opened the door first, and this time I didn't want the moment to pass.

"I know."

"Do you?" I asked. "Do you really? Because sometimes I'm not so sure you do."

I was uncertain if her lack of response was a good thing, but I could feel her listening over the phone. I had her attention and that was enough…for now.

"I haven't been happy for a while," she whispered.

I swallowed hard, unprepared for her bluntness. My stomach churned and I had trouble breathing. "I know."

"This job is sucking the life out of me," she hurried to explain. "It hasn't been good for me and it hasn't been good for you either."

"It hasn't been good for *us*," I murmured. "You can quit, you know."

"Yeah."

"We've talked about this—"

"Yeah," she said more forcefully. "It's just that they pay me a ridiculous amount of money. It's hard to give that up."

"We can afford less," I said. "We have before and we can again."

"I don't know. The bills—"

"We can do it again," I repeated. "We've gotten way too comfortable with the extra income, spending on extravagant things we don't even need. Remember our first apartment, the loft in the Village?"

"The kitchen was so small only one of us could be in it at a time."

"Which was usually me."

"Well, you're the only one who can cook," she said.

"That's only because you kept setting off the smoke detector. The neighbors complained about having to evacuate the building so often they threatened bodily harm."

"Oh, stop exaggerating."

"Exaggerating?" My voice rose in pitch, partly because I was right and partly because I was happy to lighten the mood. "Hang up and call Mrs. Alvarez right now and ask her how much I'm exaggerating."

"Mrs. Alvarez was crazy."

"No, she wasn't."

"She walked around her apartment naked."

"So did you," I pointed out.

"Not when my apartment was on the ground floor on Sixth Avenue and all the blinds were open wide."

I laughed. She had always been able to make me do that.

"It's nice to hear you laugh," she said. "I've missed it."

"Me too."

"I'm sorry—"

"It's not your fault," I insisted. "Neither of us has taken time out for the other. That needs to change, you know?"

"Yeah, I know."

We drifted back into silence, though less strained than before. I struggled to think of what to say next; wanting to talk—needing to talk—but unsure of the timing and unwilling to reverse the fragile progress we had made. I could hear scratchy static on the other end of the line, a gentle reminder of the tenuousness of our connection.

"I could go back to teaching," she said hesitantly, speaking more to herself than me.

"You used to love it," I said. "You always came home excited about your day and looked forward to the next."

"But the pay—"

"Forget about that. All that matters is that you're happy. The rest will come."

"You'll wind up having to darn my socks or something like that," she said.

"I don't knit."

"You could learn. You're fairly crafty."

"You could learn to cook," I shot back.

"So, you don't have to knit."

I smiled and was surprised to feel a tear creep down the corner of my eye and trickle into my ear.

"I love you," I blurted, and meant it so deeply, so unreservedly, I actually hurt. I sat up in bed, turned the bedside lamp on, and hugged her pillow to my chest.

"I love you too, baby," she said. "Don't worry, everything's going to be okay."

"Will it?" I asked, wanting her to believe it as much as I did, and needing to hear it in her voice.

"Yeah. I should let you get back to sleep. You've got to go to work in the morning."

"I'm not sleepy."

"You will be at six a.m., and I don't want you blaming me for your lack of sleep," she teased.

"Do I do that?" I was still sensitive to my own complicity in our unhappiness.

"Sometimes," she said softly.

"I'll be better."

"I know. We both will."

"I don't want you to go quite yet," I pleaded. "Will you stay with me until I fall asleep?"

"Anything you want."

Her reassurance loosened the slipknot that was attached to her and had tightened over the last few months the further away from me she had drifted. I hadn't realized how tightly I had clung to that line, unaware that, like the hangman's noose, it was suffocating us. For the first time in a long while my body relaxed, and in that instant, I knew I'd be able to sleep. It could only have been better had she been in bed with me, and I ached for her warmth. I snuggled into the down comforter, spooning her pillow and inhaling deeply her fragrance.

"I'll come pick you up at the airport tomorrow," I said.

"No, don't do that. It's insane getting in and out of LaGuardia. I'll grab a cab."

"But I want to. Besides, I thought we might grab something to eat afterward—nothing fast, somewhere nice. Maybe Alfredo's."

"Mmm, that sounds good. I'm a sucker for their bread pudding."

"I know," I murmured. It was quiet again, and I thought of our first date at the restaurant, how she couldn't finish her dessert and we took it home. We fed it to each other in bed after making love.

"Let's be sure and order dessert," she said hoarsely, as though reading my mind.

"Okay." I couldn't stop the yawn that stretched the word into three syllables.

"Go to sleep, baby, and I'll see you tomorrow."

"I love you," I whispered.

"I love you too. Good night."

"'Night."

I hung up and pulled her pillow tight against me. That familiar knot, my constant companion, rolled over and went to sleep.

C.J. Harte was born in New York but lived in many places while growing up. After her family finally settled in the South, she attended college in the Deep South, where she obtained her degrees as well as a significant Southern accent and a unrelenting sense of humor. Her novels with Bold Strokes include *Dreams of Bali* and the forthcoming *Magic of the Heart*.

CROSSING OVER, JORDAN
C.J. HARTE

Dinner conversation at Jordan's sorority house had become so predictable. Like most Friday nights, the topics of discussion were dates for the weekend and other social activities, things Jordan rarely participated in unless required to for an official function for her father. This particular evening her sorority sisters were more insistent than usual on discovering her plans.

"Nothing," Jordan answered. "I haven't made any plans other than studying with a friend."

"Who?" someone asked. Someone always asked.

Jordan shrugged. "A friend."

"Not that dyke tutor of yours. Do you even feel safe around her?"

Safe? The only people Jordan felt comfortable around were Mark and Drew. Drew always made her feel safe, and cared about.

"I'm studying this weekend. No other plans." She resumed eating, hoping her lack of an answer would cause the conversation to shift. She knew all too well that there was always someone who couldn't wait to announce to the world what Jordan Thompson was doing. She had grown up in the public limelight, her father's political career having begun when she was only five years old. The higher her father climbed, the more her life, and her brother's, had become public, too. How much more exposed could her life be?

Tonight, however, Jordan knew she could no longer play their game. After months of struggling, she had made a decision. Now she just needed to figure out what to do about it. As she looked around the table, she wondered if they would still be as curious if they knew what she really hoped would happen this weekend.

As soon as dinner was over, she left for her own place. One of the advantages of being Harold Thompson's daughter was that she didn't have to account for her coming and going. As long as she conformed.

Once home, she requested one of her security team drive her to Drew and Mark's house. These two medical students, she'd come to realize, were her only real friends. She instructed her driver to park someplace where the car wouldn't be noticed and requested the same of her personal security detail. Tonight she was hoping she would be staying, and she didn't want to arouse unnecessary curiosity. Tonight she needed an answer.

Mark, Drew's gay roommate, greeted her at the door. "Drew's on call until eleven. I'm due in then. Come on in. I'm heading to Miami tomorrow as soon as my ER shift is over." Mark headed back to his side of the house with Jordan following.

"I'm guessing David is also planning on taking the weekend off."

"I haven't seen him in six weeks." Mark was all smiles. "We aren't planning on going anywhere or doing anything. Just spending time together. And I'm going to catch up on my sleep."

Jordan had long admired the relationship Mark had with his lover. What amazed her most was the comfort she felt around them. Their love was obvious. It reminded her of her parents.

"Got a few minutes to talk?" Jordan asked.

"If you don't mind talking in my bedroom," Mark answered. "I've got to pack some things for the weekend."

"Sure." After a few minutes of small talk, Jordan finally gathered her courage. "Mark, when did you know?"

"I've always known. I learned early to listen to my heart." He sat on the bed next to Jordan, laughing softly. "We're Latin, you know. My mother believes in being guided by her emotions—I guess I inherited that from her. What's your heart saying?"

Jordan was not surprised by the question, just how to answer. "I've lied to myself, denied what I felt, kept this a secret for so long I almost didn't believe it was real. Tonight, at dinner, I sat listening to everyone gossip about who they were going out with, who's getting engaged, who's sleeping with what guy. I couldn't stand it. I felt so out of place, especially when they started asking me again about my plans. I don't know what to do, Mark."

"Tell her. Show her." He took her hand. "Drew's probably as nervous about this as you are."

"She's had a lot more experience with being gay than I have." Jordan's surprise had little to do with the fact that Mark had immediately known Drew was the cause of her discomfort, but more with the idea of Drew being unsure about being involved with her.

"Yes, that's true, but none of the other women were President Harold Thompson's daughter." Mark laughed. "Sorry, I was thinking about her family. They're not wild about her associating with you."

"I know." Jordan couldn't hide the pain. "What am I going to do?"

"I…" The phone rang and Mark grabbed it. "Hold on a minute while I get this. Hello." Mark paled as he listened. "Not a problem. Be there in five."

"What's going on?" Jordan asked anxiously.

"Drew's going to be late. There's a multiple motor vehicle accident coming into the ER. Sounds like a long night. I gotta go." He slipped his shoes on and kissed her on the forehead. "Go ahead and watch TV until she gets home. I'm sure she'll appreciate you being here. I just don't know when that may be." Seeing her hesitation, Mark added, "If you want to, that is."

Jordan nodded and hugged him good-bye. He was such a good friend. After he was gone, she wandered around the empty house, finally settling on his bed to watch TV and wait.

❖

An obnoxiously loud commercial on the television woke Jordan from a restless sleep. Staring at the clock, she realized it was after two in the morning. Disappointment filled her as she fought back the tears. The last few months had been difficult. She couldn't continue to ignore her feelings even though she wasn't naïve enough to believe her family and friends would understand her involvement with a woman. The very public attention she would expose her entire family to if her relationship was discovered would be the source of pain to people she loved. And the scrutiny the relationship would receive was daunting. But Drew was in her final year and if Jordan didn't make a decision soon, she might lose her and any chance for the love they might share.

Jordan started to shake with an unfamiliar longing. Her indecision was crazy-making. She needed an answer, and the one night she'd finally gathered her courage, Drew wasn't home! Her courage was fading. Discretion, and fear of making a fool of herself, dictated she leave as quickly as possible.

Jordan walked quickly through the silent house, not wanting to even imagine what could have happened. As she passed the door to Drew's bedroom, she stopped briefly and touched the door.

"Oh, Drew," she whispered, resting her head momentarily against the closed door.

The door was open earlier. I'm sure of it. Her pulse increased. *Could she have come home and I didn't hear her?* She hesitated. No sounds emerged from behind the closed door. Jordan's emotions were roiling, fear battling desire.

"I must know," she whispered and turned the knob.

The light from the living room cast a long beam bisecting the darkened room. And highlighting the naked back of Drew Hamilton. She was stretched across her bed asleep, light and shadow playing across her skin.

Jordan's heart raced, her pulse pounded, warmth traveled up the length of her body. She wanted to touch the bare skin. In the dim light she could see a scar on Drew's left shoulder. She remembered when Drew had injured that shoulder in some bull riding contest and required surgery. Jordan wanted to kiss every inch of the scar. A soft moan escaped before she could stop it. She had never wanted anything or anyone this much.

A sheet covered the lower part of Drew's body but her bare feet had crept out. She was lying on her stomach, a pillow clutched in her left arm. As she turned to her side, she pulled the pillow tight against her chest, almost as if she needed to feel safe.

Jordan slipped into the room, shutting the door, like her life, behind her. She crossed into Drew's bathroom and undressed. Seeing a T-shirt hanging on the back of the door, she slipped it on, enjoying the familiar smell. The simple act of putting on Drew's shirt warmed Jordan from the inside and gave her courage.

"Here goes," Jordan whispered, walking into the darkened room. She climbed into the bed and slowly moved up against Drew's back. Her heart raced. The reality was so much sweeter than her dreams of Drew had been. She buried her nose in dark, curly hair and smelled Drew's shampoo. She gently placed her hand on Drew's shoulder. *My parents are wrong*, she thought. *How can anything this wonderful be a sin or perversion?* She took a deep breath and basked in sensual delight. She allowed her hand to slowly move down Drew's arm.

Drew's first awareness was the warmth against her back. As if her own dreams had been answered, she turned and pulled Jordan into her arms. The familiar delicate, sweet perfume was a safe smell. She kissed Jordan's forehead, her cheek, her eyes.

The grin growing across Jordan's face could've lit up the room. She felt at home. She felt loved. She could start to put the years of being lost and awkward behind her. If Drew didn't want to be in her future, she would survive, even though she would hurt for a long time. But at last she knew she belonged in the arms of a woman. She whispered, "This woman."

Jordan lowered her head to Drew's shoulder and rested her arm across Drew's bare waist. Drew's arm pulled her closer and she sighed, allowing her body to relax into peaceful slumber.

"I'm home."

❖

Drew finally surfaced from her exhausted but trouble-free sleep. As she came fully awake, she realized a woman was draped across her. The woman moaned and cuddled closer. *Jordan!* Many evenings she and Jordan had fallen asleep on the bed watching TV, but they had both been completely dressed. Drew's breath caught as Jordan's lips moved near her breast, sending a warm breath of air across the now aroused nipple. She couldn't help but respond and moaned softly.

"Mmm. Does that mean you're in the world of the living?" Jordan shifted and kissed her. "Oh, God, Drew."

Drew smiled and Jordan sought her mouth. Their legs entwined and Jordan held her breath as Drew's tongue circled her lips. Jordan pulled back, gasping for air.

"Are you awake or asleep?" Jordan asked.

"I don't know. I don't care as long as this dream doesn't end soon." Slowly opening her eyes, Drew looked into Jordan's eyes. "Jordan, do you know what you're doing? Are you sure?"

"I wasn't sure until I was lying next to you and felt how wonderful this is. I don't know what I'm doing." Blushing, Jordan hesitated and rethought what she needed to say. "I mean I'm not sure what I'm supposed to do, but I know what I want to do. Help me." Then letting her heart lead, she said, "I love you, Drew Hamilton. And whether you want me or not, I know I am a lesbian." The familiar, dimpled smile encouraged her. "I'm just an inexperienced lesbian."

"Actually, a virgin lesbian," Drew stated. "But who cares about the details." The pained look crossing Jordan's face caused Drew to quickly add, "But I'm sure you're as fast a learner at this as you are at everything else you tackle."

The addition did little to relieve Jordan's fears. "I'm scared. Suppose I can't...I mean what if..." The blush creeping up her neck quickly covered her entire face and she tried to turn away.

Drew turned Jordan's chin back, forcing Jordan to look at her. "I'm sure everything will be fine."

"I wish I had more experience now. I'm afraid I'll screw it up."

Drew couldn't control her laughter. Jordan's obvious embarrassment was evident, but it made Drew want to protect her. "Oh, Jordan, whether we make love or not, you're my friend first and foremost, and you make me very happy. Come here."

"But I want to make love with you." Emboldened, Jordan kissed the breast beneath her lips and again heard a soft moan. Delighted at the response, she blew softly across the darkened nipple and then kissed around its edge. "Mmm. This is wonderful."

"Damn, that feels good. Are you sure you haven't been taking lessons?" Rolling her over, Drew slipped her knee between Jordan's thighs and leaned down for a kiss. "Have I told you how beautiful you are?"

"Not lately."

Drew kissed along Jordan's jaw, beginning at one ear and going to the other. When Jordan lifted her head to give easier access, Drew pushed down to the collar of Jordan's shirt and planted tender kisses across her collarbone. "I've dreamed of this for such a long time." Drew kissed her way back up Jordan's neck and to her ear. "I've wanted to kiss you and touch you for so long. I've wanted to feel you moving beneath me."

The warm breath was an electric current sending pleasant shocks along Jordan's aroused nervous system. Drew's words turned up the current and Jordan began to slide against the thigh gently pressing her crotch. She clutched Drew's shoulders and kissed her. This time with more intensity. With more urgency. "Drew, make love to me. Please."

Immediately Drew straddled Jordan, pulling her into a sitting position, never losing eye contact. The desire reflected in the gray eyes warmed her. She smiled and lifted Jordan's T-shirt, pulling it off. Drew gazed down at the full, lush body. She groaned with a rush of desire and Jordan self-consciously crossed her arms across her bare chest. Drew leaned back and gazed into Jordan's eyes. "Jordan, you're so beautiful. Let me look at you. Please."

Jordan was startled by Drew's soft words but she saw the truth and the desire on Drew's face. No one had ever thought she was beautiful. Slowly she put her arms down and leaned back, her elbows on the bed supporting her. She watched as Drew slowly caressed one breast.

"I never imagined anything as beautiful and wonderful as this. I've died and gone to heaven." Drew leaned down and briefly sucked the full breast, feeling the nipple harden in her mouth. She leaned back to watch it darken.

Jordan tilted her head, her hair falling back. She closed her eyes and concentrated on the amazing feelings her new lover was arousing. Whatever doubts and fear she might have had were quickly slipping away.

As Drew rubbed the one erect nipple with the palm of her hand, she softly stroked the other one. "God, you are so beautiful. I wish I were an artist and could paint you."

Jordan's eyes flew open. Something was stuck in her throat. She tried to swallow. Tears slipped from her eyes. She wrapped her arms around her lover's neck and pulled them both down to the bed. "I…oh, God! Drew…"

"What is it?" Drew caressed Jordan's cheek, wiping away a tear with her thumb. "What's the matter, sweetheart?"

"I've never thought I was, you know…cute." Jordan recalled some of the names she had heard growing up, especially when she had to wear glasses, but always out of range of her parents' hearing. "I…I'm overwhelmed."

"Jordan, I've always told you that you were attractive."

"Yes, but I…I had clothes on and thought I did a good job of hiding my body."

Drew's laughter brought a smile to the distraught Jordan. "Jordan, look at me." She waited until Jordan finally met her gaze. "You are a beautiful, sexy woman. I love your curves and softness." To emphasize her words she placed tender kisses on each breast, the slightly rounded stomach, the curving hips. "Even more, you're beautiful inside. Your gentleness, your tenderness. I love you, Jordan. In spite of who your parents are." Drew laughed as she added the last statement, then slowly licked salty tears from the damp eyelashes. "I love you," Drew whispered softly as she placed her hand over her heart and then moved it to Jordan's.

"I love you, Drew." Jordan placed her hand on top of Drew's. Tears, this time joyous ones, slid down her face. "I love you." She ran her hand through the thick, curly hair. "I." She kissed one eye. "Love." She kissed the other eye. "You." She kissed the soft tempting lips, this time capturing Drew in a deeper, harder kiss.

Drew felt the wetness as her thigh slid against Jordan's center. She wanted to please Jordan. She slowly rained kisses down Jordan's body, listening to her breathing, gauging her level of arousal. As she kissed down Jordan's stomach, she felt Jordan tense. She slowed her kissing and pulled herself up to enjoy Jordan's warm mouth again.

"Drew, this is incredible, but…I…" Jordan hesitated. How did she ask for what she needed if she wasn't sure what it was? "Please, I need you to help me."

"Whatever you want, or don't want, don't be afraid to tell me."

"That's the problem. I don't know what to ask for."

Smiling, Drew slowly moved her thigh and placed her hand over Jordan's center. When Jordan pushed up into her, she ran a finger softly along the length of Jordan's clit. The rapid intake of breath encouraged her. "Let me know if there is anything that bothers you."

"If you don't do something soon, I will definitely be bothered."

"I thought you already were."

Jordan pressed against Drew's hand, closing her eyes, giving herself over to the arousal now growing within her. As Drew increased the strength of her stroking, Jordan began to float. When one finger, then a second was slowly inserted, Jordan gasped. Her body began to quiver. She was glad she was sharing this moment with Drew. *With this woman*, she reminded herself. With the woman she loved and trusted.

Drew increased the pressure on Jordan's clit, her thumb circling and pushing, while she slowly slid in and out of her lover. For the first time in her life, she felt truly connected, a deep, centered emotion. She wanted more than to just please Jordan. She wanted to be the one to arouse Jordan, to take her to a place of incredible pleasure, to drown her in love. "Come," she whispered.

Jordan pushed her hips against Drew's hand, the tension within her body so taut she feared she was going to explode. Shaking with the onset of her first orgasm, she wrapped her legs and arms around Drew and tightened around the fingers inside her. She gasped and let go, her body soaring. When she was able to loosen her hold, Jordan fell back on the bed.

"Good heavens," she struggled to get out, her breathing erratic, "I don't know what happened, but I want to do that again." She paused, panting. "After I rest."

Drew smiled, her heart full. Jordan's eyes glistened, love written all over her face. "God, I love you."

"I love you," Jordan whispered and tightened her embrace. "I want to show you how much." Jordan rolled to her side, pushing Drew onto her back. Drew was lean and muscular, all angles and flat planes...and scars. She slowly touched the scar on Drew's chin, the one she had caused when they first met. She had felt so clumsy when she nearly tripped and banged into Drew's chin, blood quickly spurting everywhere. "I'm so sorry about this."

Drew clasped Jordan's hand. "And the one on the back of my head?" Jordan nodded. "And the one on my leg?" Jordan again nodded. Drew placed Jordan's hand over her left breast. "And how about the one in my heart?"

Jordan felt the nipple hardening under hand. She could barely swallow. Her excitement grew as she squeezed Drew's breast and heard her groan. "It can't be any bigger than the one in my heart." Jordan took a deep breath, this time, easily gathering her courage, knowing Drew loved her. "Help me to please you."

Her eyes closed, Drew barely whispered, "You're off to a great start." She moaned. "I doubt," she inhaled deeply as Jordan pulled on her nipple, "that there's anything you can do that won't please me."

Jordan's touches were tentative but grew bolder as she realized she was the one causing Drew's plaintive pleas. Recalling what Drew had done, she slowly explored her body. Moving her hands over Drew's stomach, she was amazed at the firmness of the muscles underlying the soft, smooth skin. When Drew moaned, Jordan felt the wetness building between her own legs again. Aroused, she wanted to make love to Drew. She wondered if Drew was as wet.

"Help me," Jordan pleaded.

"I want you to touch me." Drew pulled Jordan's hand down and placed it over her clit. "Here. Touch me here."

Jordan loved the reaction to her stroking Drew's center. Seeing and hearing the effects of her touches, Jordan's reserve faded. She became more adventurous, exploring the wetness and sliding into Drew for the first time. Her sharp intake of breath gave Jordan all the encouragement she needed. She plunged deeper and quickened her movements.

"Yes, baby. Please, I want to feel you sucking my breast as I come."

Jordan took the small, firm breast in her mouth while moving her fingers in and out. When she finally brought Drew to orgasm, Jordan felt such joy she could barely breathe.

"God, I can't believe how wonderful you feel," Drew uttered as she turned to see the morning sun peeking through the shutters. The love in her heart was nearly as bright. "I love you, Jordan Thompson." She laughed and hugged Jordan. "You are absolutely amazing."

Jordan blushed. Her face a bright red, Jordan tried to bury her head in Drew's shoulder.

Seeing this vulnerability, Drew instantly wanted to protect her. She lifted Jordan's head so that she could see into her eyes. "You are the most amazing woman I know and right now, I want to make love to you again."

Jordan's groan was all the answer she needed. Drowning Jordan in passionate kisses, Drew caressed the gentle curves and swells of Jordan's stomach and hips, dancing around the curls covering her warm center.

"Please," Jordan begged, well aware of what pleased her. She grabbed Drew's hand and moved it down.

"Anything for you." Drew found the already firm clitoris and began to stroke it. Jordan's hips joined the dance in slow, languid rhythm, an overture, a waltz of enticement. Drew's hand slipped to the warm well and one finger dipped in, teased, and retreated. Two fingers moved to the entrance. Breathing faster, the two dancers moved to the increasing beat. "You're so wet. I can't believe how good you feel."

"Drew, please. Don't stop." The pace of the dance changed. Jordan's hips thrust against her lover's hand. A faster tempo. She kissed Drew's neck, then buried her face there. "Please. Oh, Drew…" Talking was difficult. "You feel so good."

"Relax, baby. Just enjoy." Drew stroked the swollen clitoris and slipped inside. She felt Jordan tightening around her fingers. The final movement of the dance was set.

"Trust me?" Drew asked.

"Yes," Jordan answered breathlessly.

Drew slid down, kissing Jordan's stomach and thighs before sliding between her legs. She kissed Jordan's swollen clitoris, then gently sucked.

Jordan had never known such exquisite pleasure. Moving against Drew's mouth, she pushed, seeking more pressure.

"Drew, I need to feel you in me, too."

Jordan grabbed Drew's shoulders, her hips dancing to the melody her partner had set. Every nerve in her body was singing. Everywhere Drew's body touched hers, Jordan's skin was on fire. Jordan danced until finally she felt an explosive release. Her legs tightened against Drew, trapping her lover's fingers in her orgasmic spasms.

"Enough, I need to breathe," Jordan whispered. *How can this be even better? Can I die from too much?* When Drew crawled up next to her, Jordan finally collapsed on the bed. She felt strong arms pull her close, safely wrapping her in their love.

Whatever happened after today, Jordan was sure she could handle. They would have to be discreet, at least for a while—her life was constantly under inspection and this wonderful, new love needed to be sheltered and allowed time to grow. Despite the challenges, she had faith that together, they would work everything out. Until then, Drew loved her and that was all she needed.

Lisa Girolami is the author of *Love on Location* and *Run to Me*. She has been in the entertainment industry since 1979 and holds a BA in fine art and an MS in psychology. She spent ten years as production executive in the motion picture industry and another two decades producing and designing theme parks for Walt Disney and Universal Studios and is currently a counselor at a GLBTQ mental health facility in Garden Grove. Her next novel, *The Pleasure Set*, is forthcoming in 2010. www.LisaGirolami.com.

FINDING GRACE
LISA GIROLAMI

I am going tonight. I have been both dreading and anticipating this evening for weeks. How I could ever have talked myself into finding love where only sex exists is a mystery to my sense of logic and modesty. But where Grace is concerned, logic and modesty have flown right out the window.

I am going tonight because I know she will be there. She is there every Friday night. Le Spot sits in the Latin Quarter of Paris, in the fifth arrondissement, and it is a sex house. Off Rue Mouffetard and down a small, winding street, Le Spot serves as a lesbian sanctuary for clandestine and anonymous sexual encounters. This private club offers seven themed rooms for women to frequent while seeking a lover for the night, away from the pretense and negotiation that conventional coupling entails. Beds, couches, floor pillows, and other furniture provide resting places for legs and backs and pulsing bodies. Loud music throbs throughout, but moans and screams of orgasms manage to punch through the ever-present beat.

And I want none of that.

I have a membership there because that is the only way one can gain access. A two-week waiting period is required for membership in order to verify the applicants' references and to protect the club's illicit existence. I got a membership to escape my life and my failed attempts at relationships. There were too many communication struggles and misunderstandings and hurtful words. I wanted to be around women, but I didn't want to go through the technicalities of flirting or dating or even asking for a phone number. My first night there, however, I quickly realized that I wanted none of the anonymous sex either, and had decided then that my first night would be my last.

Tonight marks the fifteenth time I have gone back.

I have been going to Le Spot for four months because I see Grace each time. I have never touched another woman there, only watched. I used to watch many of the trysts and couplings through dark illumination and murky clouds of smoke, but now, all I watch is Grace.

I have fallen in love with this woman. I don't know where she lives, what she does for a living, or even how she arrives at Le Spot. But she captivated me from the first moment and I knew I had to have her in my life. I once paid the receptionist twenty francs to tell me about the woman with the black hair and red dragon back tattoo, but all I got was her first name.

I have watched Grace watching other women. She never touches any of them either. I have seen her intently gaze at the intimate pairings but I have also observed her, more often than not, sitting or standing by herself, deep in preoccupied contemplation. My attraction to her is not just from a physical sense, though she is striking. There is something about the way she holds herself, with confidence and quiet certainty. It's the way she considers everything around her with meaningful regard that compels me to know more.

Each night that I come here, I learn something new about her. In every nuance of her expression, I see a different emotion. When she inhales deeply, I sense her desire to experience life. When she elegantly lifts her fingers to glide a lock of hair behind her ear, I know that she is a gentle lover.

Tonight, as I change into the requisite blue towel, my heart beats faster, for I know that this night will not be for watching only. I have to talk with Grace. I have to finally see if this woman is all that I have imagined. I know every inch of her body, for I have seen her from afar and, at times, followed her from room to room. I have memorized her stances, I have her expressions and reactions committed to memory. But I have gleaned all I can from her exterior. Now I must know what she holds on the inside.

I long to sit down beside her and let her know that I am not doing so for a physical connection. She's too incredible for that. I want to know her life story. I want to understand her fears and grasp her dreams. I find her in the cave room, themed after the catacombs, Paris's vast network of subterranean tunnels. One lightbulb with a metal cage around it gives off just enough light to make out shapes but not enough to see faces. She is standing against the rockwork wall, a few feet away from two pairs of women who are too intent in their nameless union to notice her. Grace follows the same pattern as always, watching but not advancing, contemplating but not open to involvement.

As I move around the opposite side of the room I notice that the writhing, naked bodies serve as an abstract canvas around her. She is detached from the activities but enveloped in the ambience. I can feel her swathed in the enigmatic vibe because we both move to it in the same way.

My desire to walk toward her is strong but it is too dark, so I must wait. Next, I go to the Versailles room, its soft candlelight illuminating elegant gilded furniture and marble floors and walls. There is only one couple lying on the large bed, so I make my way over to a love seat in the corner and sit.

Closing my eyes, I feel the soft velour against my back and thighs. I picture Grace with her solid shoulders and beautiful neck. I have never been close enough to detect the color of her eyes, but I imagine them to be brown. Her black hair makes that a likely possibility, and the exact brown I picture is mahogany. Her face is slightly rounded and her mouth, though I've never seen it smile, must look exquisite when she is happy.

I open my eyes and blink suddenly. I am not prepared to see Grace standing in the doorway. Her attention is not on the prone couple. She is now contemplating me. I draw in a breath, not sure what to do next. I have made a pledge to know Grace, but my gut now tells me to stay where I am.

And then I begin to understand why. She needs time to take me in. Like a bluebird that alights in your garden, Grace requires a slow means of approach. As she watches me, I try not to change my expression. I do not want to show the craving, for I may scare her away, and I do not want to show my apprehension, for it may send the wrong message. She is not objectively scrutinizing me, nor is she staring. She is absorbing me, my body language, my soul. She is taking time to assimilate all that she has observed over these weeks and months of Fridays, and I am hopeful she will reach the same conclusion that I have.

As the bedded women begin an evident journey toward climax and their cries of pleasure begin to grow, Grace and I remain a distance away from each other, but solely connected.

For the longest time, we look at each other, her blue towel wrapped around her chest and falling to just above her knees, and I in my blue towel that hugs my waist. And then, with a slight lift of her chin, an almost imperceptible gesture but one that crashes into me with extreme significance, I know that she has completed her assessment.

I lift off the love seat, as unsure as I am sure, and I cover the distance between us in six life-changing steps.

"Your eyes are not mahogany but chestnut," I say, as if she were aware of my imaginings.

"And yours have been watching me."

"Yes." I want to tell her that I have fallen in love with her from the first day I saw her. She may think the notion is ridiculous given the fact that we have never actually met, but I cannot belie my heart. My secret truth has been at this club every Friday for four months.

"You're here every Friday," she says, piercing my eyes with hers.

I nod that she is correct.

Will she think me a stalker? I have never made advances toward her, which in a sex club is the antithesis of what one could consider normal behavior. I pray she doesn't find me discomforting for that reason. I wonder if she thinks of me as a just another shadow among the sexual players, a voyeur seeking some peculiar, solitary pleasure.

"You never talk to anyone or touch anyone." Her observation is, again, accurate.

I wait, not knowing what she will say next. My heart hammers again, just as it had when I arrived.

"When you first started coming, I noticed you right away," she says. "You fascinated me. And that night I began to hope that you would not go off with anyone. I knew that was not likely, but you didn't. I was here that first night only because I wanted to see what it was like. I would not have come back after that one visit, but then I saw you."

Could this be possible? She had experienced the same as I.

She continues. "I came back the next Friday and you were here again. And again, you didn't touch anyone."

"And I came back for the same reason," I say.

She smiles and I am right, it is exquisite.

Suddenly, we are more exposed than we have been for months. It has nothing to do with the meager towels covering our bodies. There are no secrets between us. Our true selves are now revealed without pretense or disguise.

"I want you." I am more sure than I've ever been.

"You mean my heart." It is a statement, not a question.

"Yes."

She takes my hand in hers. This first touch I will always remember. She leads me to a hallway, away from the themed rooms that are now beginning to fill up given that it is late. I know she wants to find a private place for us and I am more than willing to go anywhere with her.

We lean against the wall, face-to-face. The painted concrete is cold against my shoulder.

"I have been waiting," I say.

"For me?"

"No, for me. To finally approach you, that is." I know this conversation is profound and bordering on impractical, but I must continue. "You seem so out of place here. But this is the only frame of reference I have of you. I have never seen you in the daylight. I haven't seen you eat or run or laugh. But what I have seen, I am drawn to."

In her chestnut eyes I see welcome anticipation. She wants to see where this will go. And then she says, "May I kiss you?"

Furtively and softly, we kiss. I feel her lips part and I open my mouth to hers. Our tongues touch chastely at first, and then we grow bolder, dancing with precise harmony to the same rhythmic sonata.

I draw the warmth of her mouth into mine and I feel her from the inside. Her breath becomes mine, and our life forces merge. We offer ourselves to each other through our kisses, inhaling each other's essence, and in that moment I know more about her than a hundred coffee dates or dinners could divulge. I see her as a child, playing in her parents' backyard, and I see her in her teen years, excited about the new school year. I see all the days that led up to the first night I saw her. In one kiss, I thoroughly comprehend this woman I've just met.

Our hands stay respectfully around each other's backs, not venturing any further because a show of corporeal intent would ruin this moment. And I don't need to feel her breasts or anywhere lower because I will have time later. We are joined right now in a complete way, face-to-face, nose to nose, with the unbelievable rightness of our bodies offered to one another. Her tongue accepting mine is the deepest bond we can forge. Our awareness of each other, body and soul, is absolute.

We part lips and pull back to check each other's reaction. Her chin is down and she looks at me evocatively from under her eyebrows.

I suddenly laugh, realizing the paradox of the situation. "We've seen each other for months in a place where everyone is having sex, and yet we have just now touched."

"To do nothing all those Friday nights was to learn everything about you," she says. "And now I want to live the rest."

Could this be happening? How did it come about that a woman I had only gazed at turned into the woman I know I am to be with?

But as I look back over my weekly sojourns to this place, an incredible realization overcomes me. Simply, words and physicality did not get in our way. We did not travel down the path of anecdotes and meaningless narratives, nor did we succumb to a physical imperative, resulting only in orgasm. This total connection that we share comes purely from silent, unadorned observation. With only our eyes, we discovered our intimate truths, unclouded by subterfuge and physical need. And when we finally did touch, we were already known to each other.

Finding Grace in a French sex house is my reason for being, and we will now abide by our destiny.

CLARA NIPPER lives in Oklahoma and enjoys fine dining, bubble baths, long walks, and playing with her dogs, Virginia Woof and Bark Twain. Her Bold Strokes novels include *Femme Noir* and the forthcoming *Kiss of Noir*. Kids, stay in school!

SENTIMENTAL FOOL
CLARA NIPPER

I opened my grandmother's refrigerator for iced tea. She made the very best iced tea I had ever tasted. I noticed a bowl of nectarines on the bottom shelf.

"Grama?"

"Yes, honey?" She didn't look up from her quilting.

"Why do you always buy fifteen nectarines?"

Grama's head raised and she stared out the window with a small, sad smile on her face. "Because I'm a sentimental fool, that's why." She returned to her needlework.

"What's that?" I thought I knew what a fool was; Todd always made a fool of himself during study period, but I wasn't sure about the other. I couldn't imagine Grama acting like Todd. I loathed him. He was cute.

As I asked her, Grama's eyes were sharp behind her glasses. She put down her quilt. It was for me when she finished it. She even put bits of my favorite outgrown clothes into the pattern. Grama had told me the quilt was a double wedding ring design and I hated the sound of that, but she assured me I would appreciate it someday. I sipped my tea. You couldn't push Grama, not one inch.

"Lemons in a bowl on the counter if you're of a mind," she said.

"Okay," I answered lightly. I slowly rolled one of the plump fruit on the table to loosen its juice. I resisted the urge to add "ma'am." Grama didn't respect suck-ups. I carefully carved a slice of lemon and squeezed it into my tea. Grama made this tea just for me. She never drank it. Claimed not to like it. I waited.

"A sentimental is one who values romantic memories very highly."

"What romantic memories?" Grama had once sneaked a kiss on someone like Greg's delectable cheek during recess? Grama had once had someone like Douglas give her his art project? Grama had had valentines stuffed in her locker? Grama had had her house papered by all the boys on Halloween? Just like a grown-up, speaking in riddles. Just say it! Just tell me!

"Romantic memories like…" Grama's voice suddenly sounded like a choir of angels singing, as if they had finally been set free. "Romantic memories like…" She stopped and looked hard at me. I never felt more like an adult than I did then by not squirming under her stare.

"I don't know if you're old enough to hear this, but here goes. I want to tell it. If your mom gets mad about it, send her to me; don't let her yell at you."

"Okay." I wiggled my rear deeper into the carpet. This would be good.

"I buy fifteen nectarines at a time because I once asked someone, as a favor, to buy me a dozen nectarines, and this person brought me a lovely basket with fifteen nectarines in it. And this person told me I should always have more than I wanted."

That was it? That was romantic? I stared at my tea disappointed. The cubes floated lazily. Frost drops slid down the glass. Should I conceal my disinterest by asking questions?

Grama snorted. "That's not all, come with me." Grama shot out of her rocking chair. Grama was a tough old bird. My mother said she was still as strong as a man. I left my tea and followed her into the backyard. Grama had made it into a wildlife sanctuary. She started it years ago with one bat house and a few bird boxes, and now, it was completely alive. On different visits, I had seen lightning bugs, ladybugs, horny toads, frogs, butterflies, and hummingbirds. Grama called them hummers. She tossed me out here whenever she was sick of me watching television when I visit. Grama told me she made it into a habitat because there was nobody to mow the grass anymore. I told her about Paul, a boy in my neighborhood who did it, but she smiled, patted me on the head, and said that wasn't what she meant.

Sometimes, she let me help her weed and plant, but she was very picky. Occasionally, she was bossy and didn't even notice. But she let me eat her blackberries and strawberries as long as I left some for the birds and turtles. There is nothing like a sweet, sun-hot berry. Even with dust, it was better than candy.

We came to an old apple tree. Grama caressed the smooth bark. "See that?" Her hands were bony and roped with veins. I squinted and raised myself on tiptoes.

"Is that a heart carved there?" I looked at her in wonder. Grama smiled in satisfaction.

"Yes, that's another romantic memory."

I scratched the bark. "What's that other thing?" It looked like an eight lying down.

"The symbol for infinity, or forever." Grama's voice sounded funny and I stared at her with my mouth open. Her eyes were soft and liquidy. I got the feeling that she was pushing me to understand this. I could only drink it in gradually. Grama looked up into the tree, staring fixedly at the leaves. I was scared she would start crying. What do you do when your Grama cries? I didn't even know what she would be crying about. I held my breath.

"We had thirty-five love-filled years together," Grama stated at last. "Died the year before you were born. You, little one, helped me through the worst time of my life and you didn't know it. Your mother was generous enough to let me care for you all the time and ease my sore heart."

I swallowed and leaned against the tree. "Was it Grampa?" I whispered. I had never had one; I sometimes wondered what that would be like. A gnarled, wrinkly man with bushy eyebrows. Ornery and playful, but nice and gentle. One who taught me Old Secrets.

"No." Grama smiled strangely. I felt confused and shocked. Grama must have had a grampa because she had Mom. Who was it if not a grampa? White-haired people were supposed to be predictable and conservative.

"Who was it?" I never stopped to think I was too nosy. I had to find out.

"Sara." Grama waited for me to catch up.

"Mom? It was Mom?" That was Mom's name. My head was spinning.

"No, it wasn't your mother. I named your mother after her. Sara was my spouse, Sara Kate."

"Kate! That's my name!"

"Yes, it is, punkin, and it fits you. Your mother also loved her dearly. Sara and I were your mother's parents. I had a baby, your mom, with Sara. We raised her together."

I frowned. "But in Biology—"

"Yes, yes," Grama said impatiently. "I know. I promise I'll explain all that later. Right now, I'm explaining why I'm a sentimental fool. Come inside." Grama took off for the house without looking back.

I was slow to move from the tree. I looked at the heart and the infinity symbol again. I felt Grama had purified me somehow. Blasted all my rust off. All my thoughts were new born. I felt different. I was excited. I was on the brink of an adventure. Grama felt about a woman the way I felt about boys. That was okay. But I was richer now for knowing. Wiser and more textured. My heart felt bigger. I heard the back door slam. I hurried to follow.

I found her in an unused bedroom on the bed she kept impeccably made. She was examining the contents of a huge, dusty box. I sat down.

"What's all this?"

"More sentiment. Beautiful memories." Grama dabbed her nose with a wadded tissue. "Here." She handed me a stuffed duck like a Beatrix Potter character. "I have hundreds of ducks in every shape, size, and form. We called each other names. Do you do that with boys?"

"Kind of," I hedged with a smile.

"Well, I was her Puddles and she was my Puddleduck."

"That's cute," I said. Our eyes met over the box. I felt sad for her. I ached, wanting to fill some of Sara's void so Grama wouldn't feel so sad. How could I comfort her?

"Here are some of our love letters." Grama lifted out stacks of envelopes bound with grosgrain ribbons. "We were very prolific." She laughed, shaking her head. "Here are some souvenirs of trips we took… here's a pair of earrings she gave me…here's the shirt I wore the first time we kissed…this ring," Grama held out her hand, "is one she designed and had made for me. See that opal in the center? That's older than your mother or father. Sara gave it to me on our first anniversary."

I studied the things eagerly, wanting to inhale it all. I didn't want this story to end. I wanted to hear how they lived happily every after, and then, see Sara sitting on the bed with Grama.

Grama sure was different than my other old relatives, who sported blue hair and wiglets and were always discussing illness.

"Why is all this stuff put away?" I tenderly held a tiny, beautiful jade carving.

"Kate, when you lose someone, there's an enormous amount of pain. Sara and I didn't have nearly enough time together. When she died, it was too hard to live with these things staring at me all the time. I cherish them, and would defend this box with my life, but it was just too hard. So I put them away hoping I would go soon after her and be with her again. Then you were born. Maybe she sent you for me. But it's evident I'm not going to die soon, so I think it's time to unpack her, don't you?"

"Yes!" I felt I was discovering a long-lost sibling in Sara. Twelve years she had been waiting to come out of this box. Shyly, I said, "In Sunday school, they say angels watch over us from heaven. Maybe Sara is."

Grama put a shaking hand to her brow. "Yes, I hope so. I want to believe that. I have a talk with her every night. Sometimes, I ask her to pass messages to God. At first, all I did was cuss her for dying, but not anymore. Now I just pretend she's in bed with me, her head next to mine, and I tell her I love and miss her and just talk." Grama finally looked up and smiled. "That's why I still make tea. I'm glad you like it. Sara loved it. But do you know what was her favorite drink?"

"No…" I thought of my other ancient family. "Coffee?"

"No, green Kool-Aid!" Grama's cheeks were pink.

"Ick! Gross!" I laughed. Sara sounded cool. "My favorite is grape," I told Grama, who already knew this.

Grama shrugged. "I don't have a favorite." Her eyes twinkled.

"Grama," I took the plunge before I got scared and backed out, "isn't it gross to kiss a girl?" I stared hard at my hands. My knee trembled. Grama laughed and patted my hair. I looked up.

"Isn't kissing boys gross right now too?" she asked.

I thought about it. The fun was in being chased, and the risk of getting in trouble, and the breathless excitement. The kisses themselves were actually tight little pecks barely touching hot cheeks. And they were all I wanted for now. Anything more was icky. "Yes, I guess so," I answered.

"Well, that's natural. Later, you'll be attracted to someone and find pleasure in kissing him. So, don't worry; you won't always find it gross. And for me, Sara was the only woman I ever kissed. And we were so happy to do that. It was good for us, like vitamins. We fit together like puzzle pieces. As long as you do it with someone you love, it is never gross, always great." Grama extracted an envelope. "Look how sentimental I am." She laughed. "I even saved her hair. I cut some before she was cremated." Grama peered in the envelope. She put her nose to the edge and sniffed. She touched inside with one long thin finger. "Oh, well, that's that." She replaced the envelope.

I was scared to look at a dead person's hair. I was curious about Sara, though. "What did she look like?"

Grama rummaged in the box. "Here's one of my pictures."

The photograph was of a woman and Grama many years before. Grama had been beautiful! I looked carefully at Grama, then looked at the photo again. They had their arms around each other and the first thing that struck me was: Happy. They're happy. Grama's mouth was wide open in the kind of smile I had never seen. Sara had wise, warm green eyes that calmly met mine. She was grinning big too, and hugging hard on Grama. Sara seemed to have the strength of the earth and Grama the strength of water. They were blissful. I felt pulled into the mystery and storytelling of that photo. "Can I keep this, please?" I held it to my chest trying to be closer to Sara and this new Grama. Grama smiled softly and caressed my hair and jaw in a graceful circle.

"Of course you can. I'm glad you want it."

"You are so pretty. Am I pretty like you? Will I be when I'm finished growing?"

"Sweet baby." I had never heard Grama's voice so tender. Had she spoken to Sara that way? "You are. You are now and you will be later. You'll blossom into a helluva heartbreaker. The trick to beauty is to keep a sense of humor and to keep your heart pure."

This baffled me. But if I was pretty, okay. Everybody says Mom is beautiful; maybe it is, whatyoucallit, genetic. "Can I be a sentimental fool too?"

"Honey," Grama stretched the word into three syllables, "are you sure you want to be?"

"Yes," I answered simply.

"Then count on it. You will be."

I tapped the picture. "Tell me some more?"

"Someday." Grama closed the box and hefted it to carry downstairs. I still sat on the bed, incomplete as yet.

"Grama?" I stared mesmerized at the photo. Looking at it hard enough and long enough might bring more mature understanding. Their joy tugged at me. "Why did you save all this stuff?"

Grama turned and replaced the box on the bed. She held my chin in her hand. "Well, child, to have proof that I once loved and was loved."

SHEA GODFREY is an artist and writer working and living in the Midwest. While her formal education is in journalism and photography, she has spent most of her career thus far in 3D animation and design. Her romantic fantasy novel *Nightshade* is forthcoming from Bold Strokes in 2010.

'47 CHEVAL BLANC
SHEA GODFREY

Finn Starkweather watched Cassandra Marinos step from the limousine, the shadow she cast along the pavement lengthened further by the slant of the lights along Stockton Street.

Finn was fairly certain that should Ms. Marinos be in need of a weapon, most likely even her shadow, like the Prada heels that she wore, might come in handy. Not that Marinos was known for her violence, but she'd certainly added a few names to the walking wounded roster while she'd made her way up the food chain. *The last of which was Terry Bannon, Interpol's resident Ann Coulter with a dick.* Finn smiled with more than a touch of glee. *Two weeks, maybe more, for those tiny glass marbles to drop all over again.*

Casey spoke to the driver briefly and offered an easy smile, her blond hair brushing across her face in a cut that reminded Finn of Veronica Lake. It spilled onto the shoulders of the fawn-colored cashmere she wore against the night chill, looking sinfully soft despite the distance between them. The driver nodded and closed the door as Marinos walked toward the Campton Place Hotel. Finn leaned against the railing of the fire escape two flights up and one building over, her upper body tipping into midair as she tried to see Casey all the way in beneath the hotel awning.

"Maybe you'll fall down her dress."

"Maybe, but I wouldn't have time to see much on the way down," Finn cracked, pushing back and spinning about.

"Are you sure this is going to work?"

"Of course not."

Malik Kaseem smiled and pushed back the brim of his Manchester

United hat. "Just another day of being dragged down the street in Texas."

"Speak for yourself," Finn replied, wanting to laugh but unwilling to give him the edge.

"We could just step up the surveillance, Finn, you don't have to do this."

"We need a better view of the game, plain and simple. When the deal goes down, at the very least we have to be within spitting distance. Even with as much manpower as we can manage, we'll come up short. And besides, I can't think of anything else on such short notice that might play in our favor, can you?"

Something that wouldn't compromise your principles would be nice, Malik considered for the hundredth time. *Or that wouldn't break your heart.* "Not really."

"Let's just do it, then. I'm all grown up and taller than you besides."

"Yes, but are you wearing your clean knickers?"

"Shut up."

"Yes, sir."

"Did you pick out the waiter?"

"Yes. He seems very practiced."

"Why, because he's French and knows a lot about cheese?"

"No, because he didn't ask any questions."

"How do I look?"

Malik took a step back from his partner of eight years and gave her the once-over.

A dark navy Jil Sander suit with bluish gray lapels worn over a pristine white shirt that he and his wife, Anna, had gotten Finn for Christmas. Her matching trousers were cut low and pleated, her silver buckled belt offsetting the harness buckles and rivets on her low-heeled Gucci boots, which she only wore when she was feeling cocky and out for blood. They had been babied over the years as all good leather should be, but they added a rough edge that suited Finn completely. Her soft, black hair was short and spiky about her face and she was as handsome as all hell.

"Don't make me repeat myself. You know I hate repeating myself."

"Sex on a stick, love," Malik answered and then felt a twinge of regret, watching several different emotions darken her eyes. She flashed her trademark grin though and stepped into the punch, her right fist landing hard against Malik's shoulder.

"Go with God, my little bird," he said, wincing.

"Just don't fuck it up," Finn grumbled as she stepped from the fire escape and maneuvered through the open window. "Two weeks of surveillance and it all gets flushed because you can't recognize a magnet the size of a brick."

"That wasn't my fault," he protested beneath his breath.

"What was that?"

He smiled at Finn's raised voice somewhere behind him as he watched the traffic move along Stockton. The plan was never going to work and he knew it. Not because Finn couldn't seduce Casey Marinos into slipping up or rushing her hand, but because he knew Finn would never go through with it. It wasn't her style.

He took his phone out and dialed. "It's Malik," he said in response to the voice on the other end. "Call everyone in, we're kicking ass from the top on down. The deal fell through on this end."

❖

Finn stood just beyond the arch that led to the restaurant, watching Casey Marinos claim her reservation by one of the blue-tinted, etched windows. Her dress was cut low between her breasts and sleek, draped along her body as if the black fabric had spontaneously combusted along her skin in a burst of silk and sexuality. It was a Carolina Herrera original and Finn knew that it would somehow match Casey's dark eyes, though she'd only stared into their depths through the filter of a surveillance camera.

The headwaiter caught Finn's attention for a brief instant and she gave a nod.

Casey accepted the menu and ordered a drink, no doubt the 1998 Clos des Goisses that Finn knew was her favorite at the moment. The waiter would bring a '47 Chateau Cheval Blanc instead. It had cost Finn ten grand for the damn thing, and she'd called in a very old favor besides, but it would be worth it just to see her take that first sip.

Only the best of everything for one of the top ten thieves in the world.

Casey had never been caught and as yet, nothing had ever been proven against her. Years of investigations by private firms and Interpol as well, one after the other, and not a single scrap of evidence had ever been brought to bear. She had yet to make Interpol's Red List, and barring a disaster of epic proportions, Finn doubted she ever would. When a rare work of art went missing, however, any one of Casey's chosen names could be found on every short list in the world. Among certain circles it was no secret who she was or how she made her living.

It had started for Finn in December of 2002, and it had started with Van Gogh.

The police had captured the dynamic duo that had used a ladder splattered with old paint to break into the Van Gogh Museum in Amsterdam, not long after the theft actually, but they'd never recovered the paintings. And while Finn would not have chosen *Scheveningen* or *Nuenen* as Vincent's best, they were worth thirty million collectively and still at large. Elysian Incorporated was on a very big hook for that money and they'd issued a reward that was a dream come true for the safe return of the paintings. Every bounty hunter who could draw a breath had, in one way or another, been on the scent for years.

That was when Finn had first become aware of Cassandra Marinos, though not under that name. She'd gone by Alyssa Stavros at the time and her papers had been without reproach. It had taken Finn nearly six months to dig through the many layers of paint upon Casey's elaborate canvas in order to find the true masterpiece hiding beneath. She'd kept tabs from a distance for years now, patiently waiting for her moment. Eleven months ago that moment had presented itself, and Finn had finally met Cassandra Marinos.

Not in the flesh, never that, though after ten months of intense surveillance she knew more about Casey than she knew about her own blood. She knew what Casey's favorite breakfast food was, and how she took her coffee. She knew what movies made her laugh, and her favorite authors. And she knew that when Casey was heartbroken, she would go to the sea and bide her time until her scars had healed. Finn knew she liked Australian Blue dogs, but her real weakness was for fat cats that liked the sun and too much food. She preferred the Audi to the Lexus, but when it came to speed she went with the Aston Martin, and she had a Vantage GT2 to prove her commitment to the edge. Finn even knew what toothpaste she used.

But she'd never spoken to her face-to-face. She'd never looked into those eyes that were so dark they bordered upon black. She'd never smelled the scent of her hair or tasted the curve of her neck. She had watched her seduce more than her fair share of women over the past year. They were unworthy for the most part, in Finn's opinion. They were careless and shallow in one way or another, and never a match for the depths that Finn saw hiding within Casey, even if she was less than honorable about how she made her living. They were mostly femme and always beautiful, and Finn had yet to see a look of genuine satisfaction upon Casey's face when out and about with any one of them. She remained apart, only giving them what they needed in order to be satisfied. And if they demanded too much, Casey would quietly disappear, though not without a parting gift that might assuage any hard feelings her exodus might incur.

It was one of those gifts that had given Finn her best chance yet of proving her theory that Cassandra Marinos was in possession of what she needed most. And it had put her on Casey's trail in earnest.

A bauble of diamonds and white gold, but it was a trinket worth twenty grand that had been stolen in Amsterdam just two days before the Van Goghs went missing. In Finn's mind, it was no coincidence that a thief of Casey's caliber just happened to be in Amsterdam at the same time the museum job went down. A man named Eric Werner had fenced the remaining items of that well-timed jewel heist, and Eric Werner was the conduit through which Vincent's lost children would have to pass. He was the number one fence in central Europe, not only for Van Gogh, but Picasso, Monet, and Vermeer as well. For the past twenty years he had dealt exclusively in the underground art trade, and Finn knew that for Werner to take the time and energy to wash what would be for him a pittance in stolen ice, there had to be the deal of a lifetime waiting in the wings.

Werner was in San Francisco at that very moment, along with a veritable melting pot of possible buyers from around the world. Most were private collectors that were inclined to skate beneath the radar, but Finn knew exactly who they were despite their discretion.

As she stood there, however, it all seemed incredibly irrelevant.

She couldn't pinpoint exactly when she'd fallen in love with Casey Marinos during the past year, but fallen she had. She didn't need to be told that it was an impossible situation and she didn't stand a chance, even if the circumstances had been different. Casey might've been exactly what Finn ached for within the long dark hours of the night, but she was fairly certain that Casey had other ideas. *She's not why you're here, Finn, get a grip. Eyes on the prize, Boy-o.*

Finn straightened and walked with confidence into the dining room of the Campton Place Restaurant.

Casey Marinos watched the tall butch with a close eye, a smile pulling at her lips. She had known that she was being watched but she hadn't returned the attention, biding her time for the right opportunity. She found the woman utterly gorgeous, though she supposed some might not agree. Her features were strong and clean and from the stark cut of her suit, Casey could see that she had the lean, well-built body to back it up. There were a lot of women who would never find such a masculine energy appealing, but Casey hadn't been so instantly attracted to another woman in years. She seemed familiar, actually, though Casey couldn't quite place her. *And I'm thinking that I would remember you.*

She looked toward the window once more with considerable effort. *Another time, another place, perhaps*, she mused, *and we might play.* She closed her eyes, the storm within her head seeming to ease at just the thought of finding a respite within the strong arms of such a lover. The soft authority of the right top could sway her like nothing else, which was why women like that were far too dangerous.

Finn walked directly to the table and pulled out the empty chair, Casey looking up in genuine surprise.

Finn favored her with a crooked grin and sat down smoothly, leaning back as she crossed her legs. The waiter arrived but a second later, setting two wineglasses on the table as a second server placed the ice bucket beside Finn, the '47 Cheval Blanc nestled within and waiting.

"It's not what you ordered, I'm sure, but I have it on good authority that it's just as good as anything you might find here," Finn said, her heart beating quickly at the dark brown of Casey's eyes. *I was right…* *Sweet Jesus, they're almost black.*

Casey couldn't help but smile, her eyes filled with curiosity as they studied Finn's face close up. Flawless skin with strong features and classic lines. Her hair was a lovely, tousled mess of short, black strands and her dark caramel eyes were filled with warmth and more than a hint of challenge. It was their heat, however, that Casey found instantly compelling, so much so that for a heartbeat, it threw her completely off her game.

Finn poured them each a drink and then lifted her glass with a genuine smile. "My name is Finn O'Connell."

Casey laughed, her eyes lighting up at the sheer audacity of the scene. "O'Connell." Their glasses clinked together. "Something about the strength of a wolf, yes?"

"I don't know, it's all Irish to me," Finn replied. "All's I know is that me gran had a feud with an Angus Boyle across the fence. They used to throw potatoes and curse in Gaelic."

Casey took a drink, liking the hard, quick feel of her pulse. *"Pog mo thoin?"*

Finn laughed, a flush of heat moving along her neck. *Kiss me arse.*

"Good God!" Casey spoke in shock, eyeing her glass with pleasure. "What is this?"

Definitely worth it. "Tell me your name first."

An eyebrow was raised.

"Too bold?"

"I'd say that train left the station without you."

"Yes, but if I'd waited for you, I'd still be standing all alone."

"You think?" Casey asked, letting out a small breath at the crooked grin that moved across Finn's luxurious mouth. It seemed to be a somewhat permanent fixture on her handsome face, aside from being one of the loveliest things that Casey had encountered in a very long time.

"Tell me your name."

Samantha Drake, Casey thought but didn't say. It was on the tip of her tongue, waiting and ready, but she couldn't do it. She liked Samantha. Samantha was always in charge and never at a loss, never in doubt. Samantha was always in control. *Control is an illusion. I don't want control. But I'm thinking that's not what you see, is it, Finn O'Connell.*

"Okay, how about this," Finn offered, setting her glass down and leaning forward. "I buy you dinner and we finish the wine... We could go dancing then, if you'd like, or at least in search of some decent music. There's a place not too far from here, Biscuits an—"

"Blues." Casey smiled, finishing her sentence. "And if I were to tell you that I'm waiting for my husband?"

Finn considered the question. "I'd say..."

Casey waited patiently, wanting to laugh at the careful expression on Finn's face. "Yes?"

"No."

"No?"

"You're so gay I could feel it from across the room."

"And you're never wrong?"

Finn smiled. "Frequently, but not about this."

Casey sipped her wine, distracted by its taste once more and glancing at the bottle. The label was turned away from her, but the bottle was old, sending part of her mind down a different path in search of a vintage.

"Are you ready to order?"

Finn heard the waiter well enough, but she had no intention of looking away from those brown eyes, not now that she had them in her sights. "The salt-crusted Mediterranean branzino, two, if you please."

"Very good, sir."

Both Finn and Casey smiled, Casey looking down to keep from laughing.

Bloody Malik, Finn thought, wishing that she had punched him harder. "Perhaps I should guess, yes?"

"Perhaps you should." Casey's eyes came back up, challenging.

"I'd say Veronica, but that would be too obvious."

"True."

"And besides which, I can't really see you ending up as a bartender in some New York dive while fading into alcoholic obscurity."

"Thank you, I think."

"Don't mention it."

"Perhaps you should just give me a name."

"Rachel?"

Casey frowned.

"You're right. I knew a Rachel once, it was very unpleasant."

"First girlfriend?"

"No, that was Paula."

"What happened to Paula?"

"Too much of a top for my tastes."

"Ah. The age-old conflict of interest."

"I like what I like, and besides, it all worked out in the end."

"Really?" Casey asked. "Don't keep me in suspense, please. What happened to Paula?"

Finn's eyes lit up but she said nothing.

"Top secret?"

"Highly classified. However, I can tell you that it involved balls flying at her face."

Casey stuttered in the midst of taking another drink, swallowing awkwardly as she choked back her laughter.

"She worked the pro tennis circuit."

Casey cleared her throat and took up her napkin. "Of course."

"Football was more my sport."

"Position?"

"Tight end."

Casey resisted the urge to lean forward, an unexpected desire to be closer welling up and sending a pleasant shiver along her spine.

"Tailback?" Finn offered instead.

"No, I'd say tight end is more than fitting."

"Juliette."

"Juliette?"

"Your name." Finn spoke through her grin. "Tell me your name."

"Is that what you want, Daddy?"

Finn almost groaned, reaching for her glass instead.

Casey chuckled and watched her take a drink, liking the telltale blush of color along her neck, knowing somehow that Finn knew it was there and disliked the knowledge. She leaned forward and reached for the bottle, wanting to turn it within the ice and reveal the label.

Finn caught her by the wrist before she could get there, gentle for the most part, but firm enough to establish control. Their eyes met and

Finn changed her grip, letting the tips of her fingers find the underside of Casey's wrist. She could feel Casey's pulse beating hard beneath the soft skin and it made her smile. "Don't be naughty."

Casey pulled her hand away slowly, her fingers sliding along Finn's until they parted.

"It's not such a high price to pay," Finn said.

"It might be dangerous for you."

"Your name?"

"Perhaps."

"I was thinking the other might be more dangerous."

"The other?"

"What if you *do* have a husband?" Finn said. "Here I am making my play, and the next thing I know, someone is punching me in the throat."

Casey laughed. "It doesn't seem like such a high price to pay."

Finn sat back again. "Have you ever been punched in the throat?"

"Not that I can recall."

"It hurts."

"Well, you know what they say, the trick is not minding that it does."

"So you're saying that you're worth it?"

"Am I?"

Finn's crooked grin slipped free. "I wouldn't be sitting here if I didn't think so."

"You look as if you can take care of yourself."

"It's the boots, right? Too butch?"

"Butch, yes, but they work."

Finn leaned to the left a bit and looked at her feet. "I just polished them, actually. It felt like a betrayal of some sort." She looked across the table. "All those years to break them in properly and cultivate some character, and then I go and ruin it."

Finn, Casey thought, a start of recognition following upon the heels of the name. *Finn O'Connell*. "Who punched you in the throat?"

"Rachel's husband."

Casey felt a pleasing ache within her cheeks, uncertain of the last time she had smiled so much. "Was he big?"

Finn's brow went up. "How big do you have to be?"

"A big, bad daddy such as yourself? I'd say pretty big."

Finn said nothing, but neither did she look away. The sounds of the restaurant filled the atmosphere around them, though it did very little to invade upon their quiet connection. Several conversations could be heard, one about local politics and the other crucifying some poor bastard still trading in derivatives. The music was Bach, playing low, but it was still loud enough to be heard should anyone care to listen.

"He wasn't that big," Finn responded at last. "But he caught me by surprise."

"Didn't know, or didn't expect him?" Casey asked gently, thinking that perhaps Finn was telling the truth. Her eyes were too open and she had no reason to lie, even if they were playing.

"Didn't know, actually." Finn grinned ruefully. "I was stepping out of the shower at the time."

"Ouch."

"Not one of my better moments," Finn agreed.

"Then my name shall not be Rachel."

Finn thought she heard a tender inflection within Casey's tone, and it made her blood run hot and smooth. "Thank you."

"You're most welcome, Finn."

"Tell me your name," Finn demanded with quiet authority.

Casey was about to say it, the letters tumbling and sliding together upon her tongue and pressing eagerly toward her lips. *Casey*, she thought, willing them into life after sleeping for so very long. She was about to, but another name intruded before she had the chance. *Finnegan.*

"What?" Finn asked, seeing Casey's eyes deepen in color.

"Finn…is that your full name?"

"It's short for Finnegan, actually."

Casey considered the name in silence, never looking away as the fingers of her right hand caressed the stem of her wineglass. *Finnegan… bloody hell. Finn Starkweather.*

"I didn't pick it," Finn said, trying to decipher Casey's expression.

I thought you were a man. "Don't worry, I like it."

"I wish I could return the favor."

"Is this your usual scene, Finn?" she asked softly. "Because if it is, it's very good."

Finn considered the question and then looked down. She narrowed her eyes upon the fabric of the tablecloth, pushing a finger at a small knot within the weave. She hadn't been sure how all of this was going to pan out before she'd made her play, but now, in the midst of it, she found herself utterly certain. She could smell Casey's cologne and it was subtle and earthy, her mind clinging to the well-worn fantasy of how Casey's skin would taste. Only now that she could actually smell her cologne, things had shifted and her curiosity had been reborn with different colors and intonations. *I've got to be the dumbest fucking idiot in the world*, she thought, closing her eyes. She had wanted this for so long, just to look across the table at such a complex and beautiful woman. Though it was not just any woman that she had been wanting, it was Casey. She wanted Casey. If they were going to play, it would have to be fair.

When Finn looked up, her expression was completely without guile and the words were out of her mouth before she could stop them. "No scene, just you."

Casey felt the warmth of the expression throughout her entire body, her pulse turning thick and moving south with surprising ease. Though it wasn't just warmth this time, it was pure heat, dark and liquid and delicious. And it was the truth, she could see it, though it didn't make any sense whatsoever.

Finnegan Starkweather, former Interpol and a private investigator who had given up the game about ten years ago, as far as Casey knew. It was always a good idea to keep an eye on the other team, even if they were sitting in the stands, and they had never actually crossed paths despite being hunter and prey. She'd been a bounty hunter for several years, Casey remembered that much, but she had dropped off the grid and Casey had stopped paying attention. *Though I see I was remiss in that.*

Showing her hand like this and stepping out into the open, it was completely illogical. And though her guard was now firmly in place and the game would change by morning, Casey could not deny that she wanted more. More of what exactly, she wasn't sure, but *more* was definitely on the menu. *More of you, Finn O'Connell...or is it Starkweather?*

"You're wrong, I'm not very good at this at all." Finn pulled the wine from its resting place and set it on the table between them.

"I beg to differ," Casey said, feeling an odd twinge of panic. Finn was throwing in her hand, and she had never been so disappointed or curious in all her life. *Finally, a woman worthy of the game*, she acknowledged. *Don't give in so easily, Daddy*.

"I don't lie very well." Finn reached into her suit and pulled out a business card. She placed it beside the bottle, a simple white card with nothing but a phone number printed in dark blue ink. "Not about this."

"This?"

"You."

Casey blinked in surprise at her answer, though she pushed it aside as quickly as she could. "You're not staying for dinner?"

Finn smiled at the playful tone. "No."

"Why not?"

"Because what I really want isn't on the menu," she answered smoothly. "And the wine was for you, Casey Marinos."

Casey was torn between pleasure and protest as Finn stood up and walked away, though it was her curiosity that won out as she leaned forward and turned the bottle, finally revealing its label.

Her eyes went wide and shot up, focusing hard on Finn's back as she disappeared beneath the arch that led to the bar. She didn't know whether to be more impressed by the vintage or by the fact that Finn knew her real name.

Casey took up her glass, staring at the wine label once more and trying to decide just how much danger she was actually in, and how much dancing might be required in order to get away clean with everything that she'd come for. She had never in her wildest dreams expected a '47 Cheval Blanc to be waiting just for her.

But then I didn't expect you either...Finn.

Her slow smile filled with mischief and challenge in equal measure, her eyes finding the plain yet bold business card sitting in wait beside her impossible bottle of wine. "Finnegan."

KIM BALDWIN, a 2008 recipient of the Alice B. Readers' Appreciation Award, has published eight novels with Bold Strokes Books, including the new romantic adventure *Breaking the Ice*, set in Alaska. Four of her books have been award finalists. She has also contributed short stories to six BSB anthologies, including four in the Erotic Interludes series. Her next release is *Missing Lynx*, the third book in the Elite Operatives series co-authored with Xenia Alexiou, in 2010. A former network news executive, she lives in a cabin in the north woods of Michigan.

MEETING MY MATCH
KIM BALDWIN

I'd always had a knack for matchmaking. Put me in a room full of women and let me spend a few minutes with each, and I'd be pretty damn good at selecting which pairs would be good fits. But I was completely clueless, of course, about how to find my own special someone.

My friends realized my talents early on, and word began to spread. Before long, I began getting so many requests for help from lonely women that I started an online dating service in my spare time. Nothing big enough to compete with the major contenders out there—it was only a sideline and I got all my clients from referrals—but my success rate was phenomenal.

I had the standard questionnaire like the big boys, detailing likes and dislikes, personality quirks, goals and aspirations. And those queries certainly helped in red-flagging potential disasters in terms of who-fit-best-with-whom. No control freaks with disorganized, laid-back types. No die-hard romantics with jaded playgirls. But once you'd gotten the basics covered, I'd found that the real key in narrowing the choices for my particular clientele lay in finding compatibility in the one area that most dating Web sites don't adequately address. And that's in the answers to questions #205—*Describe in detail your sexual likes and dislikes*, and #206—*Describe in detail your ultimate sexual encounter with a stranger.*

My motives for this undertaking weren't entirely unselfish, you understand. While I took great joy in bringing two people together, I have to admit I wasn't averse to fulfilling my own appetite for passion when the opportunity arose. If a cute femme answered #206 with a fantasy that set my blood boiling, I'd find a way to make that dream come true. Personally. Of course, she never knew it was her matchmaker she was hooking up with in a dark bar or upscale hotel suite, and once the deed was done, I'd dutifully find her a prospect with long-term potential. I viewed it as a slight detour in their road to true romance. Call it my "finder's fee," if you will, because I never charged for my services. And I always delivered.

I'd never found anyone who shared my own ultimate encounter, but then again, I never really expected to. It was a little out there, I admit, and most women won't confess to fantasizing about taking—and being taken—quite that way. But two weeks ago, I got an application from a blond bombshell named Stacey, and her answers could have been my own. Just reading her detailed description to #206 worked me up. And as an added bonus, she seemed in all other ways just the type of woman I was drawn to. Sweet, smart, and funny. We had a lot of the same interests, and her honesty and openness were refreshing. I couldn't wait to meet her.

Her profile told me she worked a day job as a personal trainer, so I swung by her gym the next day to get a surreptitious 3D look at her and wasn't disappointed. She was just my height, tanned and toned, with breasts to die for and a sexy smile full of mischief. When she bent over to spot a client on the weight bench, I was in the perfect position to get a long, lingering look at her high, round ass, and it was such a fucking turn-on that my insides were already twisting in anticipation.

But it was several hours later before I was able to do anything about it. I waited patiently for the light in her bedroom to go out, then remained in my car for another hour to make sure she was well asleep. Lucky for me, she was serious enough about her fantasy that the details of her answer to #206 proved to be accurate. There was no security system in her home, and the window to her bedroom was unlatched.

I slipped in and waited a moment for my eyes to adjust. The figure beneath the light sheet in the big bed was still, and her slow, steady exhalations assured me she was asleep. She stirred slightly when I gently eased her hands near the solid brass rails of the headboard, but she didn't awaken even when I fastened the padded cuffs to her wrists and locked her to it.

As I leaned over her and put my mouth beside her ear, I was enveloped by her fragrance. Her hair smelled of vanilla and honey, and her body had a musky essence that was entirely her own. Before I spoke, I put my hand close to her mouth. Even though I knew she wanted this, I was aware that I would startle her, and a nosy neighbor calling 911 could put a definite crimp in my plans.

I gently stroked her cheek with the back of my hand to wake her. She murmured something unintelligible, rousing slowly from a deep sleep, and there was just enough ambient light from a night-light in the corner that I could see when her eyes popped open. The moment they did, before her flight response could kick in, I whispered, "Paradise." It was her safe word; she'd even included that in her questionnaire, as though she knew somehow that she was scripting her future.

I could tell the word registered, because she slumped back against the pillow and didn't fight the restraints. Even in the dim light I could see that her eyes weren't frightened, only curious.

"Shh, don't make a sound," I said, playing the role exactly as she described. I lit a single candle so that she could see me. Her fantasy stranger wore a ski mask, but after much inner debate I decided to forgo that little detail. Women seem to like my dark eyes, angular features, and crooked smile, and I didn't want to be a total stranger to her. Maybe that was part of my fantasy.

Slowly, I reached down and lightly stroked the cock that strained to be freed from my skintight jeans. Her eyes widened, and she couldn't suppress a pleased smile. The way she was looking at me sent a sharp jolt of arousal to the pit of my stomach, making me almost dizzy with anticipation.

"Are you..." She hesitated, and I knew she wanted to hold fast to her fantasy. She didn't really want confirmation that I wasn't the intruder I pretended to be. So I played along, feigning ignorance.

"Am I what?" I asked gruffly as I continued to stroke the cock. "Am I going to fuck you blind? Make you come so hard you can't move?"

I could see the reaction my words were having in the rapid rise and fall of her chest as her breathing quickened. My recitation was scripted, so she knew now with complete certainty that I was her fantasy come to life. Her words, but I felt as though she was somehow my own dream girl, conjured entirely from my imagination. Too perfect to be real.

"I won't fight you," she said shakily, and I detected an almost involuntary lift of her hips against the sheet. "Don't hurt me, and I'll do whatever you want."

I grinned my crooked smile at her and released the button at the top of my fly. Her eyes fixed on the cock, measuring its length and girth, and she licked her lips. There was a clink of metal as she tested the cuffs.

"I promise I'll be good if you let me loose," she whispered as I drew down my zipper with exquisite slowness. "These are hurting my wrists." I knew that couldn't be true, but it was part of her scene, and so I played my part.

"No. You'll be good because I say you will." I freed the cock for her appreciative eyes. Her expression was smoldering now, and when I stripped the sheet from her body, I caught the first scent of her arousal as her hips once again jerked upward.

She wore the sheerest of tank tops and string bikini briefs. From the pocket of my jeans I withdrew a sharp jackknife and carefully cut the garments free, exposing rigid nipples and a honey-blond patch of hair already glistening with moisture. No further words were spoken, but her breathing was loud and labored, and so was mine, in perfect synchronicity.

For what seemed like hours, I built her arousal to a fevered pitch, lavishing her body with slow sweeps of my tongue and teasing her with the cock between her legs but never entering her. She writhed beneath me, and her loud moans were punctuated by the clinking sound of her strains against the handcuffs.

"Please!" she begged, "I can't stand any more. Please! Let me loose!"

I was so fevered by this time I would have given in long ago were the positions reversed. She must have held this fantasy for a very long time, just like I had, and wanted it to last. With shaking hands, I withdrew the key from my pocket and released the cuffs, careful to leave the restraints open and exposed on the pillows. My voice was trembling too when I dutifully warned her not to try to escape.

"I don't want to, anymore," she promised, rubbing her wrists, and the words didn't sound as though she'd rehearsed them a hundred times in her head. "I just want to touch you, too."

I was straddling her, still fully clothed but for the exposed cock, and I could see a brief uncertainty in her eyes as she struggled with her choice. It didn't take long. Despite the temptation, she stuck close to her original script, easing slowly out from under me, eyes fixed on the cock.

"I'm not ready yet," she said, clearly a lie from the visible pool of sweet-smelling wetness at the juncture of her thighs. "Can I touch you?"

I nodded my assent with the proper wariness, and remained on my knees on the bed as she reached out to stroke the cock. Her eyes closed, and an almost animalistic grunt escaped the back of her throat as she worked it. The push-pull action did wonderful things to my groin, and I had to bite my lip to keep from coming.

She slipped her free hand beneath my black sweatshirt, and I heard her gasp when she found my bare breasts. I couldn't contain a moan of my own when she pulled and twisted first one nipple, then the other.

After pulling off the sweatshirt, she trailed her mouth over my throat and down to my breasts. She built me up so high I almost didn't notice her making her way around my body until she was snuggling up against me from behind, one hand still working the cock while the other raked nails over my flesh. She leaned against me, pushing me forward as she lazily guided my hands to grip the bedposts. It was all part of her pleasing me, and I tried not to stiffen though I knew what came next.

In a flash, I realized she must have practiced this part, because she had the cuffs fixed on me before I could blink. As soon as the restraints clamped shut, a surge of excitement shot through me and I soaked the crotch of my jeans.

"You're my prisoner now," she cooed into my ear as she pushed me down onto the bed and deftly removed my jeans. The harness followed. I craned my head around to watch her put it on. There's absolutely nothing sexier than a femme with a strap-on and I almost lost it right there.

When she was ready, her eyes met mine. And then, for a few seconds, she went entirely off script, leaning over to stroke my face with gentle hands, and whisper, "Thank you."

Our loud pants of anticipation seemed to echo off the walls. She reverted back to the fantasy and pulled me up to my knees, bent me over, and took me hard, thrusting into me so deep I had to grit my teeth to keep from yelling. I was so open and ready I couldn't hold back, and

I came with a shout. Her nails dug half-moons into my ass as I heard her echoing cry of release.

Neither her fantasy nor mine included breakfast. Or being virtually inseparable in the days to follow. I never expected that Client 451 would so quickly capture my heart as easily as she fulfilled my fantasies. But when I gave Stacey that key, I gave her control of more than my body. Lucky for me, her secret fantasy was my dream come true. And I'm wise enough to know when I've met my match.

LEA SANTOS a.k.a. Lynda Sandoval has authored twenty-four award-winning books. Her first teen novel was an ALA Quick Pick for Reluctant Young Adult Readers, a NY Public Library's "Books for the Teen Age" honoree, National Readers' Choice Award winner, and was nominated for the prestigious Colorado Book Award. Her works have garnered more than forty awards and list placements and have sold foreign rights in thirteen countries. She's been featured in *People en Español*, *Writer's Digest*, *The Denver Post Book Review*, and more.

Lea's a former cop and current 911 medical/fire dispatcher. In her spare time (ha!), Lea volunteers at Rainbow Alley, a LGBTQ teen drop-in center.

THE LIES THAT BIND
LEA SANTOS

Esme Jaramillo wiped her damp palms down the side seams of her slacks and wondered, briefly, if the taupe pantsuit her friends had insisted she wear had been the proper choice for her first—and probably only—television appearance. They'd fussed through a mountain of clothes in her hotel room that morning while she sat in the corner and reviewed her notes, amused by their fashion-plate antics. She supposed the tailored silk ensemble they'd settled on exuded a conservative enough image to offset her controversial topic: human cloning.

Now, if only she could be cloned from Jessica Biel for this talk show appearance, life would be just peachy. A smirk lifted one corner of her mouth as she glanced around the cramped makeup studio located backstage of the set of *The Barry Stillman Show*.

Four beige walls adorned with framed photos of previous guests surrounded the beauty parlor chair she occupied. A filing cabinet claimed one corner, with a CD player perched atop it. Rolling metal racks behind her held a mishmash of garments, perhaps for guests who had fashion emergencies before they were due onstage. Along with the rescue clothes hung a few smocks smeared with makeup streaks. Before her stood a long countertop stacked with more pots and jars and bottles of cosmetics than she'd ever seen, and above the counter was a huge mirror that framed the reflection of her un-made-up face.

The hot bulbs circling the mirror glared off the lenses of her supposedly hip wire-framed eyeglasses and melted the creamy cosmetics piled before her. If the makeup lights were hot, Esme could only imagine what it would feel like beneath the strong stage lights in front of All Those People. She shuddered, suddenly nervous. At least her parents and her best friends, Lilly and Pilar, would be out there for moral support. She reminded herself to look for their smiling faces in the audience the minute she got out onstage.

Speaking of faces—Esme pushed her glasses atop her head and leaned forward to squint at her own mug. Ugh.

Bland. Boring. That's how she looked.

It was always how she looked. And her hair—she twisted her head from side to side and arranged the short wisps with her fingers. The close-cropped style had looked great on Halle Berry. Not quite the same effect on Esme. She sat back in the chair until her reflection was nothing but a myopic blur and sighed. Oh well. No one expected female scientists to be attractive anyway. Still, she was grateful a professional would be applying her makeup for the show. A woman could be vain once in her life, couldn't she?

She glanced at her watch and wondered where the makeup person was. The producer had stuck her head in the room earlier and told Esme she'd go on in fifteen minutes. That didn't leave them much time.

As if on cue, the door opened, and in walked— Esme plunked her glasses back on the bridge of her nose and turned. Her breath caught. Lord, this woman was sex personified. Broad-shouldered and bronze-skinned, the woman wore faded, form-fitting Levi's, low-heeled black boots, and a tight black T-shirt emblazoned with The Barry Stillman Show in red lettering. And if her mama only knew what images the woman's shiny black ponytail brought to her mind, there'd be a chorus of Hail Marys uttered in her soul's defense within minutes.

"Dr. Jaramillo?"

"Yes?" Her hand fluttered to her throat.

"I'm Gia Mendez, your makeup artist," said the woman, her husky voice smooth as crème de menthe. "You're the brilliant scientist I've been hearing so much about, yes?" She flashed her a movie star smile and extended a long-fingered hand toward her for a handshake.

Esme nodded slowly, ignoring the heated flush she felt creeping up her neck at Gia's compliment. Disconcerted, she glanced from her face to her hand, then back at her face before she did her part to complete the handshake.

"Dios mío," she whispered more than spoke as the makeup artist's warm palm slid against hers. If women like Gia Mendez were commonplace in Chicago, she'd clone the whole darn city and become

the hero of the lesbian population. The thought curved her mouth into a smile.

Gia released her hand and asked, "Nervous?" She turned her back to switch the CD player on, filling the room with hot Celia Cruz tunes, then began assembling brushes and pencils and pots of color, her focus on the tools of her trade.

"A-a little," Esme admitted, content just to watch Gia move about the close quarters they shared. Her movements were skilled and confident, on the androgynous side, but graceful and definitely all woman. This was probably Esme's one chance in life to have a woman like Gia Mendez lay hands on her, and she was nothing if not thrilled by the prospect.

"It always seems to hit people once I come in to do their makeup." Gia winked.

Esme's heart plunged before snapping back up to lodge in her throat. *That wink should be classified as a lethal weapon.*

"You have my sympathy," Gia continued, seemingly oblivious to her admiration. "I much prefer remaining behind the scenes."

Esme pulled herself out of the lust-induced stupor and cleared her throat. "I've, ah, never been on television before." Esme chastised herself. *She probably knows that, silly.* This focused sexy female attention was rattling her composure. She wasn't used to it. "It's not too often a scientist has such an opportunity. I'm really very flattered." She nudged her glasses up with the knuckle of her pointer finger. "My parents and friends are in the audience." She cast her gaze down briefly, not wanting to appear too prideful.

Gia peered at her, her expression darkening for an instant before she turned away. Esme wondered if she'd said something wrong, but the moment quickly passed.

"Tell me about your research, Esme—may I call you that?"

"Of course."

Gia faced her, crossed toned arms over her chest, then leaned back against the counter, a position that accentuated the sculpted muscles in her upper body. The bright lights shadowed the curves of her jawline and glinted off the single diamond stud in Gia's earlobe. Esme forced her mind from its slack-jawed awe of this woman and back onto her question.

"Research? Research. Yes. Human cloning, that's what I research."

She laughed lightly, shaking her head. "And, well, it's a touchy subject."

"How so?"

"Lots of moral and religious implications. My grandmother prays daily for my soul. She thinks my colleagues and I are trying to play God. If I ever actually clone a human being, I'll probably be excommunicated from the church." Esme ran her fingers through her pixie-short locks and shrugged one shoulder.

Gia chuckled, holding several different colored lipsticks next to her cheek. "Sounds like my grandmother. Let me guess. Catholic?"

"But of course," Esme told her, tone wry. "So, I continue to do the research, but I feel guilty about it."

Gia leaned her head back and laughed, giving Esme an excellent view of her long dancer's neck, her straight white teeth. *Talk, Esme. Stay on track.*

"We're not necessarily trying to create people, though," she blurted, averting her gaze from the seductive hollow at Gia's throat. "There are a lot of other medically plausible reasons to clone human beings, but it's still a little too sci-fi for most people to swallow." She wondered when Gia would get to the part where those long fingers touched her face. She was prepped and ready to file away that particular sensory memory for frequent replays.

"Well, I'm sure there are medical reasons. But it is kind of a scary thought, having little duplicates of yourself running around," Gia conceded. She inclined her head. "Forgive my ignorance if that's a misconception. I don't know much about cloning."

"Don't apologize. There's no doubt Hollywood has put a skewed impression out there. It'll be hard for the stodgy science community to overcome."

Gia made a rumbly agreement sound deep in her throat, then said, "Take your glasses off for me, Esme."

Anything else? she wanted to ask. Her cheeks heated. She didn't usually have such wanton thoughts in the midst of a normal conversation. Then again, she'd never had a conversation with Gia Mendez before.

Esme watched, mesmerized, as Gia picked up a large makeup brush and dipped it into one of the containers. Poofs of face powder launched into the air around the brush, tiny particles dancing in the light. Gia raised perfectly peaked eyebrows at her, reminding Esme of her request. Request? Glasses. *Oh, yeah.*

"I'm sorry," she murmured. She removed her frames and folded them in her lap, then closed her eyes while Gia tickled her face with the powder brush. The sweet fragrance reminded her fondly of playing dress-up as a child, back when she still had hope she'd grow up beautiful. She wanted to smile but didn't, fearing she'd get powder-caked teeth.

When Gia finished, Esme put her glasses back on and waved her hands to fend off the cloud that still hung in the air. "I just hope the audience is open-minded about the topic and not hostile with me."

Gia stilled. "I...uh, yeah."

A thick pause ensued, prompting a seedling of discomfort to sprout in Esme's middle. Was she missing something here?

"Well, you'll knock 'em dead, I'm sure."

"I hope you're right."

Gia made careful work of capping the powder container and lining up the compacts before looking back at her. "Can I ask you something, Esme?"

"Sure."

"Do you ever...watch *The Barry Stillman Show*?"

"Oh, you would ask me that." She twisted her mouth to the side apologetically. "I'm ashamed to say that I've never seen it. I just don't have much time for television."

Gia pressed her full lips into a thin line and nodded.

"Why?" Esme asked.

"I'm... No reason. Just wondering."

It sure sounded like there was a reason behind the "no reason," but Esme didn't want to push the woman. Maybe she was just having a bad day. A fight with her undoubtedly gorgeous girlfriend at the breakfast table, perhaps. An ugly pang struck Esme at the thought, and her gaze fell to Gia's hands. No rings of any kind. No ring marks. She sighed with relief. As if it mattered. *Get a life, Esme.*

"I must say, I'm impressed, though," she told Gia. "I didn't know any of the talk shows still dealt with legitimate topics these days."

Gia didn't comment, so Esme went on. "If it's not people beating each other up or fake transvestites in love triangles, it never seems to make it to daytime TV. At least, that's what I thought until I was asked on the show." Esme glanced at her reflection, which jolted her back to the matter at hand. She pressed her fingers to her cheeks and pulled down slightly. "Aren't you going to do something with my face? I look awful."

Gia moved in between her and the mirror and spread her legs until she'd lowered herself to Esme's eye level. Esme folded her hands in her lap as her heart thunk-thunked in her chest at the proximity. Wasn't breathing supposed to be automatic? she wondered, as she reminded herself to pull in air.

Gia reached for her face slowly. Long, warm fingers danced along her cheekbones, her temples, then she smoothed the pad of her thumb over her chin. "No, Dr. Jaramillo, you don't look awful. You look anything but awful." Her voice was a gentle caress. "You look beautiful just as you are."

Her heart triple-timed. "Well…thank you, but—"

"Remember that." Gia touched the end of her nose, the gesture infinitely intimate. "Okay?"

Esme frowned, a little confused by Gia's words and spellbound by her touch. "I—sure. But I don't get it. Does that mean you aren't going to make up my face?"

The look Gia gave her seemed almost apologetic, Esme decided. "Right. I'm not going to make up your face. But it's okay. You don't need war paint."

So much for her moment of vanity. Disappointment drizzled over Esme before she shrugged it off and decided Gia was tying to tactfully tell her it wouldn't make much difference. Splashing color on her features would have probably just drawn attention to their plainness. Eh, well, it didn't matter, and she wasn't going to pout about it. At least Gia had touched her face. She inhaled the heady mingled scents of makeup and heated feminine skin, and decided a change of subject was in order. "How long have you done this kind of work, Gia?" Was that relief she saw on the other woman's beautiful face? Why?

"Three long years I've worked on this show." Gia leaned against the counter again, hands spread wide and braced on the edge, and crossed one foot over the other.

"You make it sound like a jail sentence."

Gia tilted her head to the side in a gesture of indifference. "It pays the bills, but my first love…" Doubt crossed her impeccable features. "You want to hear all this?"

"Of course," Esme assured her. "Your first love?"

"Is painting," she finished.

Esme watched in wonder as the smile lit up Gia's face. Her gaze grew distant, dreamy. She hadn't thought Gia could get much better looking. Boy, had she underestimated the woman. "War paint?" she teased, glancing back at her bare face in the mirror.

Gia chuckled. "No, not face painting. Oil painting. Art."

"An artist. Hmm. I'm not surprised." The woman had the hands of an artist, hands that made her wish she were a fresh, new canvas ripe for Gia's attention. She could almost feel the brushstrokes…

She swallowed. "It's wonderful, Gia. What do you paint?"

"Later." Esme watched a muscle tic in Gia's jaw for several moments as her dark eyes grew more serious. With a quick glance at the door and back, Gia squatted before her and sandwiched one of Esme's hands between her own. "Esme, listen to me. About the show—"

Before Gia could finish, the harried producer knocked sharply, then opened the door a crack and poked her head in. Tendrils had sprung free of her lopsided French twist into which she'd stuck two pencils and apparently forgotten them. "Dr. Jaramillo, time to go on."

Gia stood and moved away from her, sticking her hands into her back pockets. Regret socked Esme in the stomach, and she pinned the other woman with her gaze. What had she been about to say? Absurd as it was, she didn't want to leave this room, this woman. Gia was so comfortable to talk to, and so easy on the eyes. Women like Gia didn't usually give Esme a second glance. Or a first, for that matter. "I—"

"Now, Dr. Jaramillo. Please," the producer urged.

"Go on, Esme," Gia told her, treating her to another devastating wink.

"What were you going to tell me?"

"Nothing. Just, break a leg," she said, her voice husky. "That means good luck." She flashed her a thumbs-up. "I'll see you again in a few minutes."

She looked at Gia curiously as she got out of the chair and smoothed down the front of her suit. A few minutes? Hope spiked inside her. "You will?"

"I mean, I'll watch you on the monitors."

"Oh." Long awkward pause. "Well. Thank you," she told Gia, fluffing her own hair with trembling fingers and stuffing back the wave of disappointment. What did she expect from the woman, a pledge of undying love? With one last smile for Gia and a deep breath for courage, Esme turned and trailed the producer from the room.

❖

"Damnit!" Gia exclaimed as soon as the slim, soft-spoken professor was out of the makeup studio. She slumped into the chair and held her forehead in her hands as guilt assailed her gut. When the door squeaked open, she looked up to find the stage manager, Arlon, peering in at her.

Arlon raised a brow. "What's up?"

"That poor woman has no idea what she's in for," Gia muttered. "She honestly thinks she's going to talk about human cloning."

"Ah, you soft touch." Arlon snorted, leaning against the doorjamb with his clipboard cradled in his beefy arms. The remote radio headset nestled on his bald head looked like it had grown there, it was so much a part of the man. "Anyone who agrees to come onto *The Barry Stillman Show* deserves what she gets. You'd have to live in a cave to think this show bore any resemblance to legitimacy."

"She's never seen it, Arlon." Gia lunged to her feet and stalked across the small room. She punched the stop button on the CD player, then braced her palms against the wall and hung her head. Esme Jaramillo had infiltrated her domain all of what—ten minutes? And already the music reminded her of Esme. Gia could still smell her lavender scent in the air.

God, she felt like a heel.

That sweet woman with the heart-shaped face and trusting eyes didn't deserve this. Gia'd expected a renowned young scientist to be arrogant and aloof. Haughty at the very least. Instead, Esme Jaramillo had turned out to be one of the most down-to-earth, reachable women she'd met in a long time. From her inquisitive brown eyes hidden behind those endearing spectacles, to her joking manner and wide smile, Esme was nothing if not genuine.

Arlon's skeptical voice cut into Gia's thoughts. "Sure she's seen it. Everyone's seen *The Barry Stillman Show*."

"Not everyone spends their days propped in front of the boob tube, Arlon. She's a scientist. She has a life."

The stage manager whistled low. "She's got you all worked up, Mendez. Must've been some looker. No, wait"—the man turned his attention to the clipboard he held—"she couldn't be a looker if she's on this particular show. My mistake."

"She looked great." Gia growled, whirling toward her colleague. With effort, she stopped and ran her palms down her face, willing herself to relax. "Doesn't it ever get to you, Arlon?" Gia blew out a breath. "Lying to these people just to get them on the show?"

Arlon shrugged. "It's just a job, G. Television. Mindless entertainment. Besides, you were just the makeup woman. She can't blame you."

"But she will. She'll think we all lied to her, and we did. To her"—Gia pointed in the general direction of the stage—"this will be a public shaming." She clenched her jaw, fighting back those familiar bully feelings from her past. If anyone in this world did not deserve to be bullied, it was Dr. Esme Jaramillo. "We're sending an innocent lamb to the slaughter. How can we live with ourselves?"

"Don't be so melodramatic. So she gets embarrassed on television. Big deal. She'll get over it."

Gia burned him a glare. So jaded. So cavalier.

"Besides, there's nothing we can do about it now," Arlon added, pressing the earphone tighter to his ear. "Looks like the good professor just went on."

❖

The whoops and hollers from the audience surprised Esme as she walked onstage and took a seat in one of the two chairs centered on the carpeted platform. She'd expected a more demure group for a show about cloning, but at least they seemed welcoming. Behind her, an elaborate set gave the appearance of a comfortable living room. Lights mounted on scaffolding glared in her eyes, but she could vaguely make out the faces in the tiered crowd seated in a semicircle before her.

After settling into her chair, she gazed around the audience searching for her family and friends. There they were, front and center. Mama, Papa, Lilly, and Pilar, all in a row.

She smiled at them, but they looked odd.

Pilar's hands were clasped at her ample bosom, her eyes wide and serious. And Lilly? Esme could swear she looked flaming mad. Come to think of it, her father looked a little angry himself. Was Mama crying?

Perplexed, Esme squinted out at them. Yes, Mama was definitely crying. She hoped nothing bad had happened since the last time she spoke to them and fought the urge to traverse the stage and go to them. Her adrenaline level kicked up a notch. Before she could worry further, the raucous died down and Barry Stillman smiled at her from the aisle where he stood.

"Dr. Jaramillo, welcome to the show."

"Thank you," she murmured, pushing up her glasses with her knuckle. Laughter rippled through the audience, which confused her.

"Tell us a little about your research, Doctor."

She crossed one leg over the other and leaned forward. Her confidence always jumped when she could discuss her studies. She favored her host with an enthusiastic smile. "Well, I'm a professor of genetic engineering at a private college in Colorado. We're leading the country's research into cloning. Particularly human cloning, though the procedure is still not approved in the United States."

"Sounds like a job that could keep a woman pretty busy."

Apprehension began to claw its way up her spine. She glanced at the empty chair next to her and wondered who should be sitting there. They hadn't told her she would be part of a panel. And what was with Barry's inane questions? She licked her dry lips, wishing for water. "Yes, it's exhausting work."

"Probably doesn't leave you too much time for pampering, Dr. Jaramillo, does it?" More laughter from the crowd.

Suddenly defensive, Esme sat back in her chair and crossed her arms to match her entwined legs. Her skin flamed, and a rivulet of perspiration rolled down her stiff spine. "I thought we were going to discuss human cloning." This time the audience remained silent, but the pause seemed packed with gunpowder and about to explode.

"Well, Dr. Jaramillo, we aren't going to discuss human cloning. We actually have a surprise for you."

Esme blinked several times, trying to grasp what was happening to her. She glanced off into the wings and saw Gia standing there, her dark eyes urgent and pained. Their gazes met momentarily before Gia hung her head and turned away.

What in the hell was going on?

"A surprise?" Esme finally croaked out. "I don't understand."

"Maybe we can help you understand. Listen to this audio tape, Doctor, for a clue about who brought you on today's show."

Everyone fell silent, and soon a deep, accented, patronizing voice boomed through the studio. "Esme, I know you want me. But I'm here to tell you, before we have a chance, your bookworm looks have got to go. I'm doing this for your own good."

Realization filtered through Esme's disbelief like acid burning through her flesh. The phone sex voice belonged to none other than Vitoria Elizalde, her barracuda Brazilian coworker who refused to take no for an answer. Esme covered her mouth with her hand as the words slithered through her brain. *I've been duped!*

Esme had gone for coffee with Vitoria twice in the past months as a gesture of friendship. The woman was a visiting researcher from a different country, and though Esme found the woman arrogant and conceited, even predatory, she?d tried to make her feel welcome on the team. Of course Vitoria would assume a few cups of coffee meant Esme wanted more. Typical.

As the audience roared their approval, the host asked her, "Recognize that voice, Doctor?"

She couldn't even nod, let alone speak. Bookworm looks? Mortification spiked Esme to her seat as her heart sank. Hot tears stung her eyes, and as her chin started to quiver, the audience burst into applause, chanting, "Bar-ry! Bar-ry! Bar-ry! Bar-ry!"

She glanced out at her supporters, who looked as horrified as she felt. Lilly mouthed the words, "I'm so sorry."

Stillman's obnoxious voice cut in with, "Audience, what's your vote?" after which a hundred or more black placards were thrust into the air. SHE'S A BOOKWORM, most of them read in neon yellow lettering. Belatedly, Papa lifted his sign to its neon yellow flipside with shaky, liver-spotted hands. SHE'S A BEAUTY, spelled the stark black lettering. Esme was so ashamed for putting her parents into this position. If only she'd known it was all a trick—

"Audience? What do you have to say to Dr. Jaramillo?"

A hundred collective voices yelled at her, "Don't worry, Bookworm. We're going to make you over!"

Esme saw stars and gripped the chair arms so she wouldn't faint. This was a nightmare. No wonder Gia didn't make up her face. She wasn't beautiful, like the woman had claimed. Rather, Gia wanted her to look her very worst when she walked onto this stage. Esme choked back a sob. For some reason, Gia's deception cut to her core. The beautiful makeup artist had seemed so sincere. *Fooled you, Esme.*

"Welcome Professor Vitoria Elizalde to the show!" Barry hollered. From out of the wings opposite where she'd seen Gia sauntered smug, pantherlike Vitoria, her black hair perfectly coiffed. She raised her arms to the audience like a reigning queen as they clapped and cheered for her. She even took a bow.

How could she do this?

How could she bring Esme on national television, in front of God and her parents, friends? Everyone. Her staff, their colleagues. What the hell was wrong with this psycho bitch?

Before Esme could stop them, hot tears burst forth behind her glasses and blurred her vision. As Vitoria took the empty chair next to her, Esme lunged unsteadily to her feet and backed away, smearing at the tears rolling down her makeup-free face. She laid her palms on her flat, trembling abdomen.

"How could you?" she rasped, before wheeling on her stupid sensible heels and running from the stage trailed by the audience's loud booing.

Offstage, the producer with pencils in her hair caught Esme by her upper arms and held her back. "Come now, Esme. They're going to give you a makeover. It won't be so bad."

Her tears had escalated to sobs, which had prompted hiccups. Were these people for real? "Leave me"—*hiccup*—"alone, I'm not going back out"—*hiccup*—"there."

She tried to push past the woman when another man arrived to assist. The producer glanced at the man for help. "Arlon?"

"Don't, uh, cry now, miss," the man said, his stilted words proving him ill at ease with the role of comforter. He patted her upper arm and cleared his throat. "It's not so bad. We'll just get you some ice for your puffy eyes and—"

"Let. Her. Go," Gia's dead-serious voice said from behind Esme. Both the producer and the man called Arlon diverted their attention to Gia, and Esme took advantage of the moment to push between them and run through the cables and scaffolding to the hallway that would lead her out. Behind her, she heard the producer say, "Stay out of this, Mendez."

Esme wept freely, never so embarrassed in all her life.

She'd worked so hard to make her parents proud. They'd brought her to this country from Mexico when she was a toddler, hoping to provide her with better opportunities. They'd given up everything familiar—their family, friends, the language they both spoke so eloquently, the country they loved—for her. Her entire life was geared to show them she was grateful, that she'd made the most of her opportunities to become a success, a daughter they could be proud of. Now this.

Sure, she was a well-educated woman, a leader in her field, but she couldn't help thinking Mama and Papa had seen her in another light today. As a homely thirty-year-old woman who didn't even merit a date with an overblown, arrogant woman she'd never be the least bit interested in.

She shoved against the bar spanning the metal door and pushed her way into the exit hallway and wondered how she'd ever live this down, how she'd ever make it up to the parents who so valued their dignity.

"Esme! Wait!"

Gia. Esme tried to keep running, to get away before she ever had to see the woman's face again, but Gia caught her and snaked a hand around her forearm.

"Let me go," she said, staring at the ground as she tried to pull free. Part of her wished Gia would just hold her and tell her everything would be okay. The stupid part of her.

"Esme, please. I'm so sorry. Listen, let me ex—"

"Sorry?" Fury mixed with her humiliation as she hiccupped again. "Leave me alone, Gia, okay?"

Gia had pretended to be nice to her, when all the while she'd been part of the lie. She lifted her chin, pushed up her glasses, and glared at the other woman, trying her best to mask the hurt with a look of indignation. She wrenched her arm from Gia's grasp and rubbed the spot she'd held with her other hand. Her chest heaved as she stared up at the woman who'd been a major part of her humiliation.

"Just, let me go. After all this, can't you"—*hiccup*—"at least do that?" She turned and stumbled down the long, stark corridor slowly. Her limbs felt leaden, like all the energy had been leached out of her. She just wanted to go home and put sweats on and curl up with a glass of—

"I meant what I said, Esme," Gia called after her. "You are amazingly beautiful."

Her heart clenched. Another lie.

Esme never even turned back.

Telling the Barry Stillman people to take their job and shove it hadn't been difficult for Gia. But packing up her worldly goods and driving across the country in search of a woman she'd met but once, a woman who haunted her dreams—and probably hated her guts—was the biggest risk she'd ever taken.

No matter. It felt good. She'd been on the road for at least twelve hours, and as the evening skyline of Denver loomed into sight, Gia glanced down at the directions she hoped would lead her to Esme. The doctor deserved an apology, and for once, Gia would have a chance to make things right with a person she'd hurt who hadn't deserved it. Gia steered her black pickup onto Speer Boulevard South, and moved to the center lane. She rolled down her window and breathed in the cool, dry summertime air that was so different from the stifling humidity in Chicago where she'd grown up. Then again, everything about growing up had been stifling for her.

It was almost as hard for Gia to remember herself as an angry young bully as it was to remind herself she wasn't one anymore. She'd transformed, and she had her high school art teacher, Mr. Fuentes, to thank for her changed demeanor. Though rail thin and none too masculine, Fuentes wouldn't be bullied. He'd never flinched when he faced the angry young Gia toe to toe, and yet he never made her feel worthless. On the contrary, Fuentes made Gia believe in her painting, in her talent. He'd showed her how to channel her pent-up rage into art and made her understand that true happiness came from inside a person, not outside. And even though Gia hadn't gotten to the point where she could fully support herself with her painting, she'd had a couple of shows, made a few sales, and at age thirty-four, she still believed in herself.

Fuentes had won Gia's respect, and later her admiration. She'd thanked the man on more than one occasion over the years, but she'd never gone back and told any of the people she'd hurt that she was sorry. Perhaps a turned-around life was penance enough, but the open-ended guilt of her youth hung around her heart like a lead weight. She might not be able to assuage it with one apology, but at least it was a step in the right direction. And any steps that carried her closer to Dr. Esme Jaramillo were ones she definitely wanted to take.

If she was honest with herself, it wasn't just the chance for an apology that led her to the slight professor with the short, silky hair that just begged a woman to run her fingers through it. Something far more instinctual pulled her as well. It had taken one fitful night of remembering her gentle lavender scent, seeing images of her bright, dark eyes behind those glasses, hearing her wind-chime laughter, before Gia knew she had to see Esme again. If she didn't, Esme's memory would be with her forever, like a war wound. Reminding her now and then, with a stab of pain, what could possibly have been.

She glanced back down at the crinkled map in the passenger seat, brushing aside the wadded Snickers wrappers covering it. If her navigation was correct, she should be knocking on Esme's door in no time. And if fate was on her side, the doc would be willing to hear her out.

❖

Three hellish days had passed since the ill-fated appearance on *The Barry Stillman Show*. Esme—bundled in voluminous sweatpants and feeling like lukewarm death—slumped cross-legged on the floor of her living room across from her best buddies, Lilly Lujan and Pilar Valenzuela. Between them, on the dark brown carpeting, sat serving dishes filled with various comfort foods: enchilada casserole, mashed potatoes, chicken mole, and a Sara Lee cheesecake. Not to mention the pitcher of margaritas. Their forks hung limply from their hands as they took a collective break from gastronomically comforting themselves.

Esme leaned back against her slipcovered sofa and laid her hands on her distended abdomen with a groan. If only Gia Mendez could see her at this moment, she thought. How beautiful would the makeup artist claim she was now?

Esme's eyes were still tear-swollen, and she'd broken out in a rash on her neck from the stress. Her hair was smashed on one side, spiked out on the other, since she'd spent most of the last two days lying listlessly on the couch channel-surfing to kill time between her crying jags. Now she was bloated, and she just didn't care. The entire universe already knew she was ugly. No sense trying to hide it.

Oddly enough, a memory other than being humiliated on television kept popping into her mind, squeezing her heart. She'd been just a little girl, one who loved playing dress-up and watching Miss Universe on TV. She would close her eyes during commercials and picture herself accepting the crown for the USA in English, then thanking her parents in Spanish. At that point, she still believed it could happen. At that point, she still wanted it to happen.

But one summer afternoon, her aunt Luz and her mother were sharing iced tea on the front porch, while Esme played with dolls in her room. Her window was open, inviting a breeze that carried the voices of mama and Tía Luz.

"Look, Luz. Photographs of the children from the church picnic last week."

The sounds of Tía thumbing through the prints came next, and Esme's ears perked when she heard, "Ah, there's little Esme." A pause. "Such a smart girl."

"Gracias," murmured her mother, and Esme could hear the smile on Mama's face.

"Thank God for her brains. She certainly didn't get the looks. With those skinny chicken knees and thick glasses, she may never find a husband, but she'll always find a good job."

Esme froze, a crampy feeling in her stomach like when she'd eaten too much raw cookie dough the week before. She set down her dolls and curled up on her side on the floor, hoping her tummy would stop hurting. It made her want to cry. She tried to stop listening, but she couldn't help herself.

Her mama tsk-tsked. "Don't be cruel, Luz. Not everyone can

be beautiful, nor does everyone need a husband. She'll grow into her looks."

"We can only hope she's a late bloomer," Tía Luz added.

But she hadn't bloomed at all, no matter what Gia claimed about her looks three days earlier. If she had, she wouldn't have ended up as a guest on Barry Stillman's horrific bookworm makeover show. Pushing the painful memory from her mind, Esme scratched at the red bumps below her ear and hiccuped.

"You still have those?" Pilar asked.

"I get them when I'm under"—*hiccup*—"stress." She nudged up her glasses, then took to scratching the other side of her neck. "They've come and gone since the"—*hiccup*—"fiasco. I'm probably just gulping"—*hiccup*—"down my food too fast."

Pilar got up, stepped over the smorgasbord, then plopped herself onto the couch behind Esme. "I'm gonna plug your ears, and you drink your margarita. It may not get rid of 'em, but after all that tequila, you won't care."

Esme let out a mirthless chuckle, then did as she was told. It worked. She smiled up at Pilar, who'd begun playing with Esme's unruly hair, and absentmindedly brought her fingernails to her neck again.

"Honey, don't scratch your rash. You'll make it worse," Lilly told her softly. "Did you use that cream I gave you?"

Esme nodded and rested her hands in her lap. If anyone knew what being judged for your looks felt like, it was Lilly. She and Esme understood the concept from different perspectives, though. Lilly, a natural beauty with wavy, waist-length black hair and huge green eyes, had gone on to a great modeling career after being named Prettiest Girl in high school. At thirty, she was one of America's most recognizable Chicanas, having graced the pages of *Cosmo*, *Vanity Fair*, *Latina*, *Vanidades*, and *Vogue*, to name a few. In looks, she and Esme were polar opposites, always had been. But in their hearts, along with Pilar, they were soul triplets.

If only she'd looked like Lilly onstage. Maybe then Gia would have felt something for her other than pity. Lilly never lacked in attention from gorgeous women. Esme closed her eyes against the wave of embarrassment she'd relived repeatedly since the filming in Chicago.

On the airplane, she felt like everyone was staring at her. *Look! There's the ugly professor!*

She'd medicated herself with several tiny bottles of cheap, screw-cap wine during the flight, and had finally convinced herself she was being overly paranoid. Still, it had taken every ounce of her courage to walk through Denver International Airport with her head held up, even with Lilly and Pilar flanking her for much-needed moral support. Of course people had seen her. *The Barry Stillman Show* had 30 million viewers, she'd since learned via a Google search. She just wasn't sure who had seen her, and that's what scared her most.

It had felt so good to finally walk into her comfortable home in Washington Park and deadbolt the door behind her. And after a half an hour of quiet, she'd started to feel better, thinking maybe no one had seen the show. Then her phone had begun to ring. It seemed everyone she'd ever met in her life had seen the goddamn show. Her answering machine had been clogged for two days with uncomfortable messages of sympathy and pity—just what she needed. A local full-service beauty salon had even sent a courier bearing a gift certificate, much to her utter dismay.

The phone rang again, and Esme glared at it. "I could die," she whispered to her friends, chugging down another healthy dose of margarita. She wiped salt from her lips and added, "Who could that be now? The president? I think he's the only one who hasn't sent condolences for the untimely death of my dignity."

Lilly clicked her tongue and cast a beseeching look at Esme while Pilar reached over and switched off the ringer. "When we realized what they were doing, we tried our hardest to get backstage to warn you, Esme, I swear," Lilly told her.

"They wouldn't let us," Pilar added, digging her fork into the cheesecake. "Rat bastards. Your mama laid into them with a barrage of Spanish cuss words. Made my hair stand on end. I think they didn't know quite what to do with her." She popped the bite into her mouth and chewed, her eyes fixed apologetically on Esme's face.

"I don't blame you guys. It was my fault for walking into their trap." She furrowed her fingers into her hair and laid her head back against the couch. And what a trap they'd set, with a juicy enticer like Gia Mendez to lure women in. Or men, for that matter. She couldn't imagine a soul on earth who wouldn't find Gia Mendez sexy. *God, I'm so stupid.*

"It's unconscionable what they do to people, Esme. You should complain," Lilly said, dishing up another serving of enchiladas.

She shook thoughts of Gia from her mind and graced her friend with a wan smile. "Eh, it wouldn't do any good. Besides, I just want to forget it ever happened." *To forget that I entertained even one thought that a sex goddess like Gia Mendez would look twice at a woman like me.*

Miss Universe, she wasn't.

"How much time off do you have before the new semester starts?" Pilar asked.

"A little over a month." A little over four weeks until she had to face Vile Vitoria again. The thought of Elizalde made her want to fistfight. "God, that arrogant woman," she growled. "Who does she think she is, anyway?"

"That's right," Pilar said, wrapping her arms around Esme's shoulders from behind for a hug. "As if you'd ever give her the time of day anyway."

Esme didn't think she'd go that far, but she only said, "I've got to think of some way to get back at the jackass."

"Oh, revenge." Lilly nodded her head. "That's always a good, healthy way to recover from trauma."

Recognizing the sarcasm, Esme rolled her eyes. "In any case, I'm hoping by the time I go back it will be old news to everyone and my own embarrassment will have waned. I want absolutely no reminders of that debacle." Especially none of a brown-eyed artist with fingers that made a woman scream for edible body paints.

The doorbell chimed. Twice.

Esme looked from Lilly to Pilar and frowned. "Who could that be? *TMZ*?"

"Very funny. It's probably your mama," Lilly said, standing. "I'll get it."

"No, wait." Esme groaned to her feet. "Let me. It'll probably be the only exercise I get all week." Padding across the brown carpet in a tequila-induced zigzag, Esme made her way to the dark front hall leading to the door. Lord knew, she needed some fresh air.

July in Colorado heated right up, but the temperature dropped with the sun, bringing cool breezes in with the moon. Maybe she'd sit with Mama on the porch instead of bringing her in. The darkness would hide some of the puffiness around her eyes, and staying outside would prevent Mama from witnessing their little pity party on the living room carpet. The woman would be aghast that they were eating so much food from dishes set right on the floor. Mama was nothing if not proper.

Esme stopped in the dark hallway, leaned against the wall, and pulled in a long, deep breath. Just the thought of seeing her mama brought on renewed feelings of shame. Oh, her parents had handled everything much better than she had. It didn't matter—she still felt guilty. She knew, deep down, they had to be embarrassed that their daughter was known nationwide as an ugly wallflower. No matter how long it took, she was going to put the incident to rest for all of them, just as soon as her anger at Vitoria Elizalde dissipated.

Esme flipped on porch light before she threw the deadbolt back and pulled on the heavy, carved wooden door. She started speaking as the hinges squeaked.

"It's late, Mama, you shouldn't be ou—" Her words cut off as her mind grasped the realization that the lean, muscular woman looming larger than life on her porch bore no resemblance whatsoever to her mother.

She wasn't sure if her heart had stopped or was beating so fast she couldn't feel it. Either way, she looked like hell and had a guacamole smear on her sweatshirt, and here she stood face-to-face with—"Gia"—*hiccup*—"w-what are you doing here?" Amazingly calm question considering her life had just passed before her eyes. Esme hoped she wouldn't fall down, because she could no longer feel her feet. And, physiological impossibility aside, she'd just proven that a person could exist without a heartbeat or the ability to draw air into the lungs. Gia Mendez? *Here?*

"Esme. Forgive me for…just showing up." She spread her arms wide and let them drop to her sides, as if searching for what to say next. Her long, silky hair hung free of the ponytail Esme remembered, and the yellow glow of the porch light made it shine like a sheet of black gold. Gia looked just as good in dark jeans and a well-worn University of Chicago sweatshirt as she had the day Esme had met her.

Looking at her, Esme fought the ridiculous urge to sit on the floor.

Instead, she stood stock still and bunched the avocado-stained front of her sweatshirt into her fist. With her other hand, she poked her glasses up on her nose. "I…I thought I made it clear you should"—*hiccup*—"leave me alone."

To her dismay, Gia flashed a devastating, sweet smile that pulled a dimple into her left cheek. Esme hadn't noticed that the other day. "Don't tell me you've had those hiccups since you left Chicago."

She shook her head and hiccuped again.

"Esme, we need to talk." Gia took a step forward, and Esme eased the door partway closed, hiding half of her body behind it. Gia stopped, stared at her.

Her gaze dropped to Esme's neck as she swallowed. "No," she said. "We don't need to talk. I want to"—she held her breath for a moment and staved off a hiccup—"forget everything about that day." God, she wanted to be angry at Gia Mendez. She didn't want to feel her heart beating in anticipation at the mere sight of her, or worry that Gia had noticed her disheveled hair. She didn't want to smell the woman's pheromones on the night air or yearn to feel Gia's strong arms around her for comfort. "Denial is my drug of choice. I'm going to pretend it never happened."

"It shouldn't have happened, Esme." Gia laid her palm high up on the door frame, leaning toward her. "I feel just—"

"Don't." Esme held out her hand. Attraction or not, Gia had been a part of the trick; Esme couldn't forget that. "Don't apologize now, after the fact, because I really, really thought you were a nice woman, Gia Mendez. An apology will only make me want to slug you, and I've had too much trauma and too much"—*hiccup*—"tequila to resist the urge."

"It's a risk I'm willing to take," Gia said, after pausing to chew on her full, sexy lip.

Her pointed gaze, filled with inexplicable affection, flamed Esme's cheeks. She expelled a sigh and hung her head. How much could one woman take? It had been a long time since Tía Luz had pointed out her flaws, and though her glasses weren't as thick these days, her knees were just as knobby. She couldn't let a woman like Gia, a woman solidly out of her league, affect her. It would only bring her more pain. After a moment, she looked up. "Look. You were only doing your job, okay? I understand."

Gia opened her mouth to speak, but Esme waved her words away, reminding herself to be angry. Gia had tricked her. She'd shamed her. She'd left her face bare, even knowing what kind of trap Esme was walking into. "It's fine, Gia, please. Just…leave me to my life and go back to yours. There are a lot of other ugly women whose faces you can ignore, too."

"Esme?" called Lilly from the front room. "You okay?"

"Fine," she yelled back, a little too sharply, her eyes never leaving Gia's face.

"Slug me if you want, but I am sorry, Esme. More than you'll ever know. You probably don't believe that."

"Did you come here to convince me or yourself? Because you've already told me one lie. You'll have a tough job on your hands if you're working on me."

"Esme," Gia breathed her name, a pained gaze imploring.

The tall artist didn't try to touch her. Esme didn't try to move away. Time stilled between them as they stared at one another. Gia dipped her chin, Esme raised hers. Crickets chirped from the darkness beyond the porch. A gust of wind rustled the leaves on her old grand cottonwood tree and lifted a lock of Gia's long hair across her face.

"Why are you here?" she whispered. "You live in Chicago."

"Not anymore." Gia tucked her hair behind one ear as she added, "I don't work for the *Stillman Show* anymore."

"You don't?"

"You are an attractive woman, Esme." The words came out husky. "A beautiful woman. I mean it."

Esme ignored that. She had more pressing questions. "Did you get fired?"

"Quit."

Surprise fluttered through her and she let go of the door. "Why?" she asked, moving closer to lean against the jamb.

"Because I never again wanted to see hurt on a person's face like I saw on yours as you left the studio. I can't stop the show from bringing people on under false pretenses, but I can sure as hell remove myself from the situation."

Esme sighed and broke eye contact, focusing instead on Gia's low-heeled black boots. Why did she have to be so nice? So sincere? Why couldn't she leave Esme to her sulking instead of invading her doorstep with her stature and warmth, filling Esme's nostrils with the feminine scent of her skin and her ears with that silky-husky voice? "I can't feel responsible for you losing your job, Gia."

"I'm not blaming you."

She raised her gaze back to Gia's. "What will you do?"

Gia shrugged. "I'll get by. It's time to give my painting a chance, and…who knows?"

Esme shook her head slowly and reached up to scratch her neck. Gia'd quit her job. She'd quit her job and packed up her life, and now she was standing on Esme's doorstep hundreds of miles away trying to convince her she wasn't ugly.

Why?

Feeling another bout of hiccups coming on, she whispered, "I have to go."

"Can I come in?"

"No." She started to shut the door.

Gia held it open. "Esme, wait. I want to see you again."

"To assuage your own guilt? I don't think so."

"That's not why."

So she said. But, really, how would Esme ever know?

Gia reached out and ran the backs of those lovely fingers slowly down her cheek. "You have a rash."

"Adds to the whole beauty package, wouldn't you say?"

"Don't, *querida*." Gia's hand slid from Esme's cheek to her shoulder and rested there.

Esme's eyes fluttered shut, and she choked back another wave of tears. This woman could break her heart if she allowed it. "Leave me alone, Gia. Please."

"I can't."

"Esme?" Lilly and Pilar peered into the hallway, then looked from their friend to Gia, their eyes widening in surprise. Neither moved.

Esme glanced over her shoulder. "I'll be right there. Ms. Mendez was just leaving."

"No, I wasn't."

"You are now."

"We aren't finished."

"We never even started."

Gia pressed her infinitely kissable lips together and lowered her chin. Her somber gaze melted into Esme's for excruciating seconds before a smile teased that dimple into making an appearance. She winked. "Tomorrow, Esme? Can I see you then?"

"No."

"Just coffee. No pressure."

"No."

Gia shifted from boot to boot, then crossed her arms over her chest. "Need I remind you that you said you thought I was a nice woman?"

"I also said I wanted to hit you," she countered, in as haughty a tone as she could muster.

"But you didn't."

She faltered and bit her lip, which had started to tremble. "Don't do this to me. Please."

"I'm going to keep trying until you give me a chance, Esme."

Shoring up her resolve, Esme wrapped her arms around her stomach and sniffed. "You'll be wasting your time."

Gia brushed Esme's trembling bottom lip with one knuckle, then stepped back. "Ah, but you see, I'd rather waste my time on you than spend it wisely on anyone else." She nodded good night to Lilly and Pilar, who still hung behind Esme, then stepped off the porch and disappeared into the night shadows.

The standoff was only temporary. A sort of drawn-out foreplay. Though she'd never admit it, she couldn't wait to see what would come next...

L.L. RAAND has always had a fascination for the dark side—and those who dwell there.

When Hearts Run Free
Radclyffe writing as L.L. Raand

I'd only been a Werewolf for a few weeks, but I knew enough to know I shouldn't even be *looking* at the Alpha of the Adirondack *lupus* pack, let alone lusting after her. Then again, I'd never been very good at following protocol—probably if I had been, I wouldn't have found myself in a moonlit clearing deep in the mountains of upstate New York about to undergo my first fully conscious shift. If I'd been following the rules, I probably wouldn't have tried to sedate the teenager in the throes of Were fever, but by the time the police had found her in an alley she was so far gone she was seizing. She was going to die without treatment, and there wasn't time to wait for the Were medic on call to get to the ER. As it turned out, I was too late, and the girl died. But not before she bit me.

I don't remember much of what happened after her teeth sank into my wrist like two rows of razor blades, sharp and bright. Even when the flesh tore and my instruments slipped through my fingers on a river of red, I didn't feel the pain. The burn came later, at the same time as the fever. Then the dreams. Fragments of images flickered through my rioting brain, scattered patches of light and dark like broken bits of sunshine littered over the forest floor—chasing me while I ran, the hunter and the hunted. My muscles screamed, my bones shattered, and in the back of my mind always the low, throaty growl urging me to run. Run. *Run.*

When I woke, my head was clear, my stomach hollow with hunger, and everything was different. Beyond the closed door of my hospital room, I heard the staff conversing at the nurses' station at the other end of the floor as clearly as if they were standing beside my bed. I gasped and instantly gagged on the miasma of hospital smells deluging me—cafeteria food, antiseptic, disease, the living and the dead.

"Breathe slowly through your mouth for a few minutes," a voice as rich and lush as dark chocolate said from somewhere in the shadows of my room. "After a while you'll learn to filter out the sounds and smells, when you want to."

"What happened?" I asked, my memory still patchy.

A woman appeared beside my bed. She was about my age, late twenties or early thirties, and a few inches above average, putting her near my height. Blond, lithe, and on the muscular side of lean. She wore a faded green T-shirt tucked into blue jeans, and beneath the smooth skin of her exposed arms the muscles were etched and taut. "You were turned four days ago by an *insurgi*, a rogue werewolf."

"Werewolf," I said, a statement more than a question. She nodded.

"You?"

"Born and bred," she said with a hint of a grin. "My name is Sylvan. Your sponsor, Roger, will be by later. He'll help you through the transition."

"So, what's next?" I said, pushing myself up in bed and taking stock. For someone whose system had just undergone a violent, rapid mutation at the genetic, subcellular level, I felt pretty damn good. In fact, I felt terrific. I was hungry. And I was horny. I took a deep breath, and smelled female. I took another look at the blonde, noting the thrust of her small breasts beneath the green cotton, the smooth, flat plane of her abdomen, the gentle flare of her hips, the tight length of her thighs. The hunger in my belly moved lower, mutated like my cells into something fierce and untamed.

"Should I breathe slowly through my mouth *now*, too?" I said, barely containing the urge to vault over the short metal railing on the side of my bed and take her to the floor.

"That probably won't help." She didn't move back, but held my gaze steadily. "You're not human anymore. What you're feeling right now is perfectly normal for a wolf."

"How many female wolves want to mate with other females?"

A growl came from the other side of the room and I realized we weren't alone. Somehow I knew it was a bodyguard. A gravelly voice murmured, "Alpha."

I sniffed and smelled male, and my vision hazed with red. I shuddered, my spine tingling, my vocal cords quivering with a barely audible snarl.

"Alpha, please. This is not advisable," the male said, more urgently this time.

She waved her hand as if to silence the cautionary voice, and grinned again. The rims of her irises narrowed into a deep indigo band around flat black pupils. Her breasts rose and fell faster beneath her T-shirt. "More females than you might think."

"That's good to know." I clenched my fists, fighting to hold still, to force down the flames that scorched me from the inside out. Dimly, I registered a different kind of burning sensation in my palms, and when I glanced down, saw that my fingernails had elongated into short, curved dark claws. My hands bled from a series of crescent lacerations, but I felt no pain. Only want. "I think maybe you should leave. Something's happening to me." I sucked in a shaky breath. "I think I might be dangerous."

"It's your wolf," she whispered, leaning over me slightly. Her scent, a mix of burning autumn leaves cut through with cinnamon and sweet clover, grew heavier, darker. "She wants to be free. You can't hurt me."

I panted, twisting beneath the sheets. "I think I might…Jesus, I want—"

"But it's too soon for you to control her." She straightened and drifted back into the shadows. The pressure in my chest eased a fraction. "You'll learn. You have two weeks until the next full moon. Welcome to the Adirondack Timberwolf pack, whelp."

I hadn't seen her again, but I thought of her every spare minute when I wasn't being poked, prodded, and psychoanalyzed by the human physicians or being poked, prodded, and indoctrinated into Werewolf society by my sponsor. Her scent lingered like a haunting refrain, keeping me always on edge.

Tonight the moon was full.

"Ready?" Roger asked as the moon climbed to its zenith.

"Sure," I said. I wasn't. I hadn't had nearly enough time to adjust to the physical changes, let alone incorporate all the hierarchical social rules of the pack. But instinctively I knew that any show of weakness would be a mistake. I felt like I was coming out of my skin, and I guess I was.

I tried to appear casual as I followed Roger toward the pack. The whole pack, I'd been told, numbered several hundred and was spread throughout New York, Vermont, and New Hampshire. The Adirondack Pack's territory butted up against that of the Maine Silver Ridge Pack, the largest Northeastern U.S. pack.

Maybe thirty or forty males and females gathered beneath the trees, moving restlessly in the slanting shafts of silvery moonlight. All of them, male and female, moved with the powerful glide of predators. Some of them were already nude, others in the process of undressing.

"Mutia," a statuesque redhead growled as I passed.

Mutt. To the *regii*, the purebreds—the natural born Weres—I was less than a second-class citizen, I was a genetic blight. The U.S. Order of Were Affairs had agreed to sponsor, i.e. indoctrinate, any human turned accidently, as a condition for getting the Preternatural Rights Law passed. The Law granted non-humans protection from discrimination, among other more fatal things—like being shot on sight. Not everyone in the Were population was happy about being forced to accept "genetic inferiors," but living in a society is all about compromise. So they cooperated, on the surface.

I was a physician. I knew I wasn't inferior, not on any level. Once the mutation was complete, I was physiologically no different than any other *lupus* Were. Once trained, I would be able to shift at will, and I was already as fast, as strong, and potentially as deadly as any other *lupus* female my size. Maybe more so—before my turning, I'd been a trained martial artist. I could fight. I loved competitive sparring. I loved winning.

But genetically, I was different in one critical way. My somatic DNA might have mutated, but the chromosomes in my ova were still 100% human, and if those ova remained fertile, they would always be human. So my offspring at best would be half-breeds, assuming I mated with a Were male and not a human one. Assuming the offspring lived, and since the live birth rate for Weres was very low, that was a big if. Assuming a lot of things, such as my desire to mate with *any* male, human or lupine. I could have told the pack bitches who saw me as a threat that they had no worries, because I had no designs on their studs. None whatsoever. But I wasn't going to crawl on my belly to be accepted, or to avoid a fight.

I hadn't been at the bottom of the pack, any pack, since I was an intern a decade before, so keeping my gaze down when the redheaded bitch challenged me, as Roger had instructed I do when the situation arose, took all my self-discipline. The tiny hairs on the back of my neck stood up and I couldn't completely suppress the growl that resonated in my throat. She snarled and took a step closer, and if I hadn't caught a flicker of gold in the moonlight and seen *her* just at that moment, I probably would've done something stupid—like answered the bitch's challenge right then and there and gotten my ass chewed up. Literally.

Sylvan, a phalanx of Weres behind her, stalked out of the woods into the clearing. She wore skintight black jeans and nothing else. Her breasts rode high and proud, the muscles in her chest and abdomen rippling seductively beneath moon-kissed skin. I could smell her across the clearing, her scent so heady my mouth literally watered. My sex tightened and desire choked my senses.

"Sylvan." I whispered, but a whisper among Weres might as well have been a shout.

Utter silence fell over the pack.

"No," Roger said harshly as he gripped my arm, but it was too late.

She was all I could see, all I could smell, all I could sense, and I took a step forward, my eyes fixed on her face. I barely registered a blur of gold slashing through silver before my legs were cut out from under me and I fell hard, face first to the forest floor. The weight on my back crushed me into the rich loam, and I tasted blood where a tooth had cut my lip. A knee in the center of my back kept me pinned, and one iron-tight thigh rested alongside my hip. An arm bar on the back of my neck prevented me from raising my head, but I didn't need to see. I could scent her, sense her, feel her heat—some part of me beyond words, beyond thought, *knew* her.

"You forget yourself, whelp," Sylvan rasped in my ear.

I'd worn only a T-shirt and sweatpants in preparation for shifting, and I felt the hard points of her nipples against my shoulder blades as she leaned close. Flame surged from deep in my core and poured into my chest, driving my breath out on a moan.

"I'm sorry, Alpha. I'm sorry," I gasped, suddenly burning up. A soul-deep ache tore my muscle from bone, shattering my mind. A thousand knives scored my skin, flaying sanity along with my flesh. "I…oh God…I can't breathe…*hurts*…"

"You'll be all right," Sylvan whispered, her mouth soft against my ear. "Let her come." Then she rolled away, calling, "Roger!"

And I screamed. My world disintegrated in a fury of agony and all I had to cling to was her scent, the sound of her voice, the weight of her flesh on my flesh. When I came into myself once more, I was surrounded by wolves. I shook my head, took a step, and fell. A nose nuzzled my neck, as if urging me to rise. I focused on the black muzzle and large dark eyes of the hovering wolf and recognized Roger's scent. He lifted his lip in a wolfy smile, and I tried another step. Then another. I felt powerful in a way I never had before, my body and mind intimately attuned. I laughed and heard myself growl. Roger shouldered me forward. He was bigger than me, longer and taller, but glancing around, I realized that I was bigger than most of the females and some of the males. I stumbled again when I saw her, and this time, I kept my head down, stealing glances when no one was looking.

She was almost pure silver with only a few fingers of black in her thick ruff and along the ridge of her powerful back. Larger than almost all the wolves in the pack, she stalked the clearing, nosing some, growling at others, playfully nipping a few. I trembled as she drew near, but I did not drop my tail or my head as many others had done. I kept my head lower than hers, but I could not take my eyes away. She was too beautiful.

She was the pack Alpha, the leader of hundreds of Weres, not just when they were in wolf form, but in every aspect of their lives. She led not simply by might, but also by intelligence. She commanded loyalty and was given it, because she was trusted, and because she had earned it. She was my Alpha, just as I was her wolf, and even though I was there not by divinity, but by accident, I felt like I was hers.

Then with a flurry of snapping teeth and rumbling growls, she struck. And though I had never yielded in a battle, never run from a challenge, I did not fight back. Within seconds, I was on my back, her legs straddling my exposed underbelly, her teeth buried in the thick fur of my neck. I tilted my head back and gave her my throat, a soft whine escaping me. Her scent was overpowering now, enveloping me, drowning me, and still the fire inside me burned. Snarling with my throat in her jaws, she shook her head from side to side, reminding me, reminding every wolf within sight or hearing, who ruled the Adirondack pack. Then she released her vise-like grip on me, and I instinctively licked her face. Her blue eyes gleamed in the moonlight, and for just an instant, her chest and belly settled onto mine. Then she vaulted off, loped into the center of the clearing, raised her head to the moon, and howled.

Dozens of voices answered, and my heart stirred, my soul singing with them. I jumped up, shook myself, and answered her call. Then we were running, legs pounding, muscles stretching, hearts pumping. The pack broke into the forest and although I couldn't see her, I knew where she was, just as I knew how to decipher the sounds and scents of the forest. I followed her trail along with a few others, joyfully, freely, with no sense of time, no beginning, no end. Only the thrill of the hunt and the feel of her ahead, calling me. I don't how long I ran or how far, but I gradually became aware of the silence descending upon me. I caught a glimpse of silver slipping between the trees ahead, and realized that she and I had outrun the pack. We were alone in the forest. I slowed and cautiously padded forward into a small clearing. She appeared like a whisper of smoke and I halted, waiting.

She circled me, sniffed me, bumped her shoulder against mine. I waited still, shivering not from exhaustion, but excitement. She rose and set her chest on my shoulders, telling me my place—beneath her. I trembled under her weight, my heart pounding. Her hot breath teased my ear and I rumbled in pleasure. With a powerful thrust of her haunches, she dismounted and, gently setting her muzzle on top of mine, rubbed it back and forth. Then she dipped her head, but not her gaze. She would never lower her gaze to anyone—Were or human. Tentatively, I stroked the underside of my jaw over her nose. She allowed the contact only for a few seconds before backing away. Then she turned and raced toward the forest, glancing once over her shoulder, one ear flickering. An invitation. This time when I rushed to follow, she slowed until I ran by her side, and together we hunted.

When the moon slipped down and the night edged toward dawn, she led me to a shelter of fallen pines. She rested her head on her forelegs, studying me solemnly as I curled up by her side. Carefully, cautiously, I edged closer. When she didn't move away, I settled my head on her shoulder. She arched her neck over my back, and together we slept.

❖

"I need to leave," Sylvan murmured, "before the pack sees us."

I'd awakened with nude women I barely knew before, but never on a soft bed of pine needles beneath a crystal clear sky. And never had I fit so perfectly with anyone. I lay on my back with her head on my shoulder. Her hand rested in the center of my chest, her thigh over mine. I stroked her shoulder.

"How many rules are we breaking?"

"Too many for me to count." Sylvan pushed away and sat up, running her hands through her hair. "Can you find your way back?"

"I'll follow you."

She raised an eyebrow.

"I can smell you." I ran my hand over my chest, down the center of my abdomen, and watched her eyes follow the motion. They were blue, rimmed in silver, and I remembered her wolf shimmering in the moonlight, a great shining beast. "Everywhere I go, I carry you on my skin."

Her face was completely expressionless. "Don't let anyone hear you say that."

I sat up, my skin still warm where she'd lain against me. "Is there an alpha male in the wings? Is that the problem?"

"That's not for you to know." She stood quickly, her jaw set, the word *whelp* hanging unspoken in the air.

"I know I have a lot to lear—"

"Yes, you have a lot to learn." She stared down at me. "And a place to earn. You'll be challenged."

"Why?" I rose and took a step toward her, watching her muscles harden as she reacted to the threat of me in her space. I shook my head. "I'm not challenging you." I dipped my head and said softly, "Alpha."

"You're not submissive. You're not Wereborn, and…"

"And what?" I feathered my fingers over her cheek and she let me touch her for a few seconds before she edged back, a tight frown eclipsing the brief tenderness I'd glimpsed.

"And you carry my scent," she said sharply.

"Why? Why do I?"

She shook her head. "I don't know. But…" She gestured to the ground where the faint indentations of our bodies lingered. "This can't happen again."

I was powerless. I wasn't even capable of shifting at will yet. She could tear me apart if she wanted, and she would be well within her right. The pack would demand it if they knew. But I didn't care. I crossed the distance she'd put between us, cradled her face in my hands, and kissed her. After a heartbeat, her lips parted and her tongue swept over mine, strong and unhesitant. She flooded me with her wild scent, her raw power, her deep hidden tenderness. I felt her call in my deepest reaches, and I moaned, aching to answer. She grasped my wrists, forced my arms down, and broke away.

"This can never happen again," she repeated, her voice hoarse.

I touched my chest, over my heart. "I am your wolf to command, Alpha. But you cannot rule what I carry in here."

I watched her race toward the trees, as graceful and strong in human form as wolf. There would be other nights, other hunts. Until then I would carry her on my skin, in my senses, in every part of me. I would find her again, when our hearts ran free.

About the Editors

RADCLYFFE is a retired surgeon and full-time award-winning author-publisher with over thirty novels and anthologies in print. Seven of her works have been Lambda Literary finalists, including the Lambda Literary winners *Erotic Interludes 2: Stolen Moments* ed. with Stacia Seaman and the romance *Distant Shores, Silent Thunder*. She is the editor of *Best Lesbian Romance 2009* and *2010* (Cleis Press), *Erotic Interludes 2* through *5* and *Romantic Interludes 1* and *2* ed. with Stacia Seaman (BSB), and has selections in multiple anthologies. She is the recipient of the 2003 and 2004 Alice B. Readers' award for her body of work and is also the president of Bold Strokes Books, one of the world's largest independent LGBTQ publishing companies. Her latest releases are an all-Radclyffe erotica anthology, *Radical Encounters* (February 2009), the romantic intrigue novel *Justice for All* (April 2009), and the romances *Secrets in the Stone* (July 2009) and *Returning Tides* (November 2009).

STACIA SEAMAN has edited numerous award-winning titles, and with co-editor Radclyffe won a Lambda Literary Award for *Erotic Interludes 2: Stolen Moments*; an Independent Publishers Awards silver medal and a Golden Crown Literary Award for *Erotic Interludes 4: Extreme Passions*; and an Independent Publishers Awards gold medal and a Golden Crown Literary award for *Erotic Interludes 5: Road Games*. Most recently, she has essays in *Visible: A Femmethology* (Homofactus Press, 2009) and *Second Person Queer* (Arsenal Pulp Press, 2009).

Books Available From Bold Strokes Books

The Seduction of Moxie by Colette Moody. When 1930s Broadway actress Violet London meets speakeasy singer Moxie Valette, she is instantly attracted and her Hollywood trip takes an unexpected turn. (978-1-60282-114-9)

Goldenseal by Gill McKnight. When Amy Fortune returns to her childhood home, she discovers something sinister in the air—but is former lover Leone Garoul stalking her or protecting her? (978-1-60282-115-6)

Romantic Interludes 2: Secrets edited by Radclyffe and Stacia Seaman. An anthology of sensual lesbian love stories: passion, surprises, and secret desires. (978-1-60282-116-3)

Femme Noir by Clara Nipper. Nora Delaney meets her match in Max Abbott, a sex-crazed dame who may or may not have the information Nora needs to solve a murder—but can she contain her lust for Max long enough to find out? (978-1-60282-117-0)

The Reluctant Daughter by Lesléa Newman. Heartwarming, heartbreaking, and ultimately triumphant—the story every daughter recognizes of the lifelong struggle for our mothers to really see us. (978-1-60282-118-7)

Erosistible by Gill McKnight. When Win Martin arrives at a luxurious Greek hotel for a much-anticipated week of sun and sex with her new girlfriend, she is stunned to find her ex-girlfriend, Benny, is the proprietor. Aeros Ebook. (978-1-60282-134-7)

Looking Glass Lives by Felice Picano. Cousins Roger and Alistair become lifelong friends and discover their sexuality amidst the backdrop of twentieth-century gay culture. (978-1-60282-089-0)

Breaking the Ice by Kim Baldwin. Nothing is easy about life above the Arctic Circle—except, perhaps, falling in love. At least that's what pilot Bryson Faulkner hopes when she meets Karla Edwards. (978-1-60282-087-6)

It Should Be a Crime by Carsen Taite. Two women fulfill their mutual desire with a night of passion, neither expecting more until law professor Morgan Bradley and student Parker Casey meet again…in the classroom. (978-1-60282-086-9)

Rough Trade edited by Todd Gregory. Top male erotica writers pen their own hot, sexy versions of the term "rough trade," producing some of the hottest, nastiest, and most dangerous fiction ever published. (978-1-60282-092-0)

The High Priest and the Idol by Jane Fletcher. Jemeryl and Tevi's relationship is put to the test when the Guardian sends Jemeryl on a mission that puts her not only in harm's way, but back into the sights of a previous lover. (978-1-60282-085-2)

Point of Ignition by Erin Dutton. Amid a blaze that threatens to consume them both, firefighter Kate Chambers and property owner Alexi Clark redefine love and trust. (978-1-60282-084-5)

Secrets in the Stone by Radclyffe. Reclusive sculptor Rooke Tyler suddenly finds herself the object of two very different women's affections, and choosing between them will change her life forever. (978-1-60282-083-8)

Dark Garden by Jennifer Fulton. Vienna Blake and Mason Cavender are sworn enemies—who can't resist each other. Something has to give. (978-1-60282-036-4)

Late in the Season by Felice Picano. Set on Fire Island, this is the story of an unlikely pair of friends—a gay composer in his late thirties and an eighteen-year-old schoolgirl. (978-1-60282-082-1)

Punishment with Kisses by Diane Anderson-Minshall. Will Megan find the answers she seeks about her sister Ashley's murder or will her growing relationship with one of Ash's exes blind her to the real truth? (978-1-60282-081-4)

September Canvas by Gun Brooke. When Deanna Moore meets TV personality Faythe she is reluctantly attracted to her, but will Faythe side with the people spreading rumors about Deanna? (978-1-60282-080-7)

No Leavin' Love by Larkin Rose. Beautiful, successful Mercedes Miller thinks she can resume her affair with ranch foreman Sydney Campbell, but the rules have changed. (978-1-60282-079-1)

Between the Lines by Bobbi Marolt. When romance writer Gail Prescott meets actress Tannen Albright, she develops feelings that she usually only experiences through her characters. (978-1-60282-078-4)

Blue Skies by Ali Vali. Commander Berkley Levine leads an elite group of pilots on missions ordered by her ex-lover Captain Aidan Sullivan and everything is on the line—including love. (978-1-60282-077-7)

The Lure by Felice Picano. When Noel Cummings is recruited by the police to go undercover to find a killer, his life will never be the same. (978-1-60282-076-0)

Death of a Dying Man by J.M. Redmann. Mickey Knight, Private Eye and partner of Dr. Cordelia James, doesn't need a drop-dead gorgeous assistant—not until nature steps in. (978-1-60282-075-3)

Justice for All by Radclyffe. Dell Mitchell goes undercover to expose a human traffic ring and ends up in the middle of an even deadlier conspiracy. (978-1-60282-074-6)

Sanctuary by I. Beacham. Cate Canton faces one major obstacle to her goal of crushing her business rival, Dita Newton—her uncontrollable attraction to Dita. (978-1-60282-055-5)

The Sublime and Spirited Voyage of Original Sin by Colette Moody. Pirate Gayle Malvern finds the presence of an abducted seamstress, Celia Pierce, a welcome distraction until the captive comes to mean more to her than is wise. (978-1-60282-054-8)

Suspect Passions by VK Powell. Can two women, a city attorney and a beat cop, put aside their differences long enough to see that they're perfect for each other? (978-1-60282-053-1)

Just Business by Julie Cannon. Two women who come together—each for her own selfish needs—discover that love can never be as simple as a business transaction. (978-1-60282-052-4)

Sistine Heresy by Justine Saracen. Adrianna Borgia, survivor of the Borgia court, presents Michelangelo with the greatest temptations of his life while struggling with soul-threatening desires for the painter Raphaela. (978-1-60282-051-7)

Radical Encounters by Radclyffe. An out-of-bounds, outside-the-lines collection of provocative, superheated erotica by award-winning romance and erotica author Radclyffe. (978-1-60282-050-0)

Thief of Always by Kim Baldwin & Xenia Alexiou. Stealing a diamond to save the world should be easy for Elite Operative Mishael Taylor, but she didn't figure on love getting in the way. (978-1-60282-049-4)

X by JD Glass. When X-hacker Charlie Riven is framed for a crime she didn't commit, she accepts help from an unlikely source—sexy Treasury Agent Elaine Harper. (978-1-60282-048-7)

The Middle of Somewhere by Clifford Henderson. Eadie T. Pratt sets out on a road trip in search of a new life and ends up in the middle of somewhere she never expected. (978-1-60282-047-0)

Paybacks by Gabrielle Goldsby. Cameron Howard wants to avoid her old nemesis Mackenzie Brandt but their high school reunion brings up more than just memories. (978-1-60282-046-3)

Uncross My Heart by Andrews & Austin. When a radio talk show diva sets out to interview a female priest, the two women end up at odds and neither heaven nor earth is safe from their feelings. (978-1-60282-045-6)

Fireside by Cate Culpepper. Mac, a therapist, and Abby, a nurse, fall in love against the backdrop of friendship, healing, and defending one's own within the Fireside shelter. (978-1-60282-044-9)

A Pirate's Heart by Catherine Friend. When rare book librarian Emma Boyd searches for a long-lost treasure map, she learns the hard way that pirates still exist in today's world—some modern pirates steal maps, others steal hearts. (978-1-60282-040-1)

Trails Merge by Rachel Spangler. Parker Riley escapes the high-powered world of politics to Campbell Carson's ski resort—and their mutual attraction produces anything but smooth running. (978-1-60282-039-5)

Dreams of Bali by C.J. Harte. Madison Barnes worships work, power, and success, and she's never allowed anyone to interfere—that is, until she runs into Karlie Henderson Stockard. Aeros EBook (978-1-60282-070-8)

The Limits of Justice by John Morgan Wilson. Benjamin Justice and reporter Alexandra Templeton search for a killer in a mysterious compound in the remote California desert. (978-1-60282-060-9)

Designed for Love by Erin Dutton. Jillian Sealy and Wil Johnson don't much like each other, but they do have to work together—and what they desire most is not what either of them had planned. (978-1-60282-038-8)

Calling the Dead by Ali Vali. Six months after Hurricane Katrina, NOLA Detective Sept Savoie is a cop who thinks making a relationship work is harder than catching a serial killer—but her current case may prove her wrong. (978-1-60282-037-1)

Shots Fired by MJ Williamz. Kyla and Echo seem to have the perfect relationship and the perfect life until someone shoots at Kyla—and Echo is the most likely suspect. (978-1-60282-035-7)

truelesbianlove.com by Carsen Taite. Mackenzie Lewis and Dr. Jordan Wagner have very different ideas about love, but they discover that truelesbianlove is closer than a click away. Aeros EBook (978-1-60282-069-2)

Justice at Risk by John Morgan Wilson. Benjamin Justice's blind date leads to a rare opportunity for legitimate work, but a reckless risk changes his life forever. (978-1-60282-059-3)

Run to Me by Lisa Girolami. Burned by the four-letter word called love, the only thing Beth Standish wants to do is run for—or maybe from—her life. (978-1-60282-034-0)

Split the Aces by Jove Belle. In the neon glare of Sin City, two women ride a wave of passion that threatens to consume them in a world of fast money and fast times. (978-1-60282-033-3)

Uncharted Passage by Julie Cannon. Two women on a vacation that turns deadly face down one of nature's most ruthless killers—and find themselves falling in love. (978-1-60282-032-6)

Night Call by Radclyffe. All medevac helicopter pilot Jett McNally wants to do is fly and forget about the horror and heartbreak she left behind in the Middle East, but anesthesiologist Tristan Holmes has other plans. (978-1-60282-031-9)

Lake Effect Snow by C.P. Rowlands. News correspondent Annie T. Booker and FBI Agent Sarah Moore struggle to stay one step ahead of disaster as Annie's life becomes the war zone she once reported on. Aeros EBook (978-1-60282-068-5)

I Dare You by Larkin Rose. Stripper by night, corporate raider by day, Kelsey's only looking for sex and power, until she meets a woman who stirs her heart and her body. (978-1-60282-030-2)

Truth Behind the Mask by Lesley Davis. Erith Baylor is drawn to Sentinel Pagan Osborne's quiet strength, but the secrets between them strain duty and family ties. (978-1-60282-029-6)

Cooper's Deale by KI Thompson. Two would-be lovers and a decidedly inopportune murder spell trouble for Addy Cooper, no matter which way the cards fall. (978-1-60282-028-9)

Romantic Interludes 1: Discovery ed. by Radclyffe and Stacia Seaman. An anthology of sensual, erotic contemporary love stories from the best-selling Bold Strokes authors. (978-1-60282-027-2)

Homecoming by Nell Stark. Sarah Storm loses everything that matters—family, future dreams, and love—will her new "straight" roommate cause Sarah to take a chance at happiness? (978-1-60282-024-1)

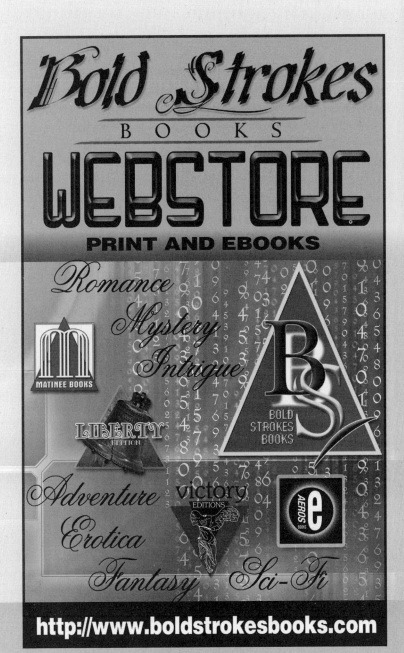

Bold Strokes

BOOKS

WEBSTORE

PRINT AND EBOOKS

Romance

Mystery

Intrigue

MATINEE BOOKS

LIBERTY EDITION

BS BOLD STROKES BOOKS

Adventure

victory EDITIONS

AEROS BOOKS

Erotica

Fantasy   Sci-Fi

http://www.boldstrokesbooks.com